# Summer Wedding Bells

## Debbie Macomber

featuring *Marriage Wanted* and *Lone Star Lovin'*

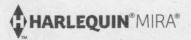
HARLEQUIN®MIRA®

Published in Great Britain 2013
Harlequin MIRA, an imprint of Harlequin (UK) Limited,
Eton House, 18-24 Paradise Road,
Richmond, Surrey, TW9 1SR

SUMMER WEDDING BELLS © Harlequin Books S.A. 2013

The publisher acknowledges the copyright holder of the individual works as follows:

*Marriage Wanted* © Debbie Macomber 1993
*Lone Star Lovin'* © Debbie Macomber 1993

ISBN 978 1 848 45235 0

58-0713

Harlequin's policy is to use papers that are natural, renewable and recyclable products and made from wood grown in sustainable forests. The logging and manufacturing processes conform to the legal environmental regulations of the country of origin.

Printed and bound by
CPI Group (UK) Ltd, Croydon, CR0 4YY

# CONTENTS

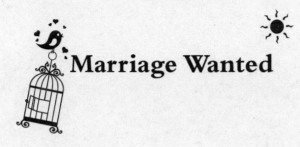

# Marriage Wanted

To Randall Toye
who has supported and encouraged me
for twenty-eight wonderful years

# One

Savannah Charles watched the young woman wandering around her bridal shop, checking prices and looking more discouraged by the moment. Her shoulders slumped and she bit her lip when she read the tag on the wedding gown she'd selected. She had excellent taste, Savannah noticed; the ivory silk-taffeta dress was one of her own favorites. A pattern of lace and pearls swirled up the puffed sleeves and bodice.

"Can I help you?" Savannah asked, moving toward her. Startled, the woman turned. "I… It doesn't look like it. This dress is almost twice as much as my budget for the whole wedding. Are you Savannah?"

"Yes."

She smiled shyly. "Missy Gilbert told me about you. She said you're wonderful to work with and that you might be able to give Kurt and me some guidance. I'm Susan Davenport." She held out her hand and Savannah shook it, liking the girl immediately.

"When's your wedding?"

"In six weeks. Kurt and I are paying for it ourselves. His

two younger brothers are still in college and his parents haven't got much to spare." Amusement turned up the corners of her mouth as she added, "Kurt's dad claims he's becoming poor by degrees."

Savannah smiled back. "What about your family?"

"There's only my brother and me. He's fifteen years older and, well…it isn't that he doesn't like Kurt. Because once you meet Kurt, it's impossible not to love him. He's kind and generous and interesting.…"

Savannah was touched by Susan's eagerness to tell her about the man she wanted to marry.

"But Nash—my brother—doesn't believe in marriage," the young woman went on to explain. "He's an attorney and he's worked on so many divorce cases over the years that he simply doesn't believe in it anymore. It doesn't help that he's divorced himself, although that was years and years ago."

"What's your budget?" Savannah asked. She'd planned weddings that went into six figures, but she was equally adept at finding reasonable alternatives. She walked back to her desk, limping on her right foot. It ached more this afternoon than usual. It always did when the humidity was this high.

Susan told her the figure she and Kurt had managed to set aside and Savannah frowned. It wasn't much, but she could work with it. She turned around and caught Susan staring at her. Savannah was accustomed to that kind of reaction to her limp, the result of a childhood accident. She generally wore pants, which disguised the scars and disfigurement, but her limp was always noticeable, and more so when she was tired. Until they knew her better, it seemed to disconcert people. Generally she ignored their hesitation and continued, hoping that her own acceptance would put them at ease.

"Even the least expensive wedding dresses would eat up the majority of the money we've worked so hard to save."

"You could always rent the dress," Savannah suggested.

"I could?" Her pretty blue eyes lit up when Savannah mentioned the rental fee.

"How many people are you inviting?"

"Sixty-seven," Susan told her, as if the number of guests had been painfully difficult to pare down. "Kurt and I can't afford more. Mostly it's his family.... I don't think Nash will even come to the wedding." Her voice fell.

Despite never having met Susan's older brother, she already disliked him. Savannah couldn't imagine a brother refusing to attend his sister's wedding, no matter what his personal views on marriage happened to be.

"Kurt's from a large family. He has aunts and uncles and, I swear, at least a thousand cousins. We'd like to invite everyone, but we can't. The invitations alone will cost a fortune."

"Have you thought about making your own invitations?"

Susan shook her head. "I'm not very artsy."

"You don't need to be." Opening a drawer, Savannah brought out a book of calligraphy. "These are fairly simple and elegant-looking and they'll add a personal touch because they're individualized." She paused. "You'll find other ideas on the internet."

"These are beautiful. You honestly think I could do this?" She looked expectantly at Savannah.

"Without a doubt," Savannah answered with a smile.

"I wish I could talk some sense into Nash," Susan muttered, then squared her shoulders as if she was ready to take him on right that minute. "He's the only family I have. We've got aunts and uncles here and there, but no one we're close to, and Nash is being so unreasonable about this. I love Kurt and nothing's going to change the way I feel. I love his family, too. It can be lonely when you don't belong to someone. That's Nash's problem. He's forgotten what it's like to belong to someone. To be in a relationship."

Loneliness. Savannah was well acquainted with the feeling. All her life she'd felt alone. The little girl who couldn't run and play with friends. The teenage girl who never got asked to the prom. The woman who arranged the happiest days of *other* people's lives.

Loneliness. Savannah knew more than she wanted to about long days and longer nights.

"I'm sure your brother will change his mind," Savannah said reassuringly—even though she wasn't sure at all.

Susan laughed. "That only goes to prove you don't know my brother. Once he's set on something, it takes an Act of Congress to persuade him otherwise."

Savannah spent the next hour with Susan, deciding on the details of both the wedding and the reception. With such a limited budget it was a challenge, but they did it.

"I can't believe we can do so much with so little," Susan said once they'd finished. Her face glowed with happiness. "A nice wedding doesn't mean as much to Kurt as it does to me, but he's willing to do whatever he can to make our day special."

Through the course of their conversation, Savannah learned that Kurt had graduated from the University of Washington with an engineering degree. He'd recently been hired by a California firm and had moved to the San Francisco area, where Susan would be joining him.

After defying her brother, Susan had moved in with Kurt's family, working part-time and saving every penny she could to help with the wedding expenses.

"I can hardly wait to talk to Kurt," Susan said excitedly as she gathered her purse and the notes she'd made. "I'll get

back to you as soon as he's had a chance to go over the contract." Susan paused. "Missy was right. You *are* wonderful."
She threw both arms around Savannah in an impulsive hug.
"I'll be back as soon as I can and you can take the measurements for the dress." She cast a dreamy look toward the silk-
and-taffeta gown and sighed audibly. "Kurt's going to die
when he sees me in that dress."

"You'll make a lovely bride."

"Thank you for everything," Susan said as she left the
store.

"You're welcome." It was helping young women like
Susan that Savannah enjoyed the most. The eager, happy
ones who were so much in love they were willing to listen
to their hearts no matter what the cost. Over the years, Savannah had worked with every kind of bride and she knew
the signs. The Susans of this world were invariably a delight.

It was highly unlikely that Savannah would ever be married herself. Men were an enigma to her. Try as she might,
she'd never been able to understand them. They invariably
treated her differently than they did other women. Savannah assumed their attitude had to do with her damaged leg.
Men either saw her as fragile, untouchable, because of it,
or they viewed her as a buddy, a confidante. She supposed
she should be flattered by the easy camaraderie they shared
with her. They sought her advice, listened politely when she
spoke, then did as they pleased.

Only a few men had seen her as a *woman*, a woman with
dreams and desires of her own. But when it came to love,
each of them had grown hesitant and afraid. Each relationship had ended awkwardly long before it had gotten close
to serious.

Maybe that wasn't a fair assessment, Savannah mused
sadly. Maybe it was her own attitude. She'd been terrified

of ever falling in love. No matter how deeply she felt about a man, she was positive that her imperfection would come between them. It was safer to hold back, to cling to her pride than risk rejection and pain later on.

A week later, Susan came breezing through the door to Savannah's shop.

"Hello," she said, smiling broadly. "I talked to Kurt and he's as excited as I am." She withdrew a debit card from her purse. "I'd like to give you the down payment now. And I have the signed contract for you."

Savannah brought out her paperwork and Susan paid her. "My brother doesn't believe we'll be able to do it without his help, but he's wrong. We're going to have a beautiful wedding, with or without Nash, thanks to you."

This was what made Savannah's job so fulfilling. "I'll order what we need right away," she told Susan. Savannah only wished there was some way she could influence the young woman's unreasonable older brother. She knew his type—cynical, distrusting, pessimistic. A man who scoffed at love, who had no respect for marriage. How very sad. Despite her irritation with the faceless Nash, Savannah couldn't help feeling sorry for him. Whether or not he realized it, he was going to lose his sister.

There were just the two of them, so she didn't understand why Nash wouldn't support his sister in her decision. Luckily Susan had Kurt's parents. Undoubtedly this was something her brother hadn't counted on, either.

Susan left soon afterward. What remained of Savannah's day was busy. The summer months used to be her overburdened time, but that hadn't held true of late. Her services were booked equally throughout the year.

Around five-thirty, when Savannah was getting ready

to close for the day, the bell chimed over her door, indicating someone had entered the shop. She looked up from her computer and found a tall, well-dressed man standing by the doorway. It had started to rain lightly; he shook off the raindrops in his hair before he stepped farther inside. She saw him glance around and scowl, as if being in such a place was repugnant to him. Even before he spoke she knew he was Susan's brother. The family resemblance was striking.

"Hello," she said.

"Hello." He slid his hands in his pockets with a contemptuous frown. Apparently he feared that even being in this place where love and romance were honored would infect him with some dread disease. It must take a good deal of energy to maintain his cynicism, Savannah thought.

"Can I help you?" she asked.

"No, thanks. I was just looking." He walked slowly through the shop. His expensive leather shoes made a tapping sound against the polished hardwood floor. She noticed that he took pains not to touch anything.

Savannah nearly laughed out loud when he passed a display of satin pillows, edged in French lace, that were meant to be carried by the ring bearer. He stepped around it, giving it a wide berth, then picked up one of her business cards from a brass holder on a small antique table.

"Are you Savannah Charles?" he asked.

"Yes," she replied evenly. "I am."

"Interesting shop you have here," he said dryly. Savannah had to admit she found him handsome in a rugged sort of way. His facial features were strong and well-defined. His mouth firm, his jaw square and stubbornly set. He walked in short, clipped steps, his impatience nearly palpable. Naturally, she might be altogether wrong and this could be someone other than Susan's brother. Savannah decided it was time to find out.

"Are you about to be married?"

"No," he said disgustedly.

"This seems like an unusual shop for you to browse through, then."

He smiled in her direction, acknowledging her shrewdness. "I believe you've been talking to my sister, Susan Davenport."

So Savannah had been right. This *was* Susan's hard-nosed older brother. His attitude had been a dead giveaway. "Yes, Susan's been in."

"I take it she's decided to go through with this wedding nonsense, then?" He eyed her suspiciously as if to suggest his sister might have changed her mind except for Savannah's encouragement and support.

"It would be best if you discussed Susan's plans with her."

Nash clasped his hands behind his back. "I would if we were on speaking terms."

How he knew his sister was working with her, Savannah hadn't a clue. She didn't even want to know.

"So," he said conversationally, "exactly what do you do here?"

"I'm a wedding coordinator."

"Wedding coordinator," he repeated, sounding genuinely curious. He nodded for her to continue.

"Basically I organize the wedding for the bride and her family so they're free to enjoy this all-important day."

"I see," he said. "You're the one who makes sure the flowers arrive at the church on time?"

"Something like that." His version oversimplified her role, but she didn't think he'd appreciate a detailed job description. After all, he wasn't interested in her, but in what he could learn about his sister and Kurt's plans.

He wandered about the shop some more, careful not to come into contact with any of the displays she'd so carefully arranged. He strolled past a lace-covered table with an elegant heart-shaped guest book and plumed pen as if he were walking past a nest of vipers. Savannah couldn't help being amused.

"Susan hasn't got the money for a wedding," he announced. "At least, not one fancy enough to hire a coordinator."

"Again, this is something you need to discuss with your sister."

He didn't like her answer; that much was obvious from the way his mouth thinned and the irritation she saw in his eyes. They were the same intense blue as his sister's, but that was where the resemblance ended. Susan's eyes revealed her love and enthusiasm for life. Nash's revealed his disenchantment and skepticism. She finished up the last of her paperwork, ignoring him as much as she could.

"You're a babe in the woods, aren't you?"

"I beg your pardon?" Savannah said, looking up.

"You actually believe all this...absurdity?"

"I certainly don't think of love and commitment as absurd, if that's what you mean, Mr. Davenport."

"Call me Nash."

"All right," she agreed reluctantly. In a few minutes she was going to show him the door. He hadn't bothered to disguise the purpose of his visit. He was trying to pump her for information and hadn't figured out yet that she refused to be placed in the middle between him and his sister.

"Did you ever stop to realize that over fifty percent of the couples who marry in this day and age end up divorcing?"

"I know the statistics."

He walked purposely toward her as if approaching a judge's bench, intent on proving his point. "Love is a lame excuse for marriage."

Since he was going to make it impossible for her to concentrate, she sat back on her stool and folded her arms. "What do you suggest couples do then, Mr. Davenport? Just live together?"

"Nash," he reminded her irritably. "And, yes, living together makes a lot more sense. If a man and woman are so hot for each other, I don't see any reason to muddy the relationship with legalities when a weekend in bed would simplify everything."

Savannah resisted the urge to roll her eyes. Rejecting marriage made as much sense to her as pushing a car over a cliff because the fender was dented. Instead she asked, "Is this what you want Susan and Kurt to do? Live together indefinitely? Without commitment?"

That gave him pause. Apparently it was perfectly fine for other couples to do that, but when it came to his little sister, he hesitated. "Yes," he finally said. "Until this infatuation passes."

"What about children?"

"Susan's little more than a child herself," he argued, although she was twenty-four—and in Savannah's estimation a mature twenty-four. "If she's smart, she'll avoid adding to her mistakes," he said stiffly.

"What about someone other than your sister?" she demanded, annoyed with herself for allowing him to draw her into this pointless discussion. "Are you suggesting our society should do away with family?"

"A wedding ring doesn't make a family," he returned just as heatedly.

Savannah sighed deeply. "I think it's best for us to agree to disagree," she said, feeling a bit sad. It was unrealistic to think she'd say anything that would change his mind. Susan was determined to marry Kurt, with or without his approval, but she loved her brother, too. That was what made this situation so difficult.

"Love is a lame excuse to mess up one's life," he said, clenching his fists at his side with impotent anger. "A lame excuse."

At his third use of the word *lame,* Savannah inwardly flinched. Because she was sitting behind her desk, he didn't realize *she* was "lame."

"Marriage is an expensive trap that destroys a man's soul," Nash went on to say, ignoring her. "I see the results of it each and every day. Just this afternoon, I was in court for a settlement hearing that was so nasty the judge had to pull both attorneys into chambers. Do you really believe I want my little sister involved in something like that?"

"Your sister is a grown woman, Mr. Davenport. She's old enough to make her own decisions."

"Mistakes, you mean."

Savannah sensed his frustration, but arguing with him would do no good at all. "Susan's in love. You should know by now that she's determined to marry Kurt."

"*In love.* Excuses don't get much worse than that."

Savannah had had enough. She stood and realized for the first time how tall Nash actually was. He loomed head and shoulders over her five-foot-three-inch frame. Standing next to him she felt small and insignificant. For all their differences, Savannah could appreciate his concerns. Nash loved his sister; otherwise he wouldn't have gone to such effort to find out her plans.

"It's been interesting," Nash said, waiting for her to walk

around her desk and join him. Savannah did, limping as she went. She was halfway across the room before she saw that he wasn't following her. Half turning around, she noticed that he was looking at her leg, his features marked by regret.

"I didn't mean to be rude," he said, and she couldn't doubt his sincerity. What surprised her was his sensitivity. She might have judged this man too harshly. His attitude had irritated her, but she'd also been entertained by him—and by the vigor of their argument.

"You didn't know." She finished her trek to the door, again surprised to realize he hadn't followed her. "It's well past my closing time," she said meaningfully.

"Of course." His steps were crisp and uniform as he marched across her shop, stopping abruptly when he reached her. A frown wrinkled his brow as he stared at her again.

"What's wrong?"

He laughed shortly. "I'm trying to figure something out."

"If it has to do with Susan and Kurt—"

"It doesn't," he cut in. "It has to do with you." An odd smile lifted his mouth. "I like you. You're impertinent, sassy and stubborn."

"Oh, really!" She might have been offended if she hadn't been struggling so hard not to laugh.

"Really."

"You're tactless, irritating and overpowering," she responded.

His grin was transformed into a full-blown smile. "You're right. It's a shame, though."

"A shame? What are you talking about?"

"You being a wedding coordinator. It's a waste. With your obvious organizational skills, you might've done something useful. Instead, your head's stuck in the clouds and you've let love and romance fog up your brain. But you know what?"

He rubbed the side of his jaw. "There just might be hope for you."

"Hope. Funny, I was thinking the same thing about you. There just might be a slim chance of reasoning with you. You're clearly intelligent and even a little witty. But unfortunately you're misguided. Now that you're dealing with your sister's marriage, however, there's a remote possibility someone might be able to get through to you."

"What do you mean?" he asked, folding his arms over his chest and resting his weight on one foot.

"Your judgment's been confused by your clients. By their anger and bitterness and separations. We're at opposite ends of the same subject. I work with couples when they're deeply in love and convinced the relationship will last forever. You see them when they're embittered and disillusioned. But what you don't seem to realize is that you need to see the glass as half-full and not half-empty."

He frowned. "I thought we were talking about marriage."

"We are. What you said earlier is true. Fifty percent of all married couples end up divorcing—which means fifty percent of them go on to lead fulfilling, happy lives."

Nash's snort was derisive. He dropped his arms and straightened, shaking his head. "I was wrong. There's no hope for you. The fifty percent who stay together are just as miserable. Given the opportunity, they'd gladly get out of the relationship."

Nash was beginning to irritate her again. "Why is it so difficult for you to believe that there's such a thing as a happy marriage?"

"Because I've never seen one."

"You haven't looked hard enough."

"Have you ever stopped to think that your head's so muddled with hearts and flowers and happy-ever-afters that you can't and won't accept what's right in front of your eyes?"

"Like I said, it's past my closing time." Savannah jerked open the shop door. The clanging bell marked the end of their frustrating conversation. Rarely had Savannah allowed anyone to get under her skin the way she had Nash Davenport. The man was impossible. Totally unreasonable…

The woman was impossible. Totally unreasonable.

Nash couldn't understand why he continued to mull over their conversation. Twenty-four hours had passed, and he'd thought about their verbal sparring match a dozen times.

Relaxing in his leather office chair, he rolled a pen between his palms. Obviously Savannah didn't know him well; otherwise, she wouldn't have attempted to convince him of the error of his views.

His eyes fell on the phone and he sighed inwardly. Susan was being stubborn and irrational. It was plain that he was going to have to be the one to mend fences. He'd hoped she'd come to her senses, but it wasn't going to happen. He was her older brother, her closest relative, and if she refused to make the first move, he'd have to do it.

He looked up Kurt Caldwell's parents' phone number. He resented having to contact her there. Luck was with him, however, when Susan herself answered.

"It's Nash," he said. When she was little, her voice rose with excitement whenever he called. Anytime he arrived home, she'd fly into his arms, so glad to see him she couldn't hold still. He sighed again, missing the child she once was.

"Hello, Nash," Susan said stiffly. No pleasure at hearing from him was evident now.

"How are you doing?" That was the purpose of this call, after all.

"Fine. How about you?" Her words were stilted, and her stubbornness hadn't budged an inch. He would have said as much, then thought better of it.

"I'm fine, too," he answered.

The silence stretched between them.

"I understand you have a wedding coordinator now," he said, hoping to come across as vaguely interested. She might have defied him, but he would always be her big brother.

"How do you know that?"

"Word, uh, gets around." In fact, he'd learned about it from a family friend. Still, he shouldn't have said anything. And he wouldn't have if Savannah hadn't dominated his thoughts from the moment he'd met her.

"You've had someone checking into my affairs, haven't you?" Susan lowered her voice to subzero temperatures. "You can't rule my life, Nash. I'm going to marry Kurt and that's all there is to it."

"I gathered as much from Savannah Charles...."

"You've talked to Savannah?"

Nash recognized his second mistake immediately. He'd blown it now, and Susan wasn't going to forgive him.

"Stop meddling in my life, Nash." His sister's voice quavered suspiciously and seconds later the line was disconnected. The phone droned in his ear before he dejectedly replaced the receiver.

Needless to say, *that* conversation hadn't gone well. He'd like to blame Savannah, but it was his fault. He'd been the one to let her name slip, a stupid error on his part.

The wedding coordinator and his sister were both too stubborn and naive for their own good. If this was how Susan wanted it, then he had no choice but to abide by her wishes. Calling her had been another mistake in a long list he'd been making lately.

His assistant poked her head in his door, and he gave her his immediate attention. He had more important things to worry about than his sister and a feisty wedding coordinator who lived in a dreamworld.

"What did my brother say?" Susan demanded.

"He wanted to know about you," Savannah said absently as she arranged champagne flutes on the display table next to the five-tier wedding cake. She'd been working on the display between customers for the past hour.

"In other words, Nash was pumping you for information?"

"Yes, but you don't need to worry, I didn't tell him anything. What I did do was suggest he talk to you." She straightened, surprised that he'd followed her advice. "He cares deeply for you, Susan."

"I know." Susan gnawed on her lower lip. "I wish I hadn't hung up on him."

"Susan!"

"I... He told me he'd talked to you and it made me so mad I couldn't bear to speak to him another second."

Savannah was surprised by Nash's slip. She would've thought their conversation was the last thing he'd mention. But from the sound of it, he didn't get an opportunity to rehash it with Susan.

"If he makes a pest of himself," Susan said righteously, "let me know and I'll...I'll do something."

"Don't worry about it. I rather enjoyed talking to him." It was true, although Savannah hated to admit it. She'd worked hard to push thoughts of Nash from her mind over the past couple of days. His attitude had annoyed her, true, but she'd found him intriguing and—it bothered her to confess this— a challenge. A smile came when she realized he probably saw her the same way.

"I have to get back to work," Susan said reluctantly. "I just wanted to apologize for my brother's behavior."

"He wasn't a problem."

On her way out the door, Susan muttered something Savannah couldn't hear. The situation was sad. Brother and sister loved each other but were at an impasse.

Savannah continued to consider the situation until the bell over the door chimed about five minutes later. Smiling, she looked up, deciding she wasn't going to get this display finished until after closing time. She should've known better than to try.

"Nash." His name was a mere whisper.

"Hello again," he said dryly. "I've come to prove my point."

# *Two*

"You want to prove your point," Savannah repeated thoughtfully. Nash Davenport was the most headstrong man she'd ever encountered. He was also one of the handsomest. That did more to confuse her than to help. For reasons as yet unclear, she'd lost her objectivity. No doubt it had something to do with that pride of his and the way they'd argued. No doubt it was also because they remained diametrically opposed on the most fundamental issues of life—love and marriage.

"I've given some thought to our conversation the other day," Nash said, pacing back and forth, "and it seems to me that I'm just the person to clear up your thinking. Besides," he went on, "if I *can* clear up your thinking, maybe you'll have some influence on Susan."

Although it was difficult, Savannah resisted the urge to laugh.

"To demonstrate my good faith, I brought a peace offering." He held up a white sack for her inspection. "Two lattes," he explained. He set the bag on the corner of her desk and opened it, handing her one of the paper cups. The smell of hot coffee blended with steamed milk was as welcome as popcorn in a theater. "Make yourself comfortable," he said next, gesturing toward the stool, "because it might take a while."

"I don't know if this is a good idea," Savannah felt obliged to say as she carefully edged onto the stool.

"It's a great idea. Just hear me out," he said smoothly.

"Oh, all right," she returned with an ungracious nod. Savannah might have had the energy to resist him if it hadn't been so late in the day. She was tired and the meeting with Susan had frustrated her. She'd come to her upset and unhappy, and Savannah had felt helpless, not knowing how to reassure the younger woman.

Nash pried off the lid of his latte, then glanced at his watch. He walked over to her door and turned over the sign so it read Closed.

"Hey, wait a minute!"

"It's—" he looked at his watch again "—5:29 p.m. You're officially closed in one minute."

Savannah didn't bother to disagree. "I think it's only fair for you to know that whatever you have to say isn't going to change my mind," she said.

"I figured as much."

The man continued to surprise her. "How do you intend to prove your point? Parade divorced couples through my wedding shop?"

"Nothing that drastic."

"Did it occur to you that I could do the same thing and have you meet with a group of blissful newlyweds?" she asked.

He grinned. "I'm way ahead of you. I already guessed

you'd enjoy introducing me to any number of loving couples who can't keep their hands off each other."

Savannah shrugged, not denying it.

"The way I figure it," he said, "we both have a strong argument to make."

"Exactly." She nodded. "But you aren't going to change my mind and I doubt I'll change yours." She didn't know what kept some couples together against all odds or why others decided to divorce when the first little problem arose. If Nash expected her to supply the answers, she had none to offer.

"Don't be so sure we won't change each other's mind." Which only went to prove that he thought there was a chance he could influence her. "We could accomplish a great deal if we agree to be open-minded."

Savannah cocked one eyebrow and regarded him skeptically. "Can you guarantee you'll be open-minded?"

"I'm not sure," he answered, and she was impressed with his honesty. "But I'm willing to try. That's all I ask of you."

"That sounds fair."

He rubbed his palms together as though eager to get started. "If you don't object, I'd like to go first."

"Just a minute," she said, holding up her hand. "Before we do, shouldn't we set some rules?"

"Like what?"

Although it was her suggestion, Savannah didn't really have an answer. "I don't know. Just boundaries of some kind."

"I trust you not to do anything weird, and you can count on the same from me," he said. "After all—"

"Don't be so hasty," she interrupted. "If we're going to put time and effort into this, it makes sense that we have rules. *And* something riding on the outcome."

His blue eyes brightened. "Now there's an interesting thought." He paused and a smile bracketed his mouth. "So you want to set a wager?"

Nash seemed to be on a one-man campaign to convince her the world would be a better place without the institution of marriage. "We might as well make it interesting, don't you think?"

"I couldn't agree more. If you can prove your point and get me to agree that you have, what would you want in exchange?"

This part was easy. "For you to attend Susan and Kurt's wedding. It would mean the world to Susan."

The easy smile disappeared behind a dark frown.

"She was in this afternoon," Savannah continued, rushing the words in her eagerness to explain. "She's anxious and confused, loving you and loving Kurt and needing your approval so badly."

Nash's mouth narrowed into a thin line of irritation.

"Would it really be so much to ask?" she ventured. "I realize I'd need to rely on your complete and total honesty, but I have faith in you." She took a sip of her latte.

"So, if you convince me my thinking is wrong on this marriage issue, you want me to attend Susan's wedding." He hesitated, then nodded slowly. "Deal," he said, and his grin reappeared.

Until that moment, Savannah was convinced Nash had no idea what he intended to use for his argument. But apparently he did. "What would you want from me?" she asked. Her question broke into his musings because he jerked his head toward her as if he'd forgotten there might be something in this for him, as well. He took a deep breath and then released it. "I don't know. Do I have to decide right now?"

"No."

"It'll be something substantial—you understand that, don't you?"

Savannah managed to hold back a smile. "I wouldn't expect anything less."

"How about home-cooked dinners for a week served on your fanciest china? That wouldn't be out of line," he murmured.

She gaped at him. Her request had been generous and completely selfless. She'd offered him an excuse to attend Susan's wedding *and* salvage his pride, and in return he wanted her to slave in the kitchen for days on end.

"That *is* out of line," she told him, unwilling to agree to anything so ridiculous. If he wanted homemade meals, he could do what the rest of the world did and cook them himself, visit relatives or get married.

Nash's expression was boyish with delight. "So you're afraid you're going to lose."

Raising her eyebrows, she said, "You haven't got a prayer, Davenport."

"Then what's the problem?" he asked, making an exaggerated gesture with both hands. "Do you agree to my terms or not?"

This discussion had wandered far from what she'd originally intended. Savannah had been hoping to smooth things over between brother and sister and at the same time prove her own point. She wasn't interested in putting her own neck on the chopping block. Any attempt to convince Nash of the error of his ways was pointless.

He finished off his latte and flung the empty container into her garbage receptacle. "Be ready tomorrow afternoon," he said, walking to the door.

Savannah scrambled awkwardly from the stool. "What for?" she called after him. She limped two steps toward him and stopped abruptly at the flash of pain that shot up her leg. She'd sat too long in the same position, something she was generally able to avoid. She wanted to rub her thigh, work the throbbing muscle, but that would reveal her pain, which she wanted to hide from Nash.

"You'll know more tomorrow afternoon," he promised, looking pleased with himself.

"How long will this take?"

"There are time restrictions? Are there any other rules we need to discuss?"

"I... We should both be reasonable about this, don't you think?"

"I *was* planning to be sensible, but I can't speak for you."

This conversation was deteriorating rapidly. "I'll be ready at closing time tomorrow afternoon, then," she said, holding her hand against her thigh. If he didn't leave soon, she was going to have to sit down. Disguising her pain had become a way of life, but the longer she stood, the more difficult it became.

"Something's wrong," he announced, his gaze hard and steady. "You'd argue with me if there wasn't."

Again she was impressed by his sensitivity. "Nonsense. I said I'd be ready. What more do you want?"

He left her then, in the nick of time. A low moan escaped as she sank onto her chair. Perspiration moistened her brow and she drew in several deep breaths. Rubbing her hand over the tense muscles slowly eased out the pain.

The phone was situated to the left of her desk and after giving the last of her discomfort a couple of minutes to ebb away, she reached for the receiver and dialed her parents' number. Apparently Nash had decided how to present his case. She had, too. No greater argument could be made than her parents' loving relationship. Their marriage was as solid as Fort Knox and they'd been devoted to each other for over thirty years. Nash couldn't meet her family and continue to discredit love and marriage.

Her father answered on the second ring, sounding delighted to hear from her. A rush of warm feeling washed over Savannah. Her family had been a constant source of love and encouragement to her through the years.

"Hi, Dad."

"It's always good to hear from you, sweetheart."

Savannah relaxed in her chair. "Is Mom around?"

"No, she's got a doctor's appointment to have her blood pressure checked again. Is there anything I can do for you?"

Savannah's hand tightened around the receiver. She didn't want to mislead her parents into thinking she was involved with Nash. But she needed to prove her point. "Is there any chance I could bring someone over for dinner tomorrow night?"

"Of course."

Savannah laughed lightly. "You might want to check Mom's calendar. It'd be just like you to agree to something when she's already made plans."

"I looked. The calendar's right here in the kitchen and tomorrow night's free. Now, if you were to ask about Friday, that's a different story."

Once more Savannah found herself smiling.

"Who do you want us to meet?"

"His name's Nash Davenport."

Her announcement was met with a short but noticeable silence. "You're bringing a young man home to meet your family? This is an occasion, then."

"Dad, it isn't like that." This was exactly what she'd feared would happen, that her family would misinterpret her bringing Nash home. "We've only just met...."

"It was like that with your mother and me," her father said excitedly. "We met on a Friday night and a week later I knew this was the woman I was going to love all my life, and I have."

"Dad, Nash is just a friend—not even a friend, really, just an acquaintance," Savannah said, trying to correct his mistaken impression. "I'm coordinating his sister's wedding."

"No need to explain, sweetheart. If you want to bring a young man for your mother and me to meet, we'd be thrilled, no matter what the reason."

Savannah was about to respond, but then decided that a lengthy explanation might hurt her cause rather than help it. "I'm not sure of the exact time we'll arrive."

"No problem. I'll light up the barbecue and that way you won't need to worry. Come whenever you can. We'll make an evening of it."

Oh, yes, it was going to be quite an evening, Savannah mused darkly. Two stubborn people, both convinced they were right, would each try to convert the other.

This was going to be so easy that Nash almost felt guilty. Almost... Poor Savannah. Once he'd finished with what he had to show her, she'd have no option but to accept the reality of his argument.

Nash loved this kind of debate, when he was certain beyond a shadow of a doubt that he was right. By the time he was done, Savannah would be eating her words.

Grabbing his briefcase, he hurried out of his office, anxious to forge ahead and prove his point.

"Nash, what's your hurry?"

Groaning inwardly, Nash turned to face a fellow attorney, Paul Jefferson. "I've got an appointment this evening," Nash explained. He didn't like Paul, had never liked Paul. What bothered him most was that this brownnoser was going to be chosen over him for the partnership position that was opening up within the year. Both Paul and Nash had come into the firm at the same time, and they were both good attorneys. But Paul had a way of ingratiating himself with the powers that be and parting the waters of opportunity.

"An appointment or a date?" Paul asked with that smug look of his. One of these days Nash was going to find an excuse to wipe that grin off his face.

He looked pointedly at his watch. "If you'll excuse me, Paul, I have to leave, otherwise I'll be late."

"Can't keep *her* waiting, now can we?" Paul said, and finding himself amusing, he laughed at his own sorry joke.

Knotting his fist at his side, Nash was happy to escape. Anger clawed at him until he was forced to stop and analyze his outrage. He'd been working with Paul for nearly ten years. He'd tolerated his humorless jokes, his conceited, self-righteous attitude and his air of superiority without displaying his annoyance. What was different now?

He considered the idea of Paul being preferred to him for the partnership. But this was nothing new. The minute he'd learned about the opening, he'd suspected Stackhouse and Serle would choose Paul. He'd accepted it as fact weeks ago.

Paul had suggested Nash was hurrying to meet a woman— which he was. Nash didn't bother to deny it. What upset him was the sarcastic way Paul had said it, as though Savannah—

His mind came to a grinding halt. Savannah.

So she was at the bottom of all this. Nash had taken offense at the edge in Paul's voice, as if his fellow attorney had implied that Savannah was, somehow, less than she should be. He knew he was being oversensitive. After all, Paul had never even met her. But still...

Nash recalled his own reaction to Savannah, his observations when he'd met her. She was small. Her dark, pixie-style hair and deep brown eyes gave her a fragile appearance, but that was deceptive. The woman obviously had a constitution of iron.

Her eyes... Once more his thoughts skidded to a halt. He'd never known a woman with eyes that were more revealing. In them he read a multitude of emotions. Pain, both physical and emotional. In them he saw a woman with courage. Nash barely knew Savannah and yet he sensed she was one of the most astonishing people he'd probably ever meet. He'd wanted to defend her, wanted to slam his colleague up against a wall and demand an apology for the slight, vague though it was. In fact, he admitted, if Paul was insulting anyone, it was more likely him than Savannah....

When he reached his car, Nash sat in the driver's seat with his key poised in front of the ignition for a moment, brooding about his colleague and the competitiveness between them.

His mood lightened considerably as he made his way through the heavy traffic to the wedding shop. He'd been looking forward to this all day.

He found a parking spot and climbed out of his car, then fed the meter. As he turned away he caught sight of Savannah in the shop window, talking to a customer. Her face was aglow with enthusiasm and even from this distance her eyes sparkled. For a reason unknown to him, his pulse accelerated as joy surged through him.

He was happy to be seeing Savannah. Any man would, knowing he was about to be proven right. But this was more than that. This happiness was rooted in the knowledge that he'd be spending time with her.

Savannah must have felt his scrutiny, because she glanced upward and their eyes met briefly before she reluctantly pulled hers away. Although she continued speaking to her customer, Nash sensed that she'd experienced the same intensity of feeling he had. It was at moments such as this that he wished he could be privy to a woman's thoughts. He would gladly have forfeited their bet to know if she was as surprised and puzzled as he felt. Nash couldn't identify the feeling precisely; all he knew was that it made him uncomfortable.

The customer was leaving just as Nash entered the shop. Savannah was sitting at her desk and intuitively he realized she needed to sit periodically because of her leg. She looked fragile and confused. When she raised her eyes to meet his, he was shocked by the strength of her smile.

"You're right on time," she said.

"You would be, too, if you were about to have home-cooked meals personally served to you for the next week."

"Don't count on it, Counselor."

"Oh, I'm counting on it," he said with a laugh. "I've already got the menu picked out. We'll start the first night with broiled New York sirloin, Caesar salad and a three-layer chocolate cake."

"You certainly love to dream," she said with an effortless laugh. "I find it amusing that you never stopped to ask if I could cook. It'll probably come as a surprise to learn that not all women are proficient in the kitchen. If by some odd quirk of fate you do happen to win this wager, you'll dine on boxed macaroni and cheese or microwave meals for seven days and like it."

Nash was stunned. She was right; he'd assumed she could cook as well as she seemed to manage everything else. Her shop was a testament to her talent, appealing to the eye in every respect. True, all those wedding gowns and satin pillows were aiding and abetting romance, but it had a homey, comfortable feel, as well. This wasn't an easy thing to admit. A wedding shop was the last place on earth Nash ever thought he'd willingly visit.

"Are you ready to admit defeat?" he asked.

"Never, but before we get started I need to make a couple of phone calls. Do you mind?"

"Not in the least." He was a patient man, and never more so than now. The longer they delayed, the better. It wasn't likely that Paul would stay late, but Nash wanted to avoid introducing Savannah to him. More important, he wanted her to himself. The thought was unwelcome. This wasn't a date and he had no romantic interest in Savannah Charles, he reminded himself.

Savannah reached for the phone and he wandered around the shop noticing small displays he'd missed on his prior visits. The first time he'd felt nervous; he didn't know what to expect from a wedding coordinator, but certainly not the practical, gutsy woman he'd found.

He trained his ears not to listen in on her conversation, but the crisp, businesslike tone of her voice was surprisingly captivating.

It was happening again—that disturbing feeling was back, deep in the pit of his stomach. He'd felt it before, several years earlier, and it had nearly ruined his life. He was in trouble. Panic shot through his blood and he felt the overwhelming urge to turn and run in the opposite direction. The last time he'd had this feeling, he'd gotten married.

"I'm ready," Savannah said, and stood.

Nash stared at her for a long moment as his brain processed what was going on.

"Nash?"

He gave himself a hard mental shake. He didn't know if he was right about what had happened here, but he didn't like it. "Do you mind riding with me?" he asked, once he'd composed himself.

"That'll be fine."

The drive back to his office building in downtown Seattle was spent in relative silence. Savannah seemed to sense his reflective mood. Another woman might have attempted to fill the space with idle chatter. Nash was grateful she didn't.

After he'd parked, he led Savannah into his building and up the elevator to the law firm's offices. She seemed impressed with the plush furnishings and the lavish view of Mount Rainier and Puget Sound from his twentieth-story window.

When she'd entered his office she'd walked directly to the window and set her purse on his polished oak credenza. "How do you manage to work with a view like this?" she asked, her voice soft with awe. She seemed mesmerized by the beauty that appeared before her.

After several years Nash had become immune to its splendor, but lately he'd begun to appreciate the solace he found there. The color of the sky reflected like a mirror on the water's surface. On a gray and hazy morning, the water was a dull shade of steel. When the sun shone, Puget Sound was a deep, iridescent greenish blue. He enjoyed watching the ferries and other commercial and pleasure craft as they intersected the waterways. In the last while, he'd often stood in the same spot as Savannah and sorted through his thoughts.

"It's all so beautiful," she said, turning back to him. Hearing her give voice to his own feelings felt oddly comforting. The sooner he presented his argument, the better. The sooner he said what had to be said and put this woman out of his mind, the better.

"You ready?" he asked, flinging opening a file cabinet

and withdrawing a handful of thick folders from the top drawer.

"Ready as I'll ever be," she said, taking a chair on the other side of his desk.

Nash slapped the files down on his credenza. "Let's start with Adams versus Adams," he muttered, flipping through the pages of the top folder. "Now, this was an interesting case. Married ten years, two sons. Then Martha learned that Bill was having an affair with a coworker, so she decided to have one herself, only she chose a nineteen-year-old boy. The child-custody battle lasted two months, destroyed them financially and ended so bitterly that Bill moved out of town and hasn't been heard from since. Last I heard, Martha was clinically depressed and in and out of hospitals."

Savannah gasped. "What about their sons?" she asked. "What happened to them?"

"Eventually they went to live with a relative. From what I understand, they're both in counseling and have been for the last couple of years."

"How very sad," she whispered.

"Don't kid yourself. This is only the beginning. I'm starting with the *A*s and working my way through the file drawer. Let me know when you've had enough." He reached for a second folder. "Anderson versus Anderson... Ah, yes, I remember this one. She attempted suicide three times, blackmailed him emotionally, used the children as weapons, wiped him out financially and then sued for divorce, claiming he was an unfit father." His back was as stiff as his voice. He tossed aside that file and picked up the next.

"Allison versus Allison," he continued crisply. "By the way, I'm changing the names to protect the guilty."

"The guilty?"

"To my way of thinking, each participant in these cases is

guilty of contributing to the disasters I'm telling you about. Each made a crucial mistake."

"You're about to suggest their first error was falling in love."

"No," he returned coldly, "it all started with the wedding vows. No two people should be expected to live up to that ideal. It isn't humanly possible."

"You're wrong, Nash. People live up to those vows each and every day, in small ways and in large ones."

Nash jabbed his finger against the stack of folders. "This says otherwise. Love isn't meant to last. Couples are kidding themselves if they believe commitment lasts beyond the next morning. Life's like that, and it's time the rest of the world woke up and admitted it."

"Oh, please!" Savannah cried, standing. She walked over to the window, her back to him, clenching and unclenching her fists. Nash wondered if she was aware of it, and doubted she was.

"Be honest, Savannah. Marriage doesn't work anymore. Hasn't in years. The institution is outdated. If *you* want to stick your head in the sand, then fine. But when others risk getting hurt, someone needs to tell the truth." His voice rose with the heat of his argument.

Slowly she turned again and stared at him. An almost pitying look came over her.

"She must have hurt you very badly." Savannah's voice was so low, he had to strain to hear.

"Hurt me? What are you talking about?"

She shook her head as though she hadn't realized she'd spoken out loud. "Your ex-wife."

The anger that burned through Nash was like acid. "Who told you about Denise?" he demanded.

"No one," she returned quickly.

He slammed the top file shut and stuffed the stack of fold-ers back inside the drawer with little care and less concern. "How'd you know I was married?"

"I'm sorry, Nash, I shouldn't have mentioned it."

"Who told you?" The answer was obvious but he wanted her to say it.

"Susan mentioned it...."

"How much did she tell you?"

"Just that it happened years ago." Each word revealed her reluctance to drag his sister into the conversation. "She wasn't breaking any confidences, if that's what you think. I'm sure the only reason she brought it up was to explain your—"

"I know why she brought it up."

"I apologize, Nash. I shouldn't have said anything."

"Why not? My file's in another attorney's cabinet, along with those of a thousand other fools just like me who were stupid enough to think love lasts."

Savannah continued to stare at him. "You loved her, didn't you?"

"As much as any foolish twenty-four-year-old loves any-one. Would you mind if we change the subject?"

"Susan's twenty-four."

"Exactly," he said, slapping his hand against the top of his desk. "And she's about to make the same foolish choice I did."

"But, Nash..."

"Have you heard enough, or do you need to listen to a few more cases?"

"I've heard enough."

"Good. Let's get out of here." The atmosphere in the of-fice was stifling. It was as though each and every client he'd represented over the years was there to remind him of the pain he'd lived through himself—only he'd come away smarter than most.

"Do you want me to drive you back to the office or would you prefer I take you home?" he asked.

"No," Savannah said as they walked out of the office. He purposely adjusted his steps to match her slower gait. "If you don't mind, I'd prefer to have our, uh, wager settled this evening."

"Fine with me."

"If you don't mind, I'd like to head for my parents' home. I want you to meet them."

"Sure, why not?" he asked flippantly. His anger simmered just below the surface. Maybe this wasn't such a brilliant idea after all....

Savannah gave him the address and directions. The drive on the freeway was slowed by heavy traffic, which frustrated him even more. By the time they reached the exit, his nerves were frayed. He was about to suggest they do this another evening when she instructed him to take a left at the next light. They turned the corner, drove a block and a half down and were there.

They were walking toward the house when a tall, burly man with a thinning hairline hurried out the front door. "Savannah, sweetheart," he greeted them with a huge grin. "So this is the young man you're going to marry."

# Three

"Dad!" Savannah was mortified. The heat rose from her neck to her cheeks, and she knew her face had to be bright red.

Marcus Charles raised his hands. "Did I say something I shouldn't have?" But there was still a smile on his face.

"I'm Nash Davenport," Nash said, offering Marcus his hand. Considering how her father had chosen to welcome Nash, his gesture was a generous one. She chanced a look in the attorney's direction and was relieved to see he was smiling, too.

"You'll have to forgive me for speaking out of turn," her father said, "but Savannah's never brought home a young man she wants us to meet, so I assumed you're the—"

"Daddy, that's not true!"

"Name one," he said. "And while you're inventing a beau, I'll take Nash in and introduce him to your mother."

"Dad!"

"Hush now or you'll give Nash the wrong impression."

*The wrong impression!* If only he knew. This meeting

couldn't have gotten off to a worse start, especially with Nash's present mood. She'd made a drastic mistake mentioning his marriage. It was more than obvious that he'd been badly hurt and was trying to put the memory behind him.

Nash had built a strong case against marriage. The more clients he described, the harder his voice became. The grief of his own experience echoed in his voice as he listed the nightmares of the cases he'd represented.

Nash and her father were already in the house by the time Savannah walked up the steps and into the living room. Her mother had redecorated the room in a Southwestern motif, with painted clay pots and Navajo-style rugs. A recent addition was a wooden folk art coyote with his head thrown back, howling at the moon.

Every time she entered this room, Savannah felt a twinge of sadness. Her mother loved the Southwest and her parents had visited there often. Savannah knew her parents had once looked forward to moving south. She also knew she was the reason they hadn't. As an only child, and one who'd sustained a serious injury—even if it'd happened years before—they worried about her constantly. And with no other immediate family in the Seattle area, they were uncomfortable leaving their daughter alone in the big city.

A hundred times in the past few years, Savannah had tried to convince them to pursue their dreams, but they'd continually made excuses. They never came right out and said they'd stayed in Seattle because of her. They didn't need to; in her heart she knew.

"Hi, Mom," Savannah said as she walked into the kitchen. Her mother was standing at the sink, slicing tomatoes fresh from her garden. "Can I do anything to help?"

Joyce Charles set aside the knife and turned to give her a

firm hug. "Savannah, let me look at you," she said, studying her. "You're working too hard, aren't you?"

"Mom, I'm fine."

"Good. Now sit down here and have something cold to
drink and tell me all about Nash."

This was worse than Savannah had first believed. She
should have explained her purpose in bringing him to meet
her family at the very beginning, before introducing him.
Giving them a misleading impression was bad enough, but
she could only imagine what Nash was thinking.

When Savannah didn't immediately answer her question, Joyce supplied what information she already knew.
"You're coordinating his sister's wedding and that's how
you two met."

"Yes, but—"

"He really is handsome. What does he do?"

"He's an attorney," Savannah said. "But, Mom—"

"Just look at your dad." Laughing, Joyce motioned toward
the kitchen window that looked out over the freshly mowed
backyard. The barbecue was heating on the brick patio and
her father was showing Nash his prize fishing flies. He'd
been tying his own for years and took real pride in the craft;
now that he'd retired, it was his favorite hobby.

After glancing out at them, Savannah sank into a kitchen
chair. Her mother had poured her a glass of lemonade. Her
father displayed his fishing flies only when the guest was
someone important, someone he was hoping to impress. Savannah should have realized when she first mentioned Nash
that her father had made completely the wrong assumption
about this meeting.

"Mom," she said, clenching the ice-cold glass. "I think
you should know Nash and I are friends. Nothing more."

"We know that, dear. Do you think he'll like my pasta

salad? I added jumbo shrimp this time. I hope he's not a fussy eater."

Jumbo shrimp! So they were rolling out the red carpet. With her dad it was the fishing flies, with her mother it was pasta salad. She sighed. What had she let herself in for now?

"I'm sure he'll enjoy your salad." And *if* his anti-marriage argument—his evidence—was stronger than hers, he'd be eating seven more meals with a member of the Charles family. Her. She could only hope her parents conveyed the success of their relationship to this cynical lawyer.

"Your father's barbecuing steaks."

"T-bone," Savannah guessed.

"Probably. I forget what he told me when he took them out of the freezer."

Savannah managed a smile.

"I thought we'd eat outside," her mother went on. "You don't mind, do you, dear?"

"No, Mom, that'll be great." Maybe a little sunshine would lift her spirits.

"Let's go outside, then, shall we?" her mother said, carrying the large wooden bowl with the shrimp pasta salad.

The early-evening weather was perfect. Warm, with a subtle breeze and slanting sunlight. Her mother's prize roses bloomed against the fence line. The bright red ones were Savannah's favorite. The flowering rhododendron tree spread out its pink limbs in opulent welcome. Robins chatted back and forth like long-lost friends.

Nash looked up from the fishing rod he was holding and smiled. At least *he* was enjoying himself. Or seemed to be, anyway. Perhaps her embarrassment was what entertained him. Somehow, Savannah vowed, she'd find a way to clarify the situation to her parents without complicating things with Nash.

A cold bottle of beer in one hand, Nash joined her, grinning as though he'd just won the lottery.

"Wipe that smug look off your face," she muttered under her breath, not wanting her parents to hear. It was unlikely they would, busy as they were with the barbecue.

"You should've said something earlier." His smile was wider than ever. "I had no idea you were so taken with me."

"Nash, please. I'm embarrassed enough as it is."

"But why?"

"Don't play dumb." She was fast losing her patience with him. The misunderstanding delighted him and mortified her. "I'm going to have to tell them," she said, more for her own benefit than his.

"Don't. Your father might decide to barbecue hamburgers instead. It isn't every day his only daughter brings home a potential husband."

"Stop it," she whispered forcefully. "We both know how you feel about marriage."

"I wouldn't object if you wanted to live with me."

Savannah glared at him so hard, her eyes ached.

"Just joking." He took a swig of beer and held the bottle in front of his lips, his look thoughtful. "Then again, maybe I wasn't."

Savannah was so furious she had to walk away. To her dismay, Nash followed her to the back of the yard. Glancing over her shoulder, she caught sight of her parents talking.

"You're making this impossible," she told him furiously.

"How's that?" His eyes fairly sparkled.

"Don't, *please* don't." She didn't often plead, but she did now, struggling to keep her voice from quavering.

He frowned. "What's wrong?"

She bit her lower lip so hard, she was afraid she'd drawn blood. "My parents would like to see me settled down and married. They…they believe I'm like every other woman and—"

"You aren't?"

Savannah wondered if his question was sincere. "I'm handicapped," she said bluntly. "In my experience, men want a woman who's whole and perfect. Their egos ride on that, and I'm flawed. Defective merchandise doesn't do much for the ego."

"Savannah—"

She placed her hand against his chest. "Please don't say it. Spare me the speech. I've accepted what's wrong with me. I've accepted the fact that I'll never run or jump or marry or—"

Nash stepped back from her, his gaze pinning hers. "You're right, Savannah," he broke in. "You *are* handicapped and you will be until you view yourself otherwise." Having said that, he turned and walked away.

Savannah went in the opposite direction, needing a few moments to compose herself before rejoining the others. She heard her mother's laughter and turned to see her father with his arms around Joyce's waist, nuzzling her neck. From a distance they looked twenty years younger. Their love was as alive now as it had been years earlier…and demonstrating that was the purpose of this visit.

She scanned the yard, looking for Nash, wanting him to witness the happy exchange between her parents, but he was busy studying the fishing flies her father had left out for his inspection.

Her father's shout alerted Savannah that dinner was ready. Reluctantly she joined Nash and her parents at the round picnic table. She wasn't given any choice but to share the crescent-shaped bench with him.

He was close enough that she could feel the heat radiating off his body. Close enough that she yearned to be closer yet. That was what surprised her, but more profoundly it terrified her. From the first moment she'd met him, Savannah suspected there was something different about him, about her reactions to him. In the beginning she'd attributed it to their disagreement, his heated argument against marriage, the challenge he represented, the promise of satisfaction if she could change his mind.

Dinner was delicious and Nash went out of his way to compliment Joyce until her mother blushed with pleasure.

"So," her father said, glancing purposefully toward Savannah and Nash, "what are your plans?"

"For what?" Nash asked.

Savannah already knew the question almost as well as she knew the answer. Her father was asking about her future with Nash, and she had none.

"Why don't you tell Nash how you and Mom met," Savannah asked, interrupting her father before he could respond to Nash's question.

"Oh, Savannah," her mother protested, "that was years and years ago." She glanced at her husband of thirty-seven years and her clear eyes lit up with a love so strong, it couldn't be disguised. "But it *was* terribly romantic."

"You want to hear this?" Marcus's question was directed to Nash.

"By all means."

In that moment, Savannah could have kissed Nash, she was so grateful. "I was in the service," her father explained. "An Airborne Ranger. A few days before I met Joyce, I received my orders and learned I was about to be stationed in Germany."

"He'd come up from California and was at Fort Lewis," her mother added.

"There's not much to tell. Two weeks before I was scheduled to leave, I met Joyce at a dance."

"Daddy, you left out the best part," Savannah complained. "It wasn't like the band was playing a number you enjoyed and you needed a partner."

Her father chuckled. "You're right about that. I'd gone to the dance with a couple of buddies. The evening hadn't been going well."

"I remember you'd been stood up," Savannah inserted, eager to get to the details of their romance.

"No, dear," her mother intervened, picking up the story, "that was me. So I was in no mood to be at any social function. The only reason I decided to go was to make sure Lenny Walton knew I hadn't sat home mooning over him, but in reality I was at the dance mooning over him."

"I wasn't particularly keen on being at this dance, either," Marcus added. "I thought, mistakenly, that we were going to play pool at a local hall. I've never been much of a dancer, but my buddies were. They disappeared onto the dance floor almost immediately. I was bored and wandered around the hall for a while. I kept looking at my watch, eager to be on my way."

"As you can imagine, I wasn't dancing much myself," Joyce said.

"Then it happened." Savannah pressed her palms together and leaned forward. "This is my favorite part," she told Nash.

"I saw Joyce." Her father's voice dropped slightly. "When I first caught sight of her, my heart seized. I thought I might be having a reaction to the shots we'd been given earlier in the day. I swear I'd never seen a more beautiful woman. She wore this white dress and she looked like an angel. For a moment I was convinced she was." He reached for her mother's hand.

"I saw Marcus at that precise second, as well," Joyce whispered. "My friends were chatting and their voices faded until the only sound I heard was the pounding of my own heart. I don't remember walking toward him and yet I must have, because when I looked up Marcus was standing there."

"The funny part is, I don't remember moving, either."

Savannah propped her elbows on the table, her dinner forgotten. This story never failed to move her, although she'd heard it dozens of times over the years.

"We danced," her mother continued.

"All night."

"We didn't say a word. I think we must've been afraid the other would vanish if we spoke."

"While we were on the dance floor I kept pinching myself to be sure this was real, that Joyce was real. It was like we were both in a dream. These sorts of things only happen in the movies.

"When the music stopped, I looked around and realized my buddies were gone. It didn't matter. Nothing mattered but Joyce."

"Oh, Dad, I never get tired of hearing this story."

Joyce smiled as if she, too, was eager to relive the events of that night. "As we were walking out of the hall, I kept thinking I was never going to see Marcus again. I knew he was in the army—his haircut was a dead giveaway. I was well aware that my parents didn't want me dating anyone in the military, and up until then I'd abided by their wishes."

"I was afraid I wasn't going to see her again," Savannah's father went on. "But Joyce gave me her name and phone number and then ran off to catch up with her ride home."

"I didn't sleep at all that night. I was convinced I'd imagined everything."

"I couldn't sleep, either," Marcus confessed. "Here I was

with my shipping orders in my pocket—this was not the time to get involved with a woman."

"I'm glad you changed your mind," Nash said, studying Savannah.

"To tell you the truth, I don't think I had much of a choice. It was as if our relationship was preordained. By the end of the following week, I knew Joyce was the woman I'd marry. I knew I'd love her all my life, and both have held true."

"Did you leave for Germany?"

"Of course. I had no alternative. We wrote back and forth for two years and then were married three months after I was discharged. There was never another woman for me after I met Joyce."

"There was never another man for me," her mother said quietly.

Savannah tossed Nash a triumphant look and was disappointed to see that he wasn't looking her way.

"It's a romantic story." He was gracious enough to admit that much.

"Apparently some of that romance rubbed off on Savannah." Her father's eyes were proud as he glanced at her. "This wedding business of hers is thriving."

"So it seems." Some of the enthusiasm left Nash's voice. He was apparently thinking of his sister, and Savannah's role in her wedding plans.

"Eat, before your dinner gets cold," Joyce said, waving her fork in their direction.

"How long did you say you've been married?" Nash asked, cutting off a piece of his steak.

"Thirty-seven years," her father told him.

"And it's been smooth sailing all that time?"

Savannah wanted to pound her fist on the table and insist that this cross-examination was unnecessary.

Marcus laughed. "Smooth sailing? Oh, hardly. Joyce and I've had our ups and downs over the years like most couples. If there's anything special about our marriage, it's been our commitment to each other."

Savannah cleared her throat, wanting to gloat. Once more Nash ignored her.

"You've never once entertained the idea of divorce?" he asked.

This question was unfair! She hadn't had the opportunity to challenge his clients about their divorces, not that she would've wanted to. Every case had saddened and depressed her.

"As soon as a couple introduces the subject of divorce, there isn't the same willingness to concentrate on communication and problem-solving. People aren't nearly as flexible," Marcus said. "Because there's always that out, that possibility."

Joyce nodded. "If there was any one key to the success of our marriage, it's been that we've refused to consider divorce an option. That's not to say I haven't fantasized about it a time or two."

"We're only human," her father agreed with a nod. "I'll admit I've entertained the notion a time or two myself— even if I didn't do anything about it."

No! It wasn't true. Savannah didn't believe it. "But you were never *serious,*" she felt obliged to say.

Marcus looked at her and offered her a sympathetic smile, as if he knew about their wager. "Your mother and I love each other, and neither of us could say we're sorry we stuck it out through the hard times, but yes, sweetheart, there were a few occasions when I didn't know if our marriage would survive."

Savannah dared not look at Nash. Her parents' timing was

incredible. If they were going to be brutally honest, why did it have to be now? In all the years Savannah was growing up she'd never once heard the word *divorce*. In her eyes their marriage was solid, always had been and always would be.

"Of course, we never stopped talking," her mother was saying. "No matter how angry we might be with each other."

Soon after, Joyce brought out dessert—a coconut cake—and coffee.

"So, what do you think of our little girl?" Marcus asked, when he'd finished his dinner. He placed his hands on his stomach and studied Nash.

"Dad, please! You're embarrassing me."

"Why?"

"My guess is Savannah would prefer we didn't give her friend the third degree, dear," Joyce said mildly.

Savannah felt like kissing her mother's cheek. She stood, eager to disentangle herself from this conversation. "I'll help with the dishes, Mom," she said as if suggesting a trip to the mall.

Nash's mood had improved considerably after meeting Savannah's parents. Obviously, things weren't going the way she'd planned. Twice now, during dinner, it was all he could do not to laugh out loud. She'd expected them to paint a rosy picture of their idyllic lives together, one that would convince him of the error of his own views.

The project had backfired in her face. Rarely had he seen anyone look more shocked than when her parents said that divorce was something they'd each contemplated at one point or another in their marriage.

The men cleared the picnic table and the two women shooed them out of the kitchen. Nash was grateful, since he had several questions he wanted to ask Marcus about Savannah.

They wandered back outside. Nash was helping Marcus gather up his fishing gear when Savannah's father spoke.

"I didn't mean to pry earlier," he said casually, carrying his fishing rod and box of flies into the garage. A motor home was parked alongside the building. Although it was an older model, it looked as good as new.

"You don't need to worry about offending me," Nash assured him.

"I wasn't worried about you. Savannah gave me 'the look' while we were eating. I don't know how much experience you have with women, young man, but take my advice. When you see 'the look,' shut up. No matter what you're discussing, if you value your life, don't say another word."

Nash chuckled. "I'll keep that in mind."

"Savannah's got the same expression as her mother. If you continue dating her, you'll recognize it soon enough." He paused. "You *are* going to continue seeing my daughter, aren't you?"

"You wouldn't object?"

"Heavens, no. If you don't mind my asking, what do you think of my little girl?"

Nash didn't mince words. "She's the most stubborn woman I've ever met."

Marcus nodded and leaned his prize fishing rod against the wall. "She gets that from her mother, too." He turned around to face Nash, hands on his hips. "Does her limp bother you?" he asked point-blank.

"Yes and no." Nash wouldn't insult her father with a half-truth. "It bothers me because she's so conscious of it herself."

Marcus's chest swelled as he exhaled. "That she is."

"How'd it happen?" Curiosity got the better of him, although he'd prefer to hear the explanation from Savannah.

Her father walked to the back of the garage where a youngster's mangled bicycle was stored. "It sounds simple to say she was hit by a car. This is what was left of her bike. I've kept it all these years as a reminder of how far she's come."

"Oh, no..." Nash breathed when he viewed the mangled frame and guessed the full extent of the damage done to the child riding it. "How'd she ever survive?"

"I'm not being facetious when I say sheer nerve. Anyone with less fortitude would have willed death. She was in the hospital for months, and that was only the beginning. The doctors initially told us she'd never walk again, and for the first year we believed it.

"Even now she still has pain. Some days are worse than others. Climate seems to affect it somewhat. And her limp is more pronounced when she's tired." Marcus replaced the bicycle and turned back to Nash. "It isn't every man who recognizes Savannah's strength. You haven't asked for my advice, so forgive me for offering it."

"Please."

"My daughter's a special woman, but she's prickly when it comes to men and relationships. Somehow, she's got it in her head that no man will ever want her."

"I'm sure that's not true."

"It is true, simply because Savannah believes it is," Marcus corrected. "It'll take a rare man to overpower her defenses. I'm not saying you're that man. I'm not even saying you should try."

"You seemed to think otherwise earlier. Wasn't it you who assumed I was going to marry your daughter?"

"I said that to get a rise out of Savannah, and it worked."
Marcus rubbed his jaw, eyes twinkling with delight.

"We've only just met." Nash felt he had to present some
explanation, although he wasn't sure why.

"I know." He slapped Nash affectionately on the back
and together they left the garage. When they returned to
the house, the dinner dishes had been washed and put away.

Savannah's mother had filled several containers with leftovers and packed them in an insulated bag. She gave Savannah detailed instructions on how to warm up the leftover
steak and vegetables. Attempting brain surgery sounded
simpler. As it happened, Nash caught a glimpse of Marcus
from the corner of his eye and nearly burst out laughing.
The older man was slowly shaking his head.

"I like the coyote, Mom," Savannah said, as Nash took
the food for her. She ran one hand over the stylized animal.
"Are you and Dad going to Arizona this winter?"

Nash felt static electricity hit the airwaves.

"We haven't decided, but I doubt we will this year," Joyce
answered.

"Why not?" Savannah asked. This was obviously an old
argument. "You love it there. More and more of your friends
are becoming snowbirds. It doesn't make sense for you to
spend your winters here in the cold and damp when you can
be with your friends, soaking up the sunshine."

"Sweetheart, we've got a long time to make that decision,"
Marcus reminded her. "It's barely summer."

She hugged them both goodbye, then slung her purse over
her shoulder, obviously giving up on the argument with her
parents.

"What was that all about?" Nash asked once they were
in his car.

It was unusual to see Savannah look vulnerable, but she

did now. He wasn't any expert on women. His sister was evidence of that, and so was every other female he'd ever had contact with, for that matter. It looked as though gutsy Savannah was about to burst into tears.

"It's nothing," she said, her voice so low it was almost nonexistent. Her head was turned away from him and she was staring out the side window.

"Tell me," he insisted as he reached the freeway's on ramp. He increased the car's speed.

Savannah clasped her hands together. "They won't leave because of me. They seem to think I need a babysitter, that it's their duty to watch over me."

"Are you sure you're not being overly sensitive?"

"I'm sure. Mom and Dad love to travel, and now that Dad's retired they should be doing much more of it."

"They have the motor home."

"They seldom use it. Day trips, a drive to the ocean once or twice a year, and that's about it. Dad would love to explore the East Coast in the autumn, but I doubt he ever will."

"Why not?"

"They're afraid something will happen to me."

"It sounds like they're being overprotective."

"They are!" Savannah cried. "But I can't force them to go, and they won't listen to me."

He sensed that there was more to this story. "What's the *real* reason, Savannah?" He made his words as coaxing as he could, not wanting to pressure her into telling him something she'd later regret.

"They blame themselves for the accident," she whispered. "They were leaving for a weekend trip that day and I was to stay with a babysitter. I'd wanted to go with them and when they said I couldn't, I got upset. In order to appease me, Dad said I could ride my bicycle. Up until that time he'd always gone with me."

Nash chanced a look at her and saw that her eyes were closed and her body was rigid with tension.

"And so they punish themselves," she continued in halting tones, "thinking if they sacrifice their lives for me, it'll absolve them from their guilt. Instead it increases mine."

"Yours?"

"Do you mind if we don't discuss this anymore?" she asked, sounding physically tired and emotionally beaten.

The silence that followed was eventually broken by Savannah's sigh of defeat.

"When would you like me to start cooking your dinners?" she asked as they neared her shop.

"You're conceding?" He couldn't keep the shock out of his voice. "Just like that, without so much as an argument? You must be more tired than I realized."

His comments produced a sad smile.

"So you're willing to admit marriage is a thing of the past and has no part in this day and age?"

"Never!" She rallied a bit at that.

"That's what I thought."

"Are *you* ready to admit love can last a lifetime when it's nourished and respected?" she asked.

Nash frowned, his thoughts confused. "I'll grant there are exceptions to every rule and your parents are clearly that. Unfortunately, the love they share doesn't exist between most married couples.

"It'd be easy to tell you I like my macaroni and cheese extra cheesy," he went on to say, "but I have a feeling you'll change your mind in the morning and demand a rematch."

Savannah smiled and pressed the side of her head against the car window.

"You're exhausted, and if I accepted your defeat, you'd never forgive me."

"What do you suggest, then?"

"A draw." He pulled into the alley behind the shop, where Savannah had parked her car. "Let's call it square. I proved what I wanted to prove and you did the same. There's no need to go back to the beginning and start over, because neither of us is going to make any progress with the other. We're both too strongminded for that."

"We should have recognized it sooner," Savannah said, eyes closed.

She was so attractive, so...delectable, Nash had to force himself to look away.

"It's very gentlemanly of you not to accept my defeat."

"Not really."

Her eyes slowly opened and she turned her head so she could meet his eyes. "Why not?"

"Because I'm about to incur your wrath."

"Really? How are you going to do that?"

He smiled. It'd been so long since he'd looked forward to anything this much. "Because, my dear wedding coordinator, I'm about to kiss you."

# *Four*

"You're...you're going to kiss me?" Savannah had been exhausted seconds earlier, but Nash's words were a shot of adrenaline that bolted her upright.

"I most certainly am," he said, parking his car behind hers in the dark alley. "Don't look so scared. The fact is, you might even enjoy this."

That was what terrified Savannah most. If ever there was a man whose touch she yearned for, it was Nash. If ever there was a man she longed to be held by, it was Nash.

He bent his head toward hers and what resistance she'd managed to amass died a sudden death as he pressed his chin to her temple and simply held her against him. If he'd been rough or demanding or anything but gentle, she might've had a chance at resisting him. She might've had the *desire* to resist him. But she didn't. A sigh rumbled through her and with heedless curiosity she lifted her hand to his face, her fingertips grazing his jaw. Her touch seemed to go through him like an electrical shock because he groaned and, as she tilted back her head, his mouth sought hers.

*Debbie Macomber*

At the blast of unexpected sensation, Savannah buckled against him and whimpered, all the while clinging to him. The kiss continued, gaining in intensity and fervor until Savannah felt certain her heart would pound straight through her chest.

Savannah closed her eyes, deep in a world of sensual pleasure.

"Savannah." Her name was a groan. His breathing, heavy and hard, came in bursts as he struggled to regain control. Savannah was struggling, too. She finally opened her eyes. Her fingers were in his hair; she sighed and relaxed her hold.

Nash raised his head and took her face between his hands, his eyes delving into hers. "I didn't mean for that to happen."

An apology. She should've expected it, should've been prepared for it. But she wasn't.

He seemed to be waiting for her to respond so she gave him a weak smile, and lowered her gaze, not wanting him to guess how strong her reaction had been.

He leaned his forehead against hers and chuckled softly. "You're a surprise a minute."

"What do you mean?"

He dropped a glancing kiss on the side of her face. "I wouldn't have believed you'd be so passionate. The way you kissed me…"

"In other words, you didn't expect someone like me to experience sensual pleasure?" she demanded righteously. "It might shock you to know I'm still a woman."

"What?" Nash said. "What are you talking about?"

"You heard me," she said, frantically searching for her purse and the bag of leftovers her mother had insisted she take home with her.

"Stop," he said. "Don't use insults to ruin something that was beautiful and spontaneous."

"I wasn't the one—"

She wasn't allowed to finish. Taking her by the arms, he hauled her toward him until his mouth was on hers. Her resistance disappeared in the powerful persuasion of his kisses.

He exhaled sharply when he finished. "Your leg has nothing to do with this. Nothing. Do you understand?"

"Why were you so surprised, then?" she asked, struggling to keep her indignation alive. It was almost impossible when she was in his arms.

His answer took a long time. "I don't know."

"That's what I thought." She broke away and held her purse against her like a shield. "We've agreed to disagree on the issue of love and marriage, isn't that correct?"

"Yes," he said without emotion.

"Then I don't see any reason for us to continue our debate. It's been a pleasure meeting you, Mr. Davenport. Goodbye." Having said that, she jerked open the car door and nearly toppled backward. She caught herself in the nick of time before she could tumble headfirst into the alley.

"Savannah, for heaven's sake, will you—"

"Please, just leave me alone," she said, furious with herself for making such a dramatic exit and with him for reasons as yet unclear.

Because he made her *feel,* she guessed sometime later, when she was home and safe. He made her feel as if she was whole and without flaws. As if she was an attractive, desirable woman. Savannah blamed Nash for pretending she could be something she wasn't and the anger simmered in her blood long after she'd readied for bed.

Neatly folding her quilt at the foot of her bed, Savannah stood, seething, taking deep breaths to keep the tears at bay.

In the morning, after she'd downed her first cup of coffee, Savannah felt better. She was determined to put the in-

cident and the man out of her mind. There was no reason
for them to see each other again, no reason for them to continue with this farce. Not that Nash would *want* to see her,
especially after the idiotic way she'd behaved, scrambling
out of his car as if escaping a murderer.

As was so often the case of late, Savannah was wrong.
Nash was waiting on the sidewalk in front of her shop, carrying a white bag, when she arrived for work.

"Another peace offering?" she asked, when she unlocked
the front door and opened it for him.

"Something like that." He handed her a latte, then walked
across the showroom and sat on the corner of her desk, dangling one leg, as though he had every right to make himself
comfortable in her place of business.

Savannah hadn't recovered from seeing him again so
soon; she wasn't prepared for another confrontation. "What
can I do for you?" she asked stiffly, setting the latte aside.
She sat down and leaned back in the swivel chair, hoping
she looked relaxed, knowing she didn't.

"I've come to answer your question," he said, leg swinging as he pried loose the lid on his cup. He was so blasé about
everything, as if the intensity of their kisses was a common
thing for him. As if she was one in a long line of conquests.
"You wanted to know what was different last night and I'm
here to tell you."

This was the last thing Savannah expected. She glanced
pointedly at her watch. "Is this going to take long? I've got
an appointment in ten minutes."

"I'll be out of here before your client arrives."

"Good." She crossed her arms, trying to hold on to her
patience. Their kisses embarrassed her now. She was determined to push the whole incident out of her mind and forget
him. It'd been crazy to make a wager with him. Fun, true,

but sheer folly nonetheless. The best she could do was forget she'd ever met the man. Nash, however, seemed unwilling to let that happen.

"Well?" she pressed when he didn't immediately speak.

"A woman doesn't generally go to my head the way you
did," he said. "When I make love to a woman I'm the one
in control."

"We weren't making love," she said heatedly, heat flushing her cheeks with instant color. Her fingers bit into the
soft flesh of her arms as she fought to keep the embarrassment to herself.

"What *do* you call it, then?"

"Kissing."

"Yes, but it would've developed into something a whole
lot more complicated if we hadn't been in my car. The last
time I made love in the backseat of a car, I was—"

"This may come as a surprise to you, but I have no interest in hearing about your sexual exploits," she interjected.

"Fine," he snapped.

"Besides, we were nowhere near making love."

Nash's responding snort sent ripples of outrage through
Savannah. "You overestimate your appeal, Mr. Davenport."

He laughed outright this time. "Somehow or other, I
thought you'd say as much. I was hoping you'd be a bit
more honest, but then, I've found truth an unusual trait in
most women."

The bell above her door chimed just then, and her appointment strolled into the shop. Savannah was so grateful
to have this uncomfortable conversation interrupted, she
almost hugged her client.

"I'd love to continue this debate," she lied, "but as you
can see, I have a customer."

"Perhaps another time," Nash suggested.

She hesitated. "Perhaps."

He snickered disdainfully as he stood and sipped from the take-out cup. "As I said, women seem to have a hard time dealing with the truth."

Savannah pretended not to hear him as she walked toward her customer, a welcoming smile on her face. "Good morning, Melinda. I'm so glad to see you."

Nash said nothing as he sauntered past her and out the door. Not until he was out of sight did Savannah relax her guard. He claimed she went to his head. What he didn't know was that his effect on her was startlingly similar. Then again, perhaps he did know....

The woman irritated him. No, Nash decided as he hit the sidewalk, his stride clipped and fast, she more than irritated him. Savannah Charles incensed him. He didn't understand this oppressive need he felt to talk to her, to explain, to hear her thoughts. He'd awakened wishing things hadn't ended so abruptly between them, wishing he'd known what to say to convince her of his sincerity. Morning had felt like a second chance.

In retrospect, he suspected he was looking for help himself in working through the powerful emotions that had evolved during their embrace. Instead, Savannah claimed he'd miscalculated her reaction. The heck he had.

He should've realized she was as confused as he was about their explosive response to each other.

Nash arrived at his office half an hour later than usual. As he walked past his assistant's desk, she handed him several telephone messages. He was due in court in twenty minutes, and wouldn't have time to return any calls until early afternoon. Shuffling through the slips, he stopped at the third one.

Susan.

His sister had called him, apparently on her cell. Without further thought he set his briefcase aside and reached for the phone, punching out the number listed.

"Susan, it's Nash," he said when she answered. If he hadn't been so eager to talk to her, he might have mulled over the reason for her call. Something must have happened; otherwise she wouldn't have swallowed her pride to contact him.

"Hello, Nash."

He waited a moment in vain for her to continue. "You called me?"

"Yes," she said abruptly. "I wanted to apologize for hanging up on you the other day. It was rude and unnecessary. Kurt and I had a...discussion about it and he said I owed you an apology."

"Kurt's got a good head on his shoulders," he said, thinking his sister would laugh and the tension between them would ease. It didn't.

"I thought about what he had to say and Kurt's right. I'm sorry for the way I reacted."

"I'm sorry, too," Nash admitted. "I shouldn't have checked up on you behind your back." If she could be so generous with her forgiveness, then so could he. After all, Susan was his little sister. He had her best interests at heart, although she wouldn't fully appreciate his concern until later in life, when she was responsible for children of her own. He wasn't Susan's father, but he was her closest relative. Although she was twenty-four, he felt she still needed his guidance and direction.

"I was thinking we might have lunch together some afternoon," she ventured, and the quaver in her voice revealed how uneasy she was making the suggestion.

Nash had missed their lunches together. "Sounds like a great idea to me. How about Thursday?"

"Same place as always?"

There was a Mexican restaurant that was their favorite, on a steep side street not far from the King County courthouse. They'd made a point of meeting there for lunch at least once a month for the past several years. The waitresses knew them well enough to greet them by name.

"All right. See you Thursday at noon."

"Great."

Grinning, Nash replaced the receiver.

He looked forward to this luncheon date with his sister the way a kid anticipates the arrival of the Easter bunny. They'd both said and done things they regretted. Nash hadn't changed his mind about his sister marrying Kurt Caldwell. Kurt was decent, intelligent, hardworking and sincere, but they were both too young for marriage. Too uninformed about it. Judging by Susan's reaction, she wasn't likely to heed his advice. He hated to think of her making the same mistakes he had, but there didn't seem to be any help for it. He might as well mend the bridges of communication before they became irreparable.

"Is something wrong?" Susan asked Savannah as they went over the details for the wedding. It bothered her how careful Susan and Kurt had to be with their money, but she admired the couple's discipline. Each decision had been painstaking.

"I'm sorry." Savannah's mind clearly wasn't on the subject at hand. It had taken a sharp turn in another direction the moment Susan had shown up for their appointment. She reminded Savannah so much of her brother. Susan and Nash had the same eye and hair color, but they were alike in other ways, as well. The way Susan smiled and her easy laugh were Nash's trademarks.

Savannah had worked hard to force all thoughts of Nash from her mind. Naively, she felt she'd succeeded, until Susan had come into the shop.

Savannah didn't know what it was about this hardheaded cynic that attracted her so strongly. She resented the fact that he was the one to ignite the spark of her sensual nature. There was no future for them. Not when their views on love and marriage were so diametrically opposed.

"Savannah," Susan asked, "are you feeling okay?"

"Of course. I'm sorry, my thoughts seem to be a thousand miles away."

"I noticed," Susan said with a laugh.

Her mood certainly seemed to have improved since their previous meeting, Savannah noticed, wishing she could say the same. Nash hadn't contacted her since their last disastrous confrontation a few days earlier. Not that she'd expected he would.

Susan had entered the small dressing room and stepped into the wedding gown. She came out, lifting her hair at the back so Savannah could fasten the long row of pearl buttons.

"I'm having lunch with Nash on Thursday," Susan announced unexpectedly.

"I'm glad you two have patched up your differences."

Susan's shoulders moved in a reflective sigh. "We haven't exactly—at least, not yet. I called him to apologize for hanging up on him. He must have been eager to talk to me because his assistant told me he was due in court and I shouldn't expect to hear from him until that afternoon. He phoned back no more than five minutes later."

"He loves you very much." Savannah's fingers expertly fastened the pearl buttons. Nash had proved he was capable of caring deeply for another human being, yet he staunchly denied the healing power of love, wouldn't allow it into his own life.

*Perhaps you're doing the same thing.*

The thought came at her like the burning flash from a laser gun, too fast to avoid, and too painful to ignore. Savannah shook her head to chase away the doubts. It was ridiculous. She'd purposely chosen a career that was steeped in romance. To suggest she was blocking love from her own life was ludicrous. Yet the accusation repeated itself over and over....

"Savannah?"

"I'm finished," she said quickly. Startled, she stepped back.

Susan dropped her arms and shook her hair free before slowly turning around to face Savannah. "Well?" she asked breathlessly. "What do you think?"

Although she was still preoccupied with a series of haunting doubts, Savannah couldn't help admiring how beautiful Nash's sister looked in the bridal gown. "Oh, Susan, you're lovely."

The young woman viewed herself in the mirror, staring at her reflection for several minutes as if she wasn't sure she could believe what she was seeing.

"I'm going to ask Nash to attend the wedding when we have lunch," she said. Then, biting her lip, she added, "I'm praying he'll agree to that much."

"He should." Savannah didn't want to build up Susan's expectations. She honestly couldn't predict what Nash would say; she only knew what she thought he *should* do.

"He seemed pleased to hear from me," Susan went on to say.

"I'm sure he was." They stood beside each other in front

of the mirror. Neither seemed inclined to move. Savannah couldn't speak for Susan, but for her part, the mirror made the reality of her situation all too clear. Her tailored pants might not reveal her scarred and twisted leg, but she remained constantly aware of it, a not-so-gentle reminder of her deficiency.

"Let me know what Nash says," Savannah said impulsively just before Susan left the shop.

"I will." Susan's eyes shone with a childlike enthusiasm as she turned and walked away.

Savannah sat at her desk and wrote down the pertinent facts about the wedding gown she was ordering for Susan, but as she moved the pen across the paper, her thoughts weren't on dress measurements. Instead they flew straight to Nash. If nothing else, he'd given her cause to think over her life and face up to a few uncomfortable truths. That wasn't a bad day's work for a skeptical divorce attorney. It was unfortunate he'd never realize the impact he'd had on her.

Nash was waiting in the booth at quarter after twelve on Thursday, anxiously glancing at his watch every fifteen seconds, convinced Susan wasn't going to show, when she strolled into the restaurant. A smile lit her face when she saw him. It was almost as if they'd never disagreed, and she was a kid again coming to her big brother for advice.

"I'm sorry I'm late," she said, slipping into the vinyl seat across from him. "I'm starved." She reached for a salted chip, weighing it down with spicy salsa.

"It's good to see you," Nash ventured, taking the first step toward reconciliation. He'd missed Susan and he said so.

"I've missed you, too. It doesn't feel right for us to fight, does it?"

"Not at all."

"You're the only real family I have."

"I feel the same way. We've both made mistakes and we should learn from them." He didn't cast blame. There was no point.

The waitress brought their menus. Nash didn't recognize the young woman, which made him consider just how long it was since he'd had lunch with Susan. Frowning, he realized she'd been the one to approach him about a reconciliation, when as the older, more mature adult, he should've been working toward that end himself.

"I brought you something," Susan said, setting her handbag on the table. She rooted through it until she found what she was looking for. Taking the envelope from her purse, she handed it to him.

Nash accepted the envelope, peeled it open and pulled out a handcrafted wedding invitation, written on antique-white parchment paper in gold letters. He didn't realize his sister knew calligraphy. Although it was obviously handmade, the effort was competent and appealing to the eye.

"I wrote it myself," Susan said eagerly. "Savannah suggested Kurt and I would save money by making our own wedding invitations. It's much more personal this way, don't you think?"

"Very nice."

"The gold ink on the parchment paper was Kurt's idea. Savannah gave me a book on calligraphy and I've been practicing every afternoon."

He wondered how many more times his sister would find an excuse to drag the wedding coordinator's name into their conversation. Each time Susan mentioned Savannah it brought up unwelcome memories of their few short times together. Memories Nash would rather forget.

"Do you like it?" Susan asked eagerly. She seemed to be waiting for something more.

"You did a beautiful job," he said.

"I'm really glad you think so."

Susan was grinning under the warmth of his praise.

The waitress returned and they placed their order, although neither of them had looked at the menu. "We're certainly creatures of habit, aren't we?" his sister teased.

"So," he said, relaxing in the booth, "how are the wedding plans going?"

"Very well, thanks to Savannah." She folded her hands on top of the table, flexing her long fingers against each other, studying him, waiting.

Nash read over the invitation a second time and saw that it had been personally written to him. So this was the purpose of her phone call, the purpose of this lunch. She was asking him if he'd attend her wedding, despite his feelings about it.

"I don't expect you to change your mind about me marrying Kurt," Susan said anxiously, rushing the words together in her eagerness to have them said. "But it would mean the world to me if you'd attend the ceremony. There won't be a lot of people there. Just a few friends and Kurt's immediate family. That's all we can afford. Savannah's been wonderful, showing us how to get the most out of our limited budget. Will you come to my wedding, Nash?"

Nash knew when he was involved in a losing battle. Susan would marry Kurt with or without his approval. His kid sister was determined to do this her way. He'd done his best to talk some sense into her, but to no avail. He'd made the mistake of threatening her, and she'd called his bluff. The past weeks had been miserable for them both.

"I'll come."

"Oh, Nash, thank you." Tears brimmed and spilled over

her lashes. She grabbed her paper napkin, holding it beneath each eye in turn. "I can't begin to tell you how much this means to me."

"I know." He felt like crying himself, but for none of the same reasons. He didn't want to see his sister hurt and that was inevitable once she was married. "I still don't approve of your marrying so young, but I can't stop you."

"Nash, you keep forgetting, I'm an adult, over twenty-one. You make me sound like a little kid."

He sighed expressively. That *was* the way he saw her, as his kid sister. It was difficult to think of her married, with a family of her own, when it only seemed a few years back that she was in diapers.

"You'll love Kurt once you get to know him better," she said excitedly, wiping the moisture from her cheek. "Look at what you've done to me," she muttered. Her mascara streaked her face in inky rows.

His hand reached for hers and he squeezed her fingers. "We'll get through this yet, kid," he joked.

Nash suspected, in the days that followed, that it was natural to feel good about making his sister so happy. All he'd agreed to do was attend the ceremony. He hadn't figured out what was going to keep him in his seat when the minister asked anyone who opposed the union to speak now or forever hold their peace. Attending the ceremony itself, regardless of his personal feelings toward marriage, was the least he could do for causing the rift between them.

The card from Savannah that arrived at his office took him by surprise. He stared at the return address on the envelope for a moment before turning it over and opening it with eager fingers. Her message was straightforward: "Thank you." Her elegant signature appeared below.

Nash gazed at the card for several minutes before slapping it down on his desk. The woman was driving him crazy.

He left the office almost immediately, shocking his assistant, who rushed after him, needing to know what she was supposed to do about his next appointment. Nash suggested she entertain him with some law journals and coffee. He promised to be back in half an hour.

Luckily he found a parking spot on the street. Climbing out of his car, he walked purposely toward the bridal shop. Savannah was sitting at her desk intent on her task. When she glanced up and saw him, she froze.

"I got your card," he said stiffly.

"I… It made Susan so happy to know you'd attend her wedding. I wanted to thank you," she said, her eyes following his every move.

He marched to her desk, not understanding even now what force had driven him to her. "How many guests is she inviting?"

"I…believe the number's around sixty."

"Change that," he instructed harshly. "We're going to be inviting three hundred or more. I'll have the list to you in the morning."

"Susan and Kurt can't afford—"

"They won't be paying for it. I will. I want the best for my sister, understand? We'll have a sit-down dinner, a dance with a ten-piece orchestra, real flowers and a designer wedding dress. We'll order invitations because there'll be too many for Susan to make herself. Have you got that?" He motioned toward her pen, thinking she should write it all down.

Savannah looked as if she hadn't heard him. "Does Susan know about all this?"

"Not yet."

"Don't you think you should clear it with her first?"

"It might be too soon, because a good deal of this hinges on one thing."

Savannah frowned. "What's that?"

"If you'll agree to attend the wedding as my date."

# Five

"Your *date?*" Savannah repeated as she leapt to her feet. No easy task when one leg was as unsteady as hers. She didn't often forget that, but she did now in her incredulity. "That's emotional blackmail," she cried, before slumping back in her chair.

"You're right, it is," Nash agreed, leaning forward and pressing his hands against the edge of her oak desk. His face was scant inches from her own, and his eyes cut straight through her defenses. "It's what you expect of me, isn't it?" he demanded. "Since I'm so despicable."

"I never said that!"

"Maybe not, but you thought it."

"No, I didn't!" she snapped, then decided she probably had. She'd been shaken by his kiss, and then he'd apologized as if he'd never meant it to happen. And, perhaps worse, maybe he wished it hadn't.

A slow, leisurely smile replaced Nash's dark scowl. "That's what I thought," he said as he raised his hand and brushed a strand of hair from her forehead. His fingertips lingered at her face. "I wish I knew what's happening to us."

"Nothing's happening," Savannah insisted, but her voice lacked conviction even to her own ears. She was fighting the powerful attraction she felt for him for all she was worth, which at the moment wasn't much. "You aren't really going to blackmail me, are you?"

He gently traced the outline of her face, pausing at her chin and tilting it upward. "Do you agree to attend the wedding with me?"

"Yes, only—"

"Then you should know I had no intention of following through with my threat. Susan can have the wedding of her dreams."

Savannah stood, awkwardly placing her weight on her injured leg. "I'm sure there are far more suitable dates for you," she said crisply.

"I want you."

He made this so difficult. "Why me?" she asked. By his own admission, there were any number of other women who'd jump at the chance to date him. Why had he insisted on singling *her* out? It made no sense.

Nash frowned as if he wasn't sure himself, which lent credence to Savannah's doubts. "I don't know. As for this wedding, it seemed to me I could be wrong. It doesn't happen often, but I have been known to make an error in judgment now and again." He gave her a quick, self-deprecating grin. "Susan's my only sister—the only family I've got. I don't want there to be any regrets between us. Your card helped, too, and the way I see it, if I'm going to sit through a wedding, I'm not going to suffer alone. I want you there with me."

"Then I suggest you ask someone who'd appreciate the invitation," she said defiantly, straightening her shoulders.

"I want to be with you," he insisted softly, his eyes revealing his confusion. "Darned if I know why. You're stubborn, defensive and argumentative."

"One would think you'd rather...oh, wrestle a rattlesnake than go out with me."

"One would think," he agreed, smiling boyishly, "but if that's the case, why do I find myself listening for the sound of your voice? Why do I look forward to spending time with you?"

"I...wouldn't know." Except that she found herself in the same situation. Nash was never far from her thoughts; she hadn't been free of him from the moment they'd met.

His eyes, dark and serious, wandered over her face. Before she could protest, he lowered his head and nuzzled her ear. "Why can't I get you out of my mind?"

"I can't answer that, either." He was going to kiss her again, in broad daylight, where they could be interrupted by anyone walking into the shop. Yet Savannah couldn't bring herself to break away, couldn't offer so much as a token resistance.

A heartbeat later, his mouth met hers. Despite her own hesitation, she kissed him back. Nash groaned, drawing her more securely into his embrace.

"Savannah," he whispered as he broke off the kiss. "I can hardly believe this, but it's even better than before."

Savannah said nothing, although she agreed. She was trembling, and prayed Nash hadn't noticed, but that was too much to ask. He slid his fingers into her hair and brought her face close to his. "You're terrified, aren't you?" he asked, his cheek touching hers.

"Don't be ridiculous," she muttered. She felt his smile

against her flushed skin and realized she hadn't fooled him any more than she had herself. "I don't know what I am."

"I don't know, either. Somehow I wonder if I ever will. I don't suppose you'd make this process a lot easier and consider just having an affair with me?"

Savannah stiffened, not knowing if he meant what he was saying. "Absolutely not."

"That's what I thought," he said with a lengthy sigh. "It's going to be the whole nine yards with you, isn't it?"

"I have no idea what you mean," she insisted.

"Perhaps not." Pulling away, he checked his watch and seemed surprised at the time. "I've got to get back to the office. I'll give Susan a call this afternoon and the three of us can get together and make the necessary arrangements."

Savannah nodded. "We're going to have to move quickly. Planning a wedding takes time."

"I know."

She smiled shyly, wanting him to know how pleased she was by his change of heart. "This is very sweet of you, Nash."

He gestured weakly with his hands, as if he wasn't sure he was doing the right thing. "I still think she's too young to be married. I can't help thinking she'll regret this someday."

"Marriage doesn't come with guarantees at any age," Savannah felt obliged to tell him. "But then, neither does life. Susan and Kurt have an advantage you seem to be overlooking."

"What's that?"

"They're in love."

"Love." Nash snickered loudly. "Generally it doesn't last more than two or three weeks."

"Sometimes that's true, but not this time," Savannah said. "However, I've worked with hundreds of couples over the years and I get a real sense about the people who come to me. I can usually tell if their marriages will last or not."

"What about Kurt and Susan?"

"I believe they'll have a long, happy life together."

Nash rubbed the side of his face, his eyes intense. He obviously didn't believe that.

"Their love is strong," she said, trying to bolster her argument.

Nash raised his eyebrows. "Spoken like a true romantic."

"I'm hoping the skeptic in you will listen."

"I'm trying."

Savannah could see the truth in that. He *was* trying, for Susan's sake and perhaps hers. He'd come a long way from where he was when they'd first met. But he had a lot farther to go.

Nash had no idea weddings could be so demanding, so expensive or so time-consuming. The one advantage of all this commotion and bother was all the hours he was able to spend with Savannah. As the weeks progressed, Nash came to know Savannah Charles, the businesswoman, as well as he did the lovely, talented woman who'd attracted him from the beginning. He had to admit she knew her stuff. He doubted anyone else could have arranged so large and lavish a wedding on such short notice. It was only because she had long-standing relationships with those involved—the florists, photographers, printers, hotel managers and so on—that Nash was able to give Susan an elaborate wedding.

As the days passed, Nash lost count of how often he asked Savannah out to dinner, a movie, a baseball game. She found a plausible excuse each and every time. A less determined man would have grown discouraged and given up.

But no more, he mused, looking out his office window.

As far as she was concerned, he held the trump card in the palm of his hand. Savannah had consented to attend Susan's wedding with him, and there was no way he was letting her out of the agreement.

He sat at his desk thinking about this final meeting scheduled for later that afternoon. He'd been looking forward to it all week. Susan's wedding was taking place Saturday evening, and Savannah had flat run out of excuses.

Nash arrived at the shop before his sister. He was grateful for these few moments alone with Savannah.

"Hello, Nash." Her face lit up with a ready smile when he walked into the shop. She was more relaxed with him now. She stood behind a silver punch bowl, decorating the perimeter with a strand of silk gardenias.

Her knack for making something ordinary strikingly beautiful was a rare gift. In some ways she'd done that with his life these past few weeks, giving him something to anticipate when he got out of bed every morning. She'd challenged him, goaded him, irritated and bemused him. It took quite a woman to have such a powerful effect.

"Susan's going to be a few minutes late," Nash told her. "I was hoping she'd changed her mind and decided to call off the whole thing." He'd hoped nothing of the sort, but enjoyed getting a reaction out of Savannah.

"Give it up. Susan's going to be a beautiful bride."

"Who's going to be working the wedding?" he asked, advancing toward her.

"I am, of course. Together with Nancy. You met her last week."

He nodded, remembering the pleasant, competent young woman who'd come to one of their meetings. Savannah often contracted her to help out at larger events.

"Since Nancy's going to be there, you can attend as my date and leave the work to her."

"Nash, will you please listen to reason? I *can't* be your date…. I know it's short notice but there are plenty of women who'd enjoy—"

"We have an agreement," he reminded her.

"I realize that, but—"

"I won't take no for an answer, Savannah, not this time."

She stiffened. Nash had witnessed this particular reaction on numerous occasions. Whenever he asked her out, her pride exploded into full bloom. Nash was well acquainted with how deeply entrenched that pride was.

"Nash, please."

He reached for her hand and raised it to his lips. His mouth grazed her fingertips. "Not this time," he repeated. "I'll pick you up just before we meet to have the pictures taken."

"Nash…"

"Be ready, Savannah, because I swear I'll drag you there in your nightgown if I have to."

Savannah was in no mood for company, nor was she keen on talking to her mother when Joyce phoned that same evening. She'd done everything she could to persuade Nash to change his plans. But he insisted she be his date for Susan's wedding. Indeed, he'd blackmailed her into agreeing to it.

"I haven't heard from you in ages," her mother said.

"I've been busy with the last-minute details of Susan Davenport's wedding."

"She's Nash's sister, isn't she?"

Her mother knew the answer to that. She was looking for an excuse to bring Nash into the conversation, which she'd done countless times since meeting him. If Savannah had to do that wager over again, she'd handle it differently. Her entire day had been spent contemplating various regrets. She wanted to start over, be more patient, finish what she'd begun, control her tongue, get out of this ridiculous "date" with Nash.

But she couldn't.

"Your father's talking about taking a trip to the ocean for a week or two."

"That sounds like an excellent idea." Savannah had been waiting all summer for them to get away.

"I'm not sure we should go...."

"For heaven's sake, why not?"

"Oh, well, I hate to leave my garden, especially now. And there've been a few break-ins in the neighborhood the last few weeks. I'd be too worried about the house to enjoy myself." The excuses were so familiar, and Savannah wanted to scream with frustration. But her mother had left out the real reason for her uncertainty. She didn't want to leave Savannah. Naturally, her parents had never come right out and said that, but it was their underlying reason for staying close to the Seattle area.

Savannah had frequently tried to discuss this with them. However, both her parents just looked at her blankly as if they didn't understand her concerns. Or they changed the subject. They didn't realize what poor liars they were.

"Have you seen much of Nash lately?" Her mother's voice rose expectantly.

"We've been working together on the wedding, so we've actually been seeing a lot of each other."

"I meant socially, dear. Has he taken you out? He's such a nice young man. Both your father and I think so."

"Mother," Savannah said, hating this, "I haven't been dating Nash."

Her mother's sigh of disappointment cut through Savannah. "I see."

"We're friends, nothing more. I've told you that."

"Of course. Be sure and let me know how the wedding goes, will you?"

Seeing that Nash had spared little expense, it would be gorgeous. "I'll give you a call early next week and tell you all about it."

"You promise?"

"Yes, Mom, I promise."

Savannah replaced the receiver with a heavy heart. The load of guilt she carried was enough to buckle her knees. How could one accident have such a negative impact on so many people for so long? It wasn't fair that her parents should continue to suffer for what had happened to her. Yet they blamed themselves, and that guilt was slowly destroying the best years of their lives.

Nash arrived at Savannah's house to pick her up late Saturday afternoon. He looked tall and distinguished in his black tuxedo and so handsome that for an awkward moment, Savannah had trouble taking her eyes off him.

"What's wrong?" he said, running his finger along the inside of his starched collar. "I feel like a concert pianist."

Savannah couldn't keep from smiling. "I was just thinking how distinguished you look."

His hand went to his temple. "I'm going gray?"

She laughed. "No."

"*Distinguished* is the word a woman uses when a man's entering middle age and losing his hair."

"If you don't get us to this wedding, we're going to miss it, and then you really *will* lose your hair." She placed her arm in his and carefully set one foot in front of the other.

She rarely wore dress shoes. It was chancy, but she didn't want to ruin the effect of her full-length dress with flats. Nash couldn't possibly know the time and effort she'd gone to for this one date, which would likely be their first *and* last. She'd ordered the dress from New York, a soft, pale pink gown with a pearl-studded yoke. The long, sheer sleeves had layered pearl cuffs. She wore complementary pearl earrings and a single-strand necklace.

It wasn't often in her life that Savannah felt beautiful, but she did now. She'd worked hard, wanting to make this evening special for Susan—and knowing it would be her only date with Nash. She suspected there was a bit of Cinderella in every woman, the need to believe in fairy tales and happy endings, in true love conquering against impossible odds. For this one night, Savannah longed to forget she was crippled. For this one night, she wanted to pretend she was beautiful. A princess.

Nash helped her across the yard and held open the door for her. She was inside the car, seat belt buckled, when he joined her. His hands gripped the steering wheel, but when he didn't start the car, she turned to him.

"Is something wrong?"

He smiled at her, but she saw the strain in his eyes and didn't understand it. "It's just that you're so beautiful, I can hardly keep my hands off you."

"Oh, Nash," she whispered, fighting tears. "Thank you."

"For what?"

She shook her head, knowing she'd never be able to explain.

The church was lovely. Savannah had rarely seen a sanctuary decorated more beautifully. The altar was surrounded with huge bouquets of pink and white roses, and their scent drifted through the room. The end of each pew was decorated with a small bouquet of white rosebuds and gardenias with pink and silver bows. The effect was charming.

Seated in the front row, Savannah closed her eyes as the organ music swelled. She stood, and from the rustle of movement behind her, she knew the church was filled to capacity.

Savannah turned to see Nash escort his sister slowly down the center aisle, their steps in tune to the music. They were followed by the bridesmaids and groomsmen, most of them recruited late, every one of them delighted to share in Susan and Kurt's happiness.

Savannah had attended a thousand or more weddings in her years as a coordinator. Yet it was always the same. The moment the music crescendoed, her eyes brimmed with tears at the beauty and emotion of it all.

This wedding was special because the bride was Nash's sister. Savannah had felt a part of it from the beginning, when Susan had approached her, desperate for assistance. Now it was all coming together and Susan was about to marry Kurt, the man she truly loved.

Nash was uncomfortable with love, and a little jealous, too, although she doubted he recognized that. Susan, the little sister he adored, would soon be married and would move to California with her husband.

When they reached the steps leading to the altar, Susan kissed Nash's cheek before placing her hand on Kurt's arm. Nash hesitated as if he wasn't ready to surrender his sister. Just when Savannah was beginning to get worried, he turned and entered the pew, standing next to her. Either by accident or design, his hand reached for hers. His grip was tight, his face strained with emotion.

Savannah was astonished to see that his eyes were bright with tears. She could easily be mistaken, though, since her own were blurred. A moment later, she was convinced she was wrong.

The pastor made a few introductory comments about the sanctity of marriage. Holding his Bible open, he stepped forward. "I'd like each couple who's come to celebrate the union of Susan and Kurt to join hands," he instructed.

Nash took both of Savannah's hands so that she was forced to turn sideways. His eyes delved into hers, and her heart seemed to stagger to a slow, uneven beat at what she read in them. Nash was an expert at disguising his feelings, yes, but also at holding on to his anger and the pain of his long-dead marriage, at keeping that bitterness alive. As he stared down at her, his eyes became bright and clear and filled with an emotion so strong, it transcended anything she'd ever seen.

Savannah was barely aware of what was going on around them. Sounds faded; even the soloist who was singing seemed to be floating away. Savannah's peripheral vision became clouded, as if she'd stepped into a dreamworld. Her sole focus was Nash.

With her hands joined to Nash's, their eyes linked, she heard the pastor say, "Those of you wishing to renew your vows, repeat after me."

Nash's fingers squeezed hers as the pastor intoned the words. "I promise before God and all gathered here this day to take you as my wife. I promise to love and cherish you, to leave my heart and my life open to you."

To Savannah's amazement, Nash repeated the vow in a husky whisper. She could hear others around them doing the same. Once again tears filled her eyes. How easy it would be to pretend he was devoting his life to hers.

"I'll treasure you as a gift from God, to encourage you to be all He meant you to be," Savannah found herself repeating a few minutes later. "I promise to share your dreams, to appreciate your talents, to respect you. I pledge myself to you, to learn from and value our differences." As she spoke, Savannah's heart beat strong and steady and sure. Excitement rose up in her as she realized that what she'd said was true. These were the very things she yearned to do for Nash. She longed for him to trust her enough to allow her into his life, to help him bury the hurts of the past. They were different, as different as any couple could be. That didn't make their relationship impossible. It added flavor, texture and challenge to their attraction. Life together would never be dull for them.

"I promise to give you the very best of myself, to be faithful to you, to be your friend and your partner," Nash whispered next, his voice gaining strength. Sincerity rang through his words.

"I offer you my heart and my love," Savannah repeated, her own heart ready to burst with unrestrained joy.

"You are my friend," Nash returned, "my lover, my wife."

It was as if they, too, were part of the ceremony, as if they, too, were pledging their love and their lives to each other.

Through the minister's words, Savannah offered Nash all that she had to give. It wasn't until they'd finished and Kurt was told to kiss his bride that Savannah remembered this wasn't real. She'd stepped into a dreamworld, the fantasy she'd created out of her own futile need for love. Nash had only been following the minister's lead. Mortified, she lowered her eyes and tugged her trembling fingers free from Nash's.

He, too, apparently harbored regrets. His hands clasped the pew in front of them until his knuckles paled. He formed a fist with his right hand. Savannah dared not look up at him, certain he'd recognize her thoughts and fearing she'd know his. She couldn't have borne the disappointment. For the next several hours they'd be forced to share each other's company, through the dinner and the dance that followed the ceremony. Savannah wasn't sure how she was going to manage it now, after she'd humiliated herself.

Thankfully she was spared having to face Nash immediately after the ceremony was over. He became a part of the reception line that welcomed friends and relatives. Savannah was busy herself, working with the woman she'd hired to help coordinate the wedding and reception. Together they took down the pew bows, which would serve as floral centerpieces for the dinner.

"I don't think I've ever seen a more beautiful ceremony," Nancy Mastell told Savannah, working furiously. "You'd think I'd be immune to this after all the weddings we attend."

"It...was beautiful," Savannah agreed. Her stomach was in knots, and her heart told her how foolish she'd been; nevertheless, she couldn't make herself regret what had happened. She'd learned something about herself, something she'd denied far too long. She needed love in her life. For years she'd cut herself off from opportunity, content to live off the happiness of others. She'd moved from one day to the next, carrying her pain and disappointment, never truly happy, never fulfilled. Pretending.

This was why Nash threatened her. She couldn't pretend with him. Instinctively he knew. For reasons she'd probably never understand, he saw straight through her.

"Let me get those," Nancy said. "You're a wedding guest."

"I can help." But Nancy insisted otherwise.

When Savannah returned to the vestibule, she found Nash waiting for her. They drove in silence to the high-end hotel, where Nash had rented an elegant banquet room for the evening.

Savannah prayed he'd say something to cut the terrible

tension. She could think of nothing herself. A long list of possible topics presented itself, but she couldn't come up with a single one that didn't sound silly or trite.

Heaven help her, she didn't know how they'd be able to spend the rest of the evening in each other's company.

Dinner proved to be less of a problem than Savannah expected. They were seated at a table with two delightful older gentlemen whom Nash introduced as John Stackhouse and Arnold Serle, the senior partners of the law firm that employed him. John was a widower, she gathered, and Arnold's wife was in England with her sister.

"Mighty nice wedding," Mr. Stackhouse told Nash.

"Thank you. I wish I could take credit, but it's the fruit of Savannah's efforts you're seeing."

"Beautiful wedding," Mr. Serle added. "I can't remember when I've enjoyed one more."

Savannah was waiting for a sarcastic remark from Nash, but one never came. She didn't dare hope that he'd changed his opinion, and guessed it had to do with the men who were seated with them.

Savannah spread the linen napkin across her lap. When she looked up, she discovered Arnold Serle watching her. She wondered if her mascara had run or if there was something wrong with her makeup. Her doubts must have shown in her eyes, because he grinned and winked at her.

Savannah blushed. A sixty-five-year-old corporate attorney was actually flirting with her. It took her a surprisingly short time to recover enough to wink back at him.

Arnold burst into loud chuckles, attracting the attention of Nash and John Stackhouse, who glanced disapprovingly at his partner. "Something troubling you, Arnold?"

"Just that I wish I were thirty years younger. Savannah here's prettier than a picture."

"You been at the bottle again?" his friend asked. "He becomes quite a flirt when he has," the other man explained. "Especially when his wife's out of town."

Arnold's cheeks puffed with outrage. "I most certainly do not."

Their salads were delivered and Savannah noted, from the corner of her eye, that Nash was studying her closely. Taking her chances, she turned and met his gaze. To her astonishment, he smiled and reached for her hand under the table.

"Arnold's right," he whispered. "Every other woman here fades compared to you." He paused. "With the exception of Susan, of course."

Savannah smiled.

The orchestra was tuning their instruments in the distance and she focused her attention on the group of musicians, feeling a surge of regret and frustration. "I need to tell you something," she said.

"What?"

"I'm sorry, I can't dance. But please don't let that stop you."

"I'm not much of a dancer myself. Don't worry about it."

"Anything wrong?" Arnold asked.

"No, no," Nash was quick to answer. "Savannah just had a question."

"I see."

"That reminds me," John began. "There's something we've been meaning to discuss with you, Nash. It's about the position for senior partner opening up at the firm," he said.

"Can't we leave business out of this evening?" Arnold asked, before Nash could respond. Arnold frowned. "It's difficult enough choosing another partner without worrying about it day and night."

Nash didn't need to say a word for Savannah to know how

much he wanted the position. She felt it in him, the way his body tensed, the eager way his head inclined. But after Arnold's protest, John hadn't continued the discussion.

The dinner dishes were cleared from the table by the expert staff. The music started, a wistful number that reminded Savannah of sweet wine and red roses. Susan, in her flowing silk gown, danced with Kurt as their guests looked on, smiling.

The following number Kurt danced with his mother and Nash with Susan. His assurances that he wasn't much of a dancer proved to be false. He was skilled and graceful.

Savannah must have looked more wistful than she realized because when the next number was announced, Arnold Serle reached for her hand. "This dance is mine."

Savannah was almost too flabbergasted to speak. "I… can't. I'm sorry, but I can't."

"Nonsense." With that, the smiling older man all but pulled her from her chair.

# *Six*

Savannah was close to tears. She couldn't dance and now she was being forced onto the ballroom-style floor by a sweet older man who didn't realize she had a limp. He hadn't even noticed it. Humiliation burned her cheeks. The wonderful romantic fantasy she was living was about to blow up in her face. Then, when she least expected to be rescued, Nash was at her side, his hand at her elbow.

"I believe this dance is mine, Mr. Serle," he said, whisking Savannah away from the table.

Relief rushed through her, until she saw that he was escorting her onto the dance floor himself. "Nash, I can't," she said in a heated whisper. "Please don't ruin this day for me."

"Do you trust me?"

"Yes, but you don't seem to understand…."

Understand or not, he led her confidently onto the crowded floor, turned and gathered her in his arms. "All I want you to do is relax. I'll do the work."

"Nash!"

"Relax, will you?"

"No... Please take me back to the table."

Instead he grasped her hands and raised them, tucking them around his neck. Savannah turned her face away from him. Their bodies fit snugly against each other and Nash felt warm and substantial. His thigh moved against hers, his chest grazed her breasts and a slow excitement began to build within her. After holding her breath, she released it in a long, trembling sigh.

"It feels good, doesn't it?"

"Yes." Lying would be pointless.

"We're going to make this as simple and easy as possible. All you have to do is hold on to me." He held her close, his hands clasped at the base of her spine. "This isn't so bad now, is it?"

"I'll never forgive you for this, Nash Davenport." Savannah was afraid to breathe again for fear she'd stumble, for fear she'd embarrass them both. She'd never been on a dance floor in her life and try as she might, she couldn't make herself relax the way he wanted. This was foreign territory to her, the girl who'd never been asked to a school dance. The girl who'd watched and envied her friends from afar. The girl who'd only waltzed in her dreams with imaginary partners. And not one of them had been anything like Nash.

"Maybe this will help," Nash whispered. He bent his head and kissed the side of her neck with his warm, moist mouth.

"Nash!" She squirmed against him.

"I've wanted to do that all night," he whispered. Goose bumps shivered up her arms as his tongue made lazy circles along one ear. Her legs felt as if they'd collapse, and she involuntarily pressed her weight against him.

"Please stop that!" she said from between clenched teeth.

"Not on your life. You're doing great." He made all the

moves and, holding her the way he was, took the weight off her injured leg so she could slide with him.

"I'll embarrass us both any minute," she muttered.

"Just close your eyes and enjoy the music."

Since they were in the middle of the floor, Savannah had no choice but to follow his instructions. Her chance to escape gracefully had long since passed.

The music was slow and easy, and when she lowered her lashes, she could pretend. This was the night, she'd decided earlier, to play the role of princess. Only she'd never expected her Cinderella fantasy to make it all the way to the ballroom floor.

"You're a natural," he whispered. "Why have you waited so long?"

She was barely moving, which was all she could manage. This was her first experience, and although she was loath to admit it, Nash was right; she was doing well. This must be a dream, a wonderful romantic dream. If so, she prayed it'd be a very long time before she woke.

As she relaxed, Nash's arms moved to a more comfortable position. She lowered her own arm just a little, and her fingers toyed with the short hair at his neck. It was a small but intimate gesture, to run her fingers through his hair, and she wondered at her courage. It might be just another facet of her fantasy, but it seemed the action of a lover or a wife.

*Wife.*

In the church, when they'd repeated the vows, Nash had called her his friend, his lover, his wife. But it wasn't real. But for now, she was in his arms and they were dancing cheek to cheek, as naturally as if they'd been partners for years. For now, she would make it real, because she so badly wanted to believe it.

"Who said you couldn't dance?" he asked her after a while.

"Shh." She didn't want to talk. These moments were much too precious to waste on conversation. This time was meant to be savored and enjoyed.

The song ended, and when the next one started almost without pause, the beat was fast. Her small bubble of happiness burst. Her disappointment must have been obvious because Nash chuckled. "Come on," he said. "If we can waltz, we can do this."

"Nash...I could do the slow dance because you were holding me, but this is impossible."

Nash, however, wasn't listening. He was dancing. Without her. His arms jerked back and forth, and his feet seemed to be following the same haphazard course. He laughed and threw back his head. "Go for it, Savannah!" He shouted to be heard above the music. "Don't just stand there. Dance!"

She was going to need to move—off the dance floor. She was about to turn away when Nash clasped her around the waist, holding her with both hands. "You can't quit now."

"Oh, yes, I can. Just watch me."

"All you need to do is move a little to the rhythm. You don't need to leap across the dance floor."

There was no talking to him, so she threw her arms in the air in abject frustration.

"That's it," he shouted enthusiastically.

"Excuse me, excuse me," Arnold Serle's voice said from behind her. "Nash, would you mind if I danced with Savannah now?" he shouted.

Nash looked at Savannah and grinned, as cheerful as a six-year-old pulling a prank on his first-grade teacher. "Savannah would love to. Isn't that right?" With that, he danced his way off the floor.

"Ready to rock 'n' roll?" Arnold asked.

Savannah didn't mean to laugh, but she couldn't stop herself. "I'm not very good at this."

"Shall we?" he said, holding out his palm to her.

Reluctantly she placed her hand in his. She didn't want to offend Nash's boss, but she didn't want to embarrass herself, either. Taking Nash's advice, she moved her arms, just a little at first, swaying back and forth, convinced she looked like a chicken attempting flight. Others around her were wiggling and twisting in every which direction. Savannah's movements, or lack of them, weren't likely to be noticed.

To her utter amazement, Mr. Serle began to twist vigorously. His dancing was reminiscent of 1960s teen movies she'd seen on TV. With each jerking motion he sank closer to the floor, until he was practically kneeling. After a moment he stopped moving. He hunkered there, one arm stretched forward, one elbow back.

"Mr. Serle, are you all right?"

"Would you mind helping me up? My back seems to have gone out on me."

Savannah looked frantically around for Nash, but he was nowhere to be seen. She was silently calling him several colorful names for getting her into this predicament. With no other alternative, she bent forward, grabbed the older man's elbow and pulled him into an upright position.

"Thanks," he said, with a bright smile. "I got carried away there and forgot I'm practically an old man. Sure felt good. My heart hasn't beaten this fast in years."

"Maybe we should sit down," she suggested, praying he'd agree.

"Not on your life, young lady. I'm only getting started."

Nash made his way back to the table, smiling to himself. He hadn't meant to embarrass Savannah. His original intent

had been to rescue her. Taking her onto the dance floor was
pure impulse. All night he'd been looking for an excuse to
hold her, and he wasn't about to throw away what might be
his only chance.

*Beautiful* didn't begin to describe Savannah. When he'd
first met her, he'd thought of her as cute. He'd dated women
far more attractive than she was. On looks alone, she wasn't
the type that stood out in a crowd. Nor did she have a vo-
luptuous body. She was small, short and proportioned ac-
cordingly. If he was looking for long shapely legs and an
ample bust, he wouldn't find either in Savannah. She wasn't
a beauty, and yet she was the most beautiful woman he'd
ever known.

That didn't make a lot of sense. He decided it was because
he'd never met anyone quite like Savannah Charles. He didn't
fully understand why she appealed to him so strongly. True,
she had a compassionate heart, determination and courage—
all qualities he admired.

"Is Arnold out there making a world-class fool of himself?" John Stackhouse asked, when Nash joined the elder
of the two senior partners at their table.

"He's dancing with Savannah."

John Stackhouse was by far the most dignified and re-
served of the two. Both were members of the executive committee, which had the final say on the appointment of the
next senior partner. Stackhouse was often the most disap-
proving of the pair. Over the years, Nash had been at odds
with him on more than one occasion. Their views on certain
issues invariably clashed. Although he wasn't particularly
fond of the older man, Nash respected him, and considered
him fair-minded.

John Stackhouse sipped from his wineglass. "Actually,
I'm pleased we have this opportunity to talk," he said to
Nash, arching an eyebrow. "A wedding's not the place to

bring up business, as Arnold correctly pointed out, but I believe now might be a good time for us to talk about the senior partnership."

Nash's breath froze in his lungs, and he nodded. "I'd appreciate that."

"You've been with the firm a number of years now, and worked hard. We've won some valuable cases because of you, and that's in your favor."

"Glad to hear that." So Paul Jefferson didn't have it sewn up the way he'd assumed.

"I don't generally offer advice..."

This was true enough. Stackhouse kept his opinions to himself until asked, and it boded well that he was willing to make a few suggestions to Nash. Although he badly wanted the position, Nash still didn't think he had a chance against Paul. "I'd appreciate any advice you care to give me."

"Arnold and a couple of the other members of the executive committee were discussing names. Yours was raised almost immediately."

Nash moved forward, perching on the end of his chair. "What's the consensus?"

"Off the record."

"Off the record," Nash assured him.

"You're liked and respected, but there's a problem, a big one as far as the firm's concerned. The fact is, I'm the one who brought it up, but the others claimed to have noticed it, as well."

"Yes?" Nash's mind zoomed over the list of potential areas of trouble.

"You've been divorced for years now."

"Yes."

"This evening's the first time I've seen you put that failure behind you. I've watched you chew on your bitterness like an old bone, digging it up and showing it off like a prized possession when it suited you. You've developed a cutting, sarcastic edge. That's fine in the courtroom, but a detriment in your professional life as well as your private life. Especially if you're interested in this senior partnership."

"I'm interested," Nash was quick to tell him, too quick perhaps because Stackhouse smiled. That happened so rarely it was worth noting.

"I'm glad to hear you say that."

"Is there anything I could do to help my chances?" This conversation was unprecedented, something Nash had never believed possible.

The attorney hesitated and glanced toward the dance floor, frowning. "How serious are you about this young woman?"

Of all the things Nash had thought he might hear, this was the one he least expected. "Ah..." Nash was rarely at a loss for words, but right now he had no idea how to answer. "I don't know. Why do you ask?"

"I realize it's presumptuous of me, and I do hope you'll forgive me, but it might sway matters if you were to marry again."

"Marry?" he repeated, as if the word was unfamiliar to him.

"It would show the committee that you've put the past behind you," John continued, "and that you're trying to build a more positive future."

"I...see."

"Naturally, there are no guarantees and I certainly wouldn't suggest you consider marriage if you weren't already thinking along those lines. I wouldn't have said anything, but I noticed the way you were dancing with the young lady and it seemed to me you care deeply for her."

"She's special."

The other man nodded. "Indeed she is. Would you mind terribly if I danced with her myself? I see no reason for Arnold to have all the fun." Not waiting for Nash to respond, he stood and made his way across the dance floor to Savannah and his friend.

Nash watched as John Stackhouse tapped his fellow attorney on the shoulder and cut in. Savannah smiled as the second man claimed her.

Marry!

Nash rubbed his face. A few months earlier, the suggestion would have infuriated him. But a few months earlier, he hadn't met Savannah.

Nor had he stood in a church, held hands with an incredible woman and repeated vows. Vows meant for his sister and the man she loved. Not him. Not Savannah. Yet these vows had come straight from his heart to hers. He hadn't intended it to be that way. Not in the beginning. All he'd wanted to do was show Savannah how far he'd come. Repeating a few words seemed a small thing at the time.

But it wasn't as simple as all that. Because everything had changed from that moment forward. He'd spoken in a haze, not fully comprehending the effect it was having on him. All he understood was that he was tired. Tired of being alone. Tired of pretending he didn't need anyone else. Tired of playing a game in which he would always be the loser. Those vows he'd recited with Savannah had described the kind of marriage she believed in so strongly. It was an ideal, an uncommon thing, but for the first time in years he was willing to admit it was possible. A man and a woman *could* share this loving, mutually respectful partnership. Savannah had made it real to him the moment she'd repeated the vows herself.

Marry Savannah.

He waited for the revulsion to hit him the way it usually did when someone mentioned the word *marriage*. Nothing happened. Of course, that was perfectly logical. He'd spent time in a wedding shop, making a multitude of decisions that revolved around Susan's wedding. He'd become immune to the negative jolt the word always struck in him.

But he expected *some* adverse reaction. A twinge, a shiver of doubt. Something.

It didn't come.

*Marriage.* He repeated it slowly in his mind. No, he'd never consider anything so drastic. Not for the sole reason of making senior partner. He'd worked hard. It was a natural progression; if he didn't get the appointment now, he would later.

Marriage to Savannah. If there was ever a time the wine was talking, it was now.

Savannah had never experienced a night she'd enjoyed more. She'd danced and drunk champagne, then danced again. Every time she'd turned around, there was someone waiting to dance with her or fill her glass.

"Oh, Nash, I had the most incredible night of my life," she said, leaning against the headrest in his car and closing her eyes. It was a mistake, because the world went on a crazy spin.

"That good, was it?"

"Yes, oh, yes. I hate to see it end."

"Then why should it? Where would you like to go?"

"You'll take me anywhere?"

"Name it."

"The beach. I want to go to the beach." She was making a fool of herself, but she didn't care. She wanted to throw out her arms and sing. Where was a mountaintop when she needed one?

"Your wish is my command," Nash said to her.

She slipped her hand around his upper arm and hugged him, resting her head on his shoulder. "That's how I feel about tonight. It's magical. I could ask for anything and somehow it would be given to me."

"I believe it would."

Excited now that her fantasy had become so real, she lowered the car window and let out a wild whoop of joy.

Nash laughed. "What was that for?"

"I'm so happy! I never dreamed I could dance like that. Did you see me? Did you see all the men who asked me?" She brought her hand to her chest. "Me. I always thought I couldn't dance, and I did, and I owe it all to you."

"I knew you could do it."

"But how…"

"You can walk, can't you?"

"Yes, but I assumed it was impossible to *dance*." The champagne had affected her, but she welcomed the light-headedness it produced. "Oh, did you see Mr. Stackhouse? I thought I'd burst out laughing. I'm convinced he's never done the twist in his life." The memory made her giggle.

"I couldn't believe my eyes," Nash said and she heard the amusement in his voice. "Neither could Arnold Serle. Arnold said they've been friends for thirty-five years and he's never seen John do anything like it, claimed he was just trying to outdo him. That's when he leapt onto the dance floor, too, and the three of you started a conga line."

"There's magic to this night, isn't there?"

"There must be," he agreed.

Her leg should be aching, and would be soon, but she hadn't felt even a twinge. Perhaps later, when adrenaline wasn't pumping through her body and she was back on planet Earth, she'd experience the familiar discomfort. But it hadn't happened yet.

"Your beach," Nash announced, edging into the parking space at Alki Beach in West Seattle. A wide expanse of sandy shore stretched before them. Seattle's lights glittered in the distance like decorations on a gaily lit Christmas tree. Gentle waves lapped the driftwood-strewn sand, and the scents of salt and seaweed hung in the air. "Make all your wishes this easy to fulfill, will you?"

"I'll do my best," she promised. Her list was short, especially for a woman who, on this one night, was a princess in disguise.

"Any other easy requests?" Nash asked. He moved closer and draped his arm across her shoulders.

"A full moon would be nice."

"Will a crescent-shaped one do, instead?"

"It'll have to."

"Perhaps I could find a way to take your mind off the moon," Nash suggested, his voice low and oddly breathless.

"Oh?" *Oh, please let him kiss me,* Savannah pleaded. The night would be perfect if only Nash were to take her in his arms and kiss her....

"Do you know what I'm thinking?" he asked.

She closed her eyes and nodded. "Kiss me, Nash. Please kiss me."

His mouth came down on hers and she thought she was ready for his sensual invasion, since she'd yearned for it so badly. But nothing could have prepared her for the greed they felt for each other. She linked her arms around his neck and gave herself to his touch.

"Why is it," Nash groaned, long minutes later as he

breathed kisses across her cheeks, "that we seem to be forever kissing in a car?"

"I...don't know."

His lips toyed with hers. "You're making this difficult."

"I am." Her effect on him made Savannah giddy. It made her feel strong, and for a woman who'd felt weak most of her life, this was a potent aphrodisiac.

"You're so beautiful," Nash whispered, just before he kissed her again.

"Tonight I'm invincible," she murmured. Privately she wondered if Cinderella had spent time like this with her prince before rushing off and leaving him with a single glass slipper. She wondered if her counterpart had the opportunity to experience such unexpected pleasure.

Nash kissed her again and again, until a host of dizzying sensations accosted her from all sides. She broke away and buried her face in his chest in a desperate effort to clear her head.

"Savannah." Taking her by the shoulders, he eased back. "Look at me."

Blindly she obeyed him, running her tongue over lips that were swollen from the urgency of their kisses. "Touch me," she pleaded, gazing at the desire in his eyes, the desire that was a reflection of her own.

Nash went still, his breathing labored. "I can't.... We're on a public beach." He closed his eyes. "That does it," he said forcefully, pulling away from her. "We're going to do this right. We're not teenagers anymore. I want to make love to you, Savannah, and I'm not willing to risk being interrupted by a policeman who'll arrest me for taking indecent liberties." He reached for the ignition and started the car. She saw how badly his hand shook.

"Where are we going?"

"My house."

"Nash…"

"Don't argue with me."

"Kiss me first," she said, not understanding his angry impatience. They had all night. She wouldn't stop being a princess for hours yet.

"I have every intention of kissing you. A lot."

"That sounds nice," she whispered, and with a soft sigh pressed her head against his shoulder.

After several minutes of silence, she said, "I'm not always beautiful." She felt she should remind him of that.

"I hate to argue with you, especially now," he said, planting one last kiss on the corner of her mouth, "but I disagree."

"I'm really not," she insisted, although she thought it was very kind of him to disagree.

"I want you more than I've ever wanted any other woman in my life."

"You do?" It was so nice of him to say such things, but it wasn't necessary. Unexpected tears filled her eyes. "No one's ever said things like that to me before."

"Stupid fools." They stopped at a red light and Nash reached for her and kissed her as if he longed to make up for a lifetime of rejection. Savannah brought her arms around his neck and sighed when he finally broke off the kiss.

"You're not drunk, are you?" Nash demanded, turning a corner sharply. He shot a wary glance at her, as if this was a recent suspicion.

"No." She was, just a little, but not enough to affect her judgment. "I know exactly what I'm doing."

"Right, but do you know what *I* intend on doing?"

"Yes, you're taking me home so we can make love in your bed. You'd prefer that to being arrested for doing it publicly."

"Smart girl."

"I'm not a girl!"

"Sorry, slip of the tongue. Trust me, I know exactly how much of a woman you are."

"No, you don't. You haven't got a clue, Nash Davenport, but that's all right because no one else does, either." Herself included, but she didn't say that.

Nash pulled into his driveway and was apparently going faster than he realized, because when he hit his brakes the car jerked to an abrupt stop. "The way I've been driving, it's a miracle I didn't get a ticket," he mumbled as he leapt out of the car. He opened her door, and Savannah smiled lazily and lifted her arms to him.

"I don't know if I can walk," she said with a tired sigh. "I can dance, though, if anyone cares to ask."

He scooped her effortlessly into his arms and carried her to his front porch. Savannah was curious to see his home, curious to learn everything she could about him. She wanted to remember every second of this incredible night.

It was a bit awkward getting the key in the lock and holding her at the same time, but Nash managed. He threw open the door and walked into the dark room. He hesitated, kicked the door closed and traipsed across the living room, not bothering to turn on the lights.

"Stop," she insisted.

"For what? Savannah, you're driving me crazy."

Languishing in his arms, she arched back her head and kissed his cheek. "What a romantic thing to say."

"Did you want something?" he asked impatiently.

"Oh, yes, I want to see your home. A person can find out a great deal about someone just by seeing the kind of furniture he buys. Little things, too, like his dishes. And books and music and art." She gave a tiny shrug. "I've been curious about you from the start."

"You want to know the pattern of my china?"

"Well, yes…"

"Can it wait until tomorrow? There are other things I'd rather be doing…."

Nash moved expertly down the darkened hallway to his room. Gently he placed her on the mattress and knelt over her. She smiled up at him. "Oh, Nash, you have a four-poster bed. But…tomorrow's too late."

"For what?"

"Us. This—being together—will only work for one night. Then the princess disappears and I go back to being a pumpkin." She frowned. "Or do I mean scullery maid?" She giggled, deciding her fracturing of the fairy tale didn't matter.

Nash froze and his eyes met hers, before he groaned and fell backward onto the bed. "You are drunk, aren't you?"

"No," she insisted. "Just happy. Now kiss me and quit asking so many questions." She was reaching for him when it happened. The pain shot like fire through her leg and, groaning, she fell onto her side.

# *Seven*

Nash recognized the effort Savannah made to hide her agony. It must have been excruciating; it was certainly too intense to disguise. Lying on her back, she squeezed her eyes tightly shut, gritted her teeth and then attempted to manage the pain with deep-breathing exercises.

"Savannah," he whispered, not wanting to break her concentration and at the same time desperately needing to do something, anything, to ease her discomfort. "Let me help," he pleaded.

She shook her head. "It'll pass in a few minutes."

Even in the moonlight, Nash could see how pale she'd become. He jumped off the bed and was pacing like a wild beast, feeling the searing grip of her pain himself. It twisted at his stomach, creating a mental torment unlike anything he'd ever experienced.

"Let me massage your leg," he insisted, and when she didn't protest he lifted the skirt of her full-length gown and ran his hands up and down her thigh. Her skin was hot to the touch and when he placed his chilled hands on her, she groaned anew.

"It'll pass." He repeated her own words, praying he was right. His heart was pounding double-time in his anxiety. He couldn't bear to see Savannah endure this unbearable pain, and stand by and do nothing.

Her whole leg was terribly scarred and his heart ached at the agony she'd endured over the years. Her muscles were tense and knotted but gradually began to relax as he gently worked her flesh with both hands, easing them up and down her thigh and calf. He saw the marks of several surgeries; the scars were testament to her suffering and her bravery.

"There are pills in my purse," she whispered, her voice barely discernible.

Nash quickly surveyed the room, jerking his head from left to right, wondering where she'd put it. He found the small clutch purse on the carpet. Grasping it, he emptied the contents on top of the bed. The brown plastic bottle filled with a prescription for pain medication rolled into view.

Hurrying into his bathroom, he ran her a glass of water, then dumped a handful of the thick chalky tablets into the palm of his hand. "Here," he said.

Levering herself up on one elbow, Savannah took three of the pills. Her hands were trembling, he noted, and he could hardly resist taking her in his arms. Once she'd swallowed the pills, she closed her eyes and laid her head on the pillow.

"Take me home, please."

"In a few minutes. Let's give those pills a chance to work first."

She was sobbing openly now. Nash lay down next to her and gathered her in his arms.

"I'm sorry," she sobbed.

"For what?"

"For ruining everything."

"You didn't ruin anything." He brushed his lips over the crown of her head.

"I...didn't want you to see my leg." Her tears came in earnest now and she buried her face in his shoulder.

"Why?"

"It's ugly."

"You're beautiful."

"For one night..."

"You're wrong, Savannah. You're beautiful every minute of every day." He cradled her head against him, whispering softly in her ear. Gradually he felt her tension diminish, and he knew by the even sound of her breathing that she was drifting off to sleep.

Nash held her for several minutes, wondering what he should do. She'd asked that he take her home, but waking her seemed cruel, especially now that the terrible agony had passed. She needed her sleep, and movement might bring back the pain.

What it came down to, he admitted reluctantly, was one simple fact. He wanted Savannah with him and was unwilling to relinquish her.

Kissing her temple, he eased himself from her arms and crawled off the bed. He got a blanket from the top shelf in his closet and covered her with it, careful to tuck it about her shoulders.

Looking down on her, Nash shoved his hands in his pockets and stared for several minutes.

He wandered into the living room, slumped into his recliner and sat in the dark while the night shadows moved against the walls.

He'd been selfish and inconsiderate, but above all he'd

been irresponsible. Bringing Savannah to his home had been the most recent in a long list of errors in judgment.

He was drunk, but not on champagne. His intoxication was strictly due to Savannah. The idealist. The romantic. Attending his sister's wedding hadn't helped matters any. Susan had been a beautiful bride and if there was ever a time he could believe in the power of love and the strength of vows, it was at her wedding.

It'd started early in the evening when he'd exchanged vows with Savannah as if *they* were the ones being married. It was a moment out of time—dangerous and unreal.

He'd attempted to understand what had happened, offered a litany of excuses, but he wasn't sure he'd ever find one that would satisfy him. He wished there was someone or something he could blame, but that wasn't likely. The best he could hope for was to forget the whole episode and pray Savannah did the same.

Savannah. She was so beautiful. He'd never enjoyed dancing with a woman like he did with her. Smiling to himself, he recalled the way he'd been caught up in the magic of her joy. Being with her, sharing this night with her, was like being drawn into a fairy tale, impossible to resist even if he'd tried. And he hadn't.

Before he knew it, they were parked at Alki Beach, kissing like there was no tomorrow. He'd never desired a woman more.

Wrong. There'd been a time, years earlier, when he'd been equally enthralled with a woman. In retrospect it was easy to excuse his naïveté. He'd been young and impressionable. And because of that, he'd fallen hopelessly in love.

*Love.* He didn't even like the sound of the word. He'd found love to be both painful and dangerous.

Nash didn't love Savannah. He refused to allow himself

to wallow in that destructive emotion a second time. He was attracted to her, but love was out of the question. Denise had taught him everything he needed to know about *that*.

He hadn't thought of her, except in passing, in years. Briefly he wondered if she was happy, and doubted his ex-wife would ever find what she was searching for. Her un-faithfulness continued to haunt him even now, years after their divorce. For too long he'd turned a blind eye to her faults, all in the glorious name of love.

He'd made other mistakes, too. First and foremost he'd married the wrong woman. His father had tried to tell him, but Nash had refused to listen, discrediting his advice, con-fident his father's qualms about Nash's choice in women were part and parcel of being too old to understand true love. Time had proved otherwise.

Looking back, Nash realized he'd shared only one thing with Denise. Incredible sex. He'd mistaken her physical de-mands for love. Within a few weeks of meeting, they were living together and their sexual relationship had become addictive.

It was ironic that she'd been the one to bring up the sub-ject of marriage. Until then she'd insisted she was a "free spirit." Not until much later did he understand this sudden need she had for commitment. With his father seriously ill, there was the possibility of a large inheritance.

They'd been happy in the beginning. Or at least Nash had attempted to convince himself of that, and perhaps they were, but their happiness was short-lived.

He'd first suspected something was wrong when he ar-rived home late one evening after a grueling day in court and caught the scent of a man's cologne. He'd asked Denise and she'd told him he was imagining things. Because he wanted to believe her, because the thought of her being unfaithful was so completely foreign, he'd accepted her word. He had no reason to doubt her.

His second clue came less than a month later when a woman he didn't know met him outside his apartment. She was petite and fragile in her full-length coat, her hands deep in the pockets, her eyes downcast. She hated to trouble him, she said, but could Nash please keep his wife away from her husband. She'd recently learned she was pregnant with their second child and wanted to keep the marriage together if she could.

Nash had been stunned. He'd tried to ask questions, but she'd turned and fled. He didn't say anything to Denise, not that night and not for a long time afterward. But that was when he started to notice the little things that should've been obvious.

Nash hated himself for being so weak. He should have demanded the truth then and there, should have kicked her out of his home. Instead he did nothing. Denial was comfortable for a week and then two, while he wrestled with his doubts.

Savannah's scarred leg was a testament to her bravery, her endless struggle to face life each and every day. His scarred emotions were a testament to his cowardice, to knowing that his wife was cheating on him and accepting it rather than confronting her with the truth.

His wife had been *cheating* on him. What an ineffectual word that was for what he felt. It sounded so…trivial. So insignificant. But the sense of betrayal was sharper than any blade, more painful than any incision. It had slashed his ego, punctured his heart and forever changed the way he viewed love and life.

Nash had loved Denise; he must have, otherwise she wouldn't have had the power to hurt him so deeply. That love had burned within him, slowly twisting itself into a bitter desire to get even.

The divorce had been ugly. Nash attempted to use legal means to retaliate for what Denise had done to him emotionally. Unfortunately there was no compensation for what he'd endured. He'd learned this countless times since from other clients. He'd wanted to embarrass and humiliate her the way she had him, but in the end they'd both lost.

Following their divorce, Denise had married again almost immediately. Her new husband was a man she'd met three weeks earlier. Nash kept tabs on her for some time afterward and was downright gleeful when he learned she was divorcing again less than a year later.

For a long while Nash was convinced he hated Denise. In some ways he did; his need for revenge had been immature. But as the years passed, he was able to put their short marriage in perspective, and he was grateful for the lessons she'd taught him. Paramount was the complete unreliability of love and marriage.

Denise had initiated him into this kind of thinking, and the hundreds of divorce cases he'd handled since then had reinforced it.

Then he'd met Savannah. In the beginning, she'd irritated him no end. With her head in the clouds, subsisting on the thin air of romance, she'd met each of his arguments as if she alone was responsible for defending the institution of marriage. As if she alone was responsible for changing his views.

Savannah irritated him—that was true enough—but she'd worn down his defenses until he was doing more than listening to her; he was beginning to believe again. It took some deep soul-searching to admit that.

He *must* believe, otherwise she wouldn't be sleeping in

his bed. Otherwise they wouldn't have come within a heart-beat of making love.

What a drastic mistake that would have been, Nash realized a second time. He didn't know when common sense had abandoned him, but it had. Perhaps he'd started breathing that impossibly thin air Savannah had existed on all these years. Apparently it had tricked him as it had her.

Nash should have known better than to bring Savannah into his home. He couldn't sleep with her and expect their relationship to remain the same. Everything would change. Savannah wasn't the type of woman to engage in casual affairs and that was all Nash had to offer. A few hours in bed would have been immensely pleasurable, but eventually disastrous to them both.

Savannah woke when dawn light crept through a nearby window. Opening her eyes, she needed a moment to orient herself. She was in a strange bed. Alone. It didn't take long to remember the events of the night before. She was in Nash's home.

Sitting up required an effort. The contents of her purse were strewn across the bed and, gathering them together as quickly as possible, she went in search of her shoes.

Nash was nowhere to be seen. If her luck held, she could call a cab and be out of his home before he realized she'd gone.

Her folly weighed heavily on her. She'd never felt more embarrassed in her life.

She moved stealthily from the bedroom into the living room. Pausing, she saw Nash asleep in his recliner. Her breath caught in her throat as she whispered a silent prayer of thanksgiving that he was asleep.

Fearing the slightest sound would wake him, she decided

to sneak out the back door, find a phone elsewhere and call for a cab. Her cell phone was at home; there hadn't been room for it in the tiny beaded purse she'd brought with her yesterday.

Her hand was on the lock to the back door, a clean escape within her reach, when Nash spoke from behind her.

"I thought you wanted to check out my china pattern."

Savannah closed her eyes in frustration. "You were sleeping," she said without turning around.

"I'm awake now."

Her face was so hot, it was painful. Dropping her hands, she did her best to smile before slowly pivoting around.

"How were you planning on getting home?" he asked.

"A taxi."

"Did you bring your cell?"

He knew perfectly well she hadn't. "No, I was going to locate a phone somewhere and call a cab."

"I see." He began to make a pot of coffee as if this morning was no different from any other. "Why did you find it so important to leave now?" he asked in what she was sure were deceptively calm tones.

"You were sleeping...."

"And you didn't want to disturb me."

"Something like that."

"We didn't make love, so there's no need to behave like an outraged virgin."

"I'm well aware of what we did and didn't do," Savannah said stiffly. He was offended that she was sneaking out of his home. That much was apparent.

Nash was an experienced lover, but she doubted he'd ever dealt with a situation similar to what had happened to them. Most women probably found pleasure in his touch, not excruciating pain. Most women sighed with enjoyment; they didn't *sob* in agony. Most women lived the life of a princess on a day-to-day basis, while her opportunity came once in a lifetime.

"How's your leg feel?"

"It's fine."

"You shouldn't have danced—"

"Nothing on this earth would have stopped me," she told him, her voice surprisingly strong. "The pain's something I live with every day. It's the price I paid for enjoying myself. I had a wonderful time last night, Nash. Don't take that away from me."

He hesitated, then said, "Sit down and have a cup of coffee. We'll talk and then I'll drive you home." He poured two cups and set them on the round kitchen table. "Cream and sugar?"

She shook her head.

He sat casually in one of the chairs.

"I... I'm not much of a conversationalist in the morning," she said.

"No problem. We can wait until afternoon if you'd rather."

She didn't and he knew that. All she wanted was to escape.

Reluctantly she pulled out the chair opposite his and sat down. The coffee was too hot to drink, but just the right temperature to warm her hands. She cradled the cup between her palms and focused her attention on it. "I want you to know how sorry I am for—"

He interrupted her. "If you're apologizing for last night, don't bother."

"All right, I won't."

"Good."

Savannah took her first tentative sip of coffee. "Well,"

she said, looking up but avoiding his eyes, "what would you suggest we talk about?"

"What happened."

"Nothing happened," she said.

"It almost did."

"I know that better than you think, Nash. So why are we acting like strangers this morning? Susan's wedding was beautiful. Dancing with you and the two gentlemen from your office was wonderful. For one incredible night I played the glamorous role of a princess. Unfortunately, it ended just a little too soon."

"It ended exactly where it should have. Our making love would have been a mistake."

Savannah was trying to put everything in perspective, but his statement felt like a slap in the face. It shouldn't have hurt so much, but it did. Unwanted tears sprang to her eyes.

"You don't agree?"

"Does it matter?" she asked, refusing to let him know how deeply he'd hurt her.

"I suppose not."

"It doesn't," she said more forcefully. She was having a difficult time holding back the tears. They threatened to spill down her face any second. "I'd like to go home now," she said.

"It wouldn't have worked, you know."

"Of course I know that," she flared.

She felt more than saw Nash's hesitation. "Are you all right?" he asked.

"I've never been better," she snapped. "But I want to go home. Sitting around here in this dress is ridiculous. Now either you drive me or I'm calling a cab."

"I'll drive you."

The ride back to her place was a nightmare for Savannah.

Nash made a couple of attempts at conversation, but she was in no mood to talk and certainly in no mood to analyze the events of the night before. She'd been humiliated enough and didn't want to make things worse.

The minute Nash pulled into her driveway, Savannah opened the car door, eager to make her escape. His hand at her elbow stopped her.

Savannah groaned inwardly and froze. But Nash didn't seem to have anything to say.

"Susan's wedding was very nice. Thank you," he finally told her.

She nodded, keeping her back to him and her head lowered.

"I enjoyed our time together."

"I…did, too." Even though that time was over now. It was daylight, and the magic of last night was gone.

"I'll give you a call later in the week."

She nodded, although she didn't believe it. This was probably a line he used often. Just another way of saying goodbye, she figured.

"What about Thursday?" he asked unexpectedly, after he'd helped her out of the car.

"What about it?"

"I'd like to take you out…. A picnic or something."

He couldn't have surprised her more. Slowly she raised her head, studying him, confident she'd misunderstood.

He met her gaze steadily. "What's wrong?"

"Are you asking me out on a date?"

"Yes," he said, taking her house keys from her lifeless hand and unlocking her front door. "Is that a problem?"

"I…I don't know."

"Would you prefer it if we went dancing instead?" he asked, his mouth lifting in a half smile.

Despite their terrible beginning that morning, Savannah smiled. "It'd be nice, but I don't think so."

"I'll see what I can arrange. I'll pick you up around six at the shop. Okay?"

Savannah was too shocked to do anything but nod.

"Good." With that he leaned forward and brushed his lips over hers. It wasn't much as kisses went, but the warmth of his touch went through her like a bolt of lightning.

Savannah stood on her porch, watching him walk away. He was at his car before he turned back. "You were a beautiful princess," he said.

Nash wasn't sure what had prompted the invitation for a picnic for Thursday. It wasn't something he'd given any thought to suggesting. In fact, he felt as surprised as Savannah looked when he'd asked her.

A date. That was simple enough. It wasn't as if he hadn't gone out on dates before, but it had been a long while since he'd formally asked a woman out. He was making more of this than necessary, he decided.

By Wednesday he would have welcomed an excuse to get out of it. Especially after John Stackhouse called him into his office. The minute he received the summons, Nash guessed this was somehow linked to Savannah.

"You wanted to see me?" Nash asked, stepping inside the senior partner's office later that afternoon.

"I hope I'm not calling you away from something important?"

"Not at all," Nash assured him. It might have been his imagination, but Stackhouse's attitude seemed unusually friendly. Although they were always polite to each other, he wasn't John's favorite, not the way Paul Jefferson was. But then, Paul wasn't prone to disagree with anyone who could advance his career.

"I have a divorce I want you to handle," his boss said casually.

These cases were often assigned to him. He'd built his reputation on them. Lately, though, they hadn't held his interest and he was hoping to diversify.

"This man is a friend of mine by the name of Don Griffin. It's a sad case, very sad." John paused, shaking his head.

"Don Griffin," Nash repeated. The name was familiar, but he couldn't place it.

"You might have heard of him. Don owns a chain of seafood restaurants throughout the Pacific Northwest."

"I think I read something about him not long ago."

"You might have," John agreed. "He's mentioned in the paper every now and then. But getting back to the divorce.... Don and Janice have been married a lot of years. They have two college-age children and then Janice learned a few years back that she was pregnant. You can imagine their shock."

Nash nodded sympathetically.

"Unfortunately the child has Down syndrome. This came as a second blow, and Don took it hard. So did Janice."

Nash couldn't blame the couple for that. "They're divorcing?"

"Yes." John's expression was filled with regret. "I don't know all the details, but apparently Janice was devoting all her time and attention to little Amy and well, in a moment of weakness, Don got involved with another woman. Janice found out and filed for divorce."

"I see. And is this what Don wants?"

The senior partner's face tightened with disappointment. "Apparently so. I'm asking you, as a personal favor, to handle this case, representing Don. My late wife and I were good friends with both Don and Janice."

"I'll help in any way I can," Nash said, but without real enthusiasm. Another divorce case, more lives ripped apart. He'd anesthetize his feelings as best he could and struggle to work out the necessary details, but only because John had asked him.

"I'll make an appointment to have Don come in for the initial consultation Friday morning, if that's agreeable?" Once more he made it a question, as if he expected Nash to decline.

This was the first personal favor Stackhouse had ever asked of him.

"I'll be happy to take the case," Nash said again. So he'd been wrong; this had nothing to do with Savannah.

"Good." John reached for his phone. "I'll let Don know I got him the best divorce attorney in town."

"Thank you." Compliments were few and far between from the eldest of the senior partners. Nash suspected he should feel encouraged that the older man trusted him with a family friend.

On his way out of the office, Nash ran into Arnold Serle. "Nash," the other man said, his face lighting up. "I haven't seen you all week."

"I've been in court."

"So I heard. I just wanted you to know how much I enjoyed your sister's wedding."

"We enjoyed having you." So he wasn't going to escape hearing about Savannah after all.

"How's Savannah?" Arnold asked eagerly.

"Very well. I'll tell her you asked about her."

"Please do. My niece is thinking about getting married. I'd like to steer her to Savannah's shop. If your sister's wedding is evidence of the kind of work Savannah does, I'd like to hire her myself." He chuckled then. "I sincerely hope you appreciate what a special woman she is."

"I do."

"Pleased to hear it," Arnold said, grinning broadly.

By Thursday evening, Nash had run through the full range of emotions. Knowing he'd be seeing Savannah later was both a curse and a blessing. He looked forward to being with her and at the same time dreaded it.

He got there right at six. Savannah was sitting at her desk, apparently working on her computer; she didn't hear him enter the shop because she didn't look up. She was probably entertaining second thoughts of her own.

"Savannah." He said her name lightly, not wanting to frighten her.

She jerked her head up, surprise written on her face. But it wasn't the shock in her eyes that unnerved him, it was the tears.

"It's Thursday," he reminded her. "We have a date."

Nash wondered if she'd forgotten.

"Are you going to tell me what's upset you so much?" he asked.

"No," she said with a warm smile, the welcome in her eyes belying her distress. "I'm glad to see you, Nash. I could do with a friend just now."

# *Eight*

Savannah hadn't forgotten about her date with Nash. She'd thought of little else in the preceding days, wondering if she should put any credence in his asking. One thing she knew about Nash Davenport—he wasn't the type to suggest something he didn't want.

"I had the deli pack us dinner," he told her. "I hope you're hungry."

"I am," she said, wiping the last tears from her face. Nash was studying her with undisguised curiosity and she was grateful he didn't press her for details. She wouldn't have known how to explain, wouldn't have found the words to tell him about the sadness and guilt she felt.

"Where are we going?" she asked, locking the shop. If ever there was a time she needed to get away, to abandon her woes and have fun, it was now.

"Lake Sammamish."

The large lake east of Lake Washington was a well-known and well-loved picnic area. Savannah had been there several times over the years, mostly in the autumn, when she went to admire the spectacular display of fall color. She enjoyed walking along the shore and feeding the ducks.

"I brought a change of clothes," she said. "It'll only take me a minute to get out of this suit."

"Don't rush. We aren't in any hurry."

Savannah moved into the dressing room and replaced her business outfit with jeans and a large sweatshirt with Einstein's image. She'd purchased it earlier in the week with this outing in mind. When she returned, she discovered Nash examining a silk wedding dress adorned with a pearl yoke. She smiled to herself, remembering the first time he'd entered her shop and the way he'd avoided getting close to anything that hinted of romance. He'd come a long way in the past few months, further than he realized, much further than she'd expected.

"This gown arrived from New York this afternoon. It's lovely, isn't it?"

She thought he'd shrug and back away, embarrassed that she'd commented on his noticing something as symbolic of love as a wedding dress.

"It's beautiful. Did one of your clients order it?"

"No. It's from a designer I've worked with in the past and I fell in love with it myself. I do that every once in a while—order a dress that appeals to me personally. Generally they sell, and if they don't, there's always the possibility of renting it out."

"Not this one," he said in a voice so low, she had to strain to hear him. He seemed mesmerized by the dress.

"Why not?" she asked.

"This is the type of wedding gown…" He hesitated.

"Yes?" she prompted.

"When a man sees the woman he loves wearing this dress, he'll cherish the memory forever."

Savannah couldn't believe what she was hearing. This was Nash? The man who'd ranted and raved that love was a wasted emotion? The man who claimed marriage was for the deluded?

"That's so romantic," Savannah murmured. "If you don't object, I'd like to advertise it that way."

Nash's eyes widened and he shook his head. "You want to use that in an ad?"

"If you don't mind. I won't mention your name, unless you want me to."

"No! I mean... Can we just drop this?"

"Of course. I'm sorry, I didn't mean to embarrass you."

"You didn't," he said when it was clear that she had. "I seem to have done this to myself." He made a point of looking at his watch. "Are you ready?"

Savannah nodded. This could prove to be an interesting picnic....

They drove to Lake Sammamish in Nash's car and he seemed extra talkative. "Arnold Serle asked about you the other day," he told her as he wove in and out of traffic.

"He's a darling," Savannah said, savoring the memories of the two older men who'd worked so hard to bolster her self-confidence, vying for her the way they had. "Mr. Stackhouse, too," she added.

"You certainly made an impression on them."

Although the night had ended in disaster, she would always treasure it. Dancing with John and Arnold. Dancing with Nash...

"What's the smile about?" Nash asked, momentarily taking his eyes off the road.

"It's nothing."

"The tears were nothing, too?"

The tears. She'd almost forgotten she'd been crying when

he arrived. "I was talking to my parents this afternoon," she said as the misery returned. "It's always the same. They talk about traveling, but they never seem to leave Seattle. Instead of really enjoying life, they smother me with their sympathy and their sacrifices, as if that could bring back the full use of my leg." She was speaking fast and furiously, and not until she'd finished did she realize how close she was to weeping again.

Nash's hand touched hers for a moment. "You're a mature adult, living independently of them," he said. "You have for years."

"Which I've explained so many times, I get angry just thinking about it. Apparently they feel that if something were to happen, no one would be here to take care of me."

"What about other relatives?"

"There aren't any in the Seattle area. I try to reassure them that I'm fine, that no disasters are about to strike and even if one did, I have plenty of friends to call on, but they just won't leave."

"Was that what upset you this afternoon?" he asked.

Savannah dropped her gaze to her hands, now clenched tightly in her lap. "They've decided to stay in Seattle this winter. Good friends of theirs asked if they'd travel with them, leaving the second week of September and touring the South before spending the winter in Arizona. My dad's always wanted to visit New Orleans and Atlanta. They said they'll go another year," Savannah muttered, "but I know they won't. They know it, too."

"Your parents love you. I understand their concern."

"How can you say that?" she demanded angrily. "They're doing this because they feel guilty about my accident. Now *I'm* the one who's carrying that load. When will it ever end?"

"I don't know," he said quietly.

"I just wish they loved me enough to trust me to take care of myself. I've been doing exactly that for a long time now."

Nodding, he exited the freeway and took the road leading into Lake Sammamish State Park. He drove around until he found a picnic table close to the parking lot. The gesture was a thoughtful one; he didn't want her to have a long way to walk.

It might not be very subtle, but Savannah didn't care. She was determined to enjoy their outing. She needed this. She knew it was dangerous to allow herself this luxury. She was well aware that Nash could be out of her life with little notice. That was something she'd always taken into account in other relationships, but her guard had slipped with Nash.

He helped her out of the car and carried the wicker basket to the bright blue picnic table. The early evening was filled with a symphony of pleasant sounds. Birds chirped in a nearby tree, their song mingling with the laughter of children.

"I'm starved," Nash said, peering inside the basket. He raised his head and waggled his eyebrows. "My, oh, my, what goodies."

Savannah spread a tablecloth across one end of the table and Nash handed her a large loaf of French bread, followed by a bottle of red wine.

"That's for show," he said, grinning broadly. "This is for dinner." He took out a bucket of fried chicken and a six-pack of soda.

"I thought you said the deli packed this."

"They did. I made a list of what I wanted and they packed it in the basket for me."

"You're beginning to sound like a tricky defense attorney," she said, enjoying this easy banter between them. It helped take her mind off her parents and their uncomfortable conversation that afternoon.

They sat across from each other and with a chicken leg in front of her mouth, Savannah looked out over the blue-green water. The day was perfect. Not too warm and not too cool. The sun was shining and a gentle breeze rippled off the lake. A lifeguard stood sentinel over a group of preschool children splashing in the water between bursts of laughter. Farther out, a group of teens dived off a large platform. Another group circled the lake in two-seater pedal boats, their wake disrupting the serenity of the water.

"You're looking thoughtful," Nash commented.

Savannah blushed, a little embarrassed to be caught so enraptured with the scene before her. "When I was a teenager I used to dream a boy would ask me to pedal one of the boats with him."

"Did anyone?"

"No…." A sadness attached itself to her heart, dredging up the memories of a difficult youth. "I can't pedal."

"Why not? You danced, didn't you?"

"Yes, but that's different."

"How?"

"Don't you remember what happened after the dance?"

"We could rent a pedal boat and I'll do the work," he said. "You just sit back and enjoy the ride."

She lowered her gaze, not wanting him to see how badly she longed to do what he'd suggested.

"Come on," he wheedled. "It'll be fun."

"We'd go around in circles," she countered. She wasn't willing to try. "It won't work if we don't each do our share of the pedaling. I appreciate what you're doing, but I simply can't hold up my part."

"You won't know that until you try," he said. "Remember, you didn't want to dance, either." His reminder was a gentle one and it hit its mark.

"We might end up looking like idiots."

"So? It's happened before. To me, anyway." He stood and offered her his hand. "You game or not?"

She stared up at him, and indecision kept her rooted to the table. "I don't know if it's a good idea."

"Come on, Savannah, prove to me that you can do this. But more importantly, prove it to yourself. I'm not going to let you overdo it, I promise."

His confidence was contagious. "If you're implying that you could've kept me off the dance floor, think again. I danced every dance."

"Don't remind me. The only way I could dance with you was to cut in on someone else. At least this way I'll have you to myself."

Savannah placed her hand firmly in his, caught up in his smile.

"If anyone else comes seeking the pleasure of your company this time," he said, "they'll have to swim."

Savannah's mood had been painfully introspective when Nash arrived. Now, for the first time in what seemed like days, she experienced the overwhelming urge to laugh. Hugging Nash was a spontaneous reaction to the lightheartedness she felt with him.

He stiffened when her arms went around him, but recovered quickly, gripping her about her waist, picking her up and twirling her around until she had to beg him to stop. Breathless, she gazed at him, and said, "You make me want to sing."

"You make me want to—"

"What?" she asked.

"Sing," he muttered, relaxing his hold enough for her feet to touch the ground.

Savannah could have sworn his ears turned red. "I make you want to do what?" she pressed.

"Never mind, Savannah," he answered. "It's better that you don't know. And please, just this once, is it too much to ask that you don't argue with me?"

"Fine," she said, pretending to be gravely disappointed. She mocked him with a deep sigh.

They walked down to the water's edge, where Nash paid for the rental of a small pedal boat. He helped her board and then joined her, the boat rocking precariously as he shifted his weight.

Savannah held tightly to her seat. She remained skeptical of this idea, convinced they were going to look like a pair of idiots once they left the shore. She didn't mind being laughed at, but she didn't want *him* laughed at because of her.

"I...don't think we should do this," she whispered, struck by an attack of cowardice.

"I'm not letting you out of this now. We haven't even tried."

"I'll embarrass you."

"Let me worry about that."

"Nash, please."

He refused to listen to her and began working the pedals, making sure the pace he set wasn't too much for her. Water rustled behind them and Savannah jerked around to see the paddle wheel churning up the water. Before she realized it, they were speeding along.

"We're moving," she shouted. "We're actually moving."

It seemed that everyone on the shore had turned to watch them. In sheer delight, Savannah waved her arms. "We're actually moving."

"I think they've got the general idea," Nash teased.

"I could just kiss you," Savannah said, resisting the urge to throw her arms around his neck and do exactly that.

"You'll need to wait a few minutes." His hand reached for hers and he entwined their fingers.

"Let's go fast," she urged, cautiously pumping her feet. "I want to see how fast we can go."

"Savannah...no."

"Yes, please, just for a little bit."

He groaned and then complied. The blades of the paddle behind them churned the water into a frothy texture as they shot ahead. Nash was doing most of the work. Her efforts were puny compared to his, but it didn't seem to matter. This was more fun than she'd dared to dream. As much fun as dancing.

Savannah laughed boisterously. "I never knew," she said, squeezing his upper arm with both hands and pressing her head against his shoulder. "I never thought I could do this."

"There's a whole world out there just waiting to be explored."

"I want to sky-dive next," Savannah said gleefully.

"Sky-dive?"

"All right, roller-skate. I wanted to so badly when I was growing up. I used to skate before the accident, you know. I was pretty good, too."

"I'm sure you were."

"All my life I've felt hindered because of my leg and suddenly all these possibilities are opening up to me." She went from one emotional extreme to the other. First joy and laughter and now tears and sadness. "Meeting you was the best thing that's ever happened to me," she said, and sniffled. "I could cry, I'm so happy."

Nash stiffened and Savannah wondered if she'd offended

him. His reaction would have been imperceptible if they hadn't been sitting side by side.

Nash was pedaling harder now; her own feet were set in motion by his efforts. "Where are we going?" she asked, noting that he seemed to be steering the craft toward shore. She didn't want to stop, not when they were just getting started. This was her one fear, that she'd embarrass him, and apparently she had.

"See that weeping willow over on the far side of the bank?" he asked, motioning down the shoreline. She did, noting the branches draped over the water like a sanctuary. It appeared to be on private property.

"Yes."

"We're headed there."

"Why?" she asked, thinking of any number of plausible reasons. Perhaps he knew the people who lived there and wanted to stop and say hello.

"Because that weeping willow offers a little more privacy than out here on the lake. And I intend to take you up on your offer, because frankly, I'm not going to be able to wait much longer."

Offer, she mused. What offer?

Nash seemed to enjoy her dilemma and raised her hand to his mouth, kissing the inside of her palm. "I seem to remember you saying you wanted to kiss me. So I'm giving you the opportunity."

"Now?"

"In a moment." He steered the boat under the drooping limbs of the tree. The dense growth cut off the sunlight and cooled the late-afternoon air.

Nash stopped and the boat settled, motionless, in the water. He turned to her and his gaze slid across her face.

"Has anyone ever told you how beautiful you are?"

Besides him and her parents? And they *had* to praise her, didn't they? No one. Not ever. "No."

"Is the rest of the world blind?"

His words were followed by silence. A silence that spanned years for Savannah. No man had looked past her flaw and seen the desirable woman she longed to be. No man but Nash.

His mouth came down on hers, shattering the silence with his hungry need, shattering the discipline she'd held herself under all these years. She wrapped herself in his embrace and returned the kiss with the potency of her own need.

Nash moaned and kissed her hard, and she responded with every ounce of her being. She kissed him as if she'd been waiting all her life for this moment, this man. In ways too numerous to count, she had been.

She moaned softly, thinking nothing seemed enough. Nash made her greedy. She wanted more. More of life. More of laughter. More of *him*.

Dragging his mouth from hers, he trailed a row of moist kisses down her neck. "If we were anyplace but here, do you know what we'd be doing now?"

"I...I think so." How odd her voice sounded.

"We'd be in bed making love."

"I..."

"What?" he prompted. "Were you about to tell me you can't? Because I'll be more than happy to prove otherwise." He directed her mouth back to his.... Then, slowly, reluctantly, as though remembering this was a public place and they could be interrupted at any time, he ended the kiss.

Savannah had more difficulty than Nash in returning to sanity. She needed the solid reality of him close to her. When he eased himself from her arms, his eyes searched out hers.

"If you say that shouldn't have happened, I swear I'll do something crazy," she whispered.

"I don't think I could make myself say it."

"Good," she breathed.

Nash pressed his forehead to hers. "I wish I knew what it is you do to me." She sensed that it troubled him that she could break through that facade of his. She was beginning to understand this man. She was physically handicapped, but Nash was crippled, too. He didn't *want* love, but he couldn't keep himself from needing it, from caring about her, and that worried him. It worried her, too.

"You don't like what I do to you." That much was obvious, but she wanted to hear him admit it.

Nash gave a short laugh. "That's the problem, I like it too much. There's never been anyone who affects me this way. Not since Denise."

"Your ex-wife?"

"Yes." He regretted mentioning her name, Savannah guessed, because he made a point of changing the subject immediately afterward.

"We should go back to the pier."

"Not yet," Savannah pleaded. "Not so soon. We just got started."

"I don't want you to strain your leg. You aren't accustomed to this much exercise."

"I won't, I promise. Just a little while longer." This was so much fun, she didn't want it to ever end. It wasn't every day that she could turn a dream into reality. It wasn't every day a man kissed her as if she were his cherished love.

Love. Love. Love. The word repeated itself in her mind. She was falling in love with Nash. It had begun weeks earlier, the first time he'd kissed her, and had been growing little by little. Love was a dangerous emotion when it came to Nash. He wouldn't be an easy man to care about.

He steered them away from the tree and into the sunlight. Savannah squinted against the glare, but it didn't seem to affect Nash. He pedaled now as if he was escaping something. The fun was gone.

"I'm ready to go back," Savannah said after several minutes of silence.

"Good." He didn't bother to disguise his relief.

The mood had changed so abruptly that Savannah had trouble taking it all in. Nash couldn't seem to get back to shore fast enough. He helped her out of the boat and placed his arm, grudgingly it seemed, around her waist to steady her. Once he was confident she had her balance, he released her.

"I think we should leave," he said when they returned to the picnic table.

"Sure," she agreed, disappointed and sad. She folded up the tablecloth and handed it to him. He carried the basket to the car and loaded it in the trunk.

Savannah knew what was coming; she'd been through it before. Whenever a man feared he was becoming—or might become—emotionally attached to her, she could count on the same speech. Generally it began with what an exceptional woman she was, talented, gifted, fun, that sort of thing. The conclusion, however, was always the same. Someday a special man would come into her life. She'd never expected her relationship with Nash to get even that far. She'd never expected to see him after Susan's wedding. This outing was an unforeseen bonus.

They were on the freeway, driving toward Seattle, before Savannah found the courage to speak. It would help if she broached the subject first.

"Thank you, Nash, for a lovely picnic."

He said nothing, which was just as well.

"I know what you're thinking," she said, clasping her hands tightly together.

"I doubt that."

She smiled to herself. "I've seen this happen with other men, so you don't need to worry about it."

"Worry about what?"

"You're attracted to me and that frightens you—probably more than the other men I've dated because a woman you once loved has deeply hurt you."

"I said I don't want to talk about Denise."

"I'm not going to ask about her, if that's what concerns you," she said quickly, wanting to relieve him about that. "I'm going to talk about us. You may not realize it now, but I'm saving you the trouble of searching for the right words."

He jerked his head away from traffic and scowled at her. "I beg your pardon?"

"You heard me right. You see, it's all familiar to me, so you needn't worry about it. This isn't the first time."

"It isn't?" The question was heavy with sarcasm.

"I've already explained it's happened before."

"Go on. I'd be interested in hearing this." The hard muscles of his face relaxed and the beginnings of a smile came into play.

"You like me."

"That should be fairly obvious," he commented.

"I like you, too."

"That's a comfort." The sarcastic edge was back, but it wasn't as biting.

"In fact, you're starting to like me a little too much."

"I'm not sure what that means, but go on."

"We nearly made love once."

"Twice," he corrected. "We were closer than you think a few minutes ago."

"Under a tree in a pedal boat?" she asked with a laugh.

"Trust me, honey, where there's a will, there's a way."

Savannah blushed and looked pointedly away. "Let's not get sidetracked."

"Good idea."

He was flustering her, distracting her train of thought. "It becomes a bit uncomfortable whenever a man finds me attractive."

"Why's that?"

"Because...well, because they have to deal with my problem, and most people are more comfortable ignoring it. If you deny that there's anything different, it might go away."

"Have I done that?" This question was more serious than the others.

"No," she admitted. "You've been accepting of my...defect. I'm just not sure—"

"I've never viewed you as defective," he interrupted.

It seemed important to him that she acknowledge that, so she did. "I'm grateful to have met you, Nash, grateful for the fun we've had."

"This is beginning to sound like a brush-off."

"It is," she murmured. "Like I said, I'm saving you the trouble of coming up with an excuse for not seeing me again. This is the better-to-be-honest-now-instead-of-cruel-later scenario."

"Saving me the trouble," he exploded, and then burst into gales of laughter. "So *that's* what this is all about."

"Yes. You can't tell me that isn't what you were thinking. I know the signs, Nash. Things got a bit intense between us and now you're getting cold feet. It happened the night of

Susan's wedding, too. We didn't make love and you were grateful, remember?"

He didn't agree or disagree.

"Just now...at the lake, we kissed, and you could feel it happening a second time, and that's dangerous. You couldn't get away from me fast enough."

"That's not entirely true."

"Your mood certainly changed."

"Okay, I'll concede that, but not for the reasons you're assuming. My mood changed because I started thinking about something and frankly it threw me for a loop."

"Thinking about what?" she pressed.

"A solution."

"To what?"

"Hold on, Savannah, because I don't know how you're going to react. Probably about the same way I did."

"Go on," she urged.

"It seems to me..."

"Yes?" she said when he didn't immediately finish.

"It seems to me that we might want to think about getting married."

# *Nine*

"Married," Savannah repeated in a husky whisper.

Nash knew he'd shocked her, but no more than he had himself. The notion of marriage went against the grain. Something was either very wrong—or very right. He hadn't decided yet.

"I don't understand." Savannah shook her head, making a vague gesture with her hands.

"Unfortunately, I don't know if I'll do a decent job of explaining it," Nash said.

"Try." Her hands were at her throat now, fingering the collar of her sweatshirt.

"This could work, Savannah, with a little effort on both our parts."

"Marriage? You hate the very word…. I've never met anyone with a more jaded attitude toward love and romance. Is this some kind of joke?"

"Trust me. I was just as shocked at the idea as you are, but the more I thought about it, the more sense it made. I wish it *was* a joke." Nash's choice of words must have been poor because Savannah recoiled from him. "It would be a marriage of convenience," he added, hoping that might reassure her—or at least not scare her off.

"What?" she cried. "In other words, you intend to take what I consider sacred and make a mockery of it."

It was difficult not to be defensive when Savannah was acting so unreasonable. "If you'll listen, you might see there are advantages for both of us."

"Take me back to my shop," she said in a icy voice.

"I'm going there now, but I was hoping we could talk first."

She said nothing, which didn't bode well. Nash wanted to explain, ease her mind, ease his own, but he wasn't sure he could. He'd spoken prematurely without giving the matter sufficient consideration. It was after they'd kissed under the weeping willow that the idea had occurred to him. It had shocked him so completely that for a time he could barely function. He'd needed to escape and now that they were on their way back into Seattle, he realized he needed to talk this over with her.

"I know this comes as a surprise," he said, looking for a way to broach the subject once again. He exited from the freeway and was within a mile of Savannah's shop.

Savannah looked steadfastly out the window, as if the houses they were passing mesmerized her.

"Say something," Nash demanded. He drove into the alley where her car was parked and turned off the engine. He kept his hands tightly on the steering wheel.

"You wouldn't want to hear what I'm thinking," Savannah told him through clenched teeth.

"Maybe not," he agreed. "But would you listen to what I have to say?"

She crossed her arms and glared at him. "I don't know if I can and keep a straight face."

"Try," he said, just as she had earlier.

"All right, go on, explain." She closed her eyes.

"When I came to pick you up this afternoon, you were upset."

She shrugged, unwilling to acknowledge even that much. It wasn't an encouraging sign. He'd been premature in mentioning marriage. He wasn't sure why he'd considered it so urgent that he couldn't take the night to sleep on it first. Perhaps he was afraid he'd change his mind. Perhaps this was what he'd always wanted, and he needed to salvage his pride with the marriage-of-convenience proposal. Either way, it didn't matter; he'd already shown his hand.

"You love your parents and want them to go after their dream, isn't that right?"

"Would you simply make your point?"

"Fine, I will," he said, his argument gaining momentum. "I'm offering you the perfect solution. You marry me."

"In other words, you're suggesting we mislead my parents into believing this is a love match?"

"I hadn't thought of it in those terms, but, yes, I guess we would be misleading them. If that makes you uncomfortable, tell them the truth. Keep your maiden name if you want. That wouldn't bother me at all. The point is, if you were married, your father and mother would feel free to move south for the winters the way they've always wanted."

"What's in this for you?" she demanded. "Don't try to tell me you're doing it out of the goodness of your heart, either. I know better."

"You're right, there're advantages to me, too."

She snickered softly. "Somehow I thought there would be."

"That's the beauty of my idea," he said, trying to keep his

irritation in check. Savannah was treating this like a joke while he was dead serious. A man didn't mention the word *marriage* lightly. Nash had been through this before, but this time marriage would be on his terms.

"Go on," Savannah snapped.

"As I said, there are certain advantages in this marriage for me, as well. The night of Susan's wedding, John Stackhouse pulled me aside and told me that I was being considered for the position of senior partner."

"But it would help if you were married."

Savannah wasn't slow-witted, that was for sure. "Something like that," he admitted. "It seems the other senior partners are afraid that my bitterness about my own divorce has spilled over into other areas of my life."

"Imagine that."

Nash tried to hide his annoyance. Savannah was making this extremely difficult.

"There're no guarantees for either of us, of course. If you agree to the terms of this marriage, that doesn't mean your parents will pack up and head south. If we did go ahead with it, there's nothing to say I'll be made senior partner. There's an element of risk for us both. You might get what you want and I might not. Or vice versa."

"Ah, now I understand," Savannah said in a slow, singsong voice. "That's where the convenience part comes into play. You want an out."

"That has nothing to do with it," Nash flared.

"Do you think I'm stupid, Nash? Of course it does. No one wants a *cripple* for a wife," she said furiously, "and if you can put an escape clause in the marriage contract, all the better."

"That's ridiculous! It has nothing to do with this."

"Would you have proposed marriage to any other woman

this way, suggesting a short-term relationship for the sake of convenience? Heaven forbid that you might feel some genuine affection for me!"

It took Nash a moment to compose himself. He'd acted on impulse, which was not only uncharacteristic but a huge mistake, one that had only led to greater confusion. "Maybe this wasn't such a bright idea after all," he began. "I should've ironed out the details before talking to you about it. If you want to find fault with me for that, then I'll accept it with a heartfelt apology, but this business about me using you because I consider you less of a woman—you couldn't be more wrong. Your suggestion insults us both."

"Why do I have a hard time believing that?" Savannah asked. She sounded suspiciously close to tears, which grieved him more than her anger had.

"All I'm looking for here is a way of being fair to us both," Nash argued. "Despite what you think, I didn't mean to insult you."

"I'm sure you didn't. You're probably thinking people will admire you. Imagine Nash Davenport taking pity on that—"

"Savannah, stop." He pressed his lips tightly together. She was making a mockery of his proposal, a mockery of herself.

"Are you saying I'm wrong?"

His self-control was stretched to the limit. "Don't even suggest that," he said.

"I have to go," Savannah whispered. She turned from him, her fingers closing around the door handle. "It'd be best if we didn't see each other again."

Nash knew that the minute she left his car it would be over between them. He couldn't allow that to happen, couldn't let her leave, not without righting the wrong. He needed to do something, anything, to convince her he was sincere.

"Not yet," Nash said, taking her by the shoulder.

"Let go of me."

"Not without this." He locked his arms around her waist and pulled her against him.

She didn't resist, not for a second. Her own arms crept around his neck, and then they were kissing again, with the same passion as before.

He didn't know how long they were in each other's arms—or what brought him back to sanity. Possibly a noise from the street, or Savannah herself. He jerked his head up and buried his face in her shoulder, which was heaving with the strength of her reaction. Her fingers were buried in his hair.

"I find it amazing," she whispered brokenly, "that you're looking for a marriage in name only."

He wasn't sure if she was being humorous or not, but he wasn't taking any chances. "We might need to revise that part of the agreement."

"There won't be any agreement, Nash."

He was afraid of that. "Would you kindly listen to reason, Savannah? I wasn't trying to insult you…I thought you'd *like* the idea."

"Think again." She was breathing deeply, clearly fighting to regain her composure.

"Are you willing to listen to reason?" he asked again, hoping he'd reached her, if on no other level than the physical.

"I've had to deal with a certain amount of cruelty in my life," she said in a low voice. "Children are often brutal with their taunts and their name-calling. It was something I became accustomed to as a child. It hurt. Sticks and stones may break your bones, but words cut far deeper."

"Savannah, stop." That she'd compare his proposal to the ridicule she'd endured as a child was too painful to hear.

She stiffened, her back straight. "I don't want to see you again."

The words hit him hard. "Why not?"

She opened the car door and stepped awkwardly into the alley. Her leg seemed to be bothering her and with some effort she shifted her weight. "I don't trust myself with you… and I don't trust you with me. I've got to take care of myself."

"I want to help you, not hurt you," he insisted.

She hung her head and Nash suspected she did so to hide the fact that she was crying. "Goodbye, Nash. Please don't try to see me again…. Don't make this any more difficult than it already is."

Two weeks later, Nash's sister, Susan, strolled into Savannah's shop. Savannah felt a sense of awe at the happiness that shone from the young woman's eyes.

"What are you doing here?" she asked. "You're supposed to be on your honeymoon."

"We've been back for several days."

Following the wedding, Savannah rarely saw her clients. Whenever someone made the effort to stop in, it was a special treat. More so with Susan because Savannah had been so actively involved in the wedding. Actively involved with Nash, if she was willing to be honest, which at the moment she wasn't.

"You look—" Savannah searched for the right word "—serene." The two women hugged and Savannah held her friend tightly as unexpected tears moistened her eyes. She didn't allow them to fall, not wanting Susan to see how emotional she'd become. "I've missed you," she said. She had, but more than that, she'd missed Nash.

"Nash said the same thing. You both knew before I was married that I'd be moving to California with Kurt. Now you're acting like it's a big shock. By the way, Kurt sends his love."

Savannah eased from Susan's embrace. "What are you doing back in Seattle so soon? Kurt's with you, isn't he?"

"Why I'm here is a long story. As to your second question, Kurt couldn't come. With the wedding and the honeymoon, he couldn't get away. It's the first time we've been apart since the wedding and I miss him dreadfully." A wistful look came over her.

"What brings you to Seattle?"

Susan hesitated just a fraction of a second. "Nash."

So her big brother had sent her. This was exactly what she should have expected from Nash. The man wasn't fair—he'd use any means at his disposal to achieve his purpose.

"He doesn't know I'm here," Susan said as if reading Savannah's thoughts. "He'd be furious if he ever found out. I phoned him when Kurt and I got home from our honeymoon and he said he was having several pieces of furniture shipped to us. Things that belonged to our parents. I was a little surprised, since we're living in a small apartment and don't have much space. Nash knows that. Kurt talked to him, too, and afterward we agreed something was wrong. The best way to handle the situation was for me to visit."

"I see." Savannah made busywork around her desk, turning off her computer, straightening papers, rearranging pens in their holder. "How is Nash?"

"Miserable. I don't know why and he's doing an admirable job of pretending otherwise. He's spending a lot of time at the office. Apparently he's tied up with an important case."

"Divorce?" Savannah asked unnecessarily. That was his specialty—driving a wedge deeper and deeper between two people who'd once loved each other, increasing misery and heartache. Each divorce he handled lent credence to his pessimistic views. That wasn't going to change, and she was a fool if she believed otherwise.

"You might have read about this case. It's the one with Don Griffin, the man who owns all those great seafood restaurants. It's really sad."

Savannah did remember reading something about it. Apparently Mr. Griffin had an affair with a much younger woman. It was a story as old as time. She hadn't realized Nash was involved, but should have. He was Seattle's top divorce attorney, and naturally a man as wealthy and influential as Don Griffin would hire the very best.

"I know the case," Savannah admitted.

"Nash's been working late every night." Susan paused and waited for Savannah to comment.

"He enjoys his work."

"He used to, but I'm not so sure anymore. Something's really bothering him."

Their conversation was making Savannah uncomfortable. "I'm sorry to hear that."

"It's more than what's going on at the law firm, though. Kurt and I both think it has something to do with you, but when I asked him, Nash nearly bit my head off. He wouldn't even talk about you."

Savannah smiled to herself. "Neither will I. Sometimes it's better to leave well enough alone. We both appreciate your love and support, but what's going on between Nash and me is our own business. Leave it at that, please."

"All right." Susan wasn't happy about it, Savannah could tell, but the last thing she and Nash wanted or needed was Susan and Kurt meddling in their lives. Susan looked regretfully at the time. "I have to get back. The movers are coming this afternoon. I'm not taking much—we simply don't have room for it. And with the stuff Nash is shipping... I don't know why he insisted on sending us the rocking horse. Dad built it for him when he was a little kid and it was understood that Nash would hand it down to his own children. It's been in the basement for years. I don't know why he sent it to me. Kurt and I aren't planning to start a family for a couple of years. Men just don't make sense sometimes."

"You're only discovering that now?" Savannah teased.

Susan laughed. "I should know better after living with my brother all those years."

They hugged and Susan left shortly afterward.

The day was exceptionally slow, and with time on her hands, Savannah sat at her desk and drew a design for a flower arrangement. Intent on her task, she worked for several minutes before she saw that it wasn't a flower arrangement that was taking shape, but a child's rocking horse.

"What do you mean Janice turned down our settlement proposal?" Don Griffin shouted. He propelled his large frame from the chair across from Nash's desk and started pacing. His movements were abrupt and disjointed. "It was a fair offer, more than fair. You said so yourself."

"That's how these things work, Mr. Griffin. As I explained earlier, if you'll recall, it was unlikely that your wife and her attorney would accept our first offer. It's just the way the game's played. Your wife's attorney wouldn't be earning his fee if he didn't raise some objections."

"How much longer is this going to drag on?" his client demanded. "I want this over with quickly. Give Janice what she wants. If she insists on taking control of the restaurants, fine, she can have them. She can have the house, the cars, our investments, too, for all I care."

"I can't allow you to do that."

"Why not?" He slammed his hand down on the desk.

"You've hired me to represent you in a court of law, to

look after your interests. If you make a decision now based on emotion, you'll regret it later. These matters take time."

"I haven't *got* time," the tall, stocky man said. Don Griffin was in his fifties, and beginning to show his age.

"Is there a reason we need to rush?" Nash hated surprises. If Don's ex-girlfriend was pregnant, he didn't want to find out about it in the courtroom.

"Yes!" the other man shouted. "There's a very good reason. I hate this constant fighting, hate having my reputation raked over the coals in the press. Twenty-seven years of marriage—and after one indiscretion, Janice makes me look like a serial murderer. The restaurant's receipts actually dropped ten percent after that story was leaked."

Nash didn't know who was responsible for that, but he could make an educated guess. Janice Griffin's attorney, Tony Pound, stirred up controversy whenever possible, especially if it helped his case.

Nash made a note of the lost revenue and decided that when he phoned Tony later this afternoon, he'd tell him Janice's compensation might not be as big as she'd hoped—not if the business failed due to negative publicity.

"If it goes on like this," Don continued, "we may be filing for bankruptcy next."

"I'll make sure Mr. Pound learns this."

"Good, and while you're at it," Don said, waving his finger at Nash, "do what you can about me seeing my daughter. Janice can't keep me away from Amy, and this bull about me being a negative influence on our daughter is exactly that—bull."

"I'll arrange visitation rights for you as soon as I can."

"See if I can have her this weekend. I'm going to the beach and Amy's always loved the beach."

"I'll see what I can do. Is there anything else?"

His client paced, rubbing his hands together. "Have you seen my wife and daughter recently?" he asked.

"No. That would be highly unusual. Is there a reason you're asking?"

"I...I was just wondering how they looked, that's all. If they're well."

It was there in his eyes, Nash saw, the way it always was. The pain, the loneliness, the sense of loss so strong it brought powerful men and women to their knees. Nash thought of these moments when clients realized they were about to lose what they'd once considered their anchor. The chains were broken. With the anchors gone, it became a struggle to keep from drifting. Storms rose up, and that was when Nash learned the truth about his clients. Some weathered these tempests and came out stronger and more confident. Others struggled to stay afloat and eventually drowned.

Sadly, he didn't know which kind of person Don Griffin would prove to be.

The urgency in her father's voice frightened Savannah. His phone call came during her busiest time of day. It took her a moment to decipher what he was saying.

"Mom's in the hospital?" Savannah repeated. Her blood ran cold at the thought.

"Yes." Her father, who was always so calm and collected, was near panic. "She collapsed at home.... I didn't know what to do so I called an aid car and they've brought her to the hospital. The doctors are with her now."

"I'll be there in five minutes," Savannah promised. Fortunately, Nancy had come in to help her, so she didn't have to close the shop.

She'd always hated the smell of hospitals, she thought as she rushed into the emergency entrance of Northend Memorial. It was a smell that resurrected memories she'd pushed to the back of her mind.

Savannah found her father in the emergency waiting room, his shoulders hunched, his eyes empty. "Daddy," she whispered, "what happened?"

"I...don't know. We were working in the yard when your mother called out to me. By the time I turned around she'd passed out. I was afraid for a moment that she was dead. I nearly panicked."

Savannah sat in the seat beside him and reached for his hand.

"I forgot about you not liking hospitals," her father said apologetically.

"It's all right. I wouldn't want to be anyplace else but here with you."

"I'm scared, sweetheart, really scared."

"I know." Savannah was, too. "Have you talked to the doctors yet?"

He shook his head. "How long will it take? She's been in there for over an hour."

"Anytime now, I'm sure." At the moment, Savannah wasn't sure of anything, least of all how her father would cope without her mother if it turned out that something was seriously wrong....

"Mr. Charles." The doctor approached them, his face revealing concern.

Automatically Savannah and her father got to their feet, bracing themselves for whatever he might say.

"Your wife's suffered a stroke."

In the past few weeks, Nash had made a habit of staying late at the office. He no longer liked spending time at the house. It'd been nearly a month since Savannah had been inside his home and he swore that whenever he walked inside, he caught a whiff of her perfume. He knew it was ridiculous, but he'd taken to placing air fresheners at strategic points.

His bed was also a problem. Savannah had left her imprint there, as well. When he woke in the morning, he could sense her presence. He could almost hear her breathing, feel her breath, her mouth scant inches from his own. It bothered him that a woman could have this powerful an effect on him.

She'd meant what she said about ending the relationship. Not that he'd expected to hear from her again. He hoped he would, but that was entirely different from *expecting* her to call.

More times than he cared to count, he'd resisted the urge to contact her. He'd considered sending flowers with a humorous note, something to break the ice, to salvage his pride and hers, then decided against it.

She'd made herself clear and he had no option but to abide by her wishes. She didn't want to see him again. So she wouldn't. The next move, if there was one, would have to be hers.

As for that absurd proposal of marriage... Seldom had he regretted anything more. It embarrassed him to think about it, so he avoided doing so whenever possible.

Someone knocked softly on his office door. He checked his watch, surprised to discover he wasn't alone at 10:00 p.m.

"Come in."

The door opened and Savannah stood there. She was pale, her features ashen, her eyes red-rimmed as if she'd recently been crying.

"Savannah," he said, hurrying around his desk. "What's wrong?" He didn't reach for her, much as he wanted to, not knowing if she'd welcome his touch.

"I've come," she said in a voice that was devoid of emotion, "to tell you I've reconsidered. I'll accept your offer of a marriage of convenience…. That is, if it's still open."

# *Ten*

"You're sure about this?" Generally Nash wasn't one to look a gift horse in the mouth, but this time was the exception. Something had happened to cause Savannah to change her mind, something drastic. Nash was convinced of that.

"I wouldn't be here if I wasn't sure." Nervously she reached inside her purse and took out a well-creased slip of paper. "I've made up a list of issues we need to discuss first…if you're willing."

"All right." He gestured toward the guest chair and sat down himself. "But first tell me what happened."

"My mother," she began, and paused as her lower lip began to tremble. She needed a moment to compose herself enough to continue speaking. "Mom's in the hospital…. She had a stroke."

"I'm sorry to hear that."

Savannah nodded. "Her prognosis for a complete recovery is excellent, but it frightened me terribly—Dad, too."

"I understand."

"Mom's stroke helped me realize I might not have my parents much longer. I refuse to allow them to sacrifice their dreams because of me."

"I see."

She unfolded the piece of paper in her hands. "Are you ready to discuss the details?"

"By all means." He reached for his gold pen and a fresh legal pad.

"There will be no...lovemaking. You mentioned earlier that you preferred this to be a marriage of convenience, and I'm in full agreement."

That had been a hasty suggestion, certainly not one he'd carefully thought out. In light of their strong physical attraction, Nash didn't believe this stipulation would hold up for more than a few days, a week at the most. The minute he kissed her, or took her in his arms, the chemistry they shared would return.

"You're sure about this?" he asked.

"Positive."

Suggesting they wouldn't be able to keep their hands off each other would inevitably trigger a heated argument. Savannah would accuse him of being arrogant. Nash decided to agree with her for the present and let time prove him right.

"Do you agree?" Her eyes challenged him to defy her.

Nash rolled the pen between his palms and relaxed in his leather chair, not wanting to give her any reason to suspect that he had reservations or what they were. "If a marriage in name only is what you want, then naturally I'll agree to those terms."

"Good." She nodded, much too enthusiastically to suit him.

"Unless we mutually agree otherwise at some point," he added.

Savannah's eyes darted back to his. "I wouldn't count

on that if I were you. I'm agreeing to this marriage for one reason and one reason only. I want to be sure you understand that."

"In other words, you don't plan to trick me into falling in love with you." He heard the edge in his own voice and regretted it. Savannah had sacrificed her pride the minute she'd walked through his door; goading wasn't necessary.

"This isn't a game to me, Nash," she said, her voice sharp. "I'm serious. If you aren't, maybe we should call it quits right now."

"I was the one who suggested this," he reminded her, not bothering to mention that it had been a spur-of-the-moment idea he'd deplored ever since. He stared at Savannah, noting the changes in her. He'd always viewed her as delicate, feminine. But there was a hardness to her now, a self-protective shell. She didn't trust him not to hurt her. Didn't trust him not to destroy her once-unshakable faith in love and marriage.

"I'll draw up the papers to read that this will be a marriage of convenience unless we mutually agree otherwise. Does that wording satisfy you?"

"All right, as long we understand each other." Her gaze fell to her list. "The second item I have here has to do with our living arrangements. I'll move in with you for a brief period of time."

"How brief?" This didn't sound any more encouraging than her first stipulation.

"Until my mother's well enough to travel south. That's the reason I'm willing to go through with this, after all. But to be as fair as possible, I'll stay with you until a senior partner's named."

"I'd appreciate that." The announcement would come within the month, Nash was certain, although it was taking much longer than he'd assumed. He'd like nothing better than to pull a fast one on Paul. The pompous ass would likely leave the firm. Nash smiled just thinking about it.

"After that there won't be any need for us to continue this farce. I'll move back to my home and we can have the marriage, such as it is, dissolved. Of course, I'll make no claims on you financially and expect the same."

"Of course," Nash agreed. Yet this talk of divorce so soon after marriage grated on him. It wouldn't look good to John Stackhouse and Arnold Serle if he was only married for a few weeks. And a quick divorce—*any* divorce—was the last thing he wanted. "For propriety's sake, I'd like to suggest we stay married a year," he said.

"A year," she repeated, making it sound as long as a lifetime. She sighed. "Fine. I'll accept that, provided we both adhere to all the other conditions."

"Anything else?" he asked, after making a second notation on the legal pad.

"Yes, as a matter of fact, I have a few more points."

Nash groaned inwardly, but presented a calm exterior.

"While I'm living with you, I insist we sleep in separate bedrooms. The less we have to do with each other, the better. You live your life the same as always and I'll live mine."

Nash wrote this down, as well, but made a point of hesitating, making sure she was aware of his uneasiness about this latest dictate. This would be the ideal setup if he was looking for a roommate, but Nash was seeking a deeper commitment.

"Since you mention propriety…" Savannah began.

"Yes?" he prompted when she didn't immediately continue.

"Although our marriage will be one of convenience, I feel strongly that we should practice a certain code of ethics."

The words were rushed, as if she thought he'd disagree. "I expect you to stop dating other women," she said, speaking more slowly now. "If I were to discover that you'd been seeing someone else, I would consider that immediate grounds for divorce."

"The same would hold true for you," he returned calmly. It made him wonder what kind of man she thought he was. "If I found out you were interested in another man, then I'd see no reason to continue our agreement."

"That isn't likely to happen," she blurted out defensively.

"Any more than it is with me."

She clamped her mouth shut and Nash guessed she didn't believe him. Where had she gotten the impression that he was a playboy? It was true that after his divorce he'd occasionally dated, but there'd never been anyone he was serious about—until Savannah. "We'll need to be convincing," she said next, her voice quavering slightly, "otherwise my parents, especially my father, will see through this whole thing in an instant. They aren't going to be easily fooled, and it's important we persuade them we're getting married because we're in love."

"I can be convincing." He'd gained his reputation swaying twelve-member juries; an elderly couple who wanted to believe he was in love with their daughter would be a piece of cake.

"I'll do my best to be the same," Savannah assured him, relaxing slightly. She neatly folded the sheet of paper, running her fingers along the crease. "Was there anything you wanted to add?"

Without time to think over their agreement, Nash was at a disadvantage. "I might later."

"I...was hoping we could come to terms quickly so I can tell my parents right away."

"We'll tell them together," Nash said. "Otherwise they'll find it odd. What do you want to do about the actual wedding ceremony?"

She looked away, then lowered her gaze. "I wasn't sure you'd agree so I hadn't given it much thought. I guess I should have, since I arrange weddings for a living."

"Don't look so chagrined. This isn't a normal, run-of-the-mill marriage."

"Exactly," she was quick to concur. "I'd like a small gathering. My parents and a few good friends—no more than ten or so. What about you?"

"About that number." He'd make sure Serle and Stackhouse received invitations.

"I'll arrange for the ceremony, then, followed by dinner. Is that agreeable?"

He shrugged, not really caring. Small and private appealed to him far more than the lavish gathering Susan had had. At least Savannah wasn't going to subject him to that, although he felt mildly guilty about cheating her out of a fancy wedding.

"How long do you think you'll need to come up with any further stipulations?" she asked.

"Not long," he promised, but he had one thought that he mentioned before he could censure it. "I'd like us to make a habit of eating dinner together."

"Dinner?" Savannah sounded incredulous.

His sole condition did seem surprising. But he felt that if they were going to the trouble of getting married, they shouldn't remain strangers. "We need to spend some time together, don't you think?"

"I don't see why that's necessary."

"It will be if we're going to create the facade of being

married. We'll need to know what's going on in each other's lives."

Her nod was reluctant. "I see your point."

"We can share the housework, so you don't need to worry about me sticking you with the cooking and the cleanup afterward. I want to be fair about this."

"That seems equitable."

"I don't intend to take advantage of you, Savannah." It was important she believe that, although it was obvious she didn't. Even married to Savannah, he didn't hold out much hope of becoming a senior partner. Not when Paul Jefferson was ingratiating himself with anyone and everyone who could advance his career. But if there was the slightest possibility that he might beat out Paul, Nash was willing to risk it. His dislike for the man increased daily, especially since Paul resented that Nash had been given the Don Griffin case and had made his feelings obvious.

"What day should I arrange the wedding for?" Savannah asked, flipping through the pages of a small pocket calendar.

"In a week, if at all possible." He could tell by the way her eyes widened that she expected more time. "Is that too soon?"

"Not really…. A week shouldn't be a problem, although people *are* going to ask questions."

"So? Does that bother you?"

"Not exactly."

"Good." Nash had little success in hiding a smile.

"In that case, I think you should write up the agreement right away," she said. "You can add whatever provisions you want and if I disagree, I'll cross them out."

"Okay. When would you like to tell your parents?"

"As soon as possible. Tomorrow evening?"

Nash stood and replaced his pen in the marble holder. "Is your mother still in the hospital?"

Savannah nodded. "Dad spends almost every minute with her. The nurses told me they tried to send him home the first night, but he refused and ended up sleeping on a cot beside her."

"He's taken this hard, hasn't he?"

Savannah nodded. "He's worried sick…. That's the main reason I decided to accept your proposal. Mom loves the sunshine and I can't think of any place she'd enjoy recuperating more than in Arizona with her friends."

"In that case, we'll do everything we can to be sure that happens."

"Oh, Savannah." Her mother's eyes glistened with the sheen of tears as she sat up in her hospital bed early the next evening. "You're going to be married."

Nash slid his arm around Savannah's waist with familiar ease and smiled down on her. "I know my timing couldn't be worse," he murmured, "but I hope you'll forgive me."

"There's nothing to forgive. We're thrilled, aren't we, Marcus?" Her mother smiled blissfully. Nash was eating up the attention, nuzzling Savannah's neck, planting kisses on her cheek when he was sure her parents would notice. These open displays of affection were unlike him and were fast beginning to irritate Savannah.

"This does seem rather sudden, though, doesn't it?" her father asked. He might have embarrassed her by acting as if Nash was practically her fiancé that first evening, but he was astute about people, and Savannah knew that convincing him would be much more difficult than persuading her mother. Nash must have realized it, too, because he was playing the role as if he expected to earn an award for his performance as the besotted lover.

"Savannah and I've been dating off and on all summer." He brought her close to his side and dropped a quick kiss on the side of her neck. The moment they were alone, she'd tell him to keep his kisses to himself. Every time he touched his lips to her skin, a shiver of awareness raced up her spine. Nash knew it; otherwise he wouldn't take every opportunity to make her so uncomfortable.

"Are you in love?" her father asked her directly.

"Marcus, what a thing to ask," her mother said with a flustered laugh. "Savannah and Nash have come to us wanting to share their wonderful news. This isn't any time to ask a lot of silly questions."

"Would I marry Nash if I didn't love him?" Savannah asked, hoping that would be enough to reassure her father.

"We'd like to have the wedding as soon as possible," Nash added, looking down at her adoringly.

"There's a rush?" her father asked.

His attitude surprised Savannah. She was prepared for a bit of skepticism, but not this interrogation. Once he was convinced Savannah loved Nash—and vice versa—she didn't figure there would be any problems.

"I want Savannah with me," Nash answered. "It took me a long time to decide to marry again and now that I have, each day without her feels like an eternity." He reached for her hand and raised it to his lips, then placed a series of soft kisses on her knuckles. He was overdoing it, making fools of them both, and Savannah fumed.

"You feel the same way about Nash?"

"Yes, Daddy," she returned smoothly.

"I've waited all my life for a woman like Savannah."

Savannah couldn't help it; she stepped on Nash's foot and he yelped, then glared at her accusingly.

"I'm sorry, darling, did I hurt you?" she asked sweetly.

"No, I'm fine." His eyes questioned her, but she ignored the silent entreaty.

Her father stood at the head of the bed, which was angled up so that her mother was in a sitting position. They were holding hands.

"Do you object to Savannah marrying Nash?" her father questioned.

Her mother's sigh was filled with relief and joy. "Savannah's far too old to require our approval, and you know it. She can do as she pleases. I don't understand why you're behaving as if this is some…some tragedy when our little girl is so happy. Isn't this what we've prayed for all these years?"

"I know it's come at you out of the blue, Daddy," Savannah whispered, the words sticking in her throat, "but you know me well enough to know I'd never marry a man I didn't love with all my heart."

"The sooner Savannah's in my life, the sooner I can be complete," Nash added with a dramatic sigh.

Although he was clearly making an effort to sound sincere, it was all Savannah could do not to elbow him in the ribs. Anyone who knew Nash would recognize that he was lying, and doing a poor job of it. Presumably he was more effective in front of a jury.

"I should be out of the hospital by Friday," her mother said excitedly. "That'll give me a couple of days to rest at home before the wedding."

"If you need a few extra days to rest, we don't mind waiting. It's important that you be there, isn't that right, darling?"

Savannah felt him nudging her and quickly nodded. "Of

course. Having you both there is more important than any-thing."

Her father shook his head. "I don't understand why you insist on having the wedding so soon. You've only known each other for a few months."

"We know each other better than you think," Nash said. The insinuation that they were lovers was clear. Savannah bit her tongue to keep from claiming otherwise. If Nash was try-ing to embarrass her, he'd surpassed his wildest expectations. Her face burned, and she couldn't meet her parents' eyes.

"I don't think we need to question Savannah and Nash any longer," her mother said. "They know their own minds. You have my blessing."

"Daddy?" Savannah whispered, holding her breath.

He didn't say anything, then nodded.

"There are a thousand things to do before Wednesday," Savannah said abruptly, bending over to kiss her mother's pale cheek. "If you don't mind, Nash and I'll leave now."

"Of course," her father said.

"Thank you so much for the wonderful news, sweetheart." Her mother was tiring; their departure came at the oppor-tune moment.

Savannah couldn't wait until they were well outside the hospital room before turning on Nash. "How dare you," she flared, hands clenched at her sides. The man had no sense of decency. She'd told him how important it was to be con-vincing, but Nash cheerfully went about making fools of them both. His behavior angered her so much she could hardly speak.

"What did I do?" he demanded, wearing a confused, in-jured look that was meant to evoke sympathy. It wouldn't work—not this time.

"You implied…you—you let my parents believe we were lovers," she sputtered. And that was just for starters.

"So?" Nash asked. "Good grief, Savannah, you're thirty years old. They know you're not a virgin."

She punched the elevator button viciously. The rush of tears was a mingling of outrage and indignation, and she blinked furiously in an effort to keep them from spilling.

Nash exhaled softly and rubbed the back of his neck. "You *are* a virgin, aren't you?"

"Do you mind if we don't discuss such private matters in a public place?" she ground out. The elevator arrived just then, and Savannah eagerly stepped on.

There were a couple of other people who stared at her. Her limp sometimes made her the center of attention, but right now she suspected it was her tears that prompted their curiosity.

She managed to keep quiet until they reached the parking lot. "As for that stupid declaration of being so crazy about me you couldn't wait another minute to make me yours—I wanted to throw up."

"Why? You should be praising me instead of getting all bent out of shape."

"*Praising* you? For what?"

"Convincing your father we're in love."

"Oh, please," Savannah whispered, gazing upward. The sun had begun to set, spreading shades of gold and pink across the sky. It was all so beautiful, when she felt so ugly. Nash was saying the things every woman longs to hear—beautiful words. Only, his were empty. Perhaps that was what troubled her so much, the fact that he didn't mean what he was saying when she wanted it to be true.

"You're not making any sense." His patience was clearly

gone as he unlocked the passenger door, then slammed it shut. "Let's have this out right here and now."

"Fine!" she shouted.

"I was doing everything I could think of to convince your parents we're madly in love. Correct me if I'm wrong, but wasn't that the objective?"

"You didn't need to lay it on so thick, did you?"

"What do you mean?"

"Did you have to hold on to me like you couldn't bear to be separated from me for a single second? The kissing has got to stop. I won't have you fawning all over me like...like a lovesick calf."

"Fine. I won't lay another hand on you as long as we're together. Not unless you ask."

"You make that sound like a distinct possibility and trust me, it's not."

He laughed shrewdly, but didn't reply. The look he gave her just then spoke volumes. Savannah found herself getting even angrier.

"You could practice being a bit more subtle, couldn't you?" she went on. "If anyone should know the power of subtlety, it's you. I thought you were this top-notch attorney. Don't you know *anything* about human nature?"

"I know a little." He went strangely quiet for a moment. "You don't think we fooled your father?"

"No, Nash, I don't," she said, calmer now. "The only people we seem capable of fooling are ourselves. I'm afraid this simply isn't going to work."

"You want out already?" he demanded, sounding shocked and surprised. "Our engagement isn't even three hours old and already you're breaking it."

"We don't have any choice," she insisted. "Anyone with sense is going to see through this charade in a heartbeat. If we can't handle announcing the news to my parents, how do you expect to get through the wedding ceremony?"

"We'll manage."

"How can you be so sure of that?"

"We did before, didn't we?" he asked softly. "At Susan's wedding."

He *would* bring that up. The man didn't fight fair. Her behavior at the wedding ceremony had been a slip of judgment and now he was waving it in front of her like a red flag, challenging her to a repeat performance. "But that wasn't real...we weren't the center of attention."

"Like I said, we'll manage very well—just wait and see." Nash walked around to the front of his car and leaned against the hood, crossing his arms. "Your parents are okay with it, so I suggest we continue as planned. Are you game?"

Savannah nodded, feeling she had no other choice. She suspected she could convince her father that she was in love with Nash; she wasn't sure he'd believe Nash was in love with her.

Nash was busy at his desk, reviewing the latest settlement offer from Don Griffin, when his secretary buzzed him and announced that a Mr. Marcus Charles was there to see him without an appointment.

"Send him in," Nash instructed. He closed the file, set it aside and stood.

Savannah's dad was a gentle, reflective man who reminded him a little of his own father. "Come in, please," Nash said pleasantly. "This is a surprise."

"I should have phoned."

"We all behave impulsively at one time or another," Nash said, hoping Savannah's father would catch his meaning. He'd tried hard to make it sound as if their wedding plans were impulsive, which was more or less the truth. He'd tried to convince her family that he was crazy in love with her and, according to Savannah, he'd overplayed his hand. Perhaps she was right.

"Do you mind if I sit down?"

"Of course not," Nash said immediately, dismayed by his own lack of manners. Apparently he was more shaken by this unforeseen visit than he'd realized. "Is there anything I can get you? Coffee, tea, a cold drink?"

"No, thanks." He claimed the chair across from Nash's and crossed his legs. "It looks like Joyce will be released from the hospital a day early."

Nash was relieved. "That's wonderful news."

"The news from you and Savannah rivaled that. The doctor seems to think it's what helped Joyce recover so quickly."

"I'm pleased to hear that."

"It's going to take several months before she's fully recovered, but that's to be expected."

Nash nodded, not thinking any comment was necessary. He was rarely nervous, but he felt that way now.

Marcus was silent for a moment. "So you want to marry Savannah."

"Yes, sir." This much was true and his sincerity must have rung clear in his response because it seemed to him that Savannah's father relaxed.

"My daughter's accident damaged her confidence, her self-image, at least in emotional situations." He paused. "Do you know what I mean?"

"Yes," he said honestly.

Marcus stood and walked over to the window. "I'm not going to ask if you love Savannah," he said abruptly. "For a number of reasons that doesn't matter to me as much as it did earlier. If you don't love her, you will soon enough.

"You came to me the other night seeking my blessing and I'm giving it to you." He turned and held out his hand.

The two men exchanged handshakes. When they'd finished, Marcus Charles reached inside his suit jacket, withdrew a business-size envelope and set it on Nash's desk.

"What's that?"

Marcus smiled. "Savannah's mother and I thought long and hard about what we should give you as a wedding present, then decided the best gift would be time alone. Inside is a map to a remote cabin in the San Juan Islands that we've rented for you. We're giving you one week of uninterrupted peace."

# *Eleven*

"What did you expect me to do?" Nash demanded as they drove off the Washington State ferry. "Refuse your parents' wedding gift?" This marriage was definitely getting off to a rocky start. They'd been husband and wife less than twelve hours and already they were squabbling.

"A remote cabin...alone together," she groaned. "I've never heard of anything more ridiculous."

"Most newlyweds would be thrilled with the idea," he said.

"We're not most newlyweds."

"I don't need you to remind me of that," Nash snapped. "You try to do someone a favor..."

"Are you insinuating that marrying me was a *favor?*" Savannah was huddled close to the door. "That you were doing it out of kindness?"

Nash prayed for patience. So this was what their marriage was going to be like—this constant barrage of insults, nit-picking, faultfinding.

"No, Savannah, I don't consider marrying you a favor and I didn't do it out of kindness. You're my wife and—"

"In name only," she said in icy tones.

"Does that mean we're enemies now?"

"Of course not."

"Then why have we been at each other's throats from the moment we left the wedding dinner? I'm sorry your family insisted on giving us a honeymoon. I'm well aware that you'd rather spend time with anyone but me. I was hoping we'd make the best of this."

She didn't respond, for which he was grateful. The silence was a welcome contrast to the constant bickering.

"It was a beautiful wedding," she said softly, unexpectedly.

"Yes, it was." Savannah was beautiful in her ivory silk suit with a short chiffon veil decorated with pearls. Nash had barely been able to take his eyes off her. It was a struggle to remember this wasn't a real, till-death-do-us-part marriage.

"I've been acting defensive," she added apologetically. "I'm sorry, Nash, for everything. It isn't your fault we're stuck together like this."

"Well, it was my idea, after all. And our marriage *could* be a good thing in lots of ways."

"You're right," she said, but she didn't sound convinced. "We might find we enjoy each other's company."

Nash was offended by the comment. He'd enjoyed being with Savannah from the beginning, enjoyed goading her, challenging her views on marriage. He'd found himself seeking her out, looking for excuses to be with her, until she'd insisted she didn't want to see him again. He'd abided by her wishes, but he'd missed her, far more than he cared to admit.

"I saw Mr. Serle and Mr. Stackhouse talking to you after the ceremony."

Nash grinned, feeling a sense of satisfaction. Both of the senior partners had been delighted to see Nash marry Savannah. She'd managed to completely captivate those two. Arnold Serle had been acutely disappointed that they'd decided against a wedding dance. He'd been counting on another spin around the floor with Savannah.

"Did they say anything about the senior partnership?" Savannah asked.

He was annoyed that she already seemed eager to get out of their arrangement. "No, but then, a wedding isn't exactly the place to be discussing business." He didn't mention that it was at his sister's reception that John Stackhouse had originally introduced the subject.

"I see." She sounded disappointed, and Nash's hands tightened on the steering wheel. Luckily the drive was a beautiful one through lush green Lopez Island. Although Nash had lived in Washington all his life, he'd never ventured into the San Juan Islands. When they drove off the ferry he was surprised by the quiet coves and breathtaking coastline. In an effort to fill their time, he'd arranged for him and Savannah to take a cruise and explore the northernmost boundary islands of Susia and Patos, which were the closest to the Canadian border. He'd wanted their honeymoon to be a memorable experience; he'd planned a shopping excursion to Friday Harbor for another day. He'd read about the quaint shops, excellent restaurants and a whale museum. Women liked those sorts of things. It seemed now that his efforts were for naught. Savannah had no intention of enjoying these days together.

"Have your parents said anything about traveling south?"

"Not yet," she said, her voice disheartened.

"They might not, you know." In other words, she could find herself living with him for the next few years, like it or not. The thought didn't appeal to him any more than it did her, especially if she continued with this attitude.

"How much farther is it to the cabin?" she asked stiffly. Nash wasn't sure. He didn't have GPS but he had a detailed map and instructions. However, since he'd never been on Lopez Island, he wasn't any expert. "Soon, I suspect."

"Good."

"You're tired?"

"A little."

It'd been a full day. First the wedding, then the dinner followed by the drive to the ferry and the ride across Puget Sound. Darkness would fall within the hour and Nash had hoped they'd be at the cabin before then.

He reached the turnoff in the road and took a winding, narrow highway for several miles. Savannah was suspiciously silent, clutching her wedding bouquet. He was surprised she'd chosen to bring it with her.

He found the dirt road that led to the cabin and slowly drove down it, grateful he'd rented a four-wheel-drive vehicle. The route was filled with ruts, which didn't lend him much confidence about this remote cabin. If this was any indication of what the house would be like, they'd be lucky to have electricity and running water.

He was wrong and knew it the minute he drove into the clearing. This was no cabin, but a luxurious house, built with a Victorian flair, even to the turret and wraparound porch.

"Oh, my...it's lovely," Savannah whispered.

The house was a sight to behold all on its own, but the view of the water was majestic.

"I'll get the luggage," Nash said, hopping out of the Jeep. He thought better of it, hurried around to Savannah's side and helped her down.

With his hands around her waist, he lifted her onto the

ground. He longed to hold her against him, to swing her into his arms and carry her over the threshold like any new husband, but he didn't dare. Savannah would assume he was making a mockery of this traditional wedding custom. That was how she seemed to be dealing with everything lately, distrusting him and his motives. She made marriage feel like an insult. If this attitude lasted much longer, they'd have the shortest marriage on record.

"I'll get the luggage," he said again, unnecessarily. At least if his hands were full, he wouldn't be tempted to reach for Savannah.

"I'll open the door," she said, and for the first time she sounded enthusiastic. She hurried ahead of him and he noticed that she favored her injured leg more than usual. Sitting for any length of time must make movement more difficult. She rarely spoke about her leg—about the accident, her long rehabilitation or the pain she still suffered. He wished he knew how to broach the subject, but every attempt had been met with bristly pride, as if she believed that sharing this imperfect part of herself would make her too vulnerable.

She had the door open when he joined her. Stepping inside the house was like stepping into the nineteenth century. The warmth and beauty of this house seemed to greet them with welcoming arms.

The living room was decorated with a mix of antiques, and huge windows created a room that glowed in the setting sun.

"Oh, Nash," Savannah said, "I don't think I've ever seen anything more beautiful."

"Me, neither."

"Dad must have seen an ad for this house, maybe on a vacation website. He knows how much I love anything Victorian, especially houses."

Nash stashed that away in his storehouse of information about Savannah. When it was time to celebrate her birthday or Christmas, he'd know what to buy her.

"I'll put these in the bedrooms," he said. He didn't like the idea of them sleeping separately, but he didn't have any choice. He'd agreed to do so until she changed her mind, and from the look of things that could be a decade from now—if ever.

The master bedroom was equally attractive, with a huge four-poster mahogany bed. French lace curtains hung from the windows and the walls were papered in pale yellow. He set down Savannah's suitcase and headed for the second bedroom, which would be his. It was originally intended as a children's room, he realized. Instead of spending his wedding night with the woman he'd just married, he was destined to stare at row after row of tin soldiers. So much for romance!

Savannah woke early the next morning. The sunlight spilling in from the window was filtered through the lace curtains until a spidery pattern reflected against the floor. She yawned and sat up in bed. Surprisingly, she'd fallen asleep right away without the sadness or tears she'd expected.

"You're a married woman," she said aloud, thinking she might believe it if she heard herself say it. Her wedding and all that led up to it was still unreal to her. Afterward she'd been awful to Nash.

It took her a long time to understand why she'd behaved in such an uncharacteristic manner. Just before she went to bed, she'd realized what was going on. She was lashing out at him, blaming him for making a farce of what she considered holy. Only, he wasn't to blame; they were in this together. Marriage was advantageous to them both.

She heard him rummaging around in the kitchen. The aroma of coffee urged her out of bed. She threw on her robe and shoved her feet into slippers.

"'Morning," she said when she joined him. He'd obviously been up for hours. His jacket hung on a peg by the back door with a pair of rubber boots on the mat. His hair was wet, and he held a mug of steaming coffee and leaned against the kitchen counter.

"'Morning," he said, grinning broadly.

"You've been exploring." It hurt a little that he'd gone outside without her, but she couldn't really fault him. She hadn't been decent company in the past week or so. And walking along the beach with her wouldn't be much fun, since her gait was slow and awkward.

"I took a walk along the beach. I found you something." He reached behind him and presented her with a perfectly formed sand dollar.

Savannah's hand closed around her prize.

"I'm not sure, but I think I saw a pod of whales. It's a little difficult to tell from this distance."

Savannah made busywork about the kitchen, pouring herself a cup of coffee and checking the refrigerator for milk, all the while struggling to hold back her disappointment. She would've loved to see a pod of whales, even from a distance.

"What would you like for breakfast?" she asked, hoping to get their day off to a better start.

"Bacon, eggs, toast and a kiss."

Savannah froze.

"You heard me right. Come on, Savannah, loosen up. We're supposed to be madly in love, remember? This isn't going to work if you act the part of the outraged virgin."

What he said was true, but that didn't make it any easier. She turned away from him and fought down a confused mixture of anger and pain. She wanted to blame him, and knew she couldn't. She longed to stamp her foot, as she had when she was a little girl, and cry out, "Stop! No more." No more discord. No more silliness. But it wouldn't do any good. She was married but resigned to a life of loneliness. These were supposed to be the happiest days of her life and here she was struggling not to weep.

Nash had moved behind her and placed his hands on her shoulders. "Do you find me so repugnant?" he whispered close to her ear.

His warm breath was moist. She shut her eyes and shook her head.

"Then why won't you let me kiss you?"

She shrugged, but was profoundly aware of the answer. If Nash kissed her, she'd remember how much she enjoyed his touch. It'd been like that from the beginning. He knew it. She knew it. Now he intended to use that against her.

He brought his mouth down to her neck and shivers of awareness moved up and down her spine. Needing something to hold on to, Savannah reached for the kitchen counter.

"One kiss," he coaxed. "Just one."

"Y-you promise?"

"Of course. Anything you say."

She made a small, involuntary movement to turn around. His hands on her shoulders aided the process. She quivered when his mouth met hers and a familiar heat began to warm her. As always, their need for each other was so hot and intense, it frightened her.

Slowly, he lifted his mouth from hers. "Do you want me to stop?" he asked in a husky whisper.

Savannah made an unintelligible sound.

"That's what I thought," he said, claiming her mouth again.

She locked her arms around his neck. Soon the kissing wasn't enough....

Savannah felt as though her body was on fire. She'd been empty and lonely for so long. No man had ever kissed her like this. No man had ever wanted her so badly.

"You don't want me to stop, do you?" he begged. "Don't tell me you want me to stop."

Incapable of a decision, she made a second unintelligible sound.

"If we continue like this, we're going to end up making love on the kitchen floor," Nash whispered.

"I don't know what I want," she whimpered.

"Yes, you do. Savannah. If it gets much hotter, we're both going to explode. Let me make love to you."

She started to protest, but he stopped her, dragging his mouth back to hers. Only she could satisfy him, his kisses seemed to be saying. Savannah didn't know if he was telling her this or if she was hearing it in her mind. It didn't matter; she got the message.

"No," she said with a whimper. She couldn't give him her body. If they made love, he'd own her completely, and she couldn't allow that to happen. Someday he was going to walk away from her. Someday he was going to announce that it was over and she was supposed to go on her merry way without him. She was supposed to pretend it didn't matter.

"You don't mean that," Nash pleaded. "You can't tell me you don't want me." The words were issued in a heated whisper. "Don't do this, Savannah."

She buried her face in his shoulder. "Please...don't. You promised. You said you'd stop...whenever I asked."

He released her then, slowly, her body dragging against

his as her feet slid back to the floor. She stepped away from him, anxious to break the contact, desperately needing room to breathe. She pressed her hand to the neckline of her gown and drew in several deep breaths.

Nash's eyes were squeezed shut as he struggled to bring himself under control. When he opened them, Savannah swore they were filled with fire.

Without a word to her, he reached for his jacket, opened the door and walked out.

She was trembling so hard, she had to pull out a chair and sit down. She didn't know how long she was there before she felt strong enough to stand, walk back into the bedroom and dress.

It was a mistake to let him kiss her; she'd known it even as she agreed, known it would be like this between them. Gnawing on her lower lip, she argued with herself. She and Nash had created an impossible situation, drawn up a list of rules and regulations and then insisted on testing each one to the limits of their endurance.

She'd just placed their coffee cups in the dishwasher when the back door opened and Nash appeared. She studied him. He looked calm and outwardly serene, but she wasn't fooled. She could see the angry glint in his eyes.

"If you're looking for an apology, you can forget it," he said.

"I'm...not."

"Good."

Now didn't seem the time to mention that he hadn't helped matters any by suggesting the kiss. Both of them knew what would happen when they started flirting with the physical aspect of their relationship.

Nash poured himself a cup of coffee. "Let's sit down and talk this over."

"I...don't know what there is to say," she said, preferring to avoid the issue completely. "It was a very human thing to happen. You're an attractive, healthy man with...needs."

"And you're a red-blooded woman. You have *needs,* too. But admitting that takes real honesty, doesn't it?"

Savannah found the remark insulting, but then, Nash didn't seem inclined to be generous with her. Since she didn't have an argument to give him, she let it pass.

"I did some thinking while I walked off my frustration."

"Oh?" She was curious about what he'd decided, but didn't want to press him.

"The way I see it, I'm setting myself up for constant frustration if we have any more bouts like this last one. If you want to come out of this marriage as pristine as the freshly fallen snow, then far be it from me to hit my head against a brick wall."

"I'm not sure I understand."

"You don't need to. You have your wish, Savannah. I won't touch you again, not until you ask me, and the way I feel right now, you're going to have to do a whole lot more than ask. You're going to have to beg."

Nash hadn't known it was possible for two human beings to live the way he and Savannah had spent the past two weeks. The so-called honeymoon had been bad enough, but back in civilization, living in his house, the situation had gone from unbearable to even worse. The electricity between them could light up a small city. Yet they continued to ignore their mutual attraction.

They lived as brother and sister. They slept in separate rooms, inquired about each other's day, sat at the dinner table every night and made polite conversation.

In two weeks Nash hadn't so much as held her hand. He

dared not for fear he'd get burned. Not by her rejection, but by their need for each other.

Part of the problem was the fact that Savannah was a virgin. She didn't know what she was missing, but she had a fairly good idea, and that added a certain amount of intrigue. He sincerely hoped she was miserable, at least as miserable as he was.

"Mr. Griffin is here to see you," his assistant announced.

Nash stood to greet his client. Don Griffin had lost weight in the past month. Nash had, too, come to think of it. He didn't have much of an appetite and was working out at the gym most nights after dinner.

"Did you hear from Janice's attorney?" Don demanded.

"Not yet."

"Does he normally take this long to return phone calls?" Agitated, Don started to pace.

"He does when he wants us to sweat," he said.

"Raise Janice's monthly allotment by five hundred dollars."

Nash sighed inwardly. This was a difficult case and not for the usual reasons. "Sit down, Mr. Griffin," he said. "Please."

Don complied and sat down. He bounced his fingers against each other and studied Nash as he leaned back in his chair.

"Janice hasn't requested any extra money," Nash said.

"She might need it. Amy, too. There are a hundred unexpected expenses that crop up. I don't want her having to scrimp. It's important to me that my wife and daughter live comfortably."

"You've been more than generous."

"Just do as I say. I'm not paying you to argue with me."

"No, you're paying me for advice and I'm about to give you some, so kindly listen. It doesn't come cheap."

Don snorted loudly. "No kidding. I just got your last bill."

Nash smiled. His clients were often shocked when they learned how expensive divorce could be. Not only financially, but emotionally. Nash had seen it happen more times than he cared to think about. Once his clients realized how costly a divorce could be, they were already embroiled in bitterness and it was impossible to undo the damage.

"Do you know what you're doing, giving Janice extra money?" he asked.

"Sure I do. I'm attempting to take care of my wife and daughter."

"You're already doing that. Offering them more money is more about easing your conscience. You want to absolve your guilt because you had an affair."

"It wasn't an affair," Don shouted. "It was a one-night thing, a momentary lapse that I've regretted every moment since. Janice would never have found out about it if it hadn't been for—never mind, that doesn't matter now. She found out about it and immediately called an attorney."

"My point is, she learned about your indiscretion and now you want to buy peace of mind. Unfortunately, it doesn't work like that."

"All I'm trying to do is get this divorce over with."

Tony Pound, Janice's attorney, wasn't a fool. He knew exactly what he was doing, dragging the proceedings out as long as possible to prolong the guilt and the agony. To Nash's way of thinking, his client had been punished enough.

"This is one mistake you aren't going to be paying monetarily for the rest of your life," Nash assured him. "And I plan to make sure of it. That's why John Stackhouse asked me to take your case. You've lost your wife, your home, your daughter. You've paid enough. Now go back to your apartment and relax. I'll contact you when I hear from Mr. Pound."

Don Griffin nodded reluctantly. "I don't know how much more of this I can take."

"It shouldn't be much longer," Nash assured him.

He rose slowly from the chair. "You'll be in touch soon?"

Nash said he would. Don left the office and Nash sat down to review his file for the hundredth time. He was missing something, he realized. That cold-blooded instinct for the kill.

He wasn't enjoying this, wasn't even close to experiencing the satisfaction he usually gained from bringing his opponents to their knees. Somewhere along the line he'd changed. He'd sensed things were different shortly after he'd met Savannah. Now there was no hiding his feelings. He'd lost it. Only, he wasn't sure what he'd found in exchange.

"Have you got a moment?" John Stackhouse stuck his head in Nash's office.

"Sure. What can I do for you?"

The senior partner was smiling from ear to ear. "Would you mind coming down to the meeting room?"

Nash's pulse accelerated wildly. The executive committee had been meeting with the other senior partners that afternoon to make their recommendation for new senior partner.

"I got the position?" Nash asked hesitantly.

"I think that would be a fair assessment," the older man said, slapping Nash on the shoulder. "It wasn't a hard decision, Nash. You're a fine attorney and an asset to this firm."

A half hour later, Nash rushed out of the office and drove directly to Savannah's shop. As luck would have it, she was busy with a customer. He tried to be patient, tried to pretend he was some stranger who'd casually strolled in.

Savannah looked at him with wide, questioning eyes and he delighted in unnerving her by blowing her a kiss.

"When did you say the wedding was?" she asked the smartly dressed businesswoman who was leafing through a book of invitations.

"In December."

"You have plenty of time, but it's a good idea to set your budget now. I'll be happy to assist you in any way I can."

"I appreciate that," Nash heard the woman say.

He wandered over to her desk and sorted through her mail. Without being obvious, Savannah walked over to where he was sitting, took the envelopes from him and gently slapped his hands. "Behave yourself," she said under her breath.

"I have a few extra expenses coming up," he said in a low whisper. "I hope you're doing well. I might need a loan."

"What expenses?" she asked in the same low voice.

"New business cards, stationery and the like."

"New stationery?" she repeated more loudly.

The customer turned around. "I'm sorry," Savannah said apologetically. "I was commenting on something my husband said."

The woman smiled graciously. "I thought you two must be married. I saw the way you looked at each other when he walked in the door."

Neither Nash nor Savannah responded.

Savannah started to walk away, when Nash caught her hand. It was the first time he'd purposely touched her since the morning after their wedding. Apparently it caught her by surprise, because she turned abruptly, her gaze seeking out his.

"I'm the new senior partner."

Savannah's eyes lit up with undisguised delight. "Nash,

oh, Nash." She covered her mouth with both hands and blinked back tears. "Congratulations."

"If you don't mind, I'll come back another time with my fiancé," Savannah's customer said.

"I'm sorry," Savannah said, limping toward the woman.

"Don't apologize. Celebrate with your husband. You both deserve it." When she reached the front door, she turned the sign to "Closed," winked at Nash and walked out of the store.

"When did you find out?" Savannah asked, rubbing her index finger beneath her eye.

"About half an hour ago. I thought we'd go out to dinner and celebrate."

"I...don't know what to say. I'm so happy for you."

"I'm happy, too." It was difficult not to take her in his arms. He stood and walked away from her rather than break his self-imposed restriction.

"Where are you going?" Savannah asked, sounding perplexed.

"I need to keep my distance from you."

"Why?"

"Because I want to hold you so much, my arms ache."

Savannah broke into a smile. "I was just thinking the same thing," she said, opening her arms to him.

# *Twelve*

Nash checked his watch for the time, set aside the paper and hurried into the kitchen. It was his night to cook and he'd experimented with a new recipe. If anyone had told him he'd be hanging around a kitchen, fretting over elaborate recipes, he would've stoutly denied such a thing could even happen.

Marriage had done this to him, and to his surprise Nash wasn't complaining. He enjoyed their arrangement, especially now that they were on much friendlier terms. The tension had lessened considerably following the evening they'd celebrated his appointment as senior partner. It felt as if the barriers were gradually being lowered.

He was bent over the oven door when he heard Savannah come into the house. She'd called him at the office to let him know she'd be late, which had become almost a nightly occurrence.

"I'm home," she said, entering the kitchen. She looked pale and worn-out. He'd never have guessed September would be such a busy month for weddings. Savannah had overbooked herself and spread her time and energy much too thin. He'd resisted the urge to lecture her, although it'd been difficult.

"Your timing couldn't be better," he said, taking the sausage, cabbage and cheese casserole out of the oven and setting it on the counter. The scent of spicy meat filled the kitchen.

"That smells delicious," Savannah said, and Nash beamed proudly. He'd discovered, somewhat to his surprise, that he enjoyed cooking. Over the years he'd learned a culinary trick or two, creating a small repertoire of dinners. Nothing, however, that required an actual recipe. Now he found himself reading cookbooks on a regular basis.

"I've got the table set if you're ready to eat," he told her.

"You must've known I was starving."

"Did you skip lunch again today?" he asked, using oven mitts to carry the glass casserole dish to the table. Once again he had to stop himself from chastising her. Their peace was too fragile to test. "Sit down and I'll bring you a plate."

It looked as if Savannah was in danger of falling asleep as he joined her at the table.

"Nash," she said after the first taste, "this is wonderful!"

"I'm glad you approve."

"Keep this up and you can do all the cooking," she teased, smiling over at him.

Nash set his fork aside and folded his hands. He couldn't keep silent any longer. "You're working too hard."

She lowered her gaze and nodded. "I know. I scheduled the majority of these weddings soon after our own. I...I thought it would be a good idea if I spent as much time at the shop as possible."

In other words, less time with him. "I hope you've changed your mind."

"I have." Her hand closed around her water glass. "I assumed our...arrangement would be awkward, but it hasn't been, not since the beginning."

"I've enjoyed spending time with you." It frustrated him, living as they did, like polite strangers, but that, too, had changed in the past couple of weeks. Their relationship had become that of good friends. Their progress was slow but steady, which gave Nash hope that eventually Savannah would be comfortable enough with him to make love. He realized his attitude was shortsighted. Breaching that barrier had been a challenge from the first, but he hadn't thought beyond it. He didn't want to think about it now.

When they finished eating, Savannah carried their plates to the sink. They had an agreement about cleanup, one of many. When one of them did the cooking, the other washed the dishes.

"Sit down," Nash ordered, "before you collapse."

"This will only take a couple of minutes," she insisted, opening the dishwasher.

Nash took her by the hands and led her into the living room. Pushing her down on the sofa, he said, "I want you to relax."

"If I do that, I'll fall asleep, and I need to go back to the shop later to finish up a few things."

"Don't even think about it, Savannah." Those were fighting words, but he counted on her being too tired to argue with him. "You're exhausted. I'm your husband, and I may not be a very good one, but I refuse to allow you to work yourself this hard."

She closed her eyes and leaned her head against the sofa cushion. She gave him a small smile. "You are a good husband, Nash. Thoughtful and considerate."

"Right." He hoped she wasn't expecting an argument. As it was, he should be awarded some kind of medal.

He reached for her legs and placed them on his lap. "Just relax," he urged again when she opened her eyes, silently questioning him. He removed her shoes and massaged her tired feet. She sighed with pleasure and wiggled her toes.

"I haven't been to my place in a week," she said, and Nash found that an odd comment until he thought about it. She was admitting how comfortable she'd gotten living with him. It was a sign, a small one, that she was willing to advance their relationship. Nash didn't intend to waste it.

"I've moved nearly all my clothes here," she continued in sleepy tones.

"That's very good, don't you think?" he asked, not expecting her to reply.

"Hmm."

He continued to rub her feet and ankles, marveling at the delicate bone structure. He let his hands venture upward over her calves. She sighed and nestled farther down in the sofa. Gaining confidence, Nash risked going higher, where her skin was silky warm and smooth. He wasn't sure how this was affecting Savannah, but it was having a strong effect on him. His breathing went shallow and his heart started to thunder in his ears. He'd promised himself that he wouldn't ask her to make love again. She'd have to come to him. He wanted her to beg—but if anyone was going to do any begging, it was him.

"It's very relaxing," Savannah murmured with a sigh.

Funny, it wasn't relaxing for him….

"Nash." His name was released on a harshly indrawn breath.

His hands froze. His heart went still and his breath caught. "Yes?" He struggled to sound expressionless, although that was nearly impossible. The less she recognized how critical his need was for her, the better.

"I think I should stop, don't you?" Where he dredged up the strength to suggest that was beyond him.

"It feels good."

"That's the problem. It feels *so* good."

"For you, too?"

Sometimes he forgot what an innocent she was. "For me, too."

Her head was propped against the back of the sofa, her eyes closed. Her mouth was slightly parted and she moistened her lips with the tip of her tongue. Nash groaned inwardly and forced himself to look away.

"Maybe we should kiss," she whispered.

Nash wasn't interested in a repeat performance of what had taken place earlier, but at the same time he wasn't about to turn down her offer. She wasn't begging, but this was close enough.

He shifted his weight and brought her into his arms.

Perspiration broke out on his forehead and he held his breath while he reined in his desire. "If we start kissing, we might not be able to stop."

"I know."

"You know that?" Something was wrong with him. He should be carrying her into the bedroom and not asking questions until afterward. A long time afterward.

"We can follow through with our agreement, can't we?" she asked. Her eyes fluttered open.

"What agreement?" His mind could only hold one thing at the moment, and that was his painful physical need for her.

"We'll separate once my parents decide to travel," she said, and it sounded more like a reassurance. "In the meantime, I'm not going to be trapped in a loveless marriage. As per the contract, we can initiate divorce proceedings when the year's up."

"Fine," he said, willing to agree to any terms. "Whatever you want."

"Do you think it would be a mistake to make love?" she asked.

"No." He sounded as if he'd choked on something. "That seems like a good idea to me," he said a couple of seconds later. He got off the sofa, reached down and scooped her into his arms.

She gave a small cry of surprise when he lifted her up and marched down the darkened hallway. He walked into his bedroom and placed her on his bed.

He was afraid of going too fast—and of not going fast enough. Afraid of not lasting long enough, of cheating her out of what lovemaking should be for her first time. His fears managed to make him feel indecisive.

"Is something wrong?" she asked, staring up at him, her eyes wide and questioning.

Unable to answer, he shook his head.

She smiled then, softly, femininely, and stretched her arms up, bringing him down next to her. He noticed that her breathing was as quick and shallow as his own. Carefully he peeled open the front of her shirt and eased it from her shoulders. Her bra and everything else soon followed....

They fell asleep afterward, their arms and legs intertwined, their bodies joined in the most elemental of ways. Nash had never known such peace, never experienced such serenity, and it lulled him into a deep sleep.

It was after midnight when he woke. The lights were still on in the living room and the kitchen. Carefully, so as not to wake Savannah, he crawled out of the bed and reached for his robe. Shuffling barefoot out of the bedroom, he yawned.

He felt good. Like he could run a marathon or swim a

mile in world-record time. He finished the dinner dishes and was turning off the kitchen light when he looked up and saw Savannah standing inside the living room. Her hair was tousled, yet he'd never seen her look more beautiful. She'd donned her blouse, which covered precious little of her body.

"I woke up and you were gone," she said in a small voice.

"I was coming back to bed."

"Good." She led him back, not that he required any coaxing. The room was dark, but streaks of moonlight floated against the wall as they made their way to the bed.

Nash held back the covers and Savannah climbed in. He followed, gathering her in his arms, cradling her head against his shoulder.

He waited for her to speak, wondering what she was thinking, afraid to ask. With utter contentment he kissed her hair. She squirmed against him, nestling in as close as possible, and breathed out a long, womanly sigh.

Although he was an experienced lover, Nash had never heard a woman sigh the way Savannah did just then. It seemed to come from deep inside her, speaking of pleasure and the surprise of mutual satisfaction.

"Thank you," he whispered.

"No," she said. "Thank you." And then she snuggled up to him again, as if she needed this closeness as much as he did. As if she craved these peaceful moments, too.

He waited a few more minutes, wanting to be sure she hadn't drifted off to sleep. "We should talk."

"I know," she whispered. "I thought about that, too."

"And?"

"I planned on discussing things with you, reassessing the issues, that sort of thing."

"Why didn't you?" He couldn't help being curious.

He felt her lips move in a smile. "When the time came, all I wanted was you."

His chest rose with an abundance of fierce male pride. "I wanted you, too."

Serenity surrounded him and he sank into its warmth.

"Should we talk now?" Savannah asked after a while.

The last thing Nash wanted right this minute was a lengthy conversation about their marriage. Words would destroy the tranquillity, and these moments were too precious to waste.

"This doesn't have to change anything, if you don't want it to," he murmured, rubbing his chin over her head, loving the silky feel of her hair.

Savannah went still, and he wondered if he'd said something wrong. "You're content with our arrangement the way it is?" she asked.

"For now I am. We don't have to make any decisions tonight, do we?"

"No," she agreed readily.

"Then relax and go back to sleep." His eyes drifted shut as he savored this closeness.

"Nash."

"Hmm?"

"It was nothing like I expected," she told him.

"Better, I hope."

"Oh, yes." And then she kissed him.

Don and Janice Griffin's meeting before Judge Wilcox was scheduled for two in the afternoon. Nash was well prepared for this final stage of the divorce proceedings.

Don Griffin arrived at his office an hour early and—in what was fast becoming a habit—started pacing the room.

"I'm ready anytime you are," his client said.

"If we leave now, we'll end up sitting outside in the hallway," Nash told him.

"I don't care. I want this over with as quickly and cleanly as possible, understand?"

"That message came through loud and clear," Nash assured him. "Settle down and relax, will you?"

Don thrust both hands into his hair. "*Relax?* Are you crazy, man? You might've gone through this a thousand times, but it's almost thirty years of my life we're throwing out the window. The stress is getting to me."

"What's this I hear about putting a divorce special on your restaurants' menu?" Nash asked in an effort to take the older man's mind off the coming proceedings. "Anyone who comes into any of your restaurants the day his divorce is final eats for free."

"That's right, and I'd rather you didn't say anything derogatory about it. I've met a number of men just like me. Some of 'em married twenty, thirty years and all of a sudden it's gone. Poof. Suddenly they're lost and alone and don't know what to do with the rest of their lives."

"I'm not going to say anything negative. I think it's a generous thing you're doing."

Don Griffin eyed him as if he wasn't sure he should believe that.

When they arrived at the courtroom, Mr. Griffin and Nash took their seats behind one table. Janice Griffin and Tony Pound sat behind the other. Nash noticed the way Don stole a look at his almost ex-wife. Next, he caught a glimpse of Janice looking at Don. It wasn't anything he hadn't seen countless times before. One last look, so to speak, before the ties were severed. A farewell. An acceptance that it was soon to be over—the end was within sight. This marriage was about to breathe its last breath.

Judge Wilcox entered the room and everyone stood. In a crisp, businesslike manner, he asked a series of questions of each party. Janice responded, her voice shaking. Don answered, sounding like a condemned man. They sat back down and the final decree was about to be pronounced when Nash vaulted out of his seat.

For a moment he didn't know what had forced him into action. "If you'll pardon me, Your Honor," he said, with his back to his client, "I'd like to say a few words."

He could hear Tony begin to object. Nash didn't give him the opportunity.

"My client doesn't want this divorce, and neither does his wife."

A string of hot words erupted behind him as Tony Pound flew out of his chair. The judge's gavel pounded several times, the noise deafening.

"Your Honor, if you'll indulge me for just a moment."

No one was more surprised than Nash when he was given permission. "Proceed."

"My client has been married for almost thirty years. He made a mistake, Your Honor. Now, he'll be the first to admit it was a foolish, stupid mistake. But he's human and so is his wife. They've both paid dearly for this blunder and it seems to me they've paid enough."

He turned to face Janice Griffin, who was shredding a tissue in her hand. "You've made mistakes in your life, too, haven't you, Mrs. Griffin?"

Janice lowered her gaze and nodded.

"You can't cross-examine my client," Pound yelled.

Nash ignored him, and thankfully so did Judge Wilcox.

"My client has loved his wife and family for nearly thirty years. He still loves her. I saw the way he looked at Mrs. Griffin when she walked into the courtroom. I also saw the way she looked at him. These two people care deeply for each other. They've been driven apart by their pain and their pride. Thirty years is a very long time out of a person's life, and I don't believe anyone should be in a rush to sign it away."

"Your Honor, I find this outburst extremely unprofessional," Tony Pound protested.

Nash didn't dare turn around.

"Don Griffin has suffered enough for his indiscretion. Mrs. Griffin has been through enough agony, too. It's time to think about rebuilding lives instead of destroying them."

There wasn't a sound in the courtroom. Having had his say, Nash returned to his seat.

Judge Wilcox held his gavel with both hands. "Is what Mr. Davenport said true, Mr. Griffin? Do you love your wife?"

Don Griffin rose slowly to his feet. "A thousand times more than I thought possible."

"Mrs. Griffin?"

She, too, stood, her eyes watering, her lips trembling. "Yes, Your Honor."

The judge glared at them both and set down the gavel. "Then I suggest you try to reconcile your differences and stop wasting the court's time."

Nash gathered together the papers he'd removed from his briefcase and slipped them back inside. Don Griffin walked behind him and was met halfway by his wife. From his peripheral vision, Nash watched as Janice Griffin, sobbing, walked into her husband's arms. They held on to each other, weeping and laughing and kissing all at once.

Not bad for an afternoon's work, Nash decided.

He picked up his briefcase and walked out of the courtroom. He hadn't taken two steps when Tony Pound joined him.

"That was quite a little drama you put on just now."

"I couldn't see two people who were obviously in love end their marriage," Nash said. They marched side by side through the halls of justice.

"It's true, then," Tony commented.

"What is?"

"That you've lost your edge, that killer instinct you're famous for. I have to admit I'm glad to see it. People said it'd happen when they learned you were married, but no one expected it to be this soon. Whoever took you on as a husband must be one heck of a woman."

Nash smiled to himself. "She is."

"It doesn't look like I'll be seeing you in court all that often."

"Probably not. I'm not taking on any new divorce cases."

"Dad, what an unexpected surprise," Savannah said, delighted that her father had decided to drop in at her store. He didn't visit often and his timing was perfect. She was about to take a break, sit down and rest her leg. "How's Mom?"

"Much better," he said, pulling out a chair as Savannah poured him a cup of coffee.

"Good."

"That's what I've come to talk to you about."

Savannah poured herself a cup and joined him. Her mother had made impressive progress in the past six weeks. Savannah called and visited often, and several times Nash had accompanied her. Joyce was growing stronger each day. She was often forgetful and that frustrated her, but otherwise she was recuperating nicely.

"I thought it'd be a good idea if I talked to you first," her father said.

"About what?"

"Your mother and I traveling."

It was the welcome news she'd been waiting to hear. At the same time it was the dreaded announcement that would end the happiest days of her life.

"I think you *should* travel. I always have."

"I was hoping to take your mother south. We might even look for a place to buy."

"Arizona," she suggested, raising the cup to her lips. "Mom's always loved the Southwest."

"The sunshine will do her good," her father agreed.

Savannah didn't know how she'd be able to pull this off, when she felt like she was dying on the inside. Over the years she'd become proficient at disguising her pain. Pain made others uncomfortable, so she'd learned to live with it.

"You wouldn't object to our going?" Her father didn't often sound hesitant but he did now.

"Of course I don't! I want you to travel and enjoy your retirement years. I've got Nash now, so there's no need to worry about me. None whatsoever."

"You're sure?"

"Dad! Go and enjoy yourselves," Savannah said and managed to laugh.

Three hours later, she sat in the middle of Nash's living room, staring aimlessly into space. All that was left now was the waiting—that, and telling him....

Nash got home shortly after six. His eyes were triumphant as he marched into the house. "Savannah," he said, apparently delighted to see her. "You didn't work late tonight."

"No," she responded simply.

He lifted her off the sofa as if she weighed nothing and twirled her around. "I had the most incredible day."

"Me, too."

"Good. We'll celebrate." Tucking his arm beneath her knees, he started for the bedroom. He stopped abruptly when he saw her suitcase sitting at the end of the hallway. His eyes were filled with questions as they met hers.

"Are you going somewhere?"

She nodded. "My parents have decided to take an extended trip south."

"So?"

"So, according to the terms of our marriage agreement, I'm moving back into my own home."

# *Thirteen*

"You're moving out just like that?" Nash asked, lowering her feet to the ground. He stepped away from her as if he needed to put some distance between them. His eyes narrowed and he studied her, his expression shocked.

Savannah hadn't expected him to look at her like that. This was what they'd decided in the beginning, it was what he said he wanted after the first time they'd made love. She'd asked, wanting to be clear on exactly what her role in his life was to be, and Nash had said that making love changed nothing.

"This shouldn't come as a surprise," she said, struggling to keep her voice as even as possible.

"Is it what you want?" He thrust his hands deep inside his pockets and glared at her icily.

"Well?" he demanded when she didn't immediately answer.

"It doesn't matter what I think. I'm keeping my end of the bargain. What do you want me to do?"

Nash gave a nonchalant shrug of his shoulders. "I'm not going to hold you prisoner here against your wishes, if that's what you're asking."

That *wasn't* what she was asking. She wanted some indication that he loved her and wanted her living with him. Some indication that he intended to throw out their stupid prenuptial agreement and make this marriage real. Apparently Nash wasn't interested.

"When are your parents leaving?"

"Friday morning, at dawn."

"So soon?"

She nodded. "Dad wanted to wait until Mom was strong enough to travel comfortably...and evidently she is now."

"I see." Nash wandered into the kitchen. "So you're planning to move out right away?"

"I...thought I'd take some clothes over to my house this evening."

"You certainly seem to be in a rush."

"Not really. I've managed to bring quite a few of my personal things here. I...imagine you'll want me out as quickly as possible." The smallest sign that he loved her would be enough to convince her to stay. A simple statement of need. A word. A look. Anything.

Nash offered nothing.

He opened the refrigerator and took out a cold soda, popping it open.

"I started dinner while I was waiting for you," she said. "The casserole's in the oven."

Nash took a long swallow of his soda. "I appreciate the effort, but I don't seem to have much of an appetite."

Savannah didn't, either. Calmly she walked over and turned off the oven. She stood with her back to Nash and bit her lip.

What a romantic fool she was, hoping the impossible would happen. She'd known when she agreed to marry him that it would be like this. He was going to break her heart.

She'd tried to protect herself from exactly this, but it hadn't worked.

These past few weeks had been the happiest of her life and nothing he said now would take them away from her. He loved her, she knew he did, as much as it was possible for Nash to love anyone. He'd never said the words, but he didn't need to. She felt them when she slept in his arms. She experienced them each time they made love.

Her heart constricted with fresh pain. She didn't want to leave Nash, but she couldn't stay, not unless he specifically asked, and it was clear he had no intention of doing so.

She heard him leave the room, which was just as well since she was having a hard time not breaking into tears.

She was angry then. Unfortunately there wasn't a door to slam or anything handy to throw. Having a temper tantrum was exactly what she felt like doing.

Dinner was a waste. She might as well throw the whole thing in the garbage. Opening the oven door, she reached inside and grabbed the casserole dish.

Intense, unexpected pain shot through her fingers as she touched the dish.

She cried out and jerked her hand away. Stumbling toward the sink, she held her fingers under cold running water.

"Savannah?" Nash rushed into the kitchen. "What happened?"

"I'm all right," she said, fighting back tears by taking deep breaths. If she was lucky, her fingers wouldn't blister, but she seemed to be out of luck lately.

"What happened?" Nash demanded again.

"Nothing." She shook her head, not wanting to answer him because that required concentration and effort, and all she could think of at the moment was pain. Physical pain.

Emotional agony. The two were intermingled until she didn't know where one stopped and the other started.

"Let me look at what you've done," he said, moving close to her.

"No," Savannah said, jerking her arm away from him. "It's nothing."

"Let me be the judge of that."

"Leave me alone," she cried, sobbing openly now, her shoulders heaving. "Just leave me alone. I can take care of myself."

"I'm your husband."

She whirled on him, unintentionally splashing him with cold water. "How can you say that when you can hardly wait to be rid of me?"

"What are you talking about?" he shouted. "*I* wasn't the one who packed my bags and casually announced I was leaving. If you want to throw out questions, then you might start by asking yourself what kind of wife *you* are!"

Savannah rubbed her uninjured hand beneath her nose. "You claimed you didn't want a wife."

"I didn't until I married you." Nash opened the freezer portion of the refrigerator and brought out a tub of ice cubes. "Sit down," he said in tones that brooked no argument. She complied. He set the tub on the table and gently placed her burned fingers inside it. "The first couple of minutes will be uncomfortable, but after that you won't feel much," he explained calmly.

Savannah continued to sob.

"What did you do?" he asked.

"I was taking out the baking dish."

Nash frowned. "Did the oven mitt slip?"

"I forgot to use one," she admitted.

He took a moment to digest this information before kneeling down at her feet. His eyes probed hers and she lowered her gaze. Tucking his finger beneath her chin, he leveled her eyes to his.

"Why?"

"Isn't it obvious? I…was upset."

"About what?"

She shrugged, not wanting to tell him the truth. "These things happen and…"

"Why?" he repeated softly.

"Because you're an idiot," she flared.

"I know you're upset about me not wanting dinner, but—"

"Dinner?" she cried, incredulous. "You think this is because you didn't want dinner? How can any man be so dense?" She vaulted to her feet, her burned fingers forgotten. "You were just going to let me walk out of here."

"Wrong."

"Wrong? And how did you plan to stop me?"

"I figured I'd move in with you."

She blinked. "I beg your pardon?"

"You heard me. The agreement, as originally written, states that you'll move out of my premises after your parents decide to travel and you—"

"I know what that stupid piece of paper says," Savannah said, frowning.

"If you don't want to live with me, then it makes perfect sense for me to—"

"I *do* want to live with you, you idiot," she broke in. "I was hoping you'd do something—anything—to convince me to stay."

Nash was quiet for a few seconds. "Let me see if I have this straight. You were going to move out, although you didn't want to. Is that right?"

She nodded.

"Why?"

"Because I wanted you to *ask* me to stay."

"Ah, I understand now. You do one thing, hoping I'll respond by asking you to do the opposite."

She shrugged, realizing how silly it sounded in the cold light of reason. "I...guess so."

"Let this be a lesson to you, Savannah Davenport," Nash said, taking her in his arms. "If you want something, all you need to do is ask for it. If you'd simply sought my opinion, you'd have learned an important fact."

"Oh?"

"I'm willing to move heaven and earth to make sure we're together for the rest of our natural lives."

"You are?"

"In case you haven't figured it out yet, I'm in love with you." A surprised look must have come over her because he added, "You honestly didn't know?"

"I...prayed you were, but I didn't dare hope you'd admit it. I've been in love with you for so long I can't remember when I didn't love you."

He kissed her gently, his mouth coaxing and warm. "Promise you won't ever stop loving me. I need you so badly. It wasn't until you were in my life that I saw how jaded I'd become. Taking on so many divorce cases didn't help my attitude any. I've made a decision that's due to your influence on me. When I graduated from law school, I specialized in tax and tax laws. I'm going back to that."

"Oh, Nash, I'm so pleased."

He kissed her with a hunger that left her weak and clinging.

"I can ask for anything?" she murmured between kisses.

"Anything."

"Throw away that stupid agreement."

He smiled boyishly and pressed his forehead against hers. "I already have.... The first night, after we made love."

"You might have told me!"

"I intended to when the time was right."

"And when did you calculate that to be?" she asked, having difficulty maintaining her feigned outrage.

"Soon. Very soon."

She smiled and closed her eyes. "But not soon enough."

"I had high hopes for us from the first. I opened my mouth and stuck my foot in it at the beginning by suggesting that ludicrous marriage-of-convenience idea. Marriage, the second time around, is a lot more frightening because you've already made one mistake."

"Our marriage isn't a mistake," she assured him. "I won't let it be."

"I felt that if I had control of the situation, I might be able to control my feelings for you, but after Susan's wedding I knew that was going to be impossible."

"Why didn't you follow your own advice and ask how *I* felt?" she said, thinking of all the weeks they'd wasted.

"We haven't been on the best of terms, have we?" he murmured.

Savannah was embarrassed now by what a shrew she'd been. She slid her arms around his neck and kissed him soundly in an effort to make up for those first weeks.

"You said I can ask for anything I want?" she said against his lips.

"Hmm…anything," he agreed.

"I'd like a baby."

Nash's eyes flew open with undisguised eagerness. "How soon?"

"Well…I was thinking we could start on the project tonight."

A slow, lazy smile came into place. "That's a very good idea. Very good indeed."

*Three years later...*

"I can't believe the changes in Nash," Susan commented to Savannah. She and Kurt had flown up from California to spend the Christmas holiday with them this year. The two women were working in the kitchen.

"He's such a good father to Jacob," Savannah said, blinking back tears. She cried so easily when she was pregnant, and she was entering her second trimester with this baby. If the ultrasound was accurate, they were going to have a little girl.

"Nash is doing so well and so are you. But don't you miss working at the shop?"

"No, I've got a wonderful manager and you can imagine how busy a fourteen-month-old keeps me. I've thought about going back part-time and then decided not to, not yet at any rate. What about you? Will you continue teaching?" Savannah softly patted Susan's slightly distended stomach.

"No, but I'll probably work on a substitute basis to keep up my credentials so when our family's complete, I can return without a lot of hassle."

"That's smart."

"She's my sister, isn't she?" Nash said, walking into the kitchen, cradling his son in his arms. Jacob babbled happily, waving his rattle in every direction. He'd been a contented baby from the first. Their joy.

Kurt's arms surrounded his wife and he flattened his hands over her stomach. "We've decided to have our two close together, the same way you and Savannah planned your family."

Savannah and Nash exchanged smiles. "Planned?" she teased her husband.

"The operative word there is *two*," Nash said, eyeing her suspiciously.

"Sweetheart, we've been over this a hundred times. I really would like four."

"Four!" Nash cried. "The last time we talked you said three."

"I've changed my mind. Four is a nice even number."

"Four children is out of the question," Nash said with a disgruntled look, then seemed to notice Kurt and Susan staring at him. "We'll talk about this later, all right? But we will talk."

"Of course we will," Savannah promised, unable to hold back a smile.

"She's going to do it," Nash grumbled to his sister and brother-in-law. "Somehow, before I've figured out how she's managed it, we'll be a family of six."

"You'll love it, Nash, I promise." The oven timer rang and Savannah glanced at the clock. "Oh, dear, I've got to get busy. Mr. Serle and Mr. Stackhouse will be here any minute."

"This is something else she didn't tell me before we were married," Nash said, his eyes shining with love. "She charms the most unexpected people...."

"They love Jacob," Savannah reminded him.

"True," Nash said wryly. "I've never seen two old men more taken with a toddler."

"And I've never seen a man more taken with his wife," Susan added. "I could almost be jealous, but there's no need." She turned to her husband and put her arms around his neck. "Still, it doesn't do any harm to keep him on his toes."

"No, it doesn't," Savannah agreed. And they all laughed.

\* \* \* \* \*

# Lone Star Lovin'

To Diane DeGooyer—a friend forever

# *One*

"You're a long way from Orchard Valley," Sherry Waterman muttered to herself as she stepped out of her PT Cruiser and onto the main street of Pepper, Texas. Heat shimmered up from the black asphalt.

Drawing a deep breath, she glanced around with an appraising eye at this town, which was to be her new home. Pepper resembled any number of small mid-Texas towns she'd driven through in the past twenty-four hours.

The sun was pounding down with a vengeance, and Sherry wiped her brow with her forearm, looking for someplace to buy a cold drink. She was a couple of weeks early; she'd actually planned it like this, hoping to get a feel for Pepper and the surrounding ranch community before she took over her assignment. In an hour or so she'd drive on to Houston, where she'd visit her friend Norah Cassidy for a couple of weeks, then double back to Pepper. Although it was considerably out of her way, she was curious about this town—and the job she'd accepted as a physician assistant, sight unseen, through a medical-employment agency.

Her car didn't have air-conditioning, and she'd rolled down both windows in an effort to create a cooling cross-draft. It had worked well enough, but along with the breeze had come a fine layer of dust, and a throat as dry as the sun-baked Texas street.

Clutching her purse and a folded state map, she headed for the Yellow Rose café directly opposite. A red neon sign in the window promised home cooking.

After glancing both ways, she jogged across the street and hurried into the, thankfully, air-conditioned café. The counter was crowded with an array of cowboy types, so she seated herself by the window and reached for the menu tucked behind the napkin canister.

A waitress wearing a pink gingham uniform with a matching ribbon in her hair strolled casually toward Sherry's table. "You're new around here, aren't you?" she asked.

"Yes," Sherry answered noncommittally, looking up from the menu. "I'll have an iced tea with extra lemon, please, and a cheeseburger, without the fries." No need to clog her arteries with extra fat. The meat and cheese were bad enough.

"Iced tea and a cheeseburger," the waitress repeated. "You wanna try our lemon meringue pie? It's the best this side of Abilene."

"Oh, sure, why not?" Sherry said, giving up the cholesterol and carbohydrate battle without a fight. The waitress left and returned almost immediately with the iced tea. Sherry drank gratefully, then spread the map across the table and charted her progress. With luck, she should be in Houston by midafternoon the following day. Right on schedule. Her friend Norah Cassidy wasn't expecting her before Wednesday, so Sherry could make a leisurely drive of it—although she'd enjoy the drive a whole lot more if it wasn't so hellishly hot.

The waitress brought Sherry's cheeseburger on a thick, old-fashioned ceramic plate. A mound of onion and tomato slices, plus lettuce and pickles, were neatly arranged next to the open burger.

"Don't see too many strangers coming this way," the waitress commented, plunking down containers of mustard and ketchup. "Most folks stick to the freeway."

"I prefer taking the back roads," Sherry said, popping a pickle slice into her mouth.

"You headed for San Antonio?"

"Houston. I'm a physician assistant and—"

"I don't suppose you're looking for a job?"

Sherry smiled to herself. "Not really. I already have one." She didn't add that the job was right here in Pepper.

"Oh." The eager grin faded. "The town council's been advertising with one of those employment agencies for over a year."

Apparently the waitress hadn't heard that they'd hired someone. "I'm also a nurse and a midwife," Sherry added, although she wasn't sure why she felt obliged to list her credentials for the woman. The physician assistant part was a recent qualification.

The waitress nodded. "I hear lots of women like to have their babies at home these days. Most everyone from around Pepper comes to the hospital, though."

"You have a hospital here?" This was welcome news. The town didn't look large enough to support more than a café, a couple of taverns and a jail.

"Actually it's a clinic. But Doc's made sure we've got the best emergency-room facilities within two hundred miles. Last year one of the high-school boys lost an arm, and Doc was able to save the arm *and* the kid. Wouldn't have been able to do it without all that fancy equipment. We're right proud of that clinic."

"You should be." Sherry gazed longingly at her lunch. If the waitress didn't stop chattering, it was going to get cold.

"You have family in Houston?"

Sherry added the rest of her condiments, folded the cheeseburger closed and raised it toward her mouth as a less-than-subtle hint. "No. A good friend."

The woman's eyes brightened. "I see." She left and returned a moment later, a tall, potbellied older man in tow.

"Howdy," he said with a lazy drawl. "Welcome to Texas."

Sherry finished chewing her first bite. "Thank you. It's a wonderful state."

"What part of the country you from?"

"Oregon," she replied. "A little town called Orchard Valley."

"I hear it's real pretty up there in Or-ee-gon."

"It's beautiful," Sherry agreed, staring down at her plate. If she was lucky, this cowpoke would get the message and leave her to her lunch.

"'Course living in Texas has a lot of advantages."

"That's what I understand."

"Suppose I should introduce myself," he said, holding out his hand. "Name's Dan Bowie. I'm Pepper's duly elected mayor."

"Pleased to meet you." Sherry wiped the mustard from her fingertips and extended her hand. He shook it, his eyes gleaming, then without waiting for an invitation, pulled out the chair opposite her and made himself comfortable.

"Donna Jo here was telling me you're a physician assistant."

"That's true."

"She also said you already have a job."

"That's true, too, but—"

"It just so happens that Pepper badly needs a qualified physician assistant. Now we've finally hired one, but she's not due to get here for a couple weeks yet. So-o-o..."

Sherry abruptly decided to discontinue her charade. "Well, she's here. It's me." She smiled brightly. "I'm early, I know, but—"

"Well, I'll be! This is great, just great. I wish you'd said something sooner. We'd've thrown a welcome party if we'd known, isn't that right, Donna Jo?"

"Actually I was on my way to Houston to visit a friend, but curiosity got the better of me," Sherry explained. "I thought I'd drive through town and get a look at Pepper."

"Well, what do you think?" He pushed back his Stetson and favored her with a wide smile. "You can stay for a while, can't you?" he asked. "Now, you finish your lunch," he said as Donna Jo set a towering piece of lemon meringue pie in front of Sherry and replenished her iced tea. "Your meal's on us," he announced grandly. "Send the tab to my office, Donna Jo."

"Thank you," Sherry began, "but—"

"Soon as you're done, Miz..."

"Waterman. Sherry Waterman."

"Soon as you're done eating, I aim to show you around town. We'll stop by the clinic, too. I want Doc Lindsey to meet you."

"Well...I suppose." Sherry hoped she didn't sound ungracious. She finished her meal quickly and in silence, acutely conscious of Mayor Bowie's rapt and unwavering gaze.

The second she put her fork down, he took hold of her elbow and practically lifted her from the chair. He'd obviously regained his voice, because he was talking enthusiastically as he guided her out the café door.

"Pepper's a sweet little town. Got its name from Jim Pepper. Don't suppose you ever heard of him up there in Or-ee-gon. He died at the Alamo, and our forefathers didn't want the world to forget what a fine man he was, so they up and named the town after him. What most folks don't know is that he was darn near blind. He couldn't have shot one of Santa Ana's men if his life depended on it, which unfortunately it did."

"I'm sure his family was proud."

They strolled down the road and turned left onto a friendly looking, tree-lined street. Sherry noticed a huge old white house with a wide porch and dark green shutters and guessed it must be the clinic.

"Doc Lindsey's going to be mighty glad to meet you," the mayor was saying as he held open the gate of the white picket fence. "He's been waiting a good long while for this. Yes, indeed. A good long while."

"I'm looking forward to meeting him, too," Sherry said politely. And it was true. She'd spent the past two years going to school part-time in order to train for this job. She was excited about beginning her new responsibilities. But not quite yet. She did want to visit Norah first.

She preceded the mayor up the porch steps to the screen door. He opened it for her, and led her inside, past a middle-aged receptionist who called out a cordial greeting.

"Doc's in, isn't he?" Dan asked over his shoulder without stopping to hear the reply.

Apparently, whether or not Doc was with a patient was of no concern to Pepper's duly elected mayor. Clasping her by the elbow, he knocked loudly on a polished oak door and let himself in.

An older white-haired man was sitting in a comfortable-looking office chair, his feet propped on the corner of a

scarred desk. His mouth was wide open; his head had fallen
back. A strangled sound came from his throat, and it took
Sherry a moment to realize he was snoring.

"Doc," Dan said loudly. "I brought someone for you to
meet." When the old man didn't respond, Dan said it again,
only louder.

"I think we should let him sleep," Sherry whispered.

"Nonsense. He'll be madder'n blazes if he misses meeting you."

Whereas the shouting hadn't interrupted Don Lindsey's
nap, Sherry's soft voice did. He dropped his feet and straightened, blinking at Sherry as if she were an apparition.

"Who in tarnation are you?"

"Sherry Waterman," she said. "Mayor Bowie wanted us
to meet."

"What ails you?"

"I'm in perfect health."

"She's that gal we hired from Or-ee-gon."

"Why in heaven's name didn't you say so?" Doc Lindsey
boomed, vaulting to his feet with the energy of a man twenty
years younger. "About time you got here."

"I'm afraid there's been a misunderstanding...." Sherry
began, but neither man was listening. Doc slapped the mayor
on the back, reached behind the door for his fishing pole and
announced he'd be back at the end of the week.

He paused on his way out of the office. "Ellie Johnson's
baby is due anytime now, but you won't have any problem
with that. More'n likely I'll be back long before she goes into
labor. She was two weeks late with her first one."

"Don't you worry," the mayor said, following Doc out the
door. "I heard Sherry tell Donna Jo she's a midwife, too."

Doc shook hands with the mayor and chortled happily.

"You outdid yourself this time, Danny-boy. See you in a week."

"Dr. Lindsey!" Sherry cried, chasing after him. He was already outside and on the sidewalk. "I'm not staying! I'm on my way to Houston to meet a friend." She scrambled down the steps so fast she nearly stumbled.

Doc didn't seem to hear her. The mayor, too, had suddenly developed a hearing problem.

Doc tossed his fishing pole into the bed of his truck and climbed into the front seat.

"I can't stay!" she shouted. "I'm not supposed to start work for another two weeks. I've made other plans!"

"Seems to me you're here now," Doc said. "Might as well stay. Good to have you on the team. I'll see you…" The roar of the engine drowned out his last words.

Sherry stood on the lawn, her heart pounding as she watched him drive away. Frowning, she clenched her fists at her sides. Neither man had taken the trouble to listen to her; they just assumed she would willingly forgo her plans. But darn it, she wasn't going to be railroaded by some hick mayor and a doctor who obviously spent more time sleeping and fishing than practicing medicine.

"I can't stay," she said, as annoyed with herself as she was with the mayor. This was what she got for being so curious.

"But you *can't* leave now," Mayor Bowie insisted. "Doc won't be back for a week. Besides, he's never been real good with time—a week could turn out to be ten days or more."

She pushed a stray lock of shiny brown hair off her forehead, and her blue eyes blazed. "That's unfortunate, because I'm meeting my friend in Houston and I can't be late." That wasn't entirely true but she didn't intend to start work until the agreed-upon date. On top of that, she couldn't shake the feeling that there was something not quite right about the situation here in Pepper.

"If you could stay the week, we'd all be mighty grateful," the mayor was saying.

"I'm sorry but no," Sherry told him emphatically, heading back down the street toward her car.

The mayor dogged her heels. "I'm sure your friend wouldn't mind. Why don't you phone and ask her? The city will pay for the call."

Great, Sherry thought, there were even perks. "No, thanks," she said firmly.

The mayor continued to plead. "I feel bad about this," he said. "But a week, why, only seven days, and Doc hasn't had time off in months."

Sherry kept walking, refusing to let him work on her sympathies. He seemed to have forgotten about the possibility of Doc's absence lasting as long as ten days, too.

"You have to understand," he went on, "that with Doc away there isn't anyone within miles for medical emergencies."

Sherry stopped and turned to glare at him. "It's too bad the pair of you didn't think of that sooner. I told you when you introduced yourself that I was on my way to Houston. My contract doesn't start for two weeks."

"I know." He removed his hat and looked at her imploringly. "Surely a week isn't too much to ask."

"Excuse me, miss." A stocky police officer dressed in a tan uniform had come out of the café and strolled over to her. The town sheriff, she decided. He was chewing on a toothpick and his thumbs were tucked in his belt buckle, which hung low under his protruding belly. "I don't suppose you happen to own that cute little Cruiser just there, do you?" He pointed at her car, about twenty feet away.

"As a matter of fact, I do."

His nod was slow and deliberate. The toothpick was smoothly transferred to the other side of his mouth. "I was afraid of that. Best I can tell, it's parked illegally."

"It most certainly is not," Sherry protested as the three of them reached the car. The slot was clearly marked and she'd pulled in between two other vehicles.

"See how your left rear tire is over the yellow line?" the sheriff asked, pointing.

"I suppose that carries a heavy fine?" Good grief, she thought. Before long some cowpoke was going to suggest they get a rope and hang her from the nearest tree. In that case she'd be okay, since she hadn't seen anything but brush for the last hundred miles.

"There isn't a fine for illegally parking your car," he said, grinning lazily. "But jaywalking does carry a hefty one, and I saw you cross that street with my very own eyes."

"There wasn't a crosswalk," she said.

"Sure there is," he said, still grinning. "It's down the street a bit, but it's there. I painted it myself no more'n ten years ago."

"You're going to fine me, then," she said, reaching into her bag for her wallet. "Great. I'll pay you and be done with it." After that she was going to head straight for the freeway, and when she got to Houston, she'd reconsider this job offer.

"There isn't any fine."

"But you just said there was!" Actually, Sherry was relieved. Her cash was running low and she doubted the sheriff would accept a check.

"No fine, but the jail term—"

"Jail term!" she exploded.

"Now, Billy Bob," the mayor said, placing himself between the two of them, "you don't really intend to put our doc's helper in jail, do you?"

Billy Bob rubbed his hand across the underside of his jaw as if needing to contemplate such a monumental decision.

"You'd give Pepper a bad name," the mayor went on, "and we wouldn't want that, would we?"

"You staying in Pepper, miss?" the officer asked.

Sherry's gaze connected with Mayor Bowie's. "It appears I don't have much choice, do I?"

The minute she had access to a phone, Sherry vowed, she was going to call her friend's husband, Rowdy Cassidy. Rowdy, the owner of one of the largest computer software companies in the world, had a large legal staff. He'd be able to pull a few strings for her. By the end of the day, these folks in Pepper would be facing so many lawsuits, they'd throw a parade when she left town.

"I'll walk you back to the clinic," the mayor said, smiling as though he didn't have a care in the world. "I'm sure Mrs. Colson'll be happy to give you a tour of the place."

Sherry ground her teeth and bit back a tart reply. Until she had the legal clout she needed, there was no point in voicing any more protests.

Instead, Sheriff Billy Bob himself escorted her down the street and around the corner to the clinic. The middle-aged receptionist introduced herself as Mrs. Colson and greeted Sherry with a warm smile. "I'm so glad you decided to stay."

"You make her welcome now," the sheriff instructed.

"You know I will," Mrs. Colson told him, standing and coming around the counter. "You can go on now," she told Billy Bob and, taking him by the elbow, escorted him out the door. She turned to Sherry. "Billy Bob can outstare a polecat, but underneath that tough hide of his, he's gentle as a baby."

Sherry swallowed a retort as the receptionist went on to extol the sheriff's virtues.

"One of those multitalented folks you read so much about. Not only does he uphold the law around these parts, but he makes the best barbecue sauce in the state. Wait till you taste it. Everyone thinks he should bottle and sell it, but I doubt he will."

"How...unfortunate," was all Sherry could manage.

Her mood didn't improve as Mrs. Colson gave her the grand tour. Despite her frame of mind, Sherry was impressed with the clinic's modern equipment and pleased with the small apartment at one end of the building that would serve as her living quarters.

"Doc's sure glad to get away for a few days," Mrs. Colson said amicably, ignoring Sherry's sour mood. "I can't even remember the last time he had more than a day to himself. He talks about fishing a lot—gets a pile of those magazines and catalogs. In the twenty years I've known him, I don't believe I've seen him livelier than he was today after you arrived. Guess he was thinking he'd best skedaddle before you changed your mind. I'm sure glad you didn't."

Sherry's answering smile was weak. Between Dan Bowie, Doc Lindsey and Billy Bob, she'd been completely hog-tied.

"So Dr. Lindsey's been practicing in Pepper for twenty years?" She wondered if, like her, he'd innocently driven into town and been snared. This could be something straight out of that old TV series, *The Twilight Zone.*

"Thirty years, in fact, maybe more. Most folks think of him as a saint."

Some saint, Sherry thought. With little more than a nod of his head, he'd abandoned Pepper and her.

Mrs. Colson led her to Doc's office. "Now make yourself at home. Do you want a cup of coffee?"

"No, thanks," Sherry answered, walking over to the desk. The telephone caught her eye. As soon as she had a minute alone, she'd call Houston.

But the moment Mrs. Colson left there was a knock at the office door. Sherry groaned. She hadn't even had time to sit down.

"Come in," she called, thinking it must be the receptionist.

In walked a tall, rawboned cowboy with skin tanned the color of a new penny. He wore jeans, a checkered shirt and a pair of scarred boots. A Stetson hat hooded his dark eyes, and somehow, with the red bandana around his neck, he looked both rough and dangerous.

"You're not Doc Lindsey," he said accusingly.

"No," she agreed tartly, "I'm not."

"Oh, good," Mrs. Colson said, following him into the room. "I see your one-o'clock appointment is here."

"*My* one o'clock appointment?"

"Where's Doc?" the cowboy demanded.

"He's gone fishing. Now you sit down," Mrs. Colson directed in steely tones. "You're Miz Waterman's first patient, and I don't want her getting a bad impression of the folks in Pepper."

"I ain't talkin' to no woman about Heather."

"Why not? A woman would be far more understanding than Doc."

The cowboy shook his head stubbornly.

Personally, Sherry agreed with him.

"Don't you argue with me, Cody Bailman," Mrs. Colson said, arms akimbo. "And don't you make trouble for Miz Waterman. She's a real sweetheart."

Cody shifted his hat farther back on his head. "It ain't gonna work."

"That's right. It ain't gonna work unless you try." The

receptionist took Cody by the elbow and marched him to the chair on the other side of the desk. "Now sit. You, too, Sherry." Neither of them bothered to comply, but that didn't disturb the receptionist. "Cody's here to talk about his daughter. She's twelve and giving him plenty of grief, and he comes here for advice because...well, because his wife died about ten years back and he's having a few problems understanding what's happening to Heather now that she's becoming a young woman."

"Which means I'm not talkin' to some stranger about my personal affairs," Cody said.

"It'll do you good to get everything out," Mrs. Colson assured him. "Now sit down," she said again. "Sherry, you sit, too. If you stand, it'll make Cody nervous."

Sherry sat. "What should I do?" she whispered.

"Listen," the older women instructed. "That's all Doc ever does. It seems to help."

Doc Lindsey apparently served as Pepper's psychologist, too. Sherry had received some training along those lines, but certainly not enough to qualify as a counselor.

"I'm not talkin' to a woman," Cody said.

"Did you ever consider that's the reason you're having so many problems with Heather?" Mrs. Colson pointed out, then stalked over to the door. As she reached for the knob, her narrowed eyes moved from Cody to Sherry, and her tight features relaxed into a smile. "You let me know if Cody gives you any problems, but I doubt he will." She dropped her voice. "What Heather really needs is a mother. In my opinion, Cody should remarry."

"You volunteering for the job, Martha?" Cody said.

Mrs. Colson's cheeks reddened. "I'm old enough to be *your* mother, and you darn well know it." With that she left the room, closing the door behind her.

Cody laughed and to Sherry's surprise sat down in the chair across from her, took off his hat and relaxed. As he rested one ankle on the opposite knee and stared at Sherry, the humor drained out of his face.

She wasn't sure what to do. If she hadn't felt so intimidated by this dark-haired cowboy, she'd have sent him on his way.

"You married?" he asked suddenly.

Her mouth fell open. When she finally managed to speak, her words stumbled over one another. "No, I'm not, I...that is..." She knew she sounded breathless and inane.

"Don't look so worried. I'm not expecting you to offer your services as my wife."

"I realize that," she said with as much dignity as she could muster. Unfortunately it wasn't much.

"Then how are you supposed to know about kids?"

"I have two younger brothers and a sister," she said, wondering why she thought she had to defend herself. She *should* be sending him on his way. She sighed. The longer this day lasted, the more convinced she was that she'd somehow stepped out of the present. The man sitting across from her might have come from another century.

"So you know about girls?"

dc "I was one not so long ago myself," she said wryly. Resigning herself to the situation, she asked, "Why don't you tell me about Heather and I'll see if I can help?"

Cody seemed to need time to think over her suggestion. Eventually he began. "Well, first off, Heather's doing things behind my back."

"What sort of things?"

"Wearing makeup and the like. The other night I went in to check up on her and I swear she had on so much silver eye shadow her eyelids glowed in the dark."

Sherry swallowed her impulse to laugh.

"No more'n about six months ago," he continued, clearly confused by his daughter's behavior, "Heather was showing signs of being one of the best cowhands I'd ever seen, but now she doesn't want anything to do with ranching. Besides that, she's, uh, getting bigger on top."

"Have you bought her a bra?"

He flushed slightly beneath his tan. "I didn't have to— she bought her own. Ordered it right off the Internet before I even knew. From what I can see, she didn't have any idea what she was doing, because the one they sent was at least five sizes too big. Instead of admitting she doesn't know about such things, she's wearing it and as best I can tell stuffing it with something. Heaven only knows what."

"My guess is tissue." That had worked for Sherry when she was a teenager.

Cody's dark eyes narrowed in concentration. "Could be. I asked her about it, and she nearly bit my head off."

Mrs. Colson was right; the poor girl did need a mother.

"Has Heather got a boyfriend?" Maybe Cody was jealous of some boy. It sounded like a good theory anyway.

Cody frowned. "Ever since she's been wearing this bra, she's got a whole passel of boys hanging around. The thing is, she doesn't like all this attention. You have to understand that until recently Heather was a tomboy."

"Heather's growing up, Cody," Sherry told him. She leaned back and crossed her arms. "She doesn't really understand what's happening to her body. She's probably frightened by the changes. Trust me, she isn't any happier about what's taking place than you are. Give her a little time and a little space, and you'll be surprised by how well she adjusts."

Cody eyed her as if he wasn't convinced he should believe her.

"Does she have any close friends?" she asked.

"Wally and Clem, but she doesn't seem to be getting along with them as well as she used to."

"What about girlfriends?"

"She has a couple, but they live here in town and we're twenty miles away. What she really needs is to talk to someone—you know, a woman, someone older than thirteen, who knows a bit more about bras and other girl stuff. And then there was this business with the 4-H—all of a sudden my daughter wants to run my life."

"The 4-H? Your life?"

"Never mind," he said, groaning heavily.

"Would you like me to talk to her?" Sherry offered. "I...I don't know if I'd be able to accomplish anything, but I'd be willing to try."

"I'd like it a whole lot," he said, his eyes softening with gratitude. He frowned again. "She's been acting like a porcupine lately, so don't be offended if she seems a bit unfriendly." Cody looked down and sighed. "Then again, she might be overly friendly. Just don't be shocked by anything she says or does, all right?"

"I won't be," Sherry promised. "We'll get along fine." She wasn't as confident as she sounded, but she found she liked Cody Bailman. It hadn't been easy for him to discuss such private matters with a stranger, a woman, no less, yet he'd put his concern for his daughter first. She was impressed.

"I found something the other day. I'm sure Heather didn't mean for me to see it."

"What was it?"

"A book. She had it tucked between the sofa cushions. It was one of those romance novels you women like so much. I tell you right now, it worries me."

"Why?"

"Well, because I don't think it's a good idea for her to be filling her head with that sort of nonsense." He muttered something else, but Sherry didn't catch it. Presumably he didn't think highly of romance.

"I'll discuss it with her if you want," Sherry said. "Of course, I won't let her know you found the book."

Cody stood. "I appreciate this, Miz..."

"Waterman. But please, call me Sherry."

"Sherry," he repeated. He held out his hand and she took it. Was it her imagination, or did he maintain contact a moment longer than necessary? Her gaze fell to their clasped hands, and he released her fingers as if he suddenly realized what he was doing. "It's been a pleasure."

"Thank you. Do you want to bring Heather in to see me tomorrow afternoon, or would you rather I paid a visit to your ranch?"

"Could you? It'd be best if this conversation seems casual. If Heather ever found out I was talking to anyone about her, she'd be madder than a mule with a mouthful of bees."

"I'll get directions from Mrs. Colson and be there shortly after lunch—say, one o'clock?"

"Great."

Cody lingered at the door and appeared to be assessing her. "Are you thinking of sticking around Pepper?"

"I was hired last month. I wasn't scheduled to start work for another two weeks, but it seems I'm starting early."

Sherry couldn't believe she'd said that. Until Cody Bailman had walked in the door, she'd been intent on demanding her two weeks. Now, she wasn't so sure.

"I'll see you tomorrow, then," Cody said, grinning broadly.

"Tomorrow," she agreed.

Still he stayed. "Might as well come by around lunchtime. The least I can do is feed you."

With a slight nod of her head, she accepted his offhand invitation.

The phone on the desk rang, breaking the silence—and the spell that had apparently descended on both of them. Then the ring was cut off. Mrs. Colson must have picked it up.

As Cody was just about to leave, the receptionist burst through the door, a look of panic in her eyes. "That was Luke Johnson. Ellie's having labor pains, and he's scared to death he's gonna have to deliver that baby on his own. You'd better get over there quick as you can."

"Where?" Sherry asked.

"Rattlesnake Ridge," Cody said. "Come on." He gripped her elbow. "I'll drive you. You'd never find it on your own."

# Two

"Rattlesnake Ridge?" Sherry muttered under her breath as she hurried with Cody toward his pickup truck. He opened the passenger door and helped her inside. Although slender, Sherry wasn't the sort of female who generally required assistance, but her comparatively meager height—five foot five, as opposed to Cody's six-two—meant she needed help this time. The tires on his truck looked as if they belonged on a tanker trailer.

It was impossible to determine the color of the vehicle, and Sherry suspected it hadn't been washed since it'd been driven off the showroom floor. Maybe, she thought, the dirt helped the rust hold the thing together.

Once she situated herself inside the cab, Cody dashed around the front and leaped in. His door made a cranking sound when he opened and closed it. He shoved the key into the ignition and the engine roared to life. She immediately noticed all the papers clipped to the dash; it looked as if he stored most of his paperwork there. She couldn't suppress a smile at his fingertip filing system.

"I'll need some things from my car," she told him. "It's parked over by the café." Cody stopped on Main Street, directly in front of her PT Cruiser and answered her unasked question.

"It's the only car I didn't recognize," he said as he opened the door and jumped down, then came around to give her a hand.

By the time Sherry was back in the pickup and fumbling with her seat belt, they were racing out of town.

Over the past few years Norah had written her long e-mails about life in Texas. One thing she'd said was that the men here were as unique as the trucks they drove. Sherry had been amused and intrigued enough to move here herself. She was beginning to understand what Norah had meant about the men.

"I wish I'd talked to Luke myself," Cody said. He glanced at Sherry as if she was somehow to blame for his friend's discomfort. "That man's so crazy about Ellie he'd lose his head completely if anything ever happened to her."

Sherry grinned. "Isn't that how a man *should* feel about his wife?"

Cody didn't answer right away. "Some men with some women, I suppose," he said a moment later.

Not wanting to discuss what he'd said or what it might imply, Sherry changed the subject. "Are there really rattlesnakes out there on Rattlesnake Ridge?" she asked conversationally.

"In Texas we tend to call a spade a spade. We don't pretty up the truth, and the truth is there's rattlers on that ridge. You'll see it isn't named Buttercup Hill."

"I see." She swallowed hard. "Are snakes a problem around here?"

"You afraid of snakes?" His gaze left the road for a few seconds.

"Not particularly," she said, trying to make her tone light. Norah hadn't said anything about snakes. "Tell me what you know about Ellie. Doc said she'd gone two weeks beyond her due date with the first pregnancy. Do you remember the baby's birth weight?"

Cody glanced at her again, his expression puzzled.

"If I'm going to be delivering this baby, any fact you can give me is helpful," she said. "Is Ellie small and delicate?"

"I guess…"

Sherry could see that Cody wasn't going to provide much information. "What else can you tell me about her?"

"Well, she's real cute."

"Young?"

"Mid-twenties. Luke wasn't interested in marriage until Ellie came to visit her grandparents a few years back. He took one look at her and he hasn't been the same since. I swear he walked around like a sick calf from the moment he met her." Cody frowned before he continued, "Unfortunately, his condition hasn't improved. It's been a long while since I've seen a man as smitten as Luke." He said this last part as if he had little patience with love or romance. "My bet is that Ellie's the calm one now."

"Her first pregnancy was normal?"

"I think so. Don't know for sure."

"Boy or girl?"

"Girl. Christina Lynn. Cute as a bug's ear, too."

"Was she a big baby?"

"Not that I recall, but then I don't know much about that sort of thing."

"How old is Christina Lynn?"

"She must be a year or so." He paused. "Is that bad?"

"Why?" His question surprised her.

"Because you frowned."

Sherry hadn't realized she had. "No, it's just that they didn't wait long before Ellie became pregnant again."

"No, but if you want the truth, I don't think this one was planned any more than Christina Lynn was. Luke's besotted—that's the only word for it. Got his head in the clouds where Ellie's concerned."

Sherry found that all rather endearing. She liked his terminology, too. *Smitten, besotted.* Here she was in her late twenties and no man had ever felt that way about her—nor she about any man. This was one of the reasons she'd decided to move out of Orchard Valley. If she stayed, she had the sinking feeling the rest of her life would have gone on just as it had been. She'd been content, but never excited. Busy, but bored. Liked, but not loved.

She'd lived her entire life in Orchard Valley, a small town where neighbors were friends and the sense of community was strong. It was one of the reasons Sherry had accepted the position in Pepper—another small town.

Norah had made the transition from Orchard Valley to Houston without difficulty, but Sherry wasn't sure she'd have done nearly as well. She didn't have a big-city mentality. But Norah's calls and e-mails about the Lone Star state had intrigued her, and if she was going to make a change, she couldn't see doing it by half measures. So she'd answered the agency's ad with a long letter and a detailed résumé. They phoned almost immediately, and she was hired so fast, without even a personal interview, her head spun. She did learn from Dr. Colby Winston, Norah's brother-in-law, that her references had been checked and this eased her mind.

They'd been driving for about twenty minutes when Cody braked suddenly to turn off the main road and onto a rugged

dirt-and-gravel one. Sherry pitched forward, and if not for
the restraint of the seat belt, would have slammed against
the dash.

"You all right?"

"Sure," she said, a bit breathless. "How much farther?"

"Ten miles or so."

Sherry groaned inwardly and forced a smile. Even if
they'd been driving at normal speed, the road would have
been a challenge. Her body jerked one way and another, and
she had to grip the seat with both hands.

When at last Cody pulled into the ranch yard, the road
smoothed out. He eased to a stop in front of a two-story
white house, which to Sherry looked like a desert oasis, a
welcoming refuge from the heat and barrenness. The windows were decorated with bright blue shutters, and brilliant
red geraniums bloomed in the boxes out front. The wraparound porch was freshly painted. Sherry watched as the
door swung open and a tall, rangy cowman barreled out
and down the steps.

"What took you so long?" he hollered. "Ellie's in pain."

Sherry was still fiddling with her seat belt when Cody
opened the door for her. His hands fit snugly around her
waist as he helped her down from the cab.

"Sherry, meet Luke," Cody said.

"Where's Doc?" Luke demanded.

"Fishing," Sherry explained, holding out her hand. "I'm
Sherry Waterman and I—"

Luke's hand barely touched hers as his gaze moved accusingly to Cody, interrupting her introduction. "You brought
some stranger out here for Ellie? Cody, this is my wife! You
can't bring just anyone to—"

"I'm a midwife, as well as a physician assistant," Sherry
supplied. "I can do just about everything Dr. Lindsey does,

including prescribe medication and deliver babies. Now, where's your wife?"

"Cody?" Luke looked at his friend uncertainly.

"Do you want to deliver Ellie's baby yourself?" Cody asked him.

Luke went visibly pale and shook his head mutely.

"That's what I thought." Cody's hand cupped Sherry's elbow as he escorted her into the house. "You'll have to forgive Luke," he whispered. "As I said earlier, he's been a bit…irrational ever since he met Ellie."

The door led into the kitchen. A toddler was sitting in a high chair grinning happily and slamming a wooden spoon against the tray.

"Christina Lynn, I assume," Sherry said.

The toddler's face broke into a wide smile. At least Luke's daughter seemed pleased to see her.

"Where's Ellie?" Sherry asked Luke.

"Upstairs. Hurry, please!" Luke strode swiftly toward the staircase.

Sherry followed, taking the stairs two at a time, Cody right behind her.

When Sherry reached the hallway, Luke led the way into the master bedroom. Ellie was braced against the headboard, her eyes closed, her teeth gnawing on her lower lip. Her hand massaged her swollen abdomen as she breathed deeply in and out.

Luke fell to his knees and took her free hand, kissing her knuckles fervently. "They're here. There's nothing to worry about now."

Ellie acknowledged Sherry's and Cody's presence with an absent nod. Sherry waited until the contraction had ebbed before she asked, "How far apart are they?"

"Five minutes," Ellie said. "They started hard, right after my water broke."

"How long ago was that?"

"An hour or so."

"I'd better check you, then." Sherry set down her bag at the foot of the bed and removed a pair of surgical gloves.

"Cody?" Once again Luke pleaded for his friend's advice.

"Cody," Ellie said, "kindly keep my big oaf of a husband entertained for a while." She motioned toward the door. "Make him tend to Christina Lynn—she shouldn't be left alone. Whatever you do, keep him out of this room."

"But, Ellie, you need me!" Luke protested.

"Not right now I don't, honey. Cody, please do as I say and keep Luke out of here."

Cody virtually pushed Luke out of the room. After the pair had left, Ellie looked at Sherry. "Whoever you are, welcome. I'm delighted to see another woman."

Sherry smiled. "Sherry Waterman. I'm new to Pepper. Doc was so excited by my arrival that he took off fishing. He said you weren't due for another couple of weeks."

"I'm not, but then we miscalculated with Christina Lynn, too."

"I'll wash my hands and be right back." By the time Sherry returned, Ellie was in the middle of another contraction. She waited until Ellie had relaxed, then adjusted her pillows to make her as comfortable as possible.

"How am I doing?" Ellie asked after the pain receded. Her brow was covered with a thin sheen of perspiration. She licked her dry lips.

"You're doing just great," Sherry murmured, wiping Ellie's face with a wet rag.

"How much longer will it take?"

"A while," Sherry said gently. "Maybe several hours."

Ellie's shoulders sagged. "I was afraid of that."

Twenty minutes later, Cody appeared after knocking lightly on the bedroom door. "How's everything going up here?"

"Fine," Sherry told him. "Ellie's an excellent patient."

"I wish I could say the same for Luke. Is there anything I can get you?"

"Pillows and a C.D. player." At his frown, she explained, "Soothing music will help Ellie relax during the contractions. I have C.D.s with me."

Cody nodded and smiled at Ellie. "Don't worry about Christina Lynn. She's in her crib and sound asleep. I phoned the ranch, and our housekeeper's staying with Heather, so everything's taken care of at my end."

"Whatever you do, make sure Luke stays out of here," Ellie said. "You'd think I was the only woman who ever had labor pains. He was a wreck when Christina Lynn was born. Doc Lindsey had to spend more time with him than with me."

"I'll keep him in line," Cody said, ducking out of the room.

Sherry remembered more than one birth where the father required full-time attention. It always touched her to see that men could be so greatly affected by the birth of their children.

A couple of minutes later, Cody brought a small C.D. player and two plump pillows. Sherry arranged the pillows behind Ellie, then put in a C.D. of soft piano music.

"That's nice," Ellie said, panting.

Sherry held her hand through a powerful contraction.

"Talk to me," Ellie requested before the next one gripped her body.

Sherry described her introduction to the good people of

Pepper. She told her about meeting Mayor Bowie and Doc
Lindsey and Billy Bob. Ellie laughed, then as the pain came
again, she rolled onto her side and Sherry massaged the
tightness from the small of her back, all the while giving
encouragement.

"I'm a transplant myself." Ellie spoke when she could. "I
was a college senior when I came here to visit my grandparents. They've lived in Pepper for as long as I can remember. I only intended to stay a few days, but then I met
Luke. I swear he was the most pigheaded, most ill-behaved
man I'd ever known. I told myself I didn't want anything to
do with him. To be truthful, I had kind of a crush on Cody
Bailman back then."

"Obviously your opinion of Luke changed."

"My sweet Luke. You've never seen anyone tougher on
the outside and so gentle on the inside. I'll never forget the
afternoon he proposed. I'd decided to drive home to Dallas—good grief, I'd spent two weeks longer than I'd originally intended. Luke didn't want me to leave, but I really
didn't have any choice. I had a job waiting for me and was
signed up for classes in the fall. Grandma sent me off with
enough food to last a month."

Sherry chuckled and waited for Ellie to breathe her way
through the next contraction.

"I was five miles out of town when I saw this man on a
horse galloping after me as if catching me was a matter of
life or death. It was Luke." She shook her head, remembering. "When I pulled over to the side of the road, he jumped
off his horse, removed his gloves, then fell to one knee and
proposed. I knew then and there I wasn't ever going to find
a man who'd love me as much as Luke Johnson. Suddenly
nothing mattered without him, not anymore. I know my par-

ents were disappointed that I didn't finish college, but I'm happy and that's what counts."

"You don't mind living so far away from town?"

"At first, just a little. Now I'm happy about it."

"That's a wonderfully romantic story."

Ellie smiled. "Is there a special man in your life?"

Sherry exhaled slowly. "I've never fallen in love. Oh, I had a few crushes. I dated a doctor for a while, but both of us knew it wasn't going anywhere." Sherry smiled to herself as she recalled how difficult it'd been for Colby Winston to admit he was in love with Valerie Bloomfield.

During the next few hours, Cody came up to check on their progress twice and give a report of his own. Luke, he said, had worn a path in the living-room carpet pacing back and forth, but thus far, Cody had been able to restrain him from racing up the stairs. He doubted Luke would have much hair left before the ordeal was over; he'd jerked his hands through it so many times there were grooves in his hairline.

"He loves me," Ellie said softly.

When Sherry walked Cody to the bedroom door, he asked quietly, "Will it be much longer? Luke's a mess."

"Another couple of hours."

Cody nodded and his eyes briefly held hers. "I'm glad you're here." He turned and headed down the stairs. A surge of emotion overwhelmed her, but she wasn't sure how to read it. All she knew was that she felt *alive,* acutely sensitive to sounds and colors, and she had the impression that Cody experienced the same thing.

"I'm glad you're here, too," Ellie said from behind her.

Sherry moved back to the bed. "Doc would've done just as well."

"Perhaps, but it helps that you're a woman."

The second stage of labor arrived shortly after midnight,

and Ellie arched against the bed at the strength of her contractions, panting in between. Sherry coached her as she had so many others. And then, at last, with a shout of triumph, Ellie delivered a strong, squalling son.

The baby was barely in his mother's arms when the door burst open and Luke barged into the room.

"A son, Luke," Ellie whispered. "We have a son."

Luke knelt beside the bed and stared down at the angry infant in his wife's arms. The baby was a bright shade of pink, his legs and arms kicking in protest. His eyes were closed and he was yelling for all he was worth. "He looks just like you when you get mad," Ellie told her husband.

Luke nodded and Sherry noticed that his eyes were bright with tears as he bent forward and kissed his son's wrinkled brow. Then he placed his hand over Ellie's cheek and kissed her, too. "Never again," he vowed. "Our family's complete now."

Ellie's eyes drifted shut. "That's what you said after Christina Lynn was born."

"True," Luke admitted, "but that was because I couldn't bear to see you suffer. This time it's for me. I don't think I could go through this again. And I nearly lost my best friend."

"You were a long way from that, partner," Cody said from the doorway.

"I don't care. Two children are plenty. Right, Ellie? I know you said you'd like four, but you agree with me, don't you?"

Sherry moved behind the big, rangy cattleman and looked down at Ellie. "You're exhausted. You need some sleep." Lifting the baby from her arms, Sherry placed him in a soft blanket, marveling at the tiny, perfectly formed person in her hands.

"Come on," Cody urged Luke. "It's time to celebrate.

Let's break open that bottle of expensive scotch you've been saving."

"She's going to do it, you know," Luke said to no one in particular. "That woman knows I can't refuse her a thing. Before I even figure out how it happened, we're going to have four kids running around this house."

Sherry finished her duties and found Luke and Cody in the living room each holding a shot of whiskey. "Ellie and Philip are both asleep," she assured them.

"Philip," Luke repeated slowly, and a brightness came into his eyes. "She decided to name him Philip, after all."

"A family name?" Cody asked him.

Luke shrugged. "Actually, it's mine. I never much cared for it as a kid and dropped it when I started school. I insisted everyone call me by my middle name."

"Ellie says your son looks like a Philip," Sherry put in.

A wide grin split Luke's face. "I think she's right—he does." He stared down into the amber liquid in his glass. "A son. I've got a son."

Sherry smiled, then yawned, covering her mouth with one hand. It had been a long day. She'd been up since dawn, not wanting to travel in the worst heat of the day, and now it was well past two in the morning.

"Come on," Cody said, setting down his glass, "I'd better drive you back into town."

Sherry nodded as another yawn escaped. She was weary through and through.

"Thank you," Luke said. He took her limp hand and pumped it several times to show his gratitude. He seemed to have forgiven her for being a stranger.

"I'll be in touch tomorrow," Sherry promised. "Ellie did a beautiful job with this baby."

"I know." Luke looked away as if embarrassed by his behavior earlier. "I knew the minute I saw that woman I was going to love her. What I didn't know was how lucky I was that I convinced her to marry me."

"From what Ellie told me, she considers herself the lucky one." Luke grinned hugely at Sherry's words.

"Come on, Sherry, you're beat," Cody said. "Good night, Luke."

"Night." Luke walked them to the front door. "Ellie's mother is on her way and should be here by morning. She'll be a big help. But thanks again."

By the time Sherry was inside Cody's truck, she was dead on her feet. She dreaded the long, rough drive back to town, but there was no alternative.

"Sherry." Her name seemed to come from far away. The bottom of a well, perhaps. It was then that she realized she'd been asleep.

She'd meant to stay awake, but she was obviously more tired than she'd realized, because she'd slept through that dreadful ten-mile stretch before they hit the main road. Cody must have driven with infinite care.

To compound her sense of disorientation, she noticed that her head was neatly tucked against his shoulder. She felt warm and comfortable there and wasn't inclined to move.

"We're in town already?" she asked, slowly opening her eyes.

"No. I couldn't see taking you all the way into Pepper when you're so tired."

Sherry straightened and looked around. They were parked outside a barn beside an enormous brick house with arched windows on the main floor and four gables on the second. The place was illuminated by several outdoor lights.

"Where are we?" she asked.

"My place, the Lucky Horseshoe. I figured you could spend what's left of the night here. I'll drive you back into town first thing in the morning."

Sherry was too tired to argue, not that she wanted to. She liked and trusted this man, and when he came around to help her from the cab, she found herself almost eager to feel his hands on her waist again.

Cody swung her down, and if he was feeling any of what Sherry was, he didn't show it.

"I hope I didn't make a pest of myself falling asleep on you that way," she said.

He mumbled something she couldn't quite make out. But apparently she hadn't bothered him. He led the way into the big country kitchen, turning on lights as he went.

Without asking, he took two large glasses from a cupboard and filled them with milk from the refrigerator. "You didn't have any dinner."

Sherry had to think about it for a moment. He was right. She hadn't had anything since the cheeseburger and pie at lunchtime. To her surprise, she wasn't the least bit hungry.

"Here," he said, handing her the glass of milk. "This'll tide you over till breakfast."

"Thanks."

He pulled out a chair for her, then twisted the one across from it around and straddled it. They didn't seem to have a lot to say to each other, yet the room was charged with electricity.

"So," he ventured, "you're planning to stay in Pepper?"

Sherry nodded. She liked the gruff quality of his voice. She liked his face, too, not that he was male-model handsome. His features were too strong and masculine for that, browned by the sun and creased with experience—some of it hard, she guessed.

"You'll like it here. Pepper's a good town."

Everything about Cody Bailman fascinated her. A few strands of thick dark hair fell over his high forehead, giving him a little-boy look. It was so appealing that Sherry had to resist leaning forward and brushing the hair away.

"The guest bedroom's upstairs," Cody said abruptly. He got to his feet, drained the last of his milk in three gulps and set the empty glass in the sink.

Sherry finished her own and stood, too. She'd almost forgotten how tired she was.

"This way," Cody whispered, leading her up the gently curving stairway off the entryway.

Sherry paused and glanced around at the expensive furnishings, the antiques and works of art. "Your home is lovely."

"Thanks."

Sherry followed him to the top of the stairs and then to a room at the far end of the hallway. He opened the door and cursed under his breath.

"Is something wrong?" Sherry asked.

"The bed isn't made up. Heather had a friend stay last night and she promised to change the sheets and remake the bed herself. Looks like she forgot. Listen, I'll sleep in here and you can use my room. Janey, our housekeeper, changed the sheets just today."

"That isn't necessary," she protested. It would only take a few minutes to assemble the bed.

"You're dead on your feet," Cody returned. "Here." He reached for her hand and guided her down to the other end of the hallway.

If she'd possessed the energy, Sherry would've continued to protest, but Cody's evaluation of her state was pretty accurate.

"Call me if you need anything, and don't argue, understand?"

Sherry nodded.

Whether it was by impulse or design, she didn't know, but before he turned away, Cody leaned down and casually brushed her lips with his.

They both seemed taken aback by the quick exchange. Neither spoke for what felt like the longest moment of Sherry's life. Her pulse was pounding wildly in her throat, and Cody pressed his fingertip to the frantic throbbing. Then, before she could encourage or dissuade him, he bent his head and brought his mouth to hers a second time.

Her moist lips quivered beneath his. He moved toward her and she toward him, and soon they were wrapped in each other's arms. The kiss took on an exploring, demanding quality, as if this moment was all they'd be granted and they'd better make the most of it.

Sherry nearly staggered when he released her. "Good night, Sherry," he said, then she watched as he strode the length of the hallway. He paused when he reached the opposite end and turned back to look at her. Even from this distance, Sherry could read the dilemma in his eyes. He didn't *want* to be attracted to her, hadn't wanted to kiss her, and now that he had, he wasn't sure what to do about it.

Sherry was experiencing many of those same feelings herself. She opened the door and stepped inside his room, angry with herself for not insisting on the guest room. Because everything about these quarters, from the basalt fireplace to the large four-poster bed, seemed to say Cody.

She pulled back the sheets and undressed. She thought she'd be asleep before her head hit the pillow, but she was wrong. She tossed and turned until dawn, the image of

Cody standing at the end of the hallway burned in her brain.
Finally she fell into a troubled sleep.

"Hot damn."

Sherry gingerly opened her eyes and saw a pretty girl of
about twelve, dressed in jeans and a red plaid shirt, standing just inside the doorway. Dark braids dangled across her
shoulders.

"Hot damn," the girl repeated, smiling as if it was Christmas morning and she'd found Santa sitting under the tree.

Sherry levered herself up on one elbow and squinted
against the light. "Hello."

"Howdy," the girl said eagerly.

"What time is it?" Sherry rubbed her eyes. It seemed she'd
only been asleep a matter of minutes. If it hadn't been rude
to do so, she would've fallen back against the pillows and
covered her face with the sheet.

"Eight-thirty. Where's Dad?"

"Uh...you're Heather?"

"So he mentioned me, did he?" she asked gleefully. The
girl walked into the room and leaped onto the mattress,
making it bounce.

"I think you have the wrong impression of what's going
on here," Sherry felt obliged to tell her.

"You're in my dad's bed, aren't you? That tells me everything I need to know. Besides, you're the first woman I've
seen him bring home. No, I think I get the picture. How'd
you two meet?" She tucked her knees up under her chin
and looped her arms around them, preparing herself for a
lengthy explanation.

"Heather!" Cody's voice boomed from the end of the
hallway.

Sherry nodded and thrust out her hand. "Call me Sherry. I'll be working with Doc Lindsey."

"Wow. That's great."

"I was with Ellie Johnson last night," Sherry said.

"Ellie had her baby?" Heather's excited gaze shot to her father.

"A boy. They named him Philip," Cody answered.

Heather slapped her hand against the mattress. "Hot damn! Luke never said anything, but I know he was hoping for a boy. But then, Luke's so crazy about Ellie he'd have been happy with a litter of kittens."

"Quit it with the swearing." Cody rubbed his forehead. "And something else—we didn't get back to the house until after two. The guest bed wasn't made up." He looked accusingly at his daughter.

"Oops." Heather pressed her fingers against her lips. "I said I'd do that, didn't I? Sorry."

Sherry gave a discreet cough. "Uh, I'd better see about getting back to town." With Doc gone she was responsible for any medical emergency that might arise. Not that she intended to be manipulated into staying. She still planned to take the time owed to her, with or without the sheriff's approval.

"You want me to see if Slim can drive her?" Heather asked her father.

"I'll do it," Cody said casually, turning away from them. "But first we'll have breakfast."

"Breakfast," Heather repeated meaningfully. She wiggled her eyebrows before slithering off the bed. "He's going to drive you back to town himself," she added, grinning at Sherry. Her smile widened and the sparkle in her eyes grew brighter. "Yup," she said. "My dad likes you. This could be interesting. It's about time he started listening to me."

"I… We only met yesterday," Sherry explained.

"So?"

"I mean, well, isn't it a little soon to be making those kinds of judgments?"

"Nope." Heather plopped herself down on the edge of the bed again. "How do you feel about him? He's kinda handsome, don't you think?"

"Ah…"

"You'll have to be patient with him, though. Dad tends to be a little dumb when it comes to women. He's got a lot to learn, but between the two of us, we should be able to teach him, don't you think?"

Sherry had gotten the impression from talking to Cody that Heather was a timid child struggling with her identity. Ha! This girl didn't have a timid bone in her body.

"I love romance," Heather said on a long drawn-out sigh. She looked behind her to be sure no one was listening, then lowered her voice. "I've been waiting for years for Dad to come to his senses about getting married again. My mom died when I was only two, so I hardly even remember her, and—"

"Heather, your father and I've only just met," Sherry reminded her. "I'm afraid you're leaping to conclusions that could be embarrassing to both your father and me."

The girl's face fell. "You think so? It's just that I'm so anxious for Dad to find a wife. If he doesn't hurry up, I'll be, like, twenty before there're any more babies. In case you haven't guessed, I really like babies. Besides, it's not much fun being an only child." She hesitated and seemed to change her mind. "Sometimes it is, but sometimes it isn't. You know what I mean?"

Sherry would have answered, given the chance, but Heather immediately began speaking again.

"You like him, don't you?"

Sherry pushed the hair away from her face with both hands. She didn't need to look in a mirror to know her cheeks were aflame. "Your father's a very nice man, but as I said before—"

"Heather!" Cody boomed again.

"He wants me to leave you alone," Heather translated with a grimace. "But we'll have a chance to talk later, okay?"

"Uh...sure." Sherry was beginning to feel dizzy, as if she'd been caught up in a whirlwind and didn't know when she'd land—or where.

It was impossible not to like Cody's daughter. She was vibrant and refreshing and fun. And not the least bit timid.

"Great. I'll talk to you soon, then."

"Right."

Fifteen minutes later, Sherry walked down the stairs and into the kitchen. Cody and Heather were sitting at the table and a middle-aged woman with thick gray braids looped on top of her head smiled a warm welcome.

"Hello," Sherry said to the small gathering.

"Sherry, this is Janey," Cody said. "She does the cooking and housekeeping around here."

"Hi, Janey." Sherry nodded and noticed the eager look exchanged between Heather and the cook. Heather, it seemed, hadn't stopped smiling from the moment she'd discovered Sherry sleeping in her father's bed. The housekeeper looked equally pleased.

"Janey's been around forever," Heather said as she stretched one arm across the table to spear a hot pancake with her fork.

Janey chuckled in a good-natured way. "I'm a bit younger than Heather believes, but not by much. Now sit down and I'll bring you some cakes hot off the griddle."

Breakfast was delicious. Cody didn't contribute much to the conversation, not that Sherry blamed him. Anything he said would be open to speculation. A comment on the weather would no doubt send Heather into a soliloquy about summer being the perfect time of year for a wedding. The girl seemed determined to do whatever she could to arrange a marriage for her father. Sherry's presence only worsened the situation.

After they'd finished eating, Cody said he needed a few minutes to check with his men. Sherry took the opportunity to phone the Johnson ranch and see how Ellie and the baby were doing. She spoke to Luke, who said that everything was well in hand, especially since Ellie's mother had arrived that morning. Once again, he thanked Sherry for her help.

"You ready?" Cody asked when she hung up the phone.

"All set. Just let me say goodbye to Janey."

When Sherry walked into the yard a few minutes later, Cody was waiting for her. Heather had come with her, and the girl paused when she saw her father standing outside the pickup. "You aren't driving her back in that old thing, are you? Dad, that truck's disgusting."

"Yes, I am," Cody said in a voice that defied argument. It didn't stop Heather, however.

"But Sherry's *special*. Don't you want to take her in the Caddie?"

"It's fine, Heather," Sherry insisted, opening the door of the truck herself. Unfortunately she was six inches too short to boost herself into the cab. Cody's aid seemed to come grudgingly. Maybe he regretted not accepting Heather's advice about which car to drive, she thought.

Sherry waved to the girl as they pulled out of the yard. Heather, with a good deal of drama, crossed her hands over her heart and collapsed, as if struck by how very sweet romance could be. With some effort, Sherry controlled her amusement.

Cody's ranch was huge. They'd been driving silently for what seemed like miles and were still on his spread. She asked him a couple of questions about the Lucky Horseshoe, to which he responded with little more than a grunt. He was obviously a grouch when he didn't get a good night's sleep.

About ten minutes outside of town he cleared his throat as if he had something important to announce. "I hope you didn't take anything Heather said seriously."

"You mean about you making an honest woman out of me?"

He snorted. "Yes."

"No, of course I didn't."

"Good."

He sounded so relieved it was all she could do not to laugh.

"The kiss, too," he added, his forehead wrinkled in a frown.

"Kisses," she said, reminding him there'd been more than one.

Despite her restless sleep, Sherry hadn't given the matter much thought. She did so now, concluding that they'd both been exhausted and high on the emotional aftermath of the birth and the roles they'd each played in the small drama. In those circumstances, being attracted to each other was completely understandable. The kisses had been a celebration of the new life they'd helped usher into the world. There hadn't been anything sexual about them...had there?

"Let's call them a breach of good judgment," Cody suggested.

"All right." That wasn't how Sherry would've defined

them, but Cody seemed comfortable with the explanation—and pleased with her understanding.

They remained silent for the rest of the trip, and Sherry considered the situation. She found she agreed with him; their evening together had been like a moment out of time. Nevertheless, disappointment spread through her—almost as though she'd been standing on the brink of a great discovery and had suddenly learned it was all a hoax.

Her entire romantic career had followed a similar sorry pattern. Just when she thought perhaps she'd connected with her life's partner in Colby Winston, she'd realized she felt no great emotion for him. Certainly nothing like what Ellie had described.

Sherry knew precious little of love. Four years earlier, she'd watched the three Bloomfield sisters back home in Orchard Valley find love, all within the space of one short summer. Love had seemed explosive and chaotic. Valerie and Colby had both been caught unawares, fighting their attraction and each other. Sherry had stood by and watched the man she'd once seriously dated fall head over heels in love. She knew that this was what she wanted for herself.

Then Valerie's sister Steffie had returned from Italy. She and Charles were brought back together after a three-year separation and they, too, had seemed unprepared for the strength of their feelings. They were married only a few weeks after Valerie and Colby.

But the Bloomfield sister who'd surprised Sherry the most was Norah. They'd been schoolmates, sharing the same interests and often the same friends. Sherry couldn't help smiling whenever she thought of Norah and Rowdy. The lanky Texan millionaire hadn't known what hit him when he fell for Norah, and the funny thing was Norah hadn't, either. All of Orchard Valley had seemed to hold its collective breath awaiting the outcome of their romance. But Norah and Rowdy made the ideal couple, in Sherry's opinion. Nothing, outside of love, would have convinced Norah to leave Orchard Valley.

In the years since Norah had left Oregon, Sherry had been busy studying and working toward her degree, too absorbed in her goal to find time for relationships. But now she was ready. She wanted the love her friends had found, the excitement, the thrill of meeting that special someone. She wanted a man who felt about her the way Luke felt about Ellie. A man who'd look at her like Colby Winston looked at Valerie Bloomfield.

Cody brought the truck to a stop behind Sherry's car. Sherry unbuckled the seat belt and reached for her purse and medical bag.

"I really appreciate the ride," she said, holding out her hand for him to shake.

"You're welcome." He briefly took her hand, then leaped from the cab and came around to help her down. When his hands circled her waist, his eyes held hers. For the longest moment she didn't move, *couldn't* move, as if his touch had caused some strange paralysis. But when he shifted his gaze away, she placed her hands on his shoulders and allowed him to set her on the ground. As she met his eyes again, she saw surprise and a twinge of regret.

Cody eased away from her, and Sherry sensed that an invisible barrier had been erected between them. Irritation seemed to flicker through him. "I'm not going to apologize for kissing you last night," he said abruptly.

"But you regret it?"

"Yes, more now than before."

The harsh edge in his voice shocked her. "Why?" Her voice fell to a whisper.

"Because it's going to be difficult not to do it again." With that, he stalked back to the driver's side of the pickup, climbed in and roared off.

Sherry got into her car and drove the short distance to the clinic, parking in the small lot behind the building. When she walked in the front door, Mrs. Colson broke into a delighted smile. "Welcome back."

"Thanks. Ellie had a beautiful baby boy."

"So I heard. Word spreads fast around here. Ellie claims she'll never have another baby without you there. She thinks you're the best thing that's happened to Pepper since we voted in sewers last November."

Sherry laughed. "I don't suppose you've heard from Doc Lindsey?"

"Yes. He called this morning to see if everything was working out."

Sherry was relieved. At least the physician had some sense of responsibility. "I want to talk to him when he phones in again."

"No problem. He wants to talk to you, too. Apparently there's been a misunderstanding—you weren't scheduled to begin work for another two weeks."

"That's what I've been trying to tell everyone," Sherry said emphatically. "I made the mistake of driving through town, and everyone figured that because I was here I was starting right away."

Mrs. Colson fiddled with a folder from the file drawer, pulling out a sheet of paper and glancing through its contents. "Doc's right. It's in the contract, plain as day. So, why *are* you here so early?"

"I was just passing through on my way to Houston," she explained patiently—and not for the first time. "Mayor Bowie assumed I was here to stay and so did Doc. Before

I could stop him, he was out the door with his fishing pole in hand."

"You should've said something."

Sherry resisted the urge to scream. "I tried, but no one would listen."

"Well, Doc told me to tell you he'll be back in town sometime this afternoon. He says the fish don't bite this early in the season, anyway."

"I'll need to call my friends and tell them I'm going to be late," Sherry said. She hadn't had a chance to phone Norah yesterday, thanks to the events of the afternoon and evening.

"Sure, go right ahead."

Sherry decided to wait until she'd showered and changed clothes before she contacted Norah. It was midmorning before she felt human again.

"I'm in Pepper," Sherry explained once she had Norah on the line. "It's a long story, but I won't be able to leave until later this afternoon, which will put me in Houston late tomorrow."

"That's no problem," Norah was quick to assure her. "I'm so glad you're coming! I've missed you, Sherry."

"I've missed you, too."

"How do you like Texas so far?" Norah wanted to know.

Given Sherry's circumstances, it was an unfair question. "I haven't been here long enough to really form an opinion. But the natives seem friendly, and with a little practice I think I'll be able to pick up the language."

Norah chuckled. "Oh, Sherry, I am *so* looking forward to seeing you! Don't worry, I'm going to give you a crash course on the state and the people once you arrive. You're going to love it—just the way I do."

Sherry didn't comment on that. "How's Rowdy?" she said instead.

"Busy as ever. That man runs circles around me. So many people want his time and attention, but that's all right. It's me he comes home to every night, me he sits across the dinner table from and me he loves. He's such a good father and an even better husband."

"Val and Steffie send their love. Your dad, too."

"Talking to you makes me miss them even more. Rowdy promised we'd fly to Orchard Valley this fall, but I doubt my dad's going to wait that long. I half expect him to drop by for a visit before the end of the summer."

Sherry chuckled. "Well, at least I'll be there before he is."

"It wouldn't matter," Norah said. "You're welcome anytime."

Sherry felt a lot better after talking to her friend. But Norah sounded so happy she couldn't quite squelch a feeling of envy. Norah and Rowdy had two small children and were adopting two more. Norah had always been a natural with children. Sherry never did understand why her friend, with her affinity for kids, hadn't chosen pediatrics.

In an effort to help pass the time until Doc's arrival, Sherry read several medical journals in his office. When she looked up, it was well past noon.

Mrs. Colson stuck her head in the door, "Do you want me to order you some lunch?" she asked.

"No, thanks." Her impatience for Doc to get back had destroyed her appetite.

"I'm going to order a salad for myself. The Yellow Rose is real good about running it over here. You sure I can't talk you into anything?"

"I'm sure."

Donna Jo stopped off fifteen minutes later with a chef's salad and sat down on a chair in the reception area. Mrs. Colson was behind the counter, and Sherry was sitting on another chair with her purse and suitcase, ready to go. "The Cattlemen's Association's in town for lunch," Donna Jo told the receptionist, removing her shoe and massaging her sore foot. She eyed Sherry with the same curiosity she had a day earlier. "I hear you delivered Ellie's baby last night."

Word had indeed gotten around. Sherry nodded.

"You must've spent the night out there with her and Luke, because Mayor Bowie came into the café this morning looking for you. You weren't at the clinic."

"Actually, Cody Bailman drove me over to his house."

"You stayed the night at Cody's?" Donna Jo asked, her interest piqued. Mrs. Colson studied Sherry with undisguised interest.

"It was after two by the time I finished. I was exhausted, and so was Cody." She certainly didn't want these two getting the wrong impression. "Nothing happened. I mean, nothing that was, uh…" She gave up trying to find the right words. "Cody was a perfect gentleman."

"Isn't he always?" Donna Jo winked at Mrs. Colson.

"Is there something wrong with my spending the night at Cody's?"

"Not in the least," Mrs. Colson immediately said. "Cody's a gentleman."

"As much of a gentleman as any Texan gets," Donna Jo amended. "Martha, are you going to tell her, or am I?"

"Tell me what?" Sherry said.

Donna Jo and Mrs. Colson shared a significant look.

"What?" Sherry demanded again.

"I don't think so," Mrs. Colson said thoughtfully. "She'll find out soon enough on her own."

"Yeah." Donna Jo nodded. "You're right."

"*What* will I find out on my own?" Sherry tried a third time, but again her question was ignored.

"Martha here tells me you're bent on leaving town," the waitress said conversationally. "Stop in at the café on your way out and I'll pack you a lunch to take along. You might not be hungry now, but you will be later."

"Thanks, I'll do that."

Doc showed up around two that afternoon, looking tired and disgruntled. "I've been up since before dawn," he muttered. "It didn't make sense that I wasn't reeling in any fifteen-inchers until I realized it was too early in the month."

"I'll be back in less than two weeks," Sherry promised, "and next time the fish are sure to be biting."

"I hope so," Doc grumbled. "You might've said something about arriving early, you know."

Sherry nearly had to swallow her tongue to keep from reminding him that she'd done everything but throw herself in front of his truck to keep him from leaving.

She'd almost passed the café when she remembered her promise to Donna Jo and pulled to a stop. The waitress was right; she should take something to eat, as well as several cold sodas. Already it was unmercifully hot. She grinned, remembering Donna Jo's remark that the locals who escaped to Colorado for the summer weren't real Texans. Apparently folks were supposed to stay in Texas and suffer.

The café was nearly empty. Sherry took a seat at the counter and reached for the menu.

"What'll you have?" Donna Jo asked.

"Let's see… A turkey sandwich with tomato and lettuce, a bag of chips and three diet sodas, all to go."

Donna Jo went into the kitchen to tell the chef. When she came back out her eyes brightened. "Howdy, Cody."

"Howdy." Cody slipped onto the stool next to Sherry's and ordered coffee.

"Hi," he said, edging up his Stetson with his index finger as if to get a better look at her.

"Hi." It was silly to feel shy with him, but Sherry did. A little like she had in junior high when Wayne Pierce, the boy she'd had a crush on, sat next to her in the school lunchroom. Her mouth went dry and she felt incapable of making conversation.

"I was wondering if I'd run into you this afternoon."

"Cody's in town for the local cattlemen's meeting," Donna Jo explained as she placed a beige ceramic mug full of steaming coffee in front of Cody.

"Doc's back," Sherry said, although she wasn't certain he understood the significance of that. "He said the fishing was terrible, but then, it generally is about now."

He shrugged. "You're having a rather late lunch, aren't you?"

Donna Jo set a brown paper bag on the counter along with the tab. "I was planning to eat on the road," Sherry said, thanking Donna Jo with a smile. She slipped her purse strap over her shoulder and opened the zipper to take out her wallet.

A frown appeared on Cody's face. "You're leaving?"

"For Houston."

His frown deepened. "So soon?"

"I'll be back in a couple of weeks." She slid off the stool and was surprised when Cody slapped a dollar bill and some coins on the counter and followed her to the register.

"Actually I was hoping to talk to you," he said, holding open the café door.

"Oh?" She headed for her car.

Cody continued to follow. "Yeah, it's about what I said this morning." His eyes refused to meet hers. "I was thinking about it on my way back to the ranch, and I realized I must've sounded pretty arrogant about the whole thing."

"I didn't notice," Sherry said. It was a lie, but only a small one. She found it charming that he wanted to correct the impression he'd made.

"It's just that Heather's on this marriage kick...."

"We both agreed it was a lapse in judgment," she told him. "Let's just forget it ever happened."

He jammed his fingers into his pockets as Sherry opened her car door. "I wish I could," he said so low Sherry wasn't sure she'd heard him accurately.

"Pardon?" she said, looking up at him and making a feeble attempt at a smile.

"Nothing," he said gruffly. "I didn't say anything."

"You wish you could what?" she pressed.

He glanced away, and his wide shoulders heaved with a labored sigh. "I wish I could forget!" he said forcefully. "There. Are you happy now?"

"No." She shook her head. "I'm confused."

"So am I. I like you, Sherry. I don't know why, but I do, and I don't mind telling you it scares the living daylights out of me. The last time I was this attracted to a woman I was—" he rubbed the side of his jaw "—a heck of a lot younger than I am now. And you're leaving."

"But I'll be back." The rush to get to Houston at the earliest possible moment left her. Nothing appealed to her more right now than exploring what was happening between her and Cody Bailman.

"But you won't be back for two weeks." He made it sound like an eternity. His face tightened. "By the time you're back it won't be the same."

"We don't know that."

"I do," he said with certainty.

Sherry was torn. "Are you asking me to stay?"

His nostrils flared at the question. "No," he said emphatically, and then more softly, "No." He moved a step closer. "Aw, what the hell," he muttered crossly. He reached for her, slipped his arm around her waist, pulled her toward him— and kissed her.

At last he drew back and sighed. "There," he said, his breath warm against her face. "Now go, before I make an even bigger fool of myself."

But Sherry wasn't sure she was capable of moving, let alone driving several hundred miles. She blinked and tried to catch her breath.

"Why'd you do that?" she demanded.

"Darned if I know," Cody admitted, sounding none too pleased with himself.

Sherry understood his consternation when she glanced around her. It seemed the entire town of Pepper, Texas, had stopped in midmotion to stare at them. A couple of men loitering outside the hardware store were watching them. Several curious faces filled the window at the Yellow Rose, including Donna Jo's. The waitress, in fact, looked downright excited and gave Sherry a thumbs-up.

"We've done it now," Cody said, scowling at her as if she were to blame. "Everyone's going to be talking."

"I'd like to remind you I wasn't the one who started this."

"Yeah, but you sure enjoyed it."

"Well, this is just fine, isn't it," she said, glad for an excuse to be on her way. "I'm outta here." Tossing her lunch bag onto the passenger seat, she slipped inside the car.

"Sherry, blast it, don't leave yet!"

"Why? What else have you got planned?"

"Okay, okay, I shouldn't have kissed you, I'll be the first

to agree." He rubbed his hand along the back of his neck. "As I said before, I like you."

"You have a funny way of showing it."

He closed his eyes and nodded. "I've already made a mess of this, and I haven't even known you for a whole day. Listen, in two weeks Pepper's going to hold its annual picnic and dance. Will you be there?" He gave her the date and the time.

She hesitated, then nodded.

"If we still feel the same way, then we'll know this has a chance," he said. He spun on his heel and walked away.

# Four

"What can I tell you about Texas?" Norah asked Sherry as they sat by the swimming pool in the yard behind her sprawling luxury home. Both three-year-old Jeff and baby Grace were napping, and Norah and Sherry were spending a leisurely afternoon soaking up the sun. "Texas is oil wells, cattle and cotton. It's grassy plains and mountains."

"And desert," Sherry added.

"That, too. Texas is chicken-fried steak, black-eyed peas and hot biscuits and gravy. Actually, I've discovered," Norah said with a grin, "that most Texans will eat just about anything. They've downed so many chili peppers over the years that they've burned out their taste buds."

"I've really come to love this state." Sherry sipped from her glass of iced tea. "Everyone's so friendly."

"It's known as the Lone Star state, but a lot of folks call it the Friendship state, too."

That didn't surprise Sherry.

"The men are hilarious," Norah continued, her eyes dancing with silent laughter. "Oh, they don't mean to be, but I swear they've got some of the craziest ideas about…well, practically everything. To give you an example, they have this sort of unwritten code, which has to do with *real* Texans versus everyone else in the world. A real Texan would or wouldn't do any number of things."

"Such as?"

"Well, a real Texan believes in law and order, except when the law insists on a fifty-five-mile-an-hour speed limit. They consider that unreasonable. And clothes… A real Texan wouldn't dream of decorating his Stetson with feathers or anything else, with the possible exception of a snake band, but only if he'd killed the snake and tanned the skin himself. And the jeans! I swear they refuse to wash them—they wear 'em until they can stand up on their own."

Sherry laughed. She'd run into a few of those types herself on her journey across the vast state. But no one could compete with the characters she'd met in Pepper. Mayor Bowie, Donna Jo and Billy Bob. The way that man had manipulated her into staying in town!

And Cody Bailman… He kept drifting into her mind, although she'd made numerous attempts to keep him out. She'd tried hard to forget their last meeting, when he'd kissed her in broad daylight in front of half the town. But nothing helped. Cody Bailman was in her head day and night. It didn't seem possible that a man she'd known for such a short while—

"Sherry."

Sherry looked up and realized Norah was waving a hand in front of her face. "You're in another world."

"Sorry, I was just thinking about, uh, the folks back in Pepper."

"More than likely it's that cattleman you were telling me about."

Sherry lowered her gaze again, not surprised Norah had

read her so easily. "I can't stop thinking about him. I thought that once I was with you, I'd be able to get some perspective on what happened between us. Not that anything really did—happen, I mean. Good heavens, I was only in town for about twenty-four hours."

"You like him, don't you?"

"That's just it," Sherry said, reaching for her drink and gripping it tightly. "I'm not sure how I feel about him. It's all messed up. I don't know Cody well enough to have an opinion, and yet..."

"And yet, you find yourself thinking about him, wishing you could be with him and missing him. All of this seems impossible because until a few days ago he wasn't even in your life."

"Yes," Sherry returned, astonished at the way Norah could clarify her thoughts. "That's *exactly* what I'm feeling."

"I thought so." Norah relaxed against the cushion on the patio chair and sighed, lifting her face to the sun. "That's how it was with me after Rowdy was released from the hospital and went home to Texas. My life felt so empty without him. He'd only been in the hospital a couple of weeks, but it seemed as if my whole world revolved around him."

"Rowdy, fortunately, felt the same way about you," Sherry said, knowing Cody was as perplexed as she was by the attraction *they* shared.

"Not at first," Norah countered. "I amused him, and being stuck in traction with that broken leg, the poor guy was desperate for some comic relief. I happened to be handy. Being Valerie's sister added to my appeal. You know, he actually came to Orchard Valley to break up her engagement to Colby! I don't think it was until much later that he fell in love with me—later than he's willing to admit now, at any rate."

"Don't be so sure." Sherry still remembered the chaos

Rowdy Cassidy had brought into the tidy world of Orchard Valley General. His plane had crashed in a nearby field and he'd been taken, seriously injured, to Emergency. He'd been a terrible patient—demanding and cantankerous. Only one nurse could handle him…. Sherry had known he was in love with Norah long before he'd ever left the hospital, even if he wasn't aware of it himself. Norah's feelings had been equally clear to her. It seemed she could judge another's emotions better than her own.

"I'm sorry, in a way, that you took this position in Pepper," Norah said. "I know it's pure selfishness on my part, but I was hoping if you moved to Texas you'd settle closer to Houston."

"I don't think I realized how large this state is. Central Texas didn't look that far from Houston on the map. I found out differently when I had to drive it."

"I wish you'd taken the time to stop in San Antonio. Rowdy took me there for our first anniversary, and we fell in love all over again. Of course, it might've had something to do with the flagstone walks, the marvelous boutiques and the outdoor cafés." Norah sighed longingly at the memory.

"It sounds wonderful."

"It was," Norah said wistfully. "We rode in a river taxi down the San Antonio River and…oh, I swear it was the most romantic weekend we've ever spent."

"I'll make a point of visiting San Antonio soon," Sherry said.

"Don't go alone," Norah insisted. "It's a place for lovers."

"Okay. I'll make sure I'm crazy in love before I make any traveling plans."

"Good." Norah gave a satisfied nod.

Rowdy returned home from the office earlier than usual with wonderful news. He and Norah were hoping to adopt two small children who'd been orphaned the year before. Because of some legal difficulties, the adoption had been held up in the courts.

"Looks like we're going to be expanding our family shortly," Rowdy said, kissing Norah before taking the chair next to her and reaching for her hand.

Sherry found it almost painful to see these two people so deeply in love. It reminded her how alone she was, how isolated her life had become as more and more of her friends got married and started families. Sherry felt like someone on the outside looking in.

"Grace's new tooth broke through this afternoon," Norah told Rowdy after she'd poured him a glass of iced tea.

"This I've got to see," he said, getting up and heading toward the house.

"Rowdy," Norah called after him. "Let her sleep. She was fussy most of the afternoon."

"I thought I'd take her and Jeff swimming."

"Yes, but wait until they wake up from their naps." Norah smiled at Sherry. "Sometimes I think Rowdy's nothing more than a big kid himself. He's looking for someone to play with."

"He's wonderful. I could almost be jealous."

"There's no need," Norah said, squeezing Sherry's arm. "Your turn's coming, and I think it's going to be sooner than you expect."

"I hope so," Sherry said, but she didn't have any faith in her friend's prediction.

"Sherry," Rowdy said, turning back from the house. "I did a bit of checking on that cattleman you mentioned the other night." He removed a slip of paper from his inside pocket. "Cody James Bailman," he read, "born thirty-five years ago, married at twenty-one, widowed, one daughter named Heather. Owns a ten-thousand-acre spread outside Pepper. He was elected president of the local Cattlemen's Association three years running."

"That's it?" Norah asked.

"He raises quarter horses, as well as cattle."

That didn't tell Sherry much more than she already knew.

"He seems like a decent guy. I spoke to a man who's known Bailman for several years and he thinks highly of him. If you want my advice, I say marry the fellow and see what happens."

"Rowdy!" Norah chastised.

"That's what we did, and everything worked out, didn't it?"

"Circumstances are just a tad different, dear," Norah said, glancing apologetically toward Sherry.

"Marriage would do them both good," Rowdy continued. He turned to Sherry and nodded as if the decision had already been made. "Marry the man."

"Marry the man." As Sherry drove toward Pepper several days later, Rowdy's words clung to her mind. Cody's parting words returned to haunt her, as well. *If we still feel the same way, then we'll know this has a chance.* But what could have changed in their two weeks apart? What could they possibly have learned?

Because of a flat tire fifty miles on the other side of nowhere, followed by a long delay at a service station, Sherry was much later than she'd hoped. In fact, she was going to miss part of the scheduled festivities, including the parade. But with any luck she'd be in town before the dance started.

She'd tried phoning Cody's ranch several times on her cell, but there hadn't been any answer. No doubt everyone was enjoying the community celebration. With nothing left to do, she drove on, not stopping for lunch, until she arrived in Pepper.

The town had put on its best dress for this community event. A banner reading "Pepper Days" was stretched across Main Street. The lampposts were decorated with a profusion of wildfowers, and red, white and blue crepe paper was strung from post to post.

Several brightly painted cardboard signs directed her to the city park and the barbecue. As soon as she turned off Main and onto Spruce, Sherry smelled the enticing aroma of mesquite and roasting beef. Various signs sent participants and onlookers to the far end of the park, where a chili cook-off was in progress. Sherry was fortunate to find a parking space on a side street. Country music blared from loudspeakers, and colorful Chinese lanterns dotted the cottonwood trees.

People were milling around the park, and Sherry didn't recognize anyone. She would've liked to freshen up before meeting Cody, but she was already late and didn't want to take the time. Besides, her calf-length denim skirt, cowboy boots and Western shirt with a white fringe were perfect for the festivities. The skirt and shirt had been a welcome-to-Texas gift from Norah.

"Sherry!"

She whirled around to see Cody's daughter waving and racing toward her. Not quite prepared for the impact as Heather flung herself at her, Sherry nearly toppled backward.

"I knew you'd come! I never doubted, not even for a second. Have you seen my dad yet?"

"No, I just got here."

"He didn't think you were going to come. Men are like that, you know. It's all a way to keep from being disappointed, don't you think?"

But Cody's attitude disappointed Sherry. "I said I'd be here."

"I know, but Dad didn't have a lot of faith that you'd show up. I did, though. Do you like my hair?" Heather looked extremely pretty with her thick dark hair loose and curling down her back. She whipped back the curls and tossed her head as if she were doing a shampoo commercial. She gazed up at Sherry, her eyes wide and guileless; she'd probably practiced the look in front of the bathroom mirror—something Sherry had done herself as a teenager. "Come on, let's go find my father," Heather said urgently.

It didn't take long for Sherry to spot Cody. He was talking to a group of men who were gathered in a circle. Their discussion seemed to be a heated one, and Sherry guessed the topic was politics. Not until she got closer did she realize they were contesting the pros and cons of adding jalapeño peppers to Billy Bob's barbecue sauce.

"They're just neighbors," Heather whispered as they approached. "Dad can talk to them anytime."

Unwilling to interrupt him, Sherry stopped the girl's progress.

"But this could go on for hours!" Heather protested, apparently loudly enough for her father to hear, because at that moment he turned and saw them.

His eyes moved from his daughter to Sherry, and he couldn't seem to believe she was really there. He excused himself to his friends and began walking toward her.

"Hello, Cody." The words seemed to stick in Sherry's throat.

"I didn't think you were going to come," he said.

"I had a flat tire on the way, and it took ages to repair. I phoned, but I guess everyone at the Lucky Horseshoe had already left for the picnic."

"Are you hungry?"

"Starved," she said.

Cody pulled a wad of bills from his pocket, peeled off several and handed them to Heather. "Bring Sherry a plate of the barbecue beef."

"But, Dad, I wanted to talk to her and—"

Cody silenced the protest with a single look.

"All right, I get it. You want to be alone with her. How long should I stay away?" The question was posed with an elaborate sigh. "An hour? Two?"

"We'll be under the willow tree," Cody said, ignoring her questions and pointing to an enormous weeping willow about fifty feet away.

"The willow tree," Heather repeated, lowering her voice suggestively. "Good choice, Dad. I couldn't have thought of a better place myself."

Cody gave a sigh of relief as Heather trotted off. "You'll have to forgive my daughter," he said, shaking his head. Then he smiled. "She was as eager for you to return as I was."

His words and smile went a long way toward reassuring Sherry. Their separation had felt like a lifetime to her. Two weeks away from a man she'd known only briefly; it didn't make sense. And yet, she couldn't deny how she felt.

All at once Sherry felt scared. Scared of all the feelings crowding inside her. Scared of being with Cody again, of kissing him again, of making more of this attraction than he intended or wanted. Her feelings were powerful, alien. At first she'd attributed them to being with Norah and Rowdy and seeing how happy they were.

Now here she was with Cody, sitting under the shadowy arms of a weeping willow, and her confusion returned a hundredfold. This man affected her in a thousand indescribable ways, but she was worried; she wasn't sure her feelings were because of Cody himself. Maybe it was the exciting promise he represented. The happiness waiting for her just around the corner, just out of reach. She desperately wanted the joy her friends had found. She was tired of being alone, tired of walking into an empty apartment. She wanted a husband, a home and a family. Was that so much to ask?

Cody spread out a blanket for them to sit on. "How were your friends?"

"Very much in love." It wasn't what Sherry had meant to say, but the first thing that sprang to her lips. She looked away, embarrassed.

"Newlyweds?"

"No." She shook her head. "They've been married four years and have two children. In a few weeks they'll be adding two adopted kids to the family."

"They sound like a compassionate, generous couple."

His words warmed her heart like a July sun. Rowdy and Norah *were* two of the most generous people Sherry had ever known. It was as if they were so secure in their love for each other that it spilled over and flowed out to those around them.

"What's wrong?"

This man seemed to sense her thoughts and emotions so accurately that nothing less than the truth would do. "I'm scared to death of seeing you again, of feeling the way I feel about you. I don't even *know* you, and I feel… That's just it, I don't know what I feel."

He laughed. "You're not alone. I keep telling myself this whole thing is nuttier than a pecan grove. I don't really know you, either. Why you, out of all the women I've met over the years?"

"I'm not interrupting anything, am I?" Heather burst

through the hanging branches and stepped onto the blanket. She crossed her legs and slowly lowered herself to the ground before handing Sherry a plate heaped high with potato salad, barbecued chicken and one of the biggest dill pickles Sherry had ever seen.

Heather tilted her head to one side. "They've run out of beef. I told Mayor Bowie this was for Sherry, and he wanted me to ask you to save a dance for him. He's been cooking all afternoon, and he says he's looking forward to seeing a pretty face, instead of a pot of Billy Bob's barbecue sauce."

"This smells heavenly," Sherry said, taking the plate and digging in.

Cody looked pointedly at his daughter, expecting her to make herself scarce, but she looked back at him just as pointedly. "So, have you come to any conclusions?" Heather asked.

"No. But then we haven't had much time *alone,* have we?"

"You've had enough."

Cody closed his eyes. "Heather, please."

"Are you going to ask Sherry to dance, or are you going to wait for Mayor Bowie to steal her away from you? Dad, you can't be so nonchalant about this business. Aren't you the one who says the early bird catches the worm? You know Mayor Bowie likes Sherry."

"The mayor's a married man."

"So?" Heather said, seeming to enjoy their exchange. "That didn't stop Russell Forester from running off with Milly You-Know-Who."

If the color in his neck was any indication, Cody's frustration level was reaching its peak. But Sherry welcomed the intrusion. She needed space and time to sort through her reactions, her feelings. Everything had become so intense so quickly. If Heather hadn't interrupted them when she had, Sherry was certain she would've been in Cody's arms—although it was too soon to cloud their feelings with sexual awareness.

"The chicken's delicious," Sherry said, licking her fingers clean of the spicy sauce. "I don't think I've ever tasted any as good as this."

"Cody Bailman, are you hiding Sherry under that tree with you?" The toes of a pair of snakeskin boots stepped on the outer edges of the blanket just under the tree's protective foliage.

Heather cast her father a righteous look and whispered heatedly, "I *told* you Mayor Bowie was going to ask her first."

Cody stood and parted the willow's hanging branches. "She's eating."

"Howdy, Mayor," Sherry said, smiling up at him, a chicken leg poised in front of her mouth. "I understand you're the chef responsible for this feed. You can cook for me anytime."

"I'm not a bad dancer, either. I thought I'd see if you wouldn't mind taking a spin with an old coot like me."

She laughed. "You're not so old."

"What'll your wife think?" Cody asked, his tone jocular, but with an underlying...what? Annoyance? Jealousy? Sherry wasn't sure.

Pepper's mayor waved his hand dismissively. "Hazel won't care. Good grief, I've been married to the woman for thirty-seven years. Besides, she's talking to her friends, and you know how that bunch loves to idle away an afternoon gossiping. I thought I'd give them something to talk about."

"Sherry?" Cody glanced at her as if he expected her to decline.

Frankly, Sherry was flattered to have two men vying for her attention, even if one of them was old enough to be her father and looked as if he'd sampled a bit too much of his own cooking over the years.

"Why, Mayor, I'd be delighted."

Cody didn't look pleased.

"I told you this was going to happen," Heather reminded him indignantly. "Your problem, Dad, is that you never listen to me. I read romance novels. I know about these things."

A laugh hovered on Sherry's lips. She hoisted herself up and accepted Mayor Bowie's hand as he led her to the dancing platform.

Cody and Heather followed close behind. Because Mayor Bowie was chatting, she couldn't quite hear the conversation between father and daughter, but it seemed to her that Heather was still chastising Cody.

Although it was early in the evening, the dance floor was crowded. Willie Nelson was crooning a melodic ballad as the mayor deftly escorted Sherry onto the large black-and-white-checkered platform. He placed one hand at her waist and held her arm out to one side, then smoothly led her across the floor.

"How're you doin', Sherry?" a woman asked.

She turned to see Donna Jo dancing with the sheriff. Sherry waved with her free hand. Doc Lindsey danced briskly by with Mrs. Colson, first in one direction and then another.

Mayor Bowie was surprisingly light on his feet, and he whirled Sherry around so many times she started to get dizzy. When the dance ended, she looked up to find Cody standing beside the mayor.

"I believe this dance is mine," he said.

"Of course." The mayor gracefully stepped aside and turned to Heather. Bowing, he asked the giggling twelve-year-old for the pleasure of the next dance.

Heather cast Sherry a proud look and responded with a dignified curtsy.

"So, we meet again," Sherry said, slipping her left arm onto Cody's shoulder.

"You should've danced with me first," he muttered.

"Why?" She wasn't sure she approved of his tone or his attitude. Mayor Bowie certainly couldn't be seen as competition!

"If you had, you would've spared me a lecture from my daughter. She seems to be doing research on romance, and apparently I've committed several blunders. According to Heather, my tactics aren't sophisticated enough." He made a wry grimace.

Sherry couldn't help noticing that they were doing little more than shuffling their feet, while other couples whirled around them. Cody seemed to notice it, too, and exhaled sharply.

"That's another thing," he said. "My own daughter suggested I take dance lessons." He snorted. "Me, as if I have time for that kind of nonsense. Listen, if you want to date a man who's good at this, you better know right now it isn't me."

Sherry had already figured that out for herself, not that it mattered. Cody sighed again.

"Is something else bothering you?" Sherry asked.

"Yes," he admitted grudgingly. "You feel good in my arms. I'm probably breaking some romance code by telling you that. Darned if I know what a man's supposed to say and what he isn't."

Sherry closed her eyes. "That was very sweet."

Cody was silent for the next few minutes. "What about you?" he asked gruffly.

Sherry pulled back enough so he could read the question in her eyes. His own were dark and troubled.

"It'd help if you told me the same thing," he said. "That you...like being with me, too." He shook his head. "I've got to tell you, I feel silly."

"I do enjoy being with you."

He didn't seem to hear. "I feel like I'm on display for everyone to inspect."

"Why's that?"

He looked away, but not before she saw his frown. "Let me just say that kissing you in public didn't improve the situation. It was the most asinine thing I've ever done in my life. I made a fool of myself in front of the entire town."

"I wouldn't say that," she whispered, close to his ear. "I liked it."

"That's the problem," he grunted. "So did I. You know what I think? This is all Heather's doing. It started with that crazy project of hers. I swear the kid's going to ruin me."

"Heather's project?"

"Forget I said that."

"Why are you so angry? Is it because I danced with the mayor?"

"Good heavens, no. This has nothing to do with that."

"Then what *does* it have to do with?"

"You," he grumbled.

Dolly Parton's tremulous tones were coming out of the speakers now. It was a fast-paced number, not that Cody noticed. He didn't alter his footwork, but continued his laborious two-step.

"Cody, maybe we should sit down."

"We can't."

"Why not?" she asked.

"Because the minute we do, someone else is gonna ask you to dance, and I can't allow that."

She stared up at him, more confused by the moment. "Why not? Cody, you're being ridiculous."

"I don't need you to tell me that. I've been ridiculous ever since I saw you holding Ellie's baby in your arms. I've been behaving like a lovesick idiot from the first time I kissed you. I can understand what caused a normally sane, sensible man like Luke Johnson to chase after a sports car on his horse because he couldn't stand to let the woman he loved leave town. And dammit, I don't like it. Not one bit."

What had first sounded rather romantic was fast losing its appeal. "I don't like what I feel for you, either, Cody Bailman. I had a perfectly good life until you barged in."

"So did I!"

"I think we should stop while we're ahead," she murmured, pulling away from him. "Before we say something we'll regret." She dropped her arms to her sides and stared up at him.

"Great," he said. "Let's just do that."

With so many couples whirling about, Sherry found it difficult to make her way off the dance floor, but she managed. To her consternation, Cody followed close behind.

Catching sight of Ellie beneath the shade of an oak tree, Sherry hurried in that direction, determined to ignore Cody. She was halfway across the park when she heard him call after her.

"Sherry! Wait up!"

She didn't bother to turn around to see what had detained

him. When she reached Ellie, the woman smiled up at her brightly.

"I see you've just tangled with the most stubborn man this side of Luke Johnson."

# *Five*

"Cody infuriates me," Sherry announced, sinking down next to Ellie Johnson on the blanket under the tree. She wrapped her arms around her knees and sighed in frustration.

"Men have infuriated women since the dawn of time. They're totally irrational beings," Ellie said calmly while patting her infant son's back. Philip was sleeping contentedly against her shoulder.

"Irrational isn't the word for it. They're *insane.*"

"That, too," Ellie agreed readily.

"No one but Cody could use a compliment to insult someone!"

"Luke did when we first started dating," Ellie told her. "He'd say things like 'You're not bad-looking for a skinny girl.'"

Despite her annoyance with Cody, Sherry laughed.

Cody had been waylaid by Luke, Sherry noticed. Luke carried Christina Lynn on his shoulders, and the toddler's arms were reaching toward the sky in an apparent effort to touch the fluffy clouds. Sherry hoped Ellie's husband was giving Cody a few pointers about relationships.

Forcing her thoughts away from the men, Sherry sighed again and watched Ellie with her baby son. Philip had awoken and she turned him in her arms, draped a receiving blanket over her shoulder, then bared her breast.

"He's thriving," Ellie said happily. "I can't thank you enough for being with me the night he was born. Having you there made all the difference in the world."

"It wasn't me doing all the work," Sherry reminded her.

"Then let's just say we make an excellent team." Ellie stroked her son's face with her index finger as he nursed greedily. "I'm really glad you're going to live in Pepper. I feel like you're a friend already."

Sherry glanced up to see Heather marching toward them, hands on hips. Her eyes were indignant as she stopped and talked briefly to her father and Luke before flinging her arms in the air and striding over to Ellie and Sherry.

"What did he do *now?*" Cody's daughter demanded. "He said something stupid, right?" In a display of complete disgust, she slapped her sides. Then she lowered herself to the blanket. "I tried to coach him, but a lot of good that did." She eyed her father angrily. "No wonder he never remarried. The man obviously needs more help than I can give him."

Ellie and Sherry exchanged a smile. "Don't try so hard, Heather," Ellie said.

"But I want Dad to remarry so I can have a baby brother or sister. Or one of each."

"Heather," Sherry began, "your father said something about a project you were involved in, and then he immediately seemed to regret mentioning it."

"He's never gonna let me forget it, either," the girl muttered. "Neither is anyone else in town."

"You have to admit, it *was* rather amusing," Ellie added.

"Oh, sure, everyone got a big laugh out of it."

"Out of what?" Sherry wanted to know.

"My 4-H project. I've been a member for a few years and every spring we work on one project for the next twelve months. One year I raised rabbits, and another year I worked with my horse, Misty. This spring I gave the whole town a big laugh when I decided my project was going to be helping my dad find a wife."

"You weren't serious!" Sherry was mortified.

"I was at the time, but now I can see it wasn't a great idea," Heather continued. "Anyway, everyone talked about it for days. That's one of the worst things about living in a small town. Dad was furious with me, which didn't help."

"That's why you were so excited when you met me," Sherry said in a thoughtful voice.

"You're darn right, especially when I found you sleeping in Dad's bed."

Sherry shot a glance at Ellie and felt her face grow warm. "Cody slept in the guest room."

"My friend Carrie Whistler spent the night before at my place, and I was supposed to change the sheets, but I forgot," Heather explained to Ellie, then turned her attention back to Sherry. "You're just perfect for Dad, and I was hoping you might grow to, you know, love him. You'd make a terrific mother."

Sherry felt tears burn the backs of her eyes. "I don't think anyone's ever paid me a higher compliment, Heather, but love doesn't work that way. I'm sorry. I can't marry your father just because you want a baby brother or sister."

"But you like him, don't you?"

"Yes, but—"

"Until he said something stupid and ruined everything." Heather's face tensed.

"Why don't you let those two figure things out for themselves?" Ellie suggested to the girl. "Your interference will only cause problems."

"But Dad won't get anything right without me!"

"He married your mother, didn't he?" Ellie reminded her. "It seems to me he'll do perfectly well all on his own."

"I *like* Sherry, though. Better than anyone, and Dad does, too. His problem is he thinks love's a big waste of time. He told me he wanted to cut to the chase and be done with it."

"He said that?" Sherry glared over at him. Cody must have sensed it, because he looked at her and grimaced at the intensity of her expression. He said something to Luke, who turned their way, too. Luke's shoulders lifted in a shrug. Then he slapped Cody's back and the two of them headed in the direction of the cook-off area.

"He said he's too busy with the ranch to date anyone or to bother with what he calls 'hearts-and-flowers' stuff."

Sherry felt like a complete fool for having constructed this wild romantic fantasy in her mind. Cody had never been interested in her. From the very first, he'd been trying to mollify his daughter. Sherry had just appeared on the scene at a convenient moment. She felt sick to her stomach. This was what happened when she allowed herself to believe in romance, to believe in love. It seemed so easy for her friends, but it wasn't for her.

"I've had a long day," Sherry said, suddenly feeling weary. "I think I'll go unpack my bags, soak in the tub and make an early night of it."

"You can't!" Heather protested. "I signed you and Dad up for the three-legged race, the egg toss and the water-balloon toss. They have the races in the evening because it's too hot in the afternoon."

"I doubt that your father wants me as a partner."

"But he does," Heather insisted. "He's won the egg toss for years and years, and it's really important to him. It's one of those ego things."

"Unfortunately, he's already got egg on his face," Sherry muttered to Ellie, who laughed outright.

"Please stay," Heather begged. "Please, please, please. If you don't, I can't see myself ever forgiving Dad for ruining this opportunity."

Sherry was beginning to understand Cody's frustration with his daughter. "Heather, don't play matchmaker. It'll do more harm than good. If your father's genuinely interested in dating me, he'll do so without you goading him into it. Promise me you'll stay out of this."

Heather looked at the ground and her pretty blue eyes grew sad. "It's just that I like you so much and we could have lots of fun together."

"We certainly don't need your father for that."

"We don't?"

"Trust me," Ellie inserted, "a man would only get in the way."

"Would you go shopping for school clothes with me? I mean, to a real town with a mall that's got more than three stores, and spend the day with me?"

"I'd love it."

Heather lowered her eyes again, then whispered, "I need help with bras and...and other stuff."

Sherry smiled. "We'll drive into Abilene and make a day of it."

Heather's eyes lit up like sparklers. "That'd be great!"

"So, I'll leave you to partner your dad on the egg toss."

The glimmer in her eyes didn't fade. "I was thinking the same thing." She looked mischievous. "This could be the year Dad loses his title as the egg champion."

"Heather," Sherry chastised, "be nice to your father."

"Oh, I will," she promised, "especially since you and I have reached an understanding."

"Good. Then I'm heading over to the clinic now."

"You're *sure* you won't stay? There's a fireworks display tonight. It's even better than the one we had on the Fourth."

"I think Sherry's seen all the fireworks she needs for one night," Ellie put in.

"You're right, I have. We'll talk soon, Heather. Bye, Ellie." She leaned over and kissed the top of Philip's head. "Let's make a point of getting together in the next little while."

"I'd like that," Ellie said.

Sherry was halfway back to her car when Cody caught up with her. He fell into step beside her. "I didn't mean to offend you," he said.

Sherry sighed and closed her eyes. "I know."

"But you're still mad?"

"No. Discouraged, perhaps, but not mad." She arrived at her car and unlocked it. "I talked to Heather and she told me about her 4-H project. It explained a lot."

"Like what?"

"Like why you're interested in me. Why you chose to drive me to the ranch instead of town after Ellie's baby was born."

"That had nothing to do with it! We were both dog-tired, and my place was a lot closer than town."

"You don't need to worry," Sherry said, unwilling to get involved in another debate with him. She was truly weary and not in the best of moods, fighting the heat, disappointment and the effects of an undernourished romantic heart. "I had a nice chat with Heather. You've done a wonderful job raising her, Cody. She's a delightful girl. Unless you object, I'd like to be her friend. She and I have already made plans to go clothes-shopping in Abilene."

"Of course I don't object."

"Thank you." She slipped inside her car and started the engine. She would've driven away, but Cody prevented her from closing the door.

He frowned darkly. "I don't mean to be obtuse, but what does all this mean?"

"Nothing, really. I'm just…cutting to the chase," she said. "I'm explaining that it isn't necessary for you to play out this charade any longer."

"What charade?"

"Of being attracted to me."

"I *am* attracted to you."

"But you wish you weren't."

He opened and closed his mouth twice before he answered. "I should've known you'd throw that back in my face. You're right. I don't have time for courtin' and buying flowers and the like. I've got a ranch to run, and this is one of the busiest months of the year."

Sherry blinked, not sure what to make of Cody. He seemed sincere about not meaning to offend her, and yet he constantly said and did things that infuriated her.

"The problem is," Cody continued, still frowning, "if I don't stake my claim on you now, there'll be ten other ranchers all vying for your attention."

*"Stake your claim?"* He made her sound like an acre of water-rich land.

"You know," he said. "Let everyone in town see you're my woman."

"I'm not *any* man's woman."

"Not yet, but I'd like you to think about being mine." He removed his hat; Sherry guessed that meant he intended her to take him seriously. "If you'd be willing to run off and get married, then—"

"Then *what?*"

"Then we'd be done with it. See, like I said, I don't have the time or energy to waste on courtin' a woman."

Sherry nodded slowly, all the while chewing the inside of her cheek to keep from saying something she'd wish she hadn't. So much for romance! So much for sipping champagne and feeding each other chocolate-covered strawberries in the moonlight, a fantasy she'd had for years. Or a romantic weekend in San Antonio, the way Norah had described. No wonder Heather was frustrated with her father. The girl must feel as if she was smacking her head against a brick wall.

"Well?" Cody demanded.

Sherry stared at him. "Are you kidding me?"

"Of course not! I meant every word." He paused to take a deep breath. "I like you. You like me. What else is there? Sure, we can spend the next few months going through all those ridiculous courtin' rituals or we can use the common sense God gave us and be done with this romance nonsense."

"And do what?" Sherry asked innocently.

"Get married, of course. I haven't stopped thinking about you in two weeks. You didn't stop thinking about me, either. I saw it in your eyes no more'n an hour ago. You know what it's like when we kiss. Instead of playing games with each other, why not admit you want me as much as I want you? I never did understand why women always complicate a basic human need. A bunch of flowery words isn't going to make any difference. If you want kids, all the better."

Sherry carefully composed her response. Apparently she took longer than he thought necessary.

"Well?" he pressed.

She looked up at him, her gaze deliberately calm. "I'd rather eat fried rattlesnake than marry a man who proposed to me the way you just did."

Cody stared at her as if not sure what to make of her response, then slammed his hat back on his head. "This is exactly the problem with you women. You want everything served to you on a silver platter. And for your information, fried rattlesnake happens to be pretty good. Doesn't taste all that different from chicken."

"Well, I wouldn't eat it even if it *was* served on a silver platter," Sherry snapped. This conversation was over. He'd frustrated her before, but now she was really angry.

"That's your decision, then?"

"That's my decision," she said tightly.

"You're rejecting my proposal?"

"Yup."

"I should've guessed," Cody said. "I knew even before I opened my mouth that you were going to be pigheaded about this."

"Don't feel bad," she said with feigned amiability. "I'm sure there are plenty of women who'd leap at your offer. I just don't happen to be one of them." She reached for the handle of the still-open door, and he was obliged to move out of the way.

"Good night, Cody."

"Goodbye," he muttered and stalked away. He turned back once as if he wanted to argue with her some more, but changed his mind. Sherry threw her car into gear and drove off.

\* \* \*

"What happened between my dad and you after we talked?" Heather asked in a whisper over the telephone. She'd called Sherry first thing the next morning.

"Heather, I'm on duty. I can't talk now."

"Who's sick?"

"No one at the moment, but—"

"If there's no one there, it won't hurt to talk to me for a couple of minutes, will it? Please?"

"Nothing happened between your dad and me." Which of course wasn't true. She'd been proposed to, if you could call it that, for the first time in her life.

"Then why is Dad acting like a wounded bear? Janey threatened to quit this morning, and she's been working for Dad since before I was born."

"Why don't you ask your father?"

"You're kidding, right? No one wants to talk to him. Even Slim's staying out of his way."

"Give him time. He'll cool down."

"If I could wait that long, I wouldn't be calling you."

"Heather," Sherry said, growing impatient, "this is between your father and me. Let's just leave it at that, shall we?"

"You don't want my help?"

"No," Sherry said emphatically. "I don't. Please, drop it, okay?"

"All right," the girl agreed reluctantly. "I won't ask any more questions about whatever it is that *didn't* happen that you don't want to talk about."

"Thank you."

"I hope you know what a sacrifice this is."

"Oh, I do."

"You might think that just because I'm a kid I don't know things. But I know more than either you or Dad realize. I—"

Sherry rolled her eyes. "I need to get off the phone."

Heather released a great gusty sigh. "All right. We're still going shopping for school clothes, aren't we? Soon, 'cause school starts in less than two weeks."

"You bet." Sherry suggested a day and a time and reminded Heather to check with her father. "I'll make reservations at a nice hotel, and we'll spend the night."

"That'll be *great!* Oh, Sherry, I really wish you and Dad could get along, because I think you're fabulous."

"I think you're pretty fabulous, too, honey. Now listen, I have to go. I can't tie up the line."

"Next time I call, I'll ask Mrs. Colson to take a message. You can call me back later when you're not on duty."

"That sounds like a good plan."

Sherry had just finished with her first patient of the afternoon, a four-year-old with a bad ear infection, when Mrs. Colson handed her a phone message. Sherry should've suspected something when the receptionist smiled so broadly.

Sherry took the slip and stuck it in the pocket of her white uniform jacket, waiting until she was alone to read it. When she did, she sank into a chair and closed her eyes. The call was from Heather. She'd talked to her father, and apparently he had business in Abilene that same weekend and was making arrangements for the three of them to travel together. He'd call her soon, Heather said.

This was going to be difficult. Knowing Cody, he'd turn a simple shopping trip into a test of her patience and endurance. She'd have to set some ground rules.

* * *

Cody was supposed to pick her up at the clinic early Saturday morning. Sherry was standing on the porch waiting. It'd been a week since she'd last seen him, four days since their stilted conversation on the phone—and a lifetime since she'd dreaded any trip more.

Her heart sank when the white Cadillac pulled to a stop in front of the clinic.

Cody got out of the car and climbed the steps. Sherry saw Heather scramble over the front seat and into the back.

"Hello," Sherry said, tightening her grip on her overnight case.

"Hello." His voice was devoid of emotion as he reached for her bag.

"I thought we should talk before we leave," she said when he was halfway down the steps.

"Fine." He didn't sound eager.

"Let's call a truce. It shouldn't be difficult to be civil to each other, should it? There's no reason for us to discuss our differences now or ever again, for that matter."

"No," he agreed, "it shouldn't be the least bit difficult to be civil."

And surprisingly, it wasn't. The radio filled in the silences during the long drive, and when the stations faded, Heather bubbled over with eager chatter. Cody seemed to go out of his way to be amiable, and Sherry found her reserve melting as the miles slipped past.

The hotel Cody chose in Abilene was situated close to a large shopping mall. Heather was ready to head for the shops the minute they checked in to their spacious two-bedroom suite.

"Hold your horses," Cody said. He had his briefcase with him. "I probably won't be back until later this evening."

"What about dinner?" Heather wanted to know.

"I've got an appointment."

"Don't worry about us," Sherry told him. "Either we'll order something from room service or eat downstairs. If we're feeling adventurous, we'll go out, but I don't imagine we'll go far."

"What time will you be back, Dad?"

Cody paused. "I can't say. I could be late, so don't wait up for me."

"Can I watch a movie?" She stood in front of the television and read over the listings offered on the printed card.

"If Sherry doesn't object, I can't see any reason why not."

Heather hugged her father and he kissed her head. "Have fun, you two."

"We will," Sherry said.

"Spend your money wisely," he advised on his way out the door, but the look he cast Sherry assured her he trusted her to guide Heather in her decisions.

The girl waited until her father was out of the room before she hurled herself onto the beige sofa and threw out both arms. "Isn't this great? You brought your swimsuit, didn't you? I did."

Sherry had, but she wasn't sure there'd be enough time for them to use the hotel pool.

"It's almost as if we're a real family."

"Heather…"

"I know, I know," she said dejectedly. "Dad already lectured me about this. I'm not supposed to say anything that might insin…insinuate that the two of you share any romantic interest in each other." She said this last bit in a tinny voice that sounded as if it were coming from a robot.

"At least your father and I understand each other."

"That's just it. You don't. He really likes you, Sherry. A

lot. He'd never admit it, though." She sighed and cocked her head. "Men have a problem with pride, don't they?"

"Women do, too," Sherry said, reaching for her purse. "Are you ready to shop till we drop, or do you want to discuss the troublesome quirks of the male psyche?"

It didn't take Heather more than a second to decide. She bolted from the sofa. "Let's shop!"

The mall close to the hotel consisted of nearly fifty stores, of which twenty sold clothing, and they made a point of visiting each and every one. When they were back in the hotel, arms laden with packages, Sherry discovered they'd bought something in more than half the stores they'd ventured into.

Heather was thrilled with her purchases. She removed the merchandise from the bags and spread the outfits over the two beds in their room, quickly running out of space. The overflow spilled onto the sofa and love seat in the living room. Two pairs of crisp jeans and several brightly colored blouses. Several T-shirts. A couple of jersey pullovers and a lovely soft cardigan. Two bras—the right size for Heather's still-developing figure—and matching panties. Sherry had talked Heather into buying a couple of dresses, too, although the girl insisted the only place she'd ever wear them was church. Their biggest extravagance had been footwear—five pairs altogether. Boots, sneakers, dress shoes—to go with her Sunday dresses—a sturdy pair for school and a pair of bedroom slippers.

Sherry wasn't immune to spending money on herself, and she'd purchased a gorgeous black crepe evening dress. Heaven only knew where she was going to wear it, but she'd been unable to resist.

"I have an idea!" Heather announced. "Let's dress up really nice for dinner. I'll wear my dress and new shoes and you can wear *your* new dress, and then we'll go down and order lobster for dinner and charge it to the room so Dad'll pay for it."

An elegant dinner to celebrate their success held a certain appeal—and gave Sherry an unexpected chance to wear her new finery—but charging it to the room didn't seem fair to Cody. "I don't know, Heather..."

"Dad won't mind," Heather said. "He's grateful you're willing to shop with me, and he'll be even happier now that I have bras that fit me. So, come on—what do you think?"

"I think dinner's a marvelous idea." They could work out the finances later.

Heather rummaged through the bags stacked on Sherry's bed until she found what she was looking for. "We should do our nails first, though, shouldn't we?"

They'd discovered the hottest shade of pink nail polish Sherry had ever seen. Heather had fallen in love with it and convinced Sherry her life wouldn't be complete without it.

"Our hair, too."

"Why not?" If they were going to dress up, there was no point in half measures. Heather was filled with such boundless enthusiasm Sherry couldn't help being infected with it, too.

Using jasmine-scented bubble bath, Sherry soaked in the tub, washed her hair and piled it high on her head, wrapping it in a white towel. Putting on a thick terry-cloth robe supplied by the hotel, she met Heather, who'd made use of the second bathroom, back in the living room.

Heather, also in a thick terry-cloth robe, eagerly set the bottle of hot-pink polish on the table.

"Only for our toes, not our fingers," Sherry instructed.

Heather was clearly disappointed, but she nodded. She balanced one foot, then the other against the edge of the coffee table, and Sherry painted the girl's toenails, then had

Heather paint hers. They were halfway through this ritual, with Heather's nail polish almost dry, when the key turned in the lock. They both looked up to see Cody stroll casually into the room.

"Dad!" Heather bounded to her feet and raced over to her father. "We had a *fabulous* day. Wait'll you see what we bought."

Cody set down his briefcase and hugged his daughter. "I take it you had a fun afternoon."

"It was wild. I spent oodles of money. Sherry did, too. She bought this snazzy black dress. It wasn't on sale, but she said she had to have it. When you see her in it, you'll know why."

Cody didn't comment on that. His eyes narrowed when he saw his daughter's feet. "What have you done to your toes?"

"Isn't it great?" Heather said rhapsodically, wiggling her toes for his inspection.

"Will they make your feet glow in the dark?"

"No, silly!"

Sherry finished painting the last of her own toenails and screwed the top back on the bottle of polish. "We were going to dress up in our new outfits and go downstairs and have dinner in the dining room," she said. "That's all right, isn't it?"

"Anything you want. Dinner's on me."

"Even lobster?" Heather asked, as though she wasn't entirely sure how far his generosity would stretch.

"Even lobster. I just sold off the main part of my herd for the best price I've gotten in years."

"Congratulations." Sherry stood, with folded tissues between her toes, and tightened the belt on her robe.

"Then you're all through with your business stuff?" Heather asked.

"I'm finished."

"That's even better! You'll join us for dinner, right? You don't mind if Dad comes, do you, Sherry?"

Cody's eyes connected with Sherry's and his smile was slightly cocky, as if to suggest the ball was in her court.

"Of course I don't mind." There wasn't anything else she could say.

"You'll wear your slinky new dress," Heather said. "Dad." She turned to her father. "Your eyeballs are going to pop out of your head when you see Sherry in it."

Cody's gaze was on his daughter when he spoke. "It's too late for that. They popped out of my head the first time I saw her."

# *Six*

Sherry wasn't sure why she felt so nervous. Maybe it had something to do with her new outfit. She suspected it was a mistake to wear that particular dress with this particular man.

She styled her glossy brown hair carefully, arranging it on top of her head with dangling wisps at her temples and neck. She wished she could tame her heart just as easily. She tried not to place any importance on this evening out, tried to convince herself it was just a meal with friends. That was all they were. Friends. The promise of more had been wiped away. Yet none of her strategies were succeeding; they hadn't even come close to succeeding. She was falling in love with this no-nonsense cattleman, despite the fact that there wasn't a romantic bone in his body.

When they'd finished dressing, the three of them met in the suite's living room. Sherry endured—and, at the same time, thrilled to—Cody's scrutiny. The dress was sleeveless with a dropped waist and a skirt that flared out at her knees

in a triple layer of sleek ruffles. The high-heeled black san-
dals were the perfect complement.

"Doesn't she look like a million bucks?" Heather asked.

Without taking his eyes from Sherry, Cody nodded. "Very
nice."

"Heather, too," Sherry said.

Cody seemed chagrined that she'd had to remind him to
compliment his daughter. His eyes widened with apprecia-
tion as he gazed at Heather.

"Wow," he murmured. "Why…you seem all grown-up."

"I'm nearly thirteen, you know, and that means I'm almost a woman."

"You certainly look like one in that pretty dress." The
glance he flashed at Sherry was filled with surprised gratitude. He seemed to be asking how she'd managed to convince his daughter to buy something other than jeans and
cowboy boots.

Seeing Cody in a smart sports jacket with a pale blue shirt
and a string tie had a curious effect on Sherry. She couldn't
look at him and not be stirred. As much as she hated to
admit it, he was a handsome man. When they'd first met,
she'd been struck by the strength and authority she sensed in
him. Those same traits were more prominent than ever now.

"Are we going to dinner, or are we going to stand around
and stare at each other all evening?" Heather asked bluntly,
looking from her father to Sherry and back again.

"By all means, let's eat," Cody said.

"Yes, let's." Sherry was shocked by how thin and wa-
very her voice sounded. Apparently she wasn't the only one
who noticed, because Heather sent her a curious look, then
grinned broadly.

Dinner truly was an elegant affair. The small dining room
was beautifully decorated with antique fixtures and furnish-

ings. The tables were covered with white linen tablecloths, and the lights were muted. Both Heather and Sherry ordered the lobster-tail dinner, while Cody chose a thick T-bone steak. When a three-piece musical ensemble started to play, Heather glanced pointedly at both her father and Sherry.

"You're going to dance, aren't you?" she said.

"The music is more for mood than dancing," Sherry explained, although she wouldn't have refused if Cody had offered. But she knew he didn't much care for dancing, so an offer wasn't likely.

Their salads arrived, all Caesars with garlicky croutons. Heather gobbled hers, and when Sherry turned to her, silently suggesting she eat more slowly, the girl wiped the dressing from the corner of her mouth and shrugged. "I'm too hungry to linger over my food like you and Dad are."

Sherry's appetite was almost nil, a stark contrast to an hour earlier—before Cody had returned to the suite. She was almost sorry he was with them, because she couldn't enjoy her food. But although she was uncomfortably aware of his presence, she was still glad to be sharing this time with him and Heather.

Their entrées were served, and Sherry was grateful to Heather, who single-handedly carried the conversation. She chattered nonstop between bites of lobster, relating the details of the afternoon. Cody concentrated on his food, occasionally murmuring a brief response to his daughter's comments.

But whatever was happening between Cody and her, if indeed anything was, felt strange to Sherry. Cody seemed withdrawn from her both physically and emotionally. A sort of sultry tension suffused the air about them, as if they were waging battles against themselves, against the strong pull of the attraction they shared. Thank goodness, she thought, for Heather's easy banter.

Sherry hardly touched her meal, but nothing went to waste, because after Heather finished her own dinner, she polished off what remained of Sherry's.

When their dinner plates had been taken away and Heather was waiting for the blueberry-swirl cheesecake she'd ordered, Sherry excused herself and retreated to the ladies' room. She applied fresh lipstick, taking her time, not ready to go back to the table yet. She was uncertain of so many things. Cody had told her how much he *didn't* want to be attracted to her, and she'd found his words somewhat insulting. Now she understood. She was attracted to him, and she didn't like it, either, didn't know how to deal with it. What troubled her most was that she seemed to be weakening toward him. She'd always thought of herself as strong-willed, but now her defenses were crumbling. She was afraid that, as the evening progressed, it would become increasingly difficult to hide her feelings—and that could be disastrous.

Sherry had rejected his less-than-flattering proposal. Cody made it sound as if he was too busy rounding up cattle to go out with her or to focus on developing a relationship. But it was much more than that. He wasn't willing to make an emotional commitment to her, and Sherry would accept nothing less.

She was on her way back into the dining room when a tall, vaguely familiar-looking man approached her. His eye caught hers, and he hesitated a moment before speaking.

"Excuse me," he said, smiling apologetically, "but don't I know you?"

Sherry studied him, thinking the same thing, but unable to decide where or when she'd met him. "I'm not from this area," she said. "This is my first time in Abilene."

He frowned and introduced himself, but that didn't help. "It'll come to me," he said. "Do I look familiar to you?"

Sherry gave him her name. "You do look familiar, but I can't place you."

"Me, neither. Well...I'm sorry to have disturbed you, Sherry."

"That's okay."

When she reached the table, Cody's eyes were full of questions. "Do you know that man?"

"I'm not sure. He said his name's Jack Burnside." She paused. "He thought we'd met before. We might have, but neither of us can remember when or where. I'm generally good about remembering people. It's a little embarrassing."

Cody snickered. "Don't you know a come-on when you hear it? That guy's never met you—he was just looking for an excuse to introduce himself. His ploy's as old as the hills. I thought you were smarter than that."

"Apparently not," Sherry said lightly, refusing to allow Cody the pleasure of irritating her.

"I think you should dance with Sherry," Heather suggested a second time, pointing at the minuscule dance floor, where several other couples were swaying to the music.

"I'm sure your father would rather we—"

"As it happens, I'd be happy to give it a try." Cody's gaze seemed to hold a challenge.

Sherry blinked. Cody had managed to surprise her once again. She stood when he pulled out her chair. His hand felt warm on the small of her back as he guided her to the polished floor.

He turned her into his arms with a flair, making her skirt fan out from her knees. Then he brought her close to him, so close she was sure she could feel his heart beating.

Sherry wasn't fooled; she knew exactly what he was

doing, although she doubted he'd ever admit it. He hadn't asked her to dance because of any great desire to twirl her around the floor, but to make sure Jack Burnside understood she was with him.

His attitude angered her, yet in some odd way pleased her, too. She was gratified to realize the attraction was mutual.

While Cody might have escorted her onto the dance floor to indicate that she was with *him,* Sherry thought he was as unprepared as she was for the impact of their physical closeness. Cody's hold on her gradually grew more possessive. His hand slid upward from her waist until his fingers splayed across her back. Of its own volition, her head moved closer to his until her temple rested against the lean strength of his jaw. Her eyes drifted shut, and she breathed in the scent of spicy aftershave. The music was pleasant, easy and undemanding. Romantic.

As soon as she realized what she was doing, allowing herself to be drawn into the magic of the moment, she pulled away and concentrated on the music. Cody didn't attempt anything beyond a mere shuffling of his feet, which suited Sherry just fine.

She quickly saw her mistake. With her head back, their eyes inevitably met, and neither seemed inclined to look away. They continued to stare at each other, attempting to gauge everything that remained unspoken between them. The longer they gazed at each other the more awkward it became. Seconds ripened into minutes….

Sherry was the first to look away. Cody's hand eased her head toward his, and she sighed as her temple again unerringly came to rest against his jaw. Her eyes had just drifted shut when, out of the blue, she remembered where she'd met Jack Burnside.

"College," she said abruptly, freeing herself from Cody's

embrace. She glanced about the restaurant until she spotted Jack. "I do know him," she said. "We met in Seattle years ago." Taking Cody by the hand, she led him off the dance floor to a table at the far side of the restaurant, where Jack was eating alone. He stood at their approach.

"Jack," she said, slightly breathless, "you're right, we do know each other. I'm Sherry Waterman. Your sister and I were roommates in our junior year at college. You were in Seattle on business and took us both to dinner. That must've been about twelve years ago."

Jack's face broke into a wide grin. "Of course. You're Angela's friend. I was sure we'd met."

"Me, too, but I couldn't remember where."

"So, how are you?"

"Fine," Sherry replied. "I'm living in Texas now."

"As a matter of fact, so am I. Small world, isn't it?" He looked fleetingly at Cody.

"Very small," Sherry agreed.

Jack seemed especially pleased to have made the connection. "I never forget a face, especially one as pretty as yours."

Sherry blushed at the compliment. "This is Cody Bailman."

The two men exchanged brisk handshakes. "Please join me," Jack invited, gesturing toward the empty chairs at his table.

"Thanks, but no," Cody said. "My daughter's with us and she's rather shy. She'd be uncomfortable around a stranger, I'm afraid." Cody refused to meet Sherry's baffled glance. Heather *shy?*

The three of them spoke for a few more minutes, and then Sherry and Cody returned to their table and an impatient Heather.

Sherry knew that the reason she'd dragged Cody off the

dance floor was more than the opportunity to prove she was right about Jack. It was a way of breaking the romantic spell they'd found themselves under. Cody had made her feel vulnerable, and she'd seized the opportunity to show him she wasn't.

"Who were you talking to?" Heather asked, craning her neck. "I didn't think you two were *ever* going to come back."

"The man who approached me earlier," Sherry said. "I remembered who he was, so we went over to speak to him. His sister and I are friends, although Jack and I only met once."

"Apparently your time with him was memorable," Cody drawled. Sherry caught the hint of sarcasm in his voice and was amused.

He paid the bill, and the three of them began to leave the dining room. Cody glanced in Jack's direction, then back at Sherry, and said stiffly, "You're welcome to stay and visit with your friend, if you like."

"I've visited enough, thanks," she said, following him and Heather to the elevators.

They weren't back in the suite thirty seconds before Heather changed out of her dress and into her pajamas and new fuzzy slippers. The girl sank down in front of the television set, studying the pay-per-view movie guide. She checked out her selection with Cody, who gave his approval.

Sherry changed out of her dress and into a comfortable pair of jeans and a cotton T-shirt, then wandered back into the living room to sit on the sofa with Heather. Her mind wasn't on the movie the girl had chosen; it was on Cody and what had happened while they were dancing.

When they'd left Pepper, the emotional distance between them had felt both wide and deep. Now she wasn't sure what to think. He was sitting at the table, with his briefcase open in front of him. He reached for the phone and ordered a pot of coffee from room service.

What made things so difficult was how strongly she was attracted to him. She realized there was little chance for a truly loving relationship between them and that saddened her. His life was ranching. He needed a woman to appease Heather—though certainly there'd be benefits. Cody would be generous with her in every way except the one that mattered. With himself.

Sherry wanted a man who cherished her, a man who was willing to do whatever he could to win her heart, even if it *was* the busiest time of the year. She wanted a husband who'd withhold none of himself from her. And Cody couldn't offer that.

"Something troubling you?" he asked, looking up from his paperwork.

The question snapped her out of her reverie. "No," she said. "What makes you ask?"

"You look like you're about to cry."

Strangely that was exactly how she felt. She managed a chuckle. "Don't be silly."

Heather fell asleep halfway through the movie. When Cody noticed that his daughter had curled up on the sofa and nestled her head in Sherry's lap, he stood, turned off the TV after a nod from Sherry, and gently lifted the girl into his arms. Heather stirred and opened her eyes as if she wanted to scold him for treating her like a little girl, but she obviously thought better of it and let him carry her to bed.

Sherry pulled back the covers, and Cody placed his daughter, who seemed to have fallen right back to sleep, on the bed. Sherry tucked her in, dropping a kiss on Heather's forehead. Silently they moved from the room, then paused as if they were suddenly aware that they were now alone.

Luckily Sherry had remembered to bring a book with her and decided to sit on the couch and bury herself in it. Although Cody sat at the table, busy with his own affairs, Sherry had never been more conscious of him. Agreeing to the suite had been a mistake. She should've insisted on two rooms—on different floors.

"Would you like some coffee?" Cody's question cut into the silence.

"No, thanks." If it wasn't so early, she'd make her excuses and go to bed too, but it would look ridiculous to turn in at nine-thirty.

Unexpectedly Cody released a beleaguered sigh. "All right," he said. "Shall we air this once and for all and be done with it?"

"Air what?" she asked, innocently.

"What's happening between us."

"I wasn't aware that anything was...now."

He closed his briefcase with a deliberate lack of haste, then stood and walked over to the sofa. He sat down on the opposite end, as far from her as he could get and still be on the same piece of furniture. "I've had more than a week to give your rejection of my proposal consideration."

Sherry spoke softly. "I shouldn't have said what I did."

He tilted his head and a hopeful expression appeared on his face. "You mean you've changed your mind and decided to marry me?"

"No." She didn't like to be so blunt, but it seemed the only way to reach Cody. "I regret saying I'd rather eat fried rattlesnake."

"Oh." His shoulders slumped. "I should've known it wouldn't be that easy." He grabbed a pen and pad. "I'd like to know exactly what you find so objectionable about me."

"Nothing. You're honest, hardworking, trustworthy. My

grandmother, if she were alive, would call you a salt-of-the-earth kind of guy, and I'd agree with her. It would be very easy to fall in love with you, Cody. Sometimes I think I already have, and that terrifies me."

"Why?" He sounded sincere.

"Because you don't love me."

His face fell. "I *like* you. I'm attracted to you. That's a lot more than many other couples start out with."

"Love frightens you, doesn't it? You lost Heather's mother, and you've guarded your heart ever since."

"Don't be ridiculous." He stood and walked to the window, shoving his hands in his pants pockets and staring out at the night. His back was to her, but that didn't prevent Sherry from hearing the pain in his voice. "Karen died ten years ago. I hardly even remember what she looked like anymore." He turned to look at her. "That's the problem with you women. You read a few magazine articles and romance novels and then think you're experts on relationships."

"You loved her, didn't you?"

"Of course I did, and I grieved when she died."

"You didn't remarry," she told him quietly, afraid of agitating him further.

"I didn't have the time, and to be truthful, my life was full enough without letting a woman dominate my time. That's why I want to set the record straight right now. I'm not about to let a wife put a collar around my neck and lead me around like a puppy."

"Karen did that?"

"No." He scowled fiercely. "But I've seen it happen to plenty of other men, including Luke."

"Ellie doesn't seem the type to do something like that."

Cody frowned. "I know—Luke put the collar around his own neck." He returned to the table, wrote on the pad and glanced at her. "I was thinking you and I might reach some sort of compromise."

"Is that possible?"

"I don't know," he answered. "But it might be if we try."

"Before we go any further, I want it understood that I have no intention of changing who you are, Cody. That's not what marriage is about."

His look told her he didn't believe her. But Sherry had no intention of arguing with him. He'd believe whatever he wanted.

"This isn't working," Cody said, thrusting his hand through his hair in frustration. "I was hoping to make a list, so I'd know what you want from me."

"For what?"

He dropped the pen he still held on the table. "So we can put an end to this foolishness and get married!"

Their conversation had taken so many twists she was no longer sure exactly what they were discussing.

"You still want to marry me?" she asked.

"Obviously. Otherwise I wouldn't risk making a fool of myself twice."

"Why?" she asked, genuinely curious.

"Damned if I know," he snapped. He took a moment to compose himself and come to grips with his temper. "Because I like the way you feel in my arms. And I like kissing you."

"That's all?" she asked.

"No. I also want to marry you because my daughter clearly adores you. On top of that, you're easy on the eyes, you're intelligent and well-read."

"Ah," Sherry said.

Her response seemed to succeed in making him angrier. "There's sparks between us—you can't deny it."

This man had the most uncanny way of insulting her with compliments. But it was impossible for her to be angry and, in fact, she was more amused than offended.

"We've only kissed twice," she reminded him.

"Only twice?" He sounded surprised. "Well, I guess you pack quite a wallop."

Sherry decided to accept that as a definite compliment, and she smiled. He was suddenly standing in front of her, his hands reaching for hers, drawing her up so that she stood before him. "I can't stop thinking about how good you taste," he whispered. His mouth was inches from her own.

Sherry knew that a kiss would muddle her reasoning, but it was already so tangled it shouldn't matter.

He pulled her closer. For one crazy moment all they did was stare at each other. Then Cody spoke. "It's been a long time since I've kissed a woman the way I want to kiss you." His words were low and heavy with need.

"I'm not afraid," Sherry said simply.

"Maybe not, but I sure am." His arms went around her, folding her against his chest. How right this felt, Sherry thought. How perfectly their bodies fit together....

His voice was ragged and oddly breathless when he said, "You kiss me."

Sherry didn't hesitate, not for an instant. She placed her hands on either side of his head and drew it down toward hers. Their lips met in an uncomplicated kiss. Sweet, gentle, undemanding. Then it changed in intensity. What had seemed so sweet and simple a moment earlier took on a magnitude and power that left her head swimming and her lungs depleted of air.

Cody groaned and his mouth slanted hard over hers.

This wasn't the type of kiss that burned itself out, that made the gradual transformation from passionate to pleasant. This kiss was a long way from being complete before it grew too hot, too heady for either of them to handle.

Sherry wasn't sure who moved first, but they broke apart and stepped back. Space, she needed space, and from the look of him, so did Cody. Sherry's chest was heaving, her heart pounding, and her emotions threatened to fly out of control.

Cody spoke first. "I think," he said raggedly, "that it's a fair assumption to say we're sexually compatible."

Sherry nodded mutely. This brief experiment with the physical aspects of their relationship had proved to be more potent than she'd thought possible. She raised her trembling fingers to her lips.

Suddenly, standing seemed to require a great deal of energy, so Sherry moved back to the sofa and sat, hoping she seemed confident and composed. She felt neither.

Cody joined her as he had earlier—sitting on the far end of the sofa where there wasn't any possibility of accidentally touching her.

He reached over to the nearby table for the same pad and pencil. "Thus far, your main objection to marrying me is…" He hesitated, then reviewed his notes and set aside the pad.

"I want to be sure of something," Sherry said when she was reasonably certain her voice would sound even and steady. "Heather's 4-H project."

Cody's gaze shot to hers.

"Your sudden desire for a wife—does it have anything to do with that?"

His shoulders squared defensively. "Yes and no. To be honest, I hadn't given much consideration to marrying again until this past year, and Heather had a lot to do with that. She's at the age now when she needs a woman's influence.

She realized it herself, I think, before I did. Otherwise she wouldn't have come up with that crazy project idea."

"I see." Sherry found the truth painful, but was glad he hadn't lied.

"That doesn't mean anything, though. I didn't meet you and immediately decide you'd be a perfect mother for Heather. I looked at you and decided you were a perfect wife for *me,* with one exception."

"What's that?"

"You want everything sugar-coated."

"Cody, it's much more than that!"

He shook his head. "I'm not the kind of guy to decorate something with a bunch of fancy words. Nor do I have the time to persuade you I'm decent enough to be your husband. If you haven't figured that out by now, flowers and candy ain't going to do it."

"Don't be so sure," she teased.

"That's what you want, is it?" He was frowning so fiercely, his lips were a tight line.

"I want a man who's willing to make an emotional commitment to me, and that includes time to come to know each other properly. I'm not willing to settle for anything less. If you're serious about marrying me, Cody, then you're going to have to prove to me you're sincere. I won't accept some... some offhand proposal."

"You're looking for *romance,* aren't you?" he asked starkly.

"If you want to call it that," she said. "I need to know I'm important to you, that this attraction isn't just a passing thing."

"I asked you to marry me, didn't I?" He sounded thoroughly disgusted. "Trust me, a man doesn't get any more serious than that."

"Perhaps not," Sherry agreed. "But a woman needs a little more than a proposal that talks about cutting to the chase and being done with it."

"You want me down on one knee with my heart on my sleeve, telling you I couldn't survive without you?"

She raised her eyebrows. "That would be a start." *If you meant it,* she added silently.

"I thought so." Cody stood and marched over to his brief-case. He threw his pen and pad inside, then slammed down the lid. "Well, you can forget it. I'm willing to compromise, but that's as far as it goes. Take it or leave it, the choice is up to you."

Sherry closed her eyes. "I believe we've both made our choices."

# *Seven*

Sherry sat in a booth at the Yellow Rose, sipping coffee and mulling over the events of the weekend in Abilene. Doubt assailed her from all sides. Twice now, she'd rejected Cody's marriage proposal.

The irony of the situation didn't escape her. For years she'd longed for a husband and family. She'd been looking for a change in her life. This was why she'd uprooted herself and moved halfway across the country.

She'd been in Texas for less than a month, and in that time she'd been held captive by a community, helped deliver a beautiful baby boy and received a marriage proposal—twice. This was some kind of state.

Cody. She wished she could think clearly about him. The fact that she'd met a man who attracted her so powerfully came as a shock. That he should feel equally drawn to her was an unexpected bonus.

Donna Jo strolled over to the booth and refilled her coffee. "You're looking a little under the weather," the waitress commented. "How'd your weekend with Cody and Heather go?"

It was no surprise that Donna Jo knew she'd spent the weekend with the Bailmans. "We had a lot of fun."

Donna Jo set the glass pot on the table. She shifted her weight, as if what she had to say was of momentous importance. "Take my word for it, honey, that man's sweet on you."

Sherry's only response was a weak smile. "I heard about Heather's 4-H project. That's what you and Mrs. Colson wanted me to find out on my own, wasn't it?"

Donna Jo did a poor job of hiding her amusement. "I wondered how long it'd take you to learn about that. Cody's kid's got a good head on her shoulders. Heather figured that suggesting *she* find him a wife would get her father's attention and by golly she was right." Donna Jo laughed at the memory. "Cody was stunned. He's lived so long without a woman that I don't think remarrying even entered his mind. You're sweet on him, too, aren't you?"

"He's a good man." Sherry tried to sound noncommittal.

"Cody's one of the best. He can be cantankerous, but then he wouldn't be a man if he wasn't. Now, I don't have any dog in this fight, but—"

Sherry stopped her. "You don't have a dog? They fight dogs in Texas?" she asked in horror.

"Of course not! It's an old Texan saying, meaning I don't have a stake in what happens between you and Cody. I've been married a whole lot of years myself, and personally I'd like to see Cody find himself a decent wife." Her smile widened. "Folks in the Yellow Rose been talking about you two, and everyone says Cody should marry you. Are we gonna have a fall wedding?"

"Uh…"

"Leave Doc's helper alone," the sheriff called out from his perch at the counter, "and bring that coffee over here."

"Hold your horses, Billy Bob. This is the kind of information folks come into the Yellow Rose for. Trust me, it isn't the liver-and-onion special they're after. It's gossip. And everyone wants to know what's happening with Cody and Sherry."

Every single person in the café seemed to be staring at Sherry, waiting for a response.

"I hear you and Heather traveled with him to Abilene," the sheriff said, twisting around to face her. "That sounds promising. Right promising."

"Sure does," someone else agreed.

"Here's how I see it," a second man intoned. Sherry hadn't formally met him, but she knew he was the local minister. "A man wasn't meant to be alone. A woman neither. Now, I know there're plenty of folks who'd argue with me, but it seems if you're both wanting the same thing, then you should get on with it."

With everyone looking at her so expectantly, Sherry felt obligated to say something, anything. "I... Thanks for the advice. I'll take it into consideration." She couldn't get out of the café fast enough. Everyone appeared to have either a question or some tidbit of wisdom.

By the time Sherry reached the clinic, she regretted opening her mouth. She had no idea so many people would be interested in her relationship with Cody.

Mrs. Colson looked up from her desk when Sherry came through the front door. "Good morning," the receptionist greeted her cheerfully, her eyes full of curiosity.

"Morning," Sherry said, hurrying past. Her eagerness to escape didn't go unnoticed.

"How was your weekend with Cody and Heather?" Mrs. Colson called after her.

"Great." Sherry got her jacket from behind the exam-room door and was buttoning it up when the receptionist let herself in. "I heard that Cody popped the question. I don't even think Donna Jo knows this yet. Is it true?"

Sherry's hands fumbled with the last button and her heart fell straight to her knees. "Who told you that?"

"Oh, you could say I heard it on the grapevine. And not just *any* grapevine."

"You should know by now how unreliable that can be," Sherry said as unemotionally as she could, unwilling to swallow the bait.

Mrs. Colson raised her brows. "Not this time. My source is dependable. I have my ways of learning things."

A "dependable" source? That had to be Janey the house-keeper. Or Heather...

"This town's worse than Orchard Valley," Sherry muttered. "I hardly know Cody Bailman. What makes you think he'd ask a casual acquaintance to marry him, and further-more, what makes you assume I'd accept?"

"Casual acquaintance, is it?" Mrs. Colson asked. "Seems to me you know him well enough to dance cheek to cheek in some fancy hotel restaurant, don't you?"

"You know about that, too?" Sherry's jaw dropped. Yes, it had to be Heather. "Is nothing sacred in this town?"

"Morning." Doc Lindsey strolled into the room; seeing Sherry, he paused and grinned broadly. "I hear you're mar-rying Cody Bailman. He's a damn good man. Congratu-lations." He patted Sherry's back and sauntered out of the room.

Sherry clenched her fists and looked up at the ceiling while she counted to ten. Apparently the folks in Pepper had nothing better to do than speculate on Cody's love life.

"Cody's waited a long time for the right woman," Mrs. Colson stated matter-of-factly on her way out the door. "I only hope his stubbornness doesn't ruin everything."

"Mrs. Colson," Sherry said, hanging the stethoscope around her neck. "I don't mean to be rude or unfriendly, but I'd rather not discuss my personal affairs with you or Donna Jo or Billy Bob or anyone else."

"The mayor's got a good ear if you change your mind."

Sherry gritted her teeth in her effort not to lose her temper. Something would have to be said, and soon; the situation was getting out of hand.

Sherry saw several patients that morning, the majority of them children having physicals before the start of the school year, which was only a week away. Rather than risk another confrontation with Donna Jo and the lunch crowd at the Yellow Rose, she ordered a chef's salad and had it delivered.

At one, Mrs. Colson ushered her into Doc's office, where a tall, regal-looking older woman in a lovely blue suit was waiting for her. The woman's hair was white, and she wore it in an elegant French roll.

"Hello," Sherry said. The older woman sat, her legs crossed, her designer purse in her lap.

"You must be Sherry. I'm Judith Bailman, Cody's mother. I've come from Dallas to meet you."

Sherry felt an overwhelming urge to sit down, too. "I'm pleased to make your acquaintance, Mrs. Bailman."

"The pleasure is mine. I understand there are several things we need to discuss."

Sherry couldn't seem to make her mouth work. She turned and pointed at the door in a futile effort to explain that she was on duty. Unfortunately, no patients were waiting at the moment.

"Mrs. Colson's arranged for us to have several minutes of privacy, so you don't need to worry we'll be interrupted."

"I...see." Sherry claimed Doc's chair, on the other side

of the desk, nearly falling into it. "What can I do for you, Mrs. Bailman?"

"I understand my son's proposed to you?" She eyed Sherry speculatively.

Sherry didn't mean to sound curt, but after everything that had happened that day, she was in no mood to review her private life with anyone. "I believe that's between Cody and me."

"I quite agree. I don't want to be nosy. I hope you'll forgive me. It's just that Cody's been single all these years, so I couldn't help getting excited when Heather mentioned—"

"Heather?" Sherry interrupted. Just as she'd expected. That explained everything.

"Why, yes. My granddaughter phoned me first thing this morning." A smile tempted the edges of her mouth. "She's concerned that her father's going to ruin her best chance at having a mom and being a big sister, and knowing my son, I'm betting she's right."

"Mrs. Bailman—"

"Please, call me Judith."

"Judith," Sherry said, "don't get me wrong, I think the world of Cody and Heather. Your son did ask me to marry him—in a rather offhand way."

The woman's mouth tightened. "That sounds like Cody."

"If you must know, I turned him down. Cody makes marriage seem about as appealing as a flu shot."

Judith laughed. "I can see I'm going to like you, Sherry Waterman."

"Thank you." She wasn't accustomed to having an entire town and now the man's mother involved in one of her relationships. At least when she lived in Orchard Valley, her life was mostly her own. The minute she'd been hired to work in Pepper, her personal business was up for grabs.

"I hope you'll forgive me for being so blunt, but are you in love with Cody?"

Sherry meant to explain that she was attracted to Judith's son, then add how much she respected and liked him, but instead, she found herself nodding.

The full impact of the truth took her by storm. She closed her eyes and waited several seconds for the torrent of emotion to pass.

Judith smiled and sighed with apparent relief. "I guessed as much. I tried speaking to him about you, but he refused. Truth be known, I would've been surprised if he *had* listened," she murmured. "That boy's more stubborn than a mule."

The description was apt, and Sherry smiled.

"If he knew I was here, he'd never forgive me, so I'm going to have to ask for your discretion."

"Of course." Sherry glanced worriedly at the door.

"You needn't worry that Martha Colson will say anything. We've been friends for years." She looked past Sherry and out the window. "Be patient with him, Sherry. He's closed himself off from love, and I know he's fighting his feelings for you with the full strength of his will. Which, I might add, is formidable."

That much Sherry knew.

"Cody deserves your love," Judith went on. "Sure he has his faults, but believe me, the woman my son loves will be happy. When he falls in love again, it'll be with his whole heart and soul. It may take some time, but I promise you the wait will be worth it."

Sherry wasn't sure how to respond. "I'll…I'll remember that," she promised.

"Now—" Judith gave a deep sigh and stood "—I should

be on my way. Remember, not a word to either my son or my granddaughter."

"I promise."

Judith hugged her and said again, "Be patient with Cody."

"I'll try," Sherry whispered.

Cody's mother left by the back door. When Mrs. Colson returned, her sparkling eyes met Sherry's and she said, "This visit will be our little secret, won't it?"

"What visit?" she replied.

Friday evening, Sherry sat out on the porch in front of the clinic enjoying the coolness. She rocked peacefully on the swing and listened to the night sounds. Crickets telegraphed greetings to one another, and music from the local tavern drifted toward her.

Evenings were her favorite time. Sherry loved to sit outside and think about her day. Her life was falling into a pattern now as she adjusted to the people of Pepper. Often she read or called family and friends or sent e-mails using her laptop computer. Norah's birthday was coming up soon, and Sherry had spent the earlier part of the evening writing her a long, chatty message.

Her heart seemed to skip a beat when Cody's pickup drew to a stop by the clinic. She got up and walked over to the steps, leaning against the support beam as he climbed out of the cab and came toward her.

"Hi, Sherry," he said, his expression a bit sheepish.

"Hi, Cody."

He looked at her for several seconds as if trying to remember the purpose of his visit. Sherry decided to make it easier for him. "Would you care to sit with me?" She motioned toward the swing.

"Don't mind if I do." He'd recently shaved and the familiar scent of his aftershave floated past her as he moved to the swing.

They sat side by side, swaying gently. Neither seemed ready to talk.

"I was on my way over to a friend's place to play poker," he said at last, "when I saw you sitting here."

"I do most evenings. Nights are so beautiful here. I love stargazing. It's one of the reasons I'd never be happy in a big city. Sometimes the sky's so full I can't stop looking."

"Have you had a good week?" he asked.

"A busy one. What about you?"

"The same." His eyes met hers. "Any problems?"

"Such as?"

He shrugged and looked past her to the street. "I thought there might've been some talk about, you know, us."

"There was definitely some heavy speculation after our trip last weekend."

"Anyone pestering you?"

"Not really. What about you?"

He laughed lightly. "You mean other than Heather and Janey?"

The bench squeaked in the quiet that followed.

"I've been thinking about what you said," he finally muttered. "About romance."

"Oh?"

"To my way of thinking, it's not necessary."

Sherry frowned. "So you've said." Countless times, but reminding him of that would have sounded petty and argumentative. The moment was peaceful, and she didn't want to ruin it.

"Tell me what you want and I'll do it," he said decisively.

"You want a *list?*"

"That'd help. I'm no good at this sort of thing, and I'm going to need a few instructions."

Sherry turned to look at him. She pressed her hand to his cheek. "That's really very sweet, Cody. I'm touched."

"If that's the only way I can convince you to marry me, then what the heck, I'll do it. Just tell me what you want, so I don't waste a lot of time."

"I…I hate to disappoint you, but giving you instructions would defeat the purpose. It has to come from your heart, Cody." She moved her hand to his chest and held it there. "Otherwise it wouldn't be sincere."

A frown quickly snapped into place. "You want me to do a few mushy things to prove I'm sincere, but you aren't willing to tell me what they are?"

"You make it sound silly."

"As far as I'm concerned, it is. Asking you to marry me is as sincere as I can get. And if that isn't good enough—"

Their peace was about to be destroyed, and Sherry was unwilling to let it happen. So she acted impulsively and stopped him the only way she knew would work.

She kissed him.

The instant her mouth covered his, she felt his anger melt away. His kiss was both tender and fierce. His breath was warm, his lips hot and eager, and the kiss left her trembling.

Then he began kissing her neck, from her chin to her shoulder. As always happened when he touched her, Sherry felt like Dorothy caught up in the tornado, spinning out of control before landing in a magical land. When he raised his head from hers, she immediately missed him. Missed his warmth, his passion, his closeness.

Cody started to say something, then changed his mind. He raised his finger to her face and brushed it down her cheek. "I have to go."

She wanted him to stay, but wouldn't ask it of him.

"The guys are waiting for me. They're counting on me."

"It's all right, Cody."

He stood and thrust his hands in his jeans pockets, as if to stop himself from reaching for her again. That thought helped lighten the melancholy she experienced at his leaving.

"It was good to see you again," he said stiffly.

"Good to see you, too," she returned just as stiffly.

He hesitated on the top step and turned back to face her. "Uh, you're sure you don't want to give me a few tips on, uh, romance?"

"I'm confident you aren't going to need them. Follow your heart, Cody, and I promise you it'll lead directly to mine."

He smiled, and Sherry swore she'd never seen anything sexier.

She didn't hear from Cody all day Saturday, which was disappointing. She'd hoped he'd taken her words to heart and understood what she'd been trying to say.

Yes, she wanted to be courted the way women had been courted for centuries. But she also wanted to be *loved*. Cody was more afraid of love than he was of marriage.

Late that night when she was in bed reading, she heard something or someone outside her bedroom window. At first she didn't know what to make of it. The noise was awful, loud and discordant. Several minutes passed before she realized it was someone playing a guitar, or rather, attempting to play a guitar.

She pulled open the blinds and looked out to see Cody standing on the lawn, crooning for all he was worth. Whatever he was singing—or thought he was singing—was completely unrecognizable to her.

"Cody!" she shouted, jerking up the window and poking her head out. "What on earth are you doing?"

He started to sing louder. Sherry winced. His singing was worse than his guitar-playing. Holding up the window with one hand, she covered her ear with the other.

"Cody!" she shouted again.

"You wanted romance," he called back and then repeatedly strummed the guitar in a burst of energy. "This comes straight from the heart, just like you wanted."

"Have you been drinking?"

He laughed and threw back his head, running his fingers over the guitar strings with hurried, unpracticed movements. "You don't honestly think I'd try this sober, do you?"

"Cody!"

The sound of a police siren in the background startled Sherry. It was the first time she'd heard one in Pepper. Apparently there was some kind of trouble, but Sherry didn't have time to think about that now, not with Cody serenading her, sounding like a sick bull.

"Cody!"

"What's the matter?" he shouted. "You said you wanted romance. Well, this is it. The best I can do."

"Give me a minute to get dressed and I'll be right out." She started to lower the window, then poked her head out again. "Don't go away, and quit playing that guitar!"

"Anything you want," he said, strumming even more wildly and discordantly than before.

Lowering the window didn't help. Cody knew as much about guitar-playing as she did about mustering cattle. Pulling on jeans and a light sweater, she slipped her feet into tennis shoes and hurried out the door. Fortunately the siren, too, had stopped.

As she came out onto the porch, she was gratified to realize he'd stopped playing. It wasn't until she'd reached the bottom step that she noticed the police car parked in front of the clinic.

Hurrying around to the side of the building, she encountered Cody and a sheriff's deputy, whose flashlight was zeroed in on her romantic idiot.

"Is there a problem here?" Sherry asked. She hadn't met this particular deputy, but the name tag above his shirt pocket read Steven Bean.

"No problem, isn't that right, Mr. Bailman?"

"None whatsoever," Cody said, looking almost sober. If it wasn't for the cocky smile he wore, it would've been impossible to tell he'd been drinking. "I only had a couple shots of whiskey," he explained. "I had to, or I'd never have had the guts to pull this off."

"Are you arresting Mr. Bailman?" Sherry asked.

"We've had three calls in the last five minutes," Deputy Bean said. "The first call said there was a wounded animal in town. The second caller thought there was a fight of some kind going on. And the third one came from Mayor Bowie. He said we had the authority to do whatever was necessary to put an end to that infernal racket. Those were his precise words."

"I may not be another Willie Nelson, but my singing isn't that bad," Cody protested.

"Trust me, Bailman, it's bad."

Cody turned to Sherry for vindication. Even though he was serenading her in the name of romance, even though he was suffering this embarrassment on her behalf, she couldn't bring herself to lie.

"I think it'd be better if you didn't sing again for a while," she suggested tactfully.

He sent her an injured look, then turned to the deputy. "Are you gonna take me to jail?" he demanded.

"I could, you know," Deputy Bean told him.

"On what grounds?" Sherry challenged.

"Disturbing the peace, for starters."

"I didn't know it was unlawful to play the guitar," Cody said, sounding aggrieved.

"It is the way you do it," Deputy Bean muttered.

"He won't be doing it again," Sherry promised, looking at Cody. "Right?"

"Right." Cody held up his hand.

The deputy sighed and lowered his flashlight. "In that case, why don't we just drop this? I'll let you off with a warning."

"Thank you," Sherry said.

The deputy began to leave, but Cody stopped him. "Will there be a report of this in the paper on Wednesday?"

The officer shrugged. "I suppose. The *Weekly* reports all police calls."

"I'd appreciate it if you could see that this one doesn't make the paper."

"I can't do that, Mr. Bailman."

"Why not?"

"I'm not the one who turns the calls over to Mr. Douglas. He comes in every morning and collects them himself."

"Then make sure he doesn't have anything to collect," Cody said.

The deputy shrugged again. "I'll do my best, but I'm not making any promises. We got three calls, you know."

Cody waited until the patrol car had disappeared into the night before he removed his Stetson and slammed it against his leg. He frowned at his mangled hat and tried to bend it back into shape.

"I've ruined the best hat I've ever had because of you," he grumbled.

*"Me?"*

"You heard me."

"Are you blaming me for this…this fiasco?"

"No!" he shouted back. "I'm blaming Luke. He was the one who said I should serenade you. He claimed it didn't matter that I couldn't play the guitar or sing. He said women go crazy for this kind of stuff. I should've known." He indignantly brushed off the Stetson before setting it back on his head, adjusting the angle.

"It was very sweet, Cody, and I do appreciate it."

"Sure you do. Women get a real kick out of seeing a grown man make a jackass out of himself in front of the whole town."

"That's not fair!"

"You know what?" Cody barked, waving his arms, "I was liked and respected in this town before you came along making unreasonable demands. All I want is a wife."

*"You're* being unreasonable."

Cody shook his head. "The way I see it, you're waiting for some prince to come along and sweep you away on his big white horse. Well, sweetheart, it isn't going to be me."

For a moment, Sherry was too shocked to respond. "I didn't ask you to serenade me. Or to sweep me away on your horse."

"Oh, no," he said, walking toward the gate. "That would've been too easy. On top of everything else, I'm supposed to be psychic or something. You won't tell me what you want. It's up to me to read your mind."

"That's not fair," she repeated.

"You said it, not me."

"Cody—" She stopped herself, not wanting to argue with

him. "You're right. I'm out of line expecting a man who wants to marry me to love me too."

Cody apparently didn't hear her, or if he did, he chose to ignore her *and* her sarcasm. "Luke. That's where I made my mistake," he said. "I assumed my best friend would know all the answers, because for all his bumbling ways, he managed to marry Ellie."

"You're absolutely right," Sherry said, marching up the steps. "You could learn a lesson or two from your friend. At least he was in love with the woman he wanted to marry and wasn't just looking for someone to warm his bed and keep his daughter happy."

Cody whirled around and shook his finger at her. "You know what I think?"

"I don't know and I don't really care."

"I'm going to tell you, anyway, so listen."

She crossed her arms and heaved an exasperated sigh.

"Cancel the whole thing!" Cody shouted. "Forget I asked you to marry me!"

"Cody!" someone hollered in the distance. Sherry looked up in time to see a head protruding from the upstairs window of the house across the street. "Either you shut up or I'm calling the sheriff again."

"Don't worry," Cody hollered back. "I'm leaving."

# *Eight*

"Is it true?" Heather asked the following morning as Sherry walked out of church. "Did you nearly get my dad arrested?"

Sherry closed her eyes wearily. "Did Cody tell you that?"

"No." Heather's eyes were huge and round. "I heard Mrs. Morgan telling Mrs. James about it. They said Dad was standing under your bedroom window singing and playing the guitar. I didn't even know Dad could play the guitar."

"He can't. I think you should ask your father about what happened last night," Sherry told her, unwilling to comment further. She couldn't. Cody would find some way of blaming her, regardless of what she said.

"He didn't come to church this morning. He had Slim drive me to town because he said his head hurt."

Served him right, thought Sherry.

"School starts the day after tomorrow," Heather announced. "Do you want to know what I'm going to wear for the first day? My new jeans, that black T-shirt and my new shoes."

"Sounds perfect," Sherry said.

"I've got to go." Heather glanced across the parking lot. "Slim's waiting for me in the pickup. When are you going to come to the house again? I was kind of hoping you would last week. I was thinking of having my hair cut and I found this really cool style in my friend Carrie's magazine. I wanted to show it to you."

"Ask your father if you can stay after school one afternoon this week, and I'll drive you home," Sherry suggested. "But tell him—" she hesitated "—I won't be able to stay. Make sure he knows that. I'll just drop you off."

"Okay," Heather said, walking backward. "That'd be great. Do you mind if Carrie comes along? She wants to meet you, too, and her place isn't that far from mine."

"Sure."

"Thanks." Heather's smile lit up her whole face. "I'll call and let you know which day is good."

Sherry waved and the girl turned and raced over to the pickup. Sighing, Sherry started toward her own car. She hadn't gone more than a few steps when she heard Ellie Johnson call her.

"Sherry," Ellie said, walking in her direction. "Have you got a minute?"

"Sure."

"I've been meaning to call you all week, but with the baby and everything, it slipped my mind. I know it's short notice, but I'd love for you to come to the house for dinner. I've got a roast in the slow cooker. Drop by in a little while and we can visit for a few hours. Luke's so busy these days I'm starved for companionship."

"I'd love to."

"That's wonderful." Ellie seemed genuinely pleased. "You won't have any problems finding your way, will you?"

Sherry told her she wouldn't. As it happened, she was

eager for a bit of female companionship, too. With Ellie, Sherry could be herself. She didn't worry that she'd have to endure an inquisition or make explanations about Cody and her.

When Sherry arrived at the ranch an hour or so later, Ellie came out onto the porch to greet her. One-year-old Christina Lynn was thrilled to have company, and she tottered excitedly over to Sherry, who scooped her up and carried her into the kitchen.

After giving Ellie's daughter the proper attention, Sherry asked about Philip. "He's sleeping," she was assured. "I fed him and put him down. Christina Lynn's due for her nap, too, but I promised she could visit with you first." Sherry sat down at the kitchen table, and the toddler climbed into her lap and investigated, with small probing fingers, the jeweled pin she wore.

It had been several weeks since Sherry had spent time with Norah and her kids, and she missed being with young children. Christina Lynn seemed equally infatuated with her.

While Sherry devoted herself to the world of a small child, Ellie poured them glasses of iced tea, which she brought to the kitchen table.

"I suppose you heard what happened?" Sherry asked, needing to discuss the events of the night before. After all, there was sure to be some sort of backlash, since Cody seemed to blame Luke as much as he did her.

"There were rumors at church this morning. Is it true Cody was almost arrested?"

"Yes. For disturbing the peace."

A smile quivered at the edges of Ellie's mouth. "I'm afraid Cody Bailman has a few lessons to learn about women."

"I would've thought his wife, Karen, had taught him all this."

"I never knew her, of course," Ellie said, reaching for her glass, "but apparently Luke did. I've asked him about her."

"What did he tell you?" Sherry was more than curious. She sensed that the key to understanding Cody was rooted in his marriage, however brief.

"From what I remember, Cody met Karen while they were in college. He was away from home for the first time and feeling lonely. Luke was surprised when he married her—at least that's what he told me. She was something of a tomboy, even at twenty. In many ways I suspect she was the perfect rancher's wife. She loved riding and working with cattle. What I heard is there wasn't anything she couldn't do." Ellie hesitated and looked away as if carefully judging her words. "Luke also said Karen wasn't very interested in being a wife or mother. She resented having to stay home with the baby." She took a deep breath.

"Luke also told me they had some huge fights about it. Karen died in a car accident after one of them. She'd threatened to leave Cody and Heather, but Luke doubts that she meant it. She mentioned divorce on a regular basis, dramatically packing her bags and lugging them out to the car. No one'll ever know if she meant it that particular time or not because she took a curve too fast and ran off the road. She died instantly."

"How sad."

"I know Cody loved Karen," Ellie continued. "I admire him for picking up the pieces of his life and moving forward."

"I do, too. I didn't realize his marriage had been so traumatic."

"It wasn't always unhappy. Don't misunderstand me. Cody cared deeply for his wife, but I don't think he was ever truly comfortable with her, if you know what I mean."

Sherry wasn't sure she did, but she let it pass.

"He's at a loss when it comes to showing a woman how he feels. The only woman he ever loved was so involved in herself that she didn't have much love left for anyone else, including him or Heather."

"He's afraid," Sherry whispered. But it wasn't for any of the reasons she'd assumed. After learning he was a widower, Sherry believed he'd buried himself in his grief. Now she understood differently. Cody feared that if he loved someone again, that love would come back to him empty and shallow.

"Be patient with him," Ellie advised.

Sherry smiled. "It's funny you should say that. A few days ago someone else said the same thing."

"Cody's so much like Luke. I'd like to shake the pair of them. Luke wasn't any different when we first met. He seemed to assume that if he loved me he'd lose part of himself. He put on this rough-and-tough exterior and was so unreasonable that...suffice it to say we had our ups and downs, as well."

"What was the turning point for you and Luke?"

Ellie leaned back in her chair, her expression thoughtful. "My first inclination is to say everything changed when I decided to leave Pepper. That's when Luke raced after my car on his horse and proposed. But it really happened about a week before that." She sighed and sipped her tea. "To hear Luke tell it, we fell in love the moment we set eyes on each other. Trust me, it wasn't like that. For most of the summer we argued. He seemed to think I was his exclusive property, which infuriated me."

"What happened?"

"Oh, there wasn't any big climactic scene when we both realized we were destined for each other. In fact, it was something small that convinced me of his love for me—and eventually mine for him.

"Luke had taken me horseback riding, and I'd dared him to do something stupid. I can't even remember what it was now, but he refused, rightly so. It made me mad and I took off at a gallop. I'm not much of a horsewoman and I hadn't gone more than a few feet before I was thrown. Luckily I wasn't hurt, but my pride had taken a beating and Luke made the mistake of laughing at me.

"I was so furious I left, figuring I'd rather walk back to the ranch than ride. Naturally, it started to rain—heavily— and I was drenched in seconds. Luke, too. I was so angry with him and myself that I wouldn't speak to him. Finally Luke got down off his horse and walked behind me, leading the two mares. He wouldn't leave me, although heaven knew I deserved it. I thought about that incident for a long time afterward, and I realized this was the kind of man I wanted to spend the rest of my life with."

"But you decided to leave Pepper shortly after that."

"Yes," Ellie admitted cheerfully. "It was the only way. He seemed to think marriage was something we could discuss in three or four years."

"It's something Cody wants to discuss every three or four minutes."

Ellie laughed. "Do you love him?"

"Yes," Sherry said in a soft voice. "But that's not the problem."

"Cody's the problem. I know what you mean."

"He wants me to marry him, but he doesn't want to get emotionally involved with me. He makes the whole thing sound like a business proposition, and I'm looking for much more than a…an arrangement."

"You frighten him."

"Good, because he frightens me, too. We met that first day I arrived in town, and my life hasn't been the same since."

Ellie patted Sherry's hand. "Tell me, what's all this about you insisting on romance? I overheard Cody talking to Luke yesterday afternoon. I wish I could've recorded the conversation, because it was quite funny. Luke was advising Cody on a variety of ways to—" she made quotation marks with her fingers "—win your heart."

Sherry rolled her eyes. "That's the thing. Cody already has my heart. He just doesn't know what to do with it."

"Give him time," Ellie said. "Cody's smarter than he looks."

A little later, Sherry helped her friend with the dinner preparations. Christina Lynn awoke from her nap and gleefully "helped" Sherry arrange the silverware around the table. A few minutes before five, Luke returned home, looking hot and dusty. He kissed his wife and daughter, showered and joined them for dinner.

They sat around the big kitchen table and after the blessing, Luke handed Sherry the bowl of mashed potatoes. He said, "So Cody came to see you last night." He cast a triumphant smile at his wife. His cocky grin implied that if Sherry and Cody were married anytime soon, he'd take the credit.

"Honey," Ellie said brightly, "Cody was nearly arrested for disturbing the peace. And from what Sherry told me, he blames you."

"*Me?* I wasn't the one out there making a first-class fool of myself."

"True, but you were the one who suggested he do it."

"That shouldn't make any difference." Luke ladled gravy over his meat and potatoes before reaching for the green beans. "As long as Sherry thought it was romantic, it shouldn't matter." He glanced at Sherry and nodded as if to accept her gratitude.

"Well, yes, it was, uh—"

"Romantic," Luke supplied, looking hopeful.

"It was…romantic, yes. Sort of."

"It was ridiculous," Ellie inserted.

"A man's willing to do ridiculous things for a woman if that's what she wants."

"I don't, and I never said I did," Sherry was quick to inform him. "It bothers me that Cody would think I wanted him to do anything so…"

"Asinine," Ellie said.

"Exactly."

Luke was grinning from ear to ear. "Isn't love grand?"

"No, it isn't," a male voice boomed from the doorway. Cody stood on the other side of the screen. He swung it open and stepped inside, eyeing Luke as if he was a traitor who ought to be dragged before a firing squad.

"Cody!" Ellie greeted him warmly. "Join us for dinner?"

"No, thanks, I just ate. I came over to have a little talk with Luke. I didn't realize you had company."

"If it makes you uncomfortable, I'll leave," Sherry offered.

"Don't," Ellie whispered.

Cody's gaze swung to Sherry and it seemed to bore into her very soul. He was angry; she could feel it.

"Come in and have a coffee at least," Ellie said, picking up the pot and pouring him a cup. Cody moved farther into the kitchen and sat down at the table grudgingly.

"I suppose you heard?" Cody's question was directed at Luke and filled with censure. "The next time I need advice about romance—or anything else—you're the last person I'm gonna see."

Sherry did her best to concentrate on her meal and ignore both men.

"I assumed because you got Ellie to marry you," Cody went on, "you'd know the secret of keeping a woman happy."

"He does!"

Three pairs of eyes moved to Ellie. "He loves me."

"Love." Cody spat the word as if the very sound of it was distasteful.

"That could be why a smart woman like Sherry is hesitant to marry you," Ellie said.

"I don't suppose she mentioned the fact that I've withdrawn my offer. I've decided the whole idea of marriage is a mistake. I don't need a woman to make a fool out of me."

"Not when you do such a good job of it yourself," Ellie said dryly.

Sherry's grip on her fork tightened at the flash of pain that went through her. It hurt her to think she'd come this close to love only to lose it.

"Anyway," Ellie said, "I'm sorry to hear you've changed your mind, Cody." Then she grinned. "I've got apple pan dowdy for dessert. Care for some?"

"Apple pan dowdy?" Cody's eyes lit up. "I think I could find room for a small serving."

Sherry wasn't sure how Ellie arranged it, but within a matter of minutes she was alone in the kitchen with Cody. Philip began to cry and Ellie excused herself. Then Luke made some excuse to leave, taking Christina Lynn with him.

"Would you like more coffee?" Sherry asked.

"Please."

She refilled his cup, then replaced the pot. Never had she been more conscious of Cody than at that moment.

"Heather said something about visiting you after school one day." He was holding his mug with both hands and refusing to look at her.

"If you don't object."

"No, of course not. You're the best thing to happen to that girl in years. I never thought anyone could convince her to wear a dress."

"She just needed a little guidance." Sherry moved around the kitchen, clearing off the table and stacking dirty dishes in the sink. At last she said, "I hope that whatever happens between you and me won't affect my relationship with Heather."

"Don't see why it should. I hope you two will always be friends."

"I hope so, too."

They didn't seem to have much to say after that.

Sherry was the first to venture into conversation again. "I'm sorry about last night."

He shrugged. "I'll get over it—someday." The beginnings of a smile touched his mouth. He stood and carried his mug to the sink. "I need to get back to the ranch. Give Ellie and Luke my regards, will you?"

Sherry nodded, not wanting him to leave but unable to ask him to stay. She walked him to the door. Cody hesitated on the top step, frowning.

"It'd help a whole lot if you weren't so pretty," he muttered before moving rapidly toward his truck.

"Cody," Sherry called after him, hurrying out the door and onto the top step. When he turned back to her, she wrapped her arms around her middle and said, "Now *that* was romantic."

"It was? That's the kind of thing you want me to say?"

"Yes," she said.

"But that was simple."

She smiled. "It came from the heart."

He seemed to stiffen. "The heart," he repeated, placing his hand on his chest. He opened the door of his truck, then looked back at her. "Do you want me to say things like 'God robbed heaven of one of its loveliest angels the day you were born' and stuff like that?"

"That's very sweet, Cody, but it sounds like a line that's been used before."

"It has been," he admitted, his eyes warming with silent laughter. "But I figured it couldn't hurt, especially since it's true."

"Now that was nice."

With an easy grace he climbed into the pickup and closed the door. Propping his elbow against the open window, he looked at her once more, grinning. "Plan on staying for dinner the night you bring Heather home."

"All right, I will. Thanks for the invitation."

Sherry watched him drive away. The dust had settled long before she realized she wasn't alone.

"He's coming around," Ellie commented. "I don't think he knows it himself yet, but he's falling in love with you hook, line and sinker."

That was exactly what Sherry wanted to hear. Hope blossomed within her and she sighed in contentment.

Monday evening, Sherry was sitting on the porch swing again, contemplating the events of the weekend. She'd sent a long e-mail to her parents, telling them all about Cody and their rocky relationship.

When she saw his Cadillac turn the corner and pull to a stop in front of the clinic, she wasn't sure what to think. Heather leaped out of the passenger side and dashed up the walkway.

"Dad needs you!"

The girl's voice was high and excited, but her smile indicated that there was no real emergency.

"It's nothing," Cody said, walking toward her. He held a box of chocolates in one hand and a bouquet of wildflowers in the other.

"The flowers are for you," Heather explained. "Dad picked them himself."

"If you don't mind, I prefer to do my own talking," Cody growled. "Here," he said, thrusting the flowers and candy at Sherry. Then he jerked up the sleeve of his shirt and started scratching his forearm.

"Both his arms are a real mess," Heather whispered.

"Heather!"

"He's in one of his moods, too."

Sherry was too flabbergasted to respond right away. "Well, thank you for the flowers. And the candy."

"That's romantic, isn't it?" his daughter prompted. "Dad asked me what I thought was romantic, and I said flowers and chocolate-covered cherries. They're my favorite, and I bet you like them, too."

"I do." She returned her gaze to Cody.

"What did you get into? Why are you so itchy?"

"This is why he needs you," Heather said in a loud whisper. A cutting look from Cody silenced her.

"Like she said, I picked the flowers myself.

"It looks like you might've tangled with something else," she said, reaching for his arm and moving him toward the light so she could get a better view. "Oh, Cody," she whispered when she saw the redness and the swelling.

"Poison ivy," he told her.

"Let me get you some calamine for that."

"He was hoping you would," Heather said. "He's real miserable. But we can't stay long, because I have to get over to Katie Butterfield's house and pick up my math book by eight o'clock."

Sherry led Cody into the clinic and got a bottle of calamine lotion, swabbing the worst of the swelling with that. She gave him an antihistamine for the itch, as well.

Heather sat in the corner of the room, the chocolates in her lap. "Janey says you should give Dad an *A* for effort. I think so, too." This last bit was added between bites of candy.

"Heather, I didn't buy those for you," Cody said irritably.

"I know, but Sherry doesn't mind sharing them, do you?"

"Help yourself."

"She already has," Cody muttered.

Sherry put the lotion away while Cody rolled down his sleeves and snapped them closed at the wrists. "Heather, don't you have something to occupy yourself with outside?"

"No."

"Yes, you do," he said pointedly.

"I do? Oh, I get it, you want to be alone with Sherry. Gee, Dad, why didn't you just say so?"

"I want to be alone with Sherry."

"Great." Heather checked her watch. "Is fifteen minutes enough, or do you need longer? Don't forget I have to be at Katie's by eight."

Cody sighed expressively, and Sherry could tell his patience was in tatters. "Fifteen minutes will be fine. I'll meet you on the porch."

"I can take the chocolates?"

"Heather!"

"All right, all right." She threw him an injured look on her way outside. "I know when I'm not wanted."

"Not soon enough, you don't," her father said.

Now that they were alone, Cody didn't seem to know what he wanted to say. He paced the room restlessly, without speaking.

"Cody?"

"I'm thinking."

"This sounds serious," Sherry said, amused.

"It *is* serious. Sit down." He pulled out a chair, escorted her to it and sat her down, then stood facing her.

"I'm sorry about the poison ivy," Sherry ventured.

He shrugged. "My own fault. I should've noticed it, but my head was in the clouds thinking about you."

"I know it's painful. The poison ivy, I mean."

"It won't be as bad as the razzing I'm going to get when folks learn about this—on top of my behavior Saturday night."

"Oh, Cody," she whispered, feeling genuinely contrite, aware that her insistence that he be "romantic" and demonstrate his feelings had led directly to his actions. He was trying hard to give her what she wanted, yet he didn't seem to understand what that really was. Yes, she wanted the sweet endearing things a man did for a woman he was courting, but more than that, she needed him to trust her, to open up to her.

"Listen, the other day I said I was withdrawing my proposal of marriage, but we both know I wasn't serious."

Sherry hadn't known that at all, but was pleased he was willing to say so.

"I'm not sure what to do anymore, and every time I try to give you what you say you need, it turns into another disaster."

He crouched before her and took both her hands in his. She saw how callused they were, the knuckles chafed, yet to her they were the most beautiful male hands she'd ever seen.

"You wanted romance, and I swear to you, Sherry, I've given it my best shot. If it's romantic to nearly get arrested for a woman, then I should receive some kind of award."

She nodded, trying not to smile.

"I don't blame you for the poison ivy—that was my own fault. I wanted to impress you with the wildflowers. I could've bought you a bouquet of carnations and that fancy grass from the market. Les Gilles sells them for half price after seven, but I figured you'd think those wildflowers were more romantic."

"I do. They're beautiful. Thank you."

"I've done every romantic thing I can think of for you. I don't know what else you want. I've sung to you, I've brought you candy—I know Heather's the one eating it, but I'll buy you another box."

"Don't worry about it."

"I am worried, but not about the chocolates." He stared at the floor for a moment. "I know you're concerned that Heather was the one who prompted my proposal, her wanting a brother or sister and all. In a way I suppose she did— at first. I'm asking you to marry me again, only this time it's for me."

"Five minutes." Heather's voice trilled from the other side of the clinic door.

Cody closed his eyes, stood and marched over to the door. "Heather, I asked for some time alone with Sherry, remember?"

"I'm just telling you that you've used up ten minutes, and you only have five more. I can't be late, Dad, or Katie will be gone—and so will my book."

"I remember."

"Dad, you've wasted another whole minute lecturing me."

Cody shook his head helplessly and returned to Sherry's side. "Now, where was I?"

"We were discussing your proposal."

"Right." He wiped his face. "I guess what I have to tell you is that I don't know how to be romantic. All I know is how to be me. I'm wondering if that'll ever be good enough for you."

"Stop." She raised both hands. "Go back to what you were saying before Heather interrupted you."

He looked confused.

"You said you were asking me to marry you, not for Heather's sake, but for yours."

"So?"

"So," she said, straightening in her chair, "are you trying to tell me you love me?"

He rubbed his hand along the back of his neck. "I'm not going to lie to you, Sherry. I don't know if I love you, but I do know there hasn't been a woman in the last decade who makes me feel the things you do. I've swallowed my pride for you, nearly been arrested for you. I'm suffering a bout of poison ivy because all I think about is you."

His words sounded like the lyrics of a love song. Sherry was delighted. But before she could speak, they were interrupted.

"Dad!"

"All right, all right," Cody said impatiently. "I'm coming."

Sherry got to her feet, not wanting him to leave. "I'll be over at the ranch one afternoon this week," she volunteered hastily. "That'll give us both time to think about what we want."

Cody smiled and briefly touched her face. "I'll do what I can to keep Heather out of our hair."

"I heard that!"

Cody chuckled and, leaning forward, kissed Sherry gently on the lips. "Your kisses are sweeter than any chocolate-covered cherries."

"Hey, Dad, that was good," Heather announced on her way through the door. "I didn't help him with that, either," she told Sherry.

# Nine

"I hate to impose on you," Ellie said for the third time.

"You're not imposing," Sherry insisted also for the third time. "Christina Lynn and I will get along fine, and Philip won't even know you're gone." As if to confirm her words, Christina Lynn crawled into Sherry's lap and planted a wet kiss on her cheek. "Now go," Sherry said. She stood up, with the toddler tucked against her hip, and escorted Ellie to the door. "Your husband wants to celebrate your anniversary."

"I can't believe he arranged all this without me knowing!"

Luke appeared then, dressed in a dark suit, his hair still damp beneath his hat. His arm went around Ellie's waist. "We haven't been out to dinner in months."

"I know, but…"

"Go and enjoy yourself," Sherry insisted. The more time she spent with Luke and Ellie, the more she grew to like them, individually and as a couple. Luke wasn't as easy to know as his wife, but Sherry was touched by the strength of his love for Ellie and his family. Luke had called her on Tuesday morning to ask if she'd mind staying with the children Wednesday night while he took Ellie out for a surprise dinner to celebrate their third wedding anniversary. Sherry had been honored that he'd want her to look after his kids. He then told her there wasn't anyone he'd trust more.

Later, when she arrived at the ranch and Ellie was putting the finishing touches on her makeup, Luke had proudly shown Sherry the gold necklace he'd purchased for his wife. Sherry suspected her friend would be moved to tears when she saw it and told him so. Luke had beamed with pleasure.

"If Philip wakes up," Ellie said, "there's a bottle in the fridge."

"Ellie," Luke said pointedly, edging her toward the door. "We have a dinner reservation for six."

"But—"

"Go on, Ellie," Sherry urged. "Everything will be fine."

"I know. It's just that I've never left Philip before, and it seems a bit soon to be cutting the apron strings."

Sherry laughed and bounced Christina Lynn on her hip. "We're going to have a nice quiet evening all by ourselves."

"You're sure—"

*"Go,"* Sherry said again. She stood on the porch with Christina Lynn as Luke and Ellie drove off. The little girl waved madly.

For the first half hour, Christina Lynn was content to show Sherry her toys. She dragged them into the living room and proudly demonstrated how each one worked. Sherry oohed and ahhed at all the appropriate moments. When the toddler had finished, Sherry helped her return the toys to the chest that Luke had made for his daughter.

Having grown tired of her game, Christina Lynn lay down on the floor and started to fuss. "Mama!" she demanded as if suddenly realizing that her mother wasn't there.

"Mommy and Daddy have gone out to eat," Sherry explained patiently. Thinking Christina Lynn might be hungry, she heated her dinner and set the little girl in her high chair. But apparently Christina Lynn wasn't hungry, because the meal landed on the floor in record time.

"Mama!" Christina yelled, banging her little fists on the high-chair tray.

"Mommy's out with Daddy, sweetheart."

Christina Lynn's lower lip started to wobble.

"Don't cry, honey," Sherry pleaded but to no avail. Within seconds Christina Lynn was screaming.

Sherry lifted her from the high chair and carried her into the living room. She sat in the rocker trying to soothe her, but Christina Lynn only wept louder.

Inevitably her crying woke Philip. With Christina Lynn clinging to her leg, Sherry took the whimpering infant from his bassinet and changed his diaper. Holding him against her shoulder, she gently patted his back, hoping to urge him back to sleep.

That, however, proved difficult, especially with Christina Lynn still at full throttle. The little girl was wrapped around Sherry's leg and both she and Philip were wailing loudly enough to bring the house down. Sherry was in despair, trying to soothe both children to no avail.

That was how Cody found her.

She didn't hear him come in, so she was surprised to discover him standing in the hallway outside the children's bedroom, grinning hugely.

"Hi," he said. "Luke told me you were sitting with the kids tonight. Looks like you could use a little help."

"Christina Lynn," Sherry said gratefully. "Look—Uncle Cody's here."

Cody moved into the room and dislodged the toddler from

Sherry's leg, lifting her into his arms. Christina Lynn hid her face in his shoulder and continued her tearful performance.

"What's wrong with Philip?" Cody asked over the din.

"I think he might be hungry. If you'll keep Christina Lynn occupied, I'll go heat his bottle."

They met in the living room, Sherry carrying the baby and the bottle. Cody was down on the floor, attempting to interest the toddler in a five-piece wood puzzle, but the little girl wanted none of it.

Philip apparently felt the same way about the bottle. "He's used to his mother nursing him," Sherry said. "Besides, I don't think he's all that hungry, after all. If he was, he'd accept the bottle quickly enough."

She returned it to the kitchen and sat down in the chair with Philip, rocking him until his cries abated. Christina Lynn's wails turned to soft sobs as she buried her face in the sofa cushions.

"You've got your hands full."

Sherry gave a weary sigh. "Imagine Ellie handling them both, day in and day out. The woman's a marvel."

"So are you."

"Hardly." Sherry didn't mean to discount his compliment, but she was exhausted, and Luke and Ellie hadn't been gone more than a couple of hours. "I don't know how Ellie does it."

"Or Luke," Cody added. He slumped onto the end of the sofa and lifted an unresisting Christina Lynn into his arms. She cuddled against him, and at last silence reigned.

"Come sit by me," Cody said, stretching his arm along the back of the couch.

Sherry was almost afraid to move for fear Philip would wake up, but her concern was groundless. The infant didn't so much as sigh as she tiptoed over to the couch. As soon as she was comfortable, Cody dropped his arm to her shoulder and pulled her closer. It was wonderful to be sitting with him this way, so warm and intimate.

"Ah, peace," he whispered. "Do I dare kiss you?"

Sherry smiled. "You like to live dangerously, don't you?" She raised her head and Cody's mouth brushed hers. Softly at first, then he deepened the kiss, until she was so involved in what was happening between them she nearly forgot Philip was in her arms.

She broke off the kiss and exhaled on a ragged sigh. "You're one powerful kisser."

"It isn't me, Sherry. It's *us*."

"Whoever or whatever, it's dangerous." She nestled her head against his shoulder. "I don't think we should do that again."

"Oh, I plan to do it again soon."

"Cody," she said, lifting her head so their eyes could meet, "I'm not here to, uh, make out with you."

"Shh." He pressed his finger to her lips.

She pressed her head against his shoulder again. His arm was around her. She enjoyed the feeling of being linked to him, of being close, both physically and emotionally. It was what she'd sought from the beginning, this bonding, this intimacy.

When she felt his breathing quicken, she straightened and read the hunger in his eyes, knowing it was a reflection of her own. Cody lowered his mouth to hers, claiming her with a kiss that left her weak.

She was trembling inside and out. Neither of them spoke as they kissed again and again, each kiss more potent than the last. After many minutes, Sherry pulled back, almost gasping with pleasure and excitement.

"I can't believe we're doing this," she whispered. Each

held a sleeping child. They were in their friends' home and could be interrupted at any time.

"I can't believe it, either," Cody agreed. "Damn, but you're beautiful."

They didn't speak for a few minutes, just sat and savored the silence and each other.

"Sherry, listen—" Cody began.

He was interrupted by the shrill ringing of the telephone. Philip's piercing cry joined that of the phone. Christina Lynn woke, too, and after taking one look at Cody and Sherry, burst into tears and cried out for her mom.

Cody got up to answer the phone. He was back on the couch in no time. He cast Sherry a frustrated look. "That was my daughter. She heard I was over here helping you babysit Christina Lynn and Philip, and she's mad that I left her at home."

"I think," Sherry said, patting Philip's back, "she got her revenge."

Cody grinned. "It was selfish of me not to bring her, but I wanted to be alone with you."

"We aren't exactly alone," she said. She looked down at Luke and Ellie's children, who had miraculously calmed again and seemed to be drifting off.

"True, but I was counting on them both being asleep. Luke thought they'd be and—"

"Luke," Sherry broke in, pretending to be offended. "Do you mean to tell me this was all prearranged between you and Luke?"

"Well…"

"Did you?" Sherry could have sworn Cody was blushing.

"This all came about because of you and the fuss you made over wanting romance. Luke got a bit whimsical and thought he'd like to do something special for his anniversary. Then he got worried that Ellie wouldn't go because she wouldn't want to leave the children. It's hard to be romantic with a couple of kids around."

Sherry looked at Christina Lynn and Philip and smiled. "They didn't seem to deter us."

"True, but we're the exception." After a pause he said, "Put your head back on my shoulder." He slid his arm around her. "It feels good to have you this close."

"It feels good to me, too."

He kissed the crown of her head. Sherry closed her eyes, never dreaming she'd fall asleep, but she must have, because the next thing she heard was Luke and Ellie whispering.

She opened her eyes and her gaze met Ellie's. "They were a handful, weren't they?" she asked with a smile.

"Not really," Sherry whispered.

"All four of you are worn to a frazzle. Even Cody's asleep."

"I'm not now," he said, yawning loudly.

Ellie removed Philip from Sherry's arms, and Luke took his daughter from Cody's. They disappeared down the hallway to the children's room, returning soon after.

"How was your dinner?" Sherry asked.

"Fantastic." Ellie's eyes were dreamy. She sat in the rocking chair while Luke went into the kitchen. He reappeared a few minutes later carrying a tray with four mugs of coffee.

"I can't remember an evening I've enjoyed more." Ellie's hand went to her throat and the single strand of gold Luke had given her for their anniversary. "Thank you, Sherry."

"I'll be happy to watch the kids anytime."

"I don't mean for watching the kids—I...I certainly appreciate it, but there's more. Luke told me I should thank you because it was Cody talking to him about love and romance that made him realize he wanted our anniversary to be extra-special this year."

Luke stood behind the rocking chair and leaned forward to kiss his wife's cheek.

"I think it's time we left," Cody suggested, "before this turns into something, uh, private."

"You could be right," Sherry agreed.

With eyes only for each other, Ellie and Luke didn't seem to notice they were leaving until Sherry was out the front door.

"Stick around, you two," Luke protested. "You haven't finished your coffee."

"Another time," Cody answered, leading Sherry down the steps.

"Night," Sherry called to her friends.

"Night, and thanks again," Ellie said, standing in the doorway, her arm around her husband's waist, her head against his shoulder.

Cody escorted Sherry to her car, then hesitated before turning away. "I'll see you soon," he said, frowning.

She was puzzled by the frown. She watched as his gaze swung back to Luke in the doorway and then to her again. Then he sighed and stepped away.

Sherry would have given her first month's wages to know what Cody was thinking.

"Dad was furious with me," Heather said when she stopped in at the clinic the next afternoon. Doc was out doing house calls, like the old-fashioned country doctor he was.

"Hi, Heather," Sherry greeted her. "Why was he mad?"

"He told me I had the worst sense of timing of anyone he's ever known. First the night he brought you the candy and flowers, and then when you were watching Christina Lynn and Philip."

"It's all right," Sherry assured her. "Your father and I'll get everything straightened out sooner or later." But Cody hadn't said anything about marriage lately, and Sherry was beginning to wonder.

"I'm not supposed to butt into Dad's business or yours, and I don't mean to, but I hope you decide to marry us. I don't even care about the babies so much anymore. I really like you, Sherry, and it'd be so much fun if you were always around."

"I'd enjoy that, too."

"You would?" Sherry instantly brightened. "Can I tell Dad you said that, 'cause I know he'd like it and—"

"That might not be a good idea." Sherry removed her white jacket and tossed it in the laundry hamper. She was finished for the day and eager to see Cody.

"I thought your friend Carrie was going to come by with you," she said.

"She couldn't. That's why I can't show you the way I want my hair cut."

"Oh, well. I'll see the magazine another time."

"Especially if you're going to stay around." Heather pressed her books against her as her eyes grew wistful. "I can hardly wait for you to move in with us."

"I didn't say I was moving in with you, Heather. Remember what Ellie told you at the picnic?"

Heather rolled her eyes in exasperation, as if reciting it for the hundredth time. "If I interfere with you and Dad, I could hurt more than help."

"You got it."

Before leaving the clinic, Sherry ran a brush through her

hair and touched up her makeup. "You're sure Janey and your father are expecting me tonight?"

"Of course. Dad specifically said I should stop by today and invite you, but if you can't come, that's fine, too, 'cause Slim's in town and he can take me home."

The phone rang just then, and Sherry let Mrs. Colson answer it. The receptionist came back for Sherry.

"It's a nice-sounding man asking for you."

This surprised Sherry. The only "nice-sounding man" who interested her was Cody Bailman, but Mrs. Colson would have recognized his voice.

She walked into her office and picked up the receiver. "This is Sherry Waterman."

"Sherry, it's Rowdy Cassidy. I know it's short notice, but I was wondering if you could fly to Houston for dinner tonight?"

"Fly to Houston? Tonight?"

"It's Norah's birthday, and I'd love to surprise her."

"But there isn't a plane for me to catch, and it'd take you hours to fly to Pepper to get me."

"I'm here now, at the airstrip outside town."

"Here?"

"Yeah, I flew into Abilene this morning and I got to thinking on my way home that I should bring you back with me. I know it's a lot to ask, but it'd give Norah such a boost. She loves Texas, but after your visit, she got real homesick. It'd mean a lot to her if you'd come and help celebrate her birthday."

Sherry hesitated and looked at Heather, not wanting to disappoint Cody's daughter, either. "I need to be back by nine tomorrow morning."

"No problem. I can have one of my staff fly you back first thing. What do you say?"

"Uh..." Sherry wished she had more time to think this over. "Sure," she said finally. "Why not?" Norah was her best friend, and she missed her, too.

They made the arrangements to meet, and Sherry hung up. "You heard?" she asked Heather.

Heather lowered her head dejectedly.

"It's for a surprise birthday dinner. Norah's the reason I moved to Texas, and she'd do it for me. Besides, you said Slim can take you back to the ranch."

"Yeah, I know."

"How about if you stop by after school tomorrow?" Sherry asked, hating to disappoint Heather. "It'd be even better, wouldn't it, because Carrie might be able to come."

Heather nodded, but not with a lot of enthusiasm. "You're right. It's just that I was really looking forward to having you out at the ranch again. I think Dad was, too."

"There'll be plenty of other times, I promise. You'll explain to your father, won't you?"

Heather nodded. Sherry dropped her off at the feed store, where Slim's pickup was parked. She stayed long enough to be sure the older man was available to drive Heather to the ranch.

From there she drove to the landing strip. Rowdy was waiting for her, and after greetings and hugs, Sherry boarded his company jet and settled back in the cushioned seat.

"So how's Pepper been treating you?" Rowdy asked.

"Very well. I love Texas."

"Any progress with that cattleman?"

She smiled. "Some."

"Norah's going to be glad to hear that." He grinned with satisfaction. "She's going to be very surprised to see you, but even more surprised to see her father. He arrived earlier this afternoon. My driver picked him up at the airport and is giving him a quick tour of Houston and Galveston Island. If everything goes according to schedule, we should get to the house at about the same time."

"You thought all this up on your own?"

"Yep." He looked extremely proud of himself. "I talked to Norah's father a couple months back about flying out, but as I said, having you join us was a spur-of-the-moment idea. Norah's going to be thrilled."

To say that Norah was thrilled—or surprised—was putting it mildly. As Rowdy had predicted, David Bloomfield arrived within minutes of her and Rowdy. They'd waited in the driveway for him, and the three of them walked into the house together.

Rowdy stood in the entryway and, his eyes twinkling, called, "Norah, I'm home!"

Norah appeared and Rowdy threw open his arms. "Happy birthday!" he shouted and stepped aside to reveal David Bloomfield and Sherry, standing directly behind him.

"Daddy!" Norah cried, enthusiastically hugging her father first. "Sherry!" Norah wrapped both arms around her, eyes bright with tears.

"You thought I forgot your birthday, didn't you?" Rowdy crowed.

Norah wiped the tears from her face and nodded. "I really did. I had the most miserable day. The kids were both fussy, and I felt like I'd moved to the ends of the earth and *everyone* had forgotten me."

"This is a long way from Orchard Valley," her father said, putting his arm around his youngest daughter, "but it isn't the end of the earth—although I think I can see it from here."

Norah chuckled. "Oh, Dad, that's an old joke."

"You laughed, didn't you?"

"Come on in and make yourselves comfortable," Rowdy

invited, ushering them into the living room. "I certainly hope you didn't go to any trouble for dinner," he said to Norah.

"No. I was feeling sorry for myself and thought we'd order pizza. It's been that kind of day."

"Good—" Rowdy paused and looked at his watch "—because the caterer should get here in about ten minutes."

Norah was floored. "Is there anything else I should know about?"

"This?" He removed a little velvet box from his pocket, then put it back. "Think I'll save that for later when we're alone."

David laughed and glanced around. "Now, where are those precious grandchildren of mine?"

"Sleeping. They're both exhausted. But if you promise to be quiet, I'll take you upstairs for a peek. How long are you staying? A week, I hope."

David and Sherry followed Norah upstairs and tiptoed into the children's rooms. Sherry was fond of David Bloomfield and loved watching his reaction as he looked at his grandchildren. Sherry remembered several years back, when David had suffered a heart attack and almost died. His recovery had been nothing short of miraculous.

By the time they came back downstairs, the caterer was there and the table had been set for an elegant dinner. The candles were lit, the appetizers served and champagne poured.

"Rowdy did this once before," Norah said, reaching for her husband's hand. Rowdy brought her fingers to his mouth and brushed his lips over them. "He wanted something from me then. Dinner was all part of a bribe to get me to leave Orchard Valley and be his private nurse."

Rowdy laughed. "It didn't work. Norah didn't believe I loved her, and I can't say I blame her, since I didn't know it myself. All I knew was that I couldn't imagine my life without her. You led me on quite a merry chase—but I wouldn't have had it any different."

"Are you trying to bribe my daughter this time?" David asked.

Rowdy shook his head. "Nope. I have everything I need."

The shrimp appetizer was followed by a heart-of-palm salad. Norah turned to Sherry. "How's everything going with you and Cody?"

Sherry shrugged, unsure how much she should say. "Better, I guess."

"I have to tell you, I got a kick out of your last e-mail. He actually proposed to you by saying he wanted to cut to the chase?"

"Sounds like a man who knows what he wants," Rowdy commented.

"Cody's come a long way since then. He's trying to understand what I want, but I don't think he's quite figured it out." She lowered her gaze and sighed. "Currently he's suffering from the effects of poison ivy. He ran into a patch of it while picking wildflowers for me."

"Well, as you say, he's certainly trying hard."

"I wish now I'd been more specific," Sherry said, smoothing her napkin. "I love Cody and I want romance, yes, but more than that, I want him to share himself with me, his thoughts and ideas, his dreams for the future. What worries him most is the fear that if he loves me he'll lose his identity. He says he isn't willing to let any woman put a collar around his neck."

"Sounds reasonable," David said.

"He's really a darling." Sherry wanted to be sure everyone understood her feelings.

"You love him?"

Sherry nodded. "I did almost from the first."

"Let me talk to him," Rowdy offered.

"It wouldn't do any good," Sherry said. "His best friend, who's happily married, already tried, and Cody just thinks Luke's lost his marbles."

"He'll feel differently once he's married himself."

"Didn't you tell me Cody has a twelve-year-old daughter?" Norah asked.

Sherry nodded. "I don't know a lot about his marriage, just enough to know they were both pretty immature. His wife was killed in a car accident years ago."

"And he's never thought about marrying again until now?" David inquired.

"Heather had a lot to do with his proposal, but—" She stopped, remembering how Cody had told her that the first time he'd asked her to marry him had been for Heather's sake, but now it was for his own. "With time, I believe he'll understand it isn't flowers that interest me or serenading me in the dead of night—it's trusting and sharing. It's a sense of belonging to each other."

"It's sitting up together with a sick baby," Norah murmured.

"And loving your partner enough to allow him to be himself," Rowdy continued. "And vice versa."

"And looking back over the years you were together, knowing they were the best ones of your life," David added thoughtfully.

Sherry hoped that eventually Cody would understand all of this. His mother had asked her to be patient, and Ellie had given her the same advice. It was difficult at times, but she held on to the promise of a future together.

Sherry left early the next morning. Norah walked out to

the car with her, dressed in her robe, her eyes sleepy. "I wish you could stay longer."

"I do, too."

"If you ever want to get away for a weekend, let me know, and I'll have Rowdy send a plane for you."

"I will. And thank you."

The flight back to Pepper seemed to take only half the time the trip into Houston had. She glanced at her watch as she walked to her car, pleased to see she had plenty of time before she went on duty at the clinic.

Driving down Main Street, Sherry was struck once more by the welcome she felt in Pepper. It was as if this was her home and always would be. The sight of Cody's pickup in front of the clinic came as a surprise. She pulled around to the back of the building, parking in her appointed slot, and hurried inside.

Cody wasn't anywhere in sight. "Mrs. Colson," she asked, walking out to the reception area. "Have you seen Cody?"

"No, I was wondering that myself. His truck's here, but he doesn't seem to be around."

Stepping onto the porch, Sherry glanced around. A movement, ever so slight, from Cody's truck caught her eye. She ran down the walkway to discover Cody fast asleep in the cab.

"Cody," she called softly through the open window, not wanting to startle him. "What are you doing here?"

"Sherry?" He bolted upright, banging his head on the steering wheel. "Damn!" he muttered, rubbing the injured spot. He opened the door and nearly fell onto the street in his eagerness.

"Have you been drinking?" she demanded.

"No," he returned angrily. "Where the hell have you been all night?"

"With my friend in Houston," she told him, "although where I was or who I was with is none of your business."

"Some hotshot with a Learjet, from what I heard."

"Yes. As I understand it, Rowdy's a legend in the corporate world."

"I see." Cody slammed his hat onto his head. "What are you trying to do? Make me jealous?"

"Oh, for crying out loud, that's the stupidest thing you've ever said to me, Cody Bailman, and you've said some real doozies. Rowdy's married."

"So you're flying off with married men now?"

"Rowdy's married to my best friend, Norah. It was her birthday yesterday, and on his way home from Abilene, he decided to surprise Norah by bringing me back with him."

Cody frowned as if he didn't believe her. "That's not the story Heather gave me. She said I had to do something quick, because you were seeing another man." Cody paced the sidewalk in front of her. "This is it, Sherry. I'm not willing to play any more games with you. I've done everything I can to prove to you I'm sincere, so if you want to run off with a married man at this point—"

"I didn't run off with a married man!" she said hotly. "For you to even suggest it is ridiculous."

"I spent the entire night sleeping in my pickup, waiting for you to get back, so if I happen to be a bit short-tempered, you can figure out why."

"Then maybe you should just go home and think this through before you start throwing accusations at me."

"Maybe I should," he growled.

Sherry was mortified to find out that they had an audience. Mrs. Colson was standing on the porch, enthralled with their conversation. The woman across the street, who'd been watering her roses, had long since lost interest in them and was inadvertently hosing down the sidewalk. Another couple rocking on their porch seemed to be enjoying the show, as well.

"I'm serious, Sherry. This is the last time I'm going to ask." Cody jerked open the truck door and leaped inside. "Are you going to marry me or not? Because I've had it."

"That proposal's about as romantic as the first one."

"Well, you know what I think of romance." He started the engine and ground the gears.

He'd just pulled away from the curb when she slammed her foot down on the pavement. "Yes, you idiot!" she screamed after him. "I'll marry you!"

# *Ten*

"I don't think he heard you, dear," the lady watering the roses called out to her.

"I don't think he did, either," the older man on the porch agreed, standing up and walking to his gate to get a better look at Sherry.

"I can't believe he drove away," Mrs. Colson said. "That man's beside himself for want of you. Cody may be stubborn, but he isn't stupid. Mark my words, he'll come to his senses soon."

Sherry wasn't sure she wanted him to. He was too infuriating. Imagine—suggesting she was seeing a married man behind his back!

"Do you want me to phone Cody for you, dear, and explain?" Mrs. Colson suggested as Sherry marched up the steps and in the front door.

Sherry turned and glared angrily at the receptionist.

"It was only a suggestion," Mrs. Colson muttered.

"I can do my own talking."

"Of course," Mrs. Colson said pleasantly, clearly not offended by the reprimand. "I'm positive everything will work out between you and Cody. Don't give a moment's heed to what he said earlier. Everyone knows how stubborn he can be."

"I'm not the least bit positive about *anything* having to do with that man," Sherry returned. Cody had been telling her for weeks that this was her last opportunity to marry him, that he wasn't going to ask her again.

A half hour later, when Sherry came out of her office reading a file Doc Lindsey had left for her to review, she heard Mrs. Colson speaking quietly into the phone.

"I swear you've never seen anyone so angry in all your life as Cody Bailman was this morning," she said. "He just peeled out of here, and all because he's so crazy about—"

"Mrs. Colson," Sherry said.

The receptionist placed her hand over the receiver, but didn't even glance upward. "I'll be with you in a minute." She put the receiver to her ear again and continued, "And dear, dear Sherry. Why, she's so overwrought she can hardly—"

Suddenly Mrs. Colson froze, swallowed once, and then looked at Sherry. "Is there anything I can do for you?" she managed, her face flushing crimson.

"Yes," Sherry said. "You can stop gossiping about me."

"Oh, I was afraid of that. You've got the wrong impression. I never gossip—ask anyone. I *have* been known to pass on information, but I don't consider that gossiping." Abruptly she replaced the receiver.

Sherry scowled at the phone, wondering what the person on the other end was thinking.

"I was only trying to help," Mrs. Colson insisted. "Donna Jo's known Cody all his life and—"

"You were speaking to Donna Jo?" Sherry wondered how anyone got any work done in this town.

"Why, yes. Donna Jo's friends with Cody's mother, same as I am. She has a vested interest in what happens between you two. So do Mayor Bowie and the sheriff, and we both know those two spend a lot of time over at the Yellow Rose."

"What's my schedule like this morning?" Sherry asked wearily.

Mrs. Colson flipped through the pages of the appointment book. "Mrs. O'Leary's due at ten, but she's been coming to see Doc for the past three years for the same thing."

"What's her problem?"

Mrs. Colson sighed heavily. "Mrs. O'Leary's over seventy and, well, she wants a nose job. She's convinced she lost Earl Burrows because her nose was too big, and that was more'n fifty years ago."

"Didn't marry someone else?"

"Oh, yes. She married Larry O'Leary, but I don't think it was a happy union, although she bore him eight sons. Doc says it's the most ridiculous thing he's ever heard of, a woman getting her nose done at the age of seventy. When she comes in, he asks her to think about it for another six months. She's been coming back faithfully every six months for three years."

"If she sees me, I'll give her a referral. If she's that set on a new nose, then she should have it."

"I told Doris you'd feel that way—that's why I set the appointment up with you," Mrs. Colson said. She looked pleased with herself. "If you want, I can save Doris the trouble of coming in and give her the name of the referral."

"All right. I'll make a few calls and get back to you in a couple of minutes. Am I scheduled to see anyone else?"

"Not until this afternoon." The receptionist seemed almost

gleeful at the news. "You're free to go for a long drive, if you like." She looked both ways, then added, "No one would blame you for slipping out for a few hours...."

Sherry wasn't sure if she was slipping out or flipping out. She made a couple of calls, gave Mrs. Colson the names of three plastic surgeons to pass on to her first patient of the day, then reached for her purse.

She was halfway to the door when it burst open and Donna Jo rushed in. "I'm so glad I caught you!" she said excitedly. "You poor, poor girl, you must be near crazy with worry."

"Worry?"

"About losing Cody. Now, you listen here, I've got some advice for you." She paused, inhaled deeply and pressed her hand to her generous bosom. "Sherry Waterman, fight for your man. You love him—folks in town have known that for weeks—and we're willing to forgive you for leaving in that fancy jet with that handsome cowboy. By the way, who *was* that?"

"Rowdy Cassidy, and before you say another word, I didn't leave with him like you're implying."

"We know that, dear."

"Rowdy Cassidy?" Martha Colson whispered. "Not *the* Rowdy Cassidy?"

"That's who she said," Donna Jo muttered irritably. "Now let her talk."

"There's nothing more to say." Sherry didn't want to spend what free time she had talking about her excursion of the night before, although both women were eager for details. "I'm going to do as you suggest and take a long drive this morning."

"Now you be sure to stop in at the café and let me know what happens once you're through talking to Cody," Donna Jo instructed.

"Who said I was going to talk to Cody?"

"You *are* going to him, aren't you?" Donna Jo said. "You have to. That poor boy's all thumbs when it comes to love and romance. Personally, I thought you did a smart thing, asking for a little romance first, but everyone agrees that it's time for you to put Cody out of his misery."

"He's suffered enough," Mrs. Colson added.

"Who would've believed Cody Bailman would be like this with a woman. I will say it took a mighty special one," Donna Jo concluded, winking at Sherry.

With half the town awaiting the outcome of her trip to Cody's ranch, Sherry hopped in her car and drove to the Lucky Horseshoe. Odds were he'd be out on the range somewhere, so she didn't know what good her visit would do. Nevertheless, she had to try.

She saw Cody almost immediately. He was working with a gelding in the corral when she arrived, leading him around the enclosed area. Several other men stood nearby, watching and talking among themselves.

Climbing out of her car, Sherry walked over to the fence and stood there for a few minutes, waiting for Cody to notice her. He seemed preoccupied with his task, putting the gelding through his paces. Sherry was sure he knew she was there, and she was willing to be ignored for only so long.

Five of the slowest minutes of her life passed before she stepped onto the bottom rung of the fence and braced her arms on the top one.

"Cody!"

He turned to face her, his eyes blank.

This was much harder than Sherry had expected. On the drive out to his ranch, she'd envisioned Cody's eyes lighting up with pleasure at the sight of her. She'd imagined him hugging her, lifting her from the ground and swinging her around, his eyes filled with love and promises.

"Yes?" he said at last.

"When you drove away this morning, I...I didn't think you heard me," she said weakly.

Cody led the gelding over to one of his hands, removed his hat long enough to wipe his forehead, then strolled toward her as if he had all the time in the world.

Sherry found it impossible to sense what he thought, what he felt. He revealed no emotion.

"I...guess you're not ready to talk yet," Sherry said.

"You were the one who told me to go home."

"I know, but I was hoping you'd have thought things out by now and realized I'd never fool around with my best friend's husband." Or anyone else when she was so desperately in love with Cody. It seemed as if their evening with Christina Lynn and Philip had been forgotten.

"It was Rowdy Cassidy you left with, wasn't it?"

Sherry nodded.

"You certainly have friends in high places."

"It's Norah I know, not Rowdy."

"So you left on a moment's notice with a man who's virtually a stranger?"

Sherry closed her eyes and prayed for patience. "Would you stop being so stubborn! If you honestly believe I'm the type of woman who'd run around with a married man, then you don't know me at all!"

"*I'm* stubborn!" he exploded. "Do you realize what I've gone through because of you? I've been the butt of everyone's jokes for weeks. My reputation with the other ranchers is in shambles—and I'm still scratching." He removed his glove, rolled up a sleeve and scraped his fingernails across his forearm. "I've done everything I can to earn your love, and I'm done."

"That's the problem. You want my love, but you aren't willing to give me yours. It wasn't really romance I was looking for, Cody, it was *love*. I wanted you to care about me, enough that you'd be willing to do whatever it took to win my heart." She said the words seriously, earnestly. "You never understood that. From the very first, you've been looking for a shortcut, because you didn't want to be bothered. Well, guess what? No woman wants to be considered an annoyance."

"So that's what you think."

"What am I supposed to think with the things you've been saying?"

"That's just fine."

He turned away as if this was the end of their conversation, as if everything that needed to be said had been said. Sherry knew a brush-off when she saw one. Anything else she might say would fall on deaf ears.

She walked over to her car, climbed in and started the engine. She'd shifted into gear and begun to drive away when she changed her mind. Easing the car into Reverse, she pulled alongside the corral fence and stuck her head out the open window, intending to shout at him—but no words came.

She drove out of the yard, tires screeching. It'd been a mistake to try to reason with Cody. Her better judgment insisted she wait several days and let him cool down before she attempted to reopen communications. She should've listened to her own heart instead of Mrs. Colson's and Donna Jo's eagerly offered advice.

Sherry wasn't sure what made her look in her rearview mirror, but when she did, her breath jammed in her throat.

Cody was riding bareback, chasing after her on the gelding he'd been working with minutes earlier. The horse was in full gallop, and Sherry was astonished that he managed to stay on.

She came to a stop, and so did the gelding. Cody slid off his back and jerked open her car door.

"Are you going to marry me or not?" he demanded. He was panting hard.

Sherry eyed him calmly. "Do you love me?"

"After everything I've been through, how can you ask me a question like that!" he snapped. "Yes, I love you. What does it take to convince you I mean it? Blood?"

"No," she whispered, biting her lower lip.

"I love you, Sherry Waterman," he said. "Would you do me the honor of becoming my wife?"

She nodded through her tears.

"Hot damn!" he shouted, then hauled Sherry into his arms so fast her breath fled her lungs. A second later, his mouth was on hers.

His kiss left her trembling. "Cody…" she said, breaking away from him. "You maniac! You chased after my car on a horse just the way Luke came after Ellie, and you always said that was such a stupid thing to do."

He opened his mouth as though to deny it, but didn't say a word. He blinked, then smiled sheepishly. "So I did. Guess this is what love does to a man."

"Do you really love me?"

"Love you?" he cried. "Yes, Sherry, I love you."

"But you—"

"Don't even say it." He kissed her again, this kiss far less urgent, more…loving. After a few minutes he released her and said, "Let's go."

"Where?" she asked.

"Where else? A preacher. I'm not giving you the opportunity to change your mind."

She threw her arms around his neck again. "I'm not going to, not ever." It was Sherry who initiated the kissing this time, and when they finished, Cody was leaning against the side of her car. His eyes were closed and his breathing was labored. Then he reached for her again and swung her off the ground.

"Put me down," Sherry said. "I'm too heavy."

"No, you're not," Cody declared. "I'm calling the preacher right now and we'll get the license this afternoon."

"Cody," she said, "put me down!"

He finally did, then looked at her firmly. "I've waited ten long years for you, and I'm not putting this wedding off another day. If you want one of those big fancy shindigs, then..." He paused.

"A small ceremony is fine." She grinned.

"With a reception big enough to fill the state of Texas, if that's what you want."

"I want my family here."

"I'll have airplane tickets for them by noon."

"Cody, are we crazy?"

"Yes, for each other, and that's just how it's supposed to be. Luke told me that, and I didn't understand it until I met you." He grimaced comically. "Sherry Waterman, what took you so long?"

She stared at him and felt the laughter bubble up inside her. Flinging her arms around his neck, she kissed him soundly. "For the life of me I don't know."

Sherry returned to the office sometime later to find both Mrs. Colson and Donna Jo standing on the porch waiting for her.

Sherry greeted them as she strolled past.

"How'd it go with Cody?" Donna Jo asked urgently. The pair followed her into the clinic.

"Everything went fine," Sherry said. She couldn't help it; she enjoyed keeping them guessing.

*"Fine?"* Mrs. Colson repeated. She looked at Donna Jo. "What does *fine* tell us?"

"Nothing," the waitress responded. "I learned a long time ago not to listen to the words, but to study the expression. *Fine,* the way Sherry just said it, tells me there's going to be a wedding in Pepper soon."

"Isn't the lunch crowd at the café by now?" Sherry asked.

"Ellen can handle it," Donna Jo said, sitting in the closest chair.

"She's not wearing a diamond," Martha Colson pointed out.

"No diamond?" Donna Jo looked incredulous. "I was sure you'd come back sporting the biggest rock this side of Mexico."

"You mean one like this?" Sherry dug into her purse and pulled out the ring Cody had given her. She slipped it on her finger, feeling heady with joy and excitement. Mrs. Colson and Donna Jo screamed delightedly and Sherry hugged them both.

"When's the wedding?"

"Soon, just like you said," Sherry told them, her heart warming. She and Cody had called Sherry's family and made what arrangements they could over the phone. Afterward, Cody had given her the ring, one he'd been patiently carrying with him for weeks.

Sherry wasn't able to explain more. The door opened, and Heather let out a cry and vaulted into her arms.

"Who told you?" Sherry asked when she caught her

breath. Cody had planned to pick up his daughter after school and bring her over to the clinic so they could tell her together.

"Dad," Heather explained. "He came by the school. Men are so funny—they can't keep a secret at all."

Cody walked into the clinic behind her, looking sheepish. "You don't mind, do you?"

"Of course not." Sherry hugged her soon-to-be daughter.

"Hey, I need a hug, too," Cody said, wrapping his arms around Sherry and holding her against him.

"Now *that's* romantic," Mrs. Colson sighed.

"I could just cry," Sherry heard Donna Jo say.

"How soon do you think it'll be before Sherry has a baby?" Heather whispered.

"A year," Mrs. Colson whispered back.

"A year?" Cody lifted his head. He smiled down at Sherry and winked. "I don't think it'll take nearly that long."

* * * * *

# Laughter, sunshine and love—
# spend summer in Orchard Valley

Falling in love is the last thing on Valerie's mind.
And with Dr Colby Winston, of all people! Her dad's
heart surgeon—they're complete opposites in
every way.

The Bloomfield sisters, Valerie, Stephanie and Norah,
have all returned home to help look after their
father, but romance seems to be blossoming
in Orchard Valley…

*Make time for friends.*
*Make time for Debbie Macomber.*

M276_SIOV

*Debbie Macomber invites you
to come and meet the best
friends you could ever make...*

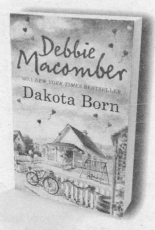

Lindsay Snyder is a newcomer to Buffalo Valley, the
little town struggling to make ends meet. She might
be an outsider, but she's also a breath of fresh air and
she can see that, while the houses need a coat
of paint, there's also a spirit of hope.

Lindsay was never expecting small-town life to
be for her. But she's starting to discover all
the best reasons to stay...

Collect the trilogy
*Dakota Born* ✱ *Dakota Home* ✱ *Always Dakota*

# Debbie Macomber welcomes you to the little town with love in the air!

Maddy Washburn needs a change in her life. She's seen her best friend Lindsay Snyder settle into the little community of Buffalo Valley and how the magic of the town has imbued her spirit. So Maddy decides to up stakes and join her, taking over the dilapidated grocery store and throwing all her energy into reviving the business.

Buffalo Valley is surviving on a lot of luck as it starts to flourish once more; perhaps some of that will rub off on Maddy…

Collect the trilogy
*Dakota Born* ∗ *Dakota Home* ∗ *Always Dakota*

# Debbie Macomber sweeps you away to a place where dreams come true

While Margaret has inherited her father's prosperous ranch and is doing really well for herself, her dream is to fall in love. But when Matt Eilers catches her eye, everyone in Buffalo Valley is quick to tell her that Matt's bad news. Her friends are trying to protect her, but soon the gossips whisper that Matt's only with her for her money. And maybe he is? Or maybe there's something more…

Collect the trilogy
*Dakota Born* ∗ *Dakota Home* ∗ *Always Dakota*